Peach Fuzz

Vol. 3

by

Lindsay Cibos
and
Jared Hodges

TOKYOPOP®

HAMBURG // LONDON // LOS ANGELES // TOKYO

Spotlight

visit us at www.abdopublishing.com

Reinforced library bound edition published in 2009 by Spotlight, a division of ABDO Publishing Group, 8000 West 78th Street, Edina, Minnesota 55439. This edition reprinted by arrangement with TOKYOPOP Inc. www.tokyopop.com

Lettering	Lucas Rivera, Lindsay Cibos and Jared Hodges
Cover Design	Monalisa De Asis
Editor	Alexis Kirsch
Digital Imaging Manager	Chris Buford

Library of Congress Cataloging-in-Publication Data

Cibos, Lindsay.
Peach Fuzz / by Lindsay Cibos and Jared Hodges.
v. cm.
Summary: When Amanda begs her parents for a pet and they relent and get her a ferret, the previously calm household turns chaotic, and even worse, the ferret learns to fear Amanda, who knows nothing about how to take care of a pet.
Contents: Vol. 1. Peach Fuzz -- Vol. 2. Show & tell -- Vol. 3. Prince Edwin.
ISBN 978-1-59961-573-8 (vol. 3: Prince Edwin)
1. Graphic novels. [1. Graphic novels. 2. Ferrets as pets--Fiction. 3. Pets--Fiction.] I. Hodges, Jared. II. Title.
PZ7.7.C53Pe 2008
[Fic]--dc22

2008002197

Spotlight

All Spotlight books have reinforced library binding and are manufactured in the United States of America.

Table of Contents

History of the Valley

Welcome to an enchanted land of astonishing mountains that envelop the horizon and mushrooms that spring from the earth like magic. In 1866, a group of hapless settlers, bound for riches further west, found themselves trapped in Mushroom Valley. Hemmed in and low on supplies, the starving settlers found salvation in the ever renewing mushrooms that carpeted the valley floor.

The "Miracle of the Mushrooms" led to the eventual settlement of the land, and the foundation of a unique fungus-based religion that's followed even today.

Times may be a'changin', but the city's old-fashioned settler charm will stay here forever. Won't you stay for a while?

In more recent history

Two residents of Mushroom Valley, a young girl named Amanda and her ferret Peach, have been through a lot together, from bite training to escape attempts. Through their struggles, Amanda has learned how to better care for Peach, and in turn, Peach has grown to better understand her "No-Fur."

Amanda craves attention from her peers. She turns to her trend-setting friend Kim for help, and together they hatch a scheme to win friends and influence people. Their creation: a ferret costume. Unfortunately, the plan backfires when a pair of bullies convinces her classmates that Amanda is wearing the costume because she thinks she's better than them. Even though she's teased and tormented by her fellow classmates, Amanda manages to turn their opinions of her around when she bravely volunteers to save the class hamsters from a rogue snake.

Meanwhile, Peach's encounter with Kim's pompous new ferret, Pavaratty, leaves her with an identity crisis and a longing to find the ferret of her dreams. Peach escapes from her cage to undertake a series of princess- affirming trials. In short order, she rounds up a menagerie of servants, sets up a thriving monarchy, and transforms a stolen sock into a beautiful gown.

Her fledgling kingdom still in need of resources, Peach sneaks a ride into the Handra stronghold in search of treasure. Her greedy nature leads to her recapture by the Handra, but only after a bizarre showdown with a lively runaway snake.

Unfortunately for Peach, despite her determination, no prince has come calling...yet.

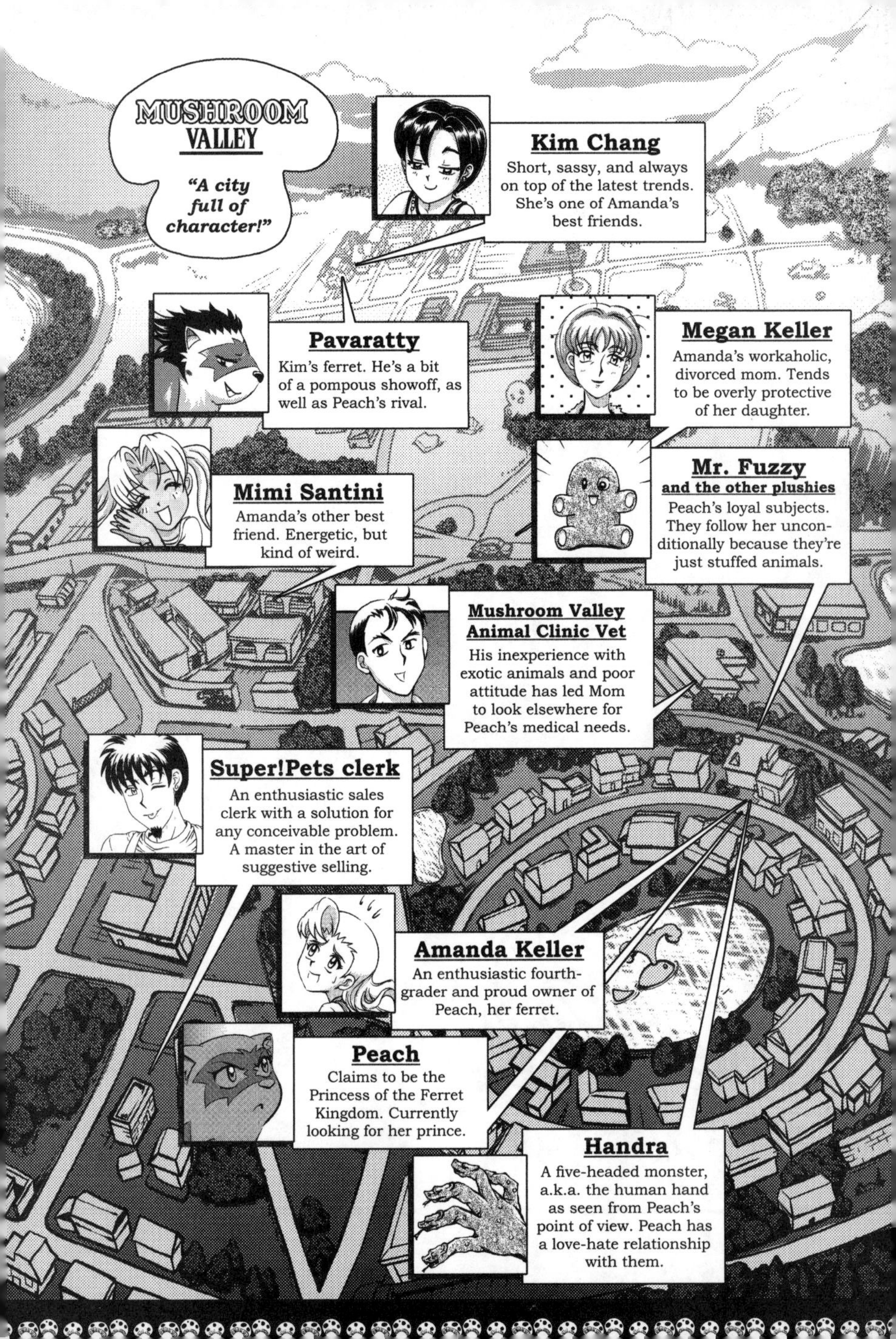
MUSHROOM VALLEY
"A city full of character!"
Kim Chang
Short, sassy, and always on top of the latest trends. She's one of Amanda's best friends.
Pavaratty
Kim's ferret. He's a bit of a pompous showoff, as well as Peach's rival.
Megan Keller
Amanda's workaholic, divorced mom. Tends to be overly protective of her daughter.
Mimi Santini
Amanda's other best friend. Energetic, but kind of weird.
Mr. Fuzzy
and the other plushies
Peach's loyal subjects. They follow her unconditionally because they're just stuffed animals.
Mushroom Valley Animal Clinic Vet
His inexperience with exotic animals and poor attitude has led Mom to look elsewhere for Peach's medical needs.
Super!Pets clerk
An enthusiastic sales clerk with a solution for any conceivable problem. A master in the art of suggestive selling.
Amanda Keller
An enthusiastic fourth-grader and proud owner of Peach, her ferret.
Peach
Claims to be the Princess of the Ferret Kingdom. Currently looking for her prince.
Handra
A five-headed monster, a.k.a. the human hand as seen from Peach's point of view. Peach has a love-hate relationship with them.

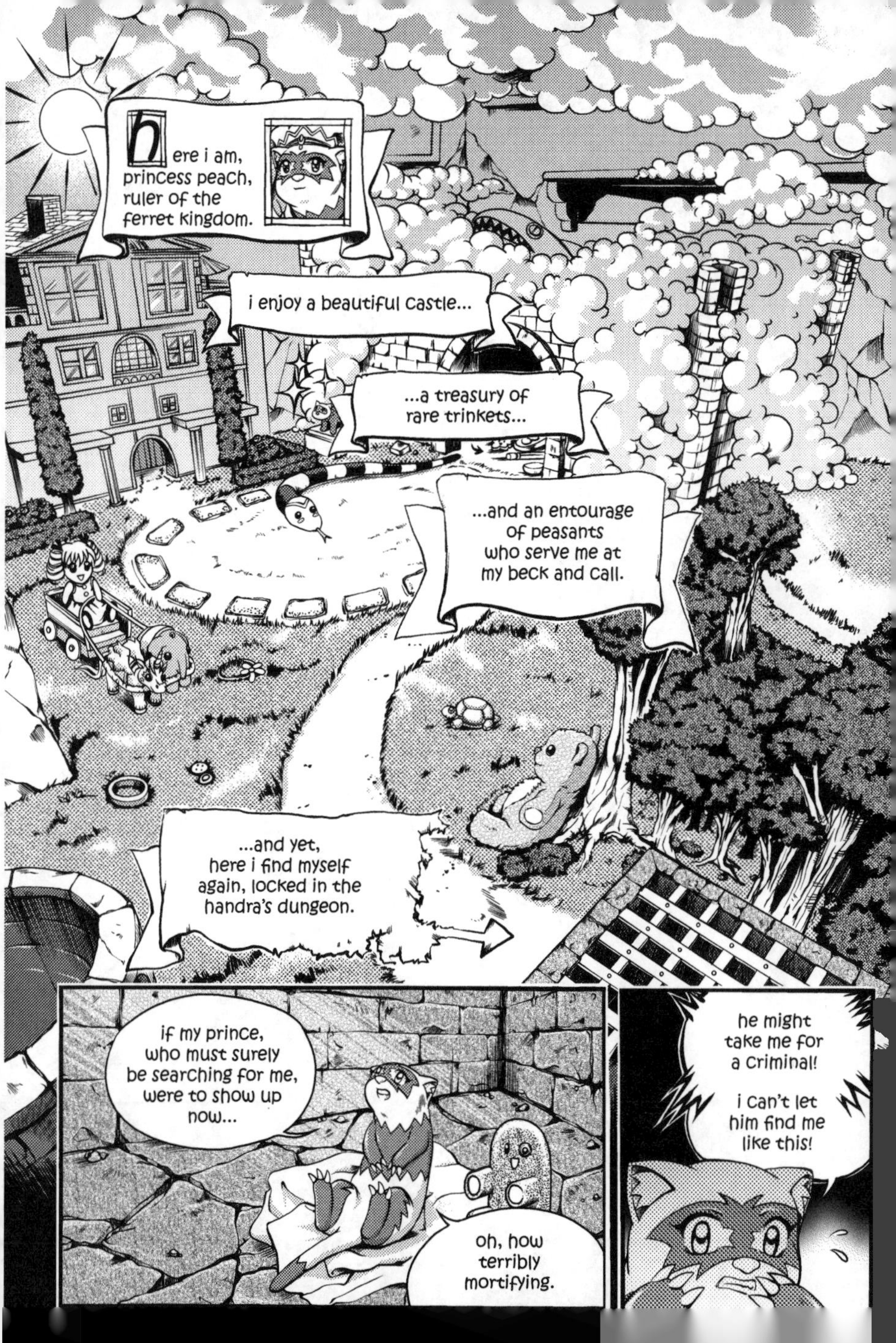
here i am, princess peach, ruler of the ferret kingdom.
i enjoy a beautiful castle...
...a treasury of rare trinkets...
...and an entourage of peasants who serve me at my beck and call.
...and yet, here i find myself again, locked in the handra's dungeon.
if my prince, who must surely be searching for me, were to show up now...
oh, how terribly mortifying.
he might take me for a criminal!
i can't let him find me like this!

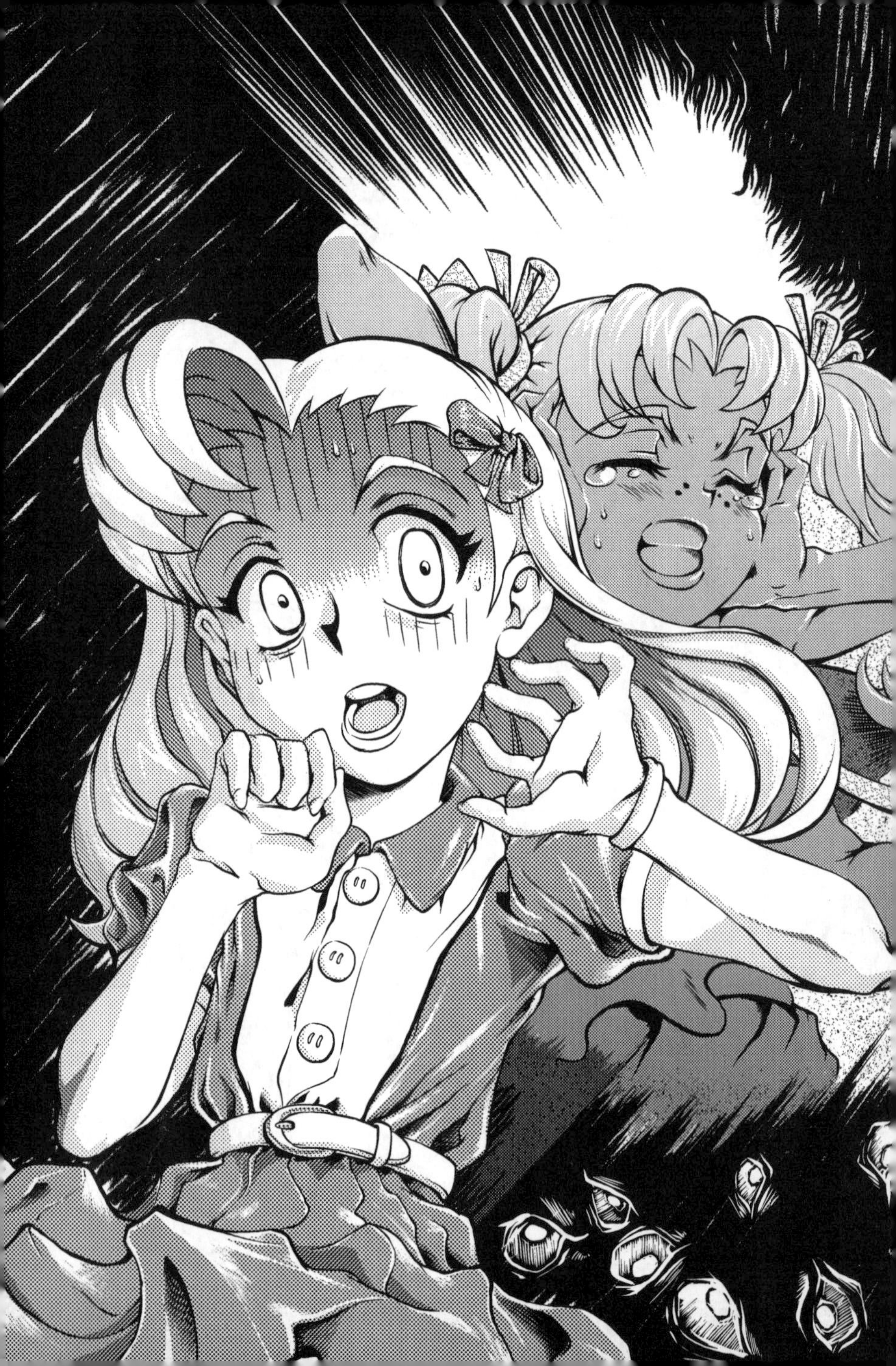

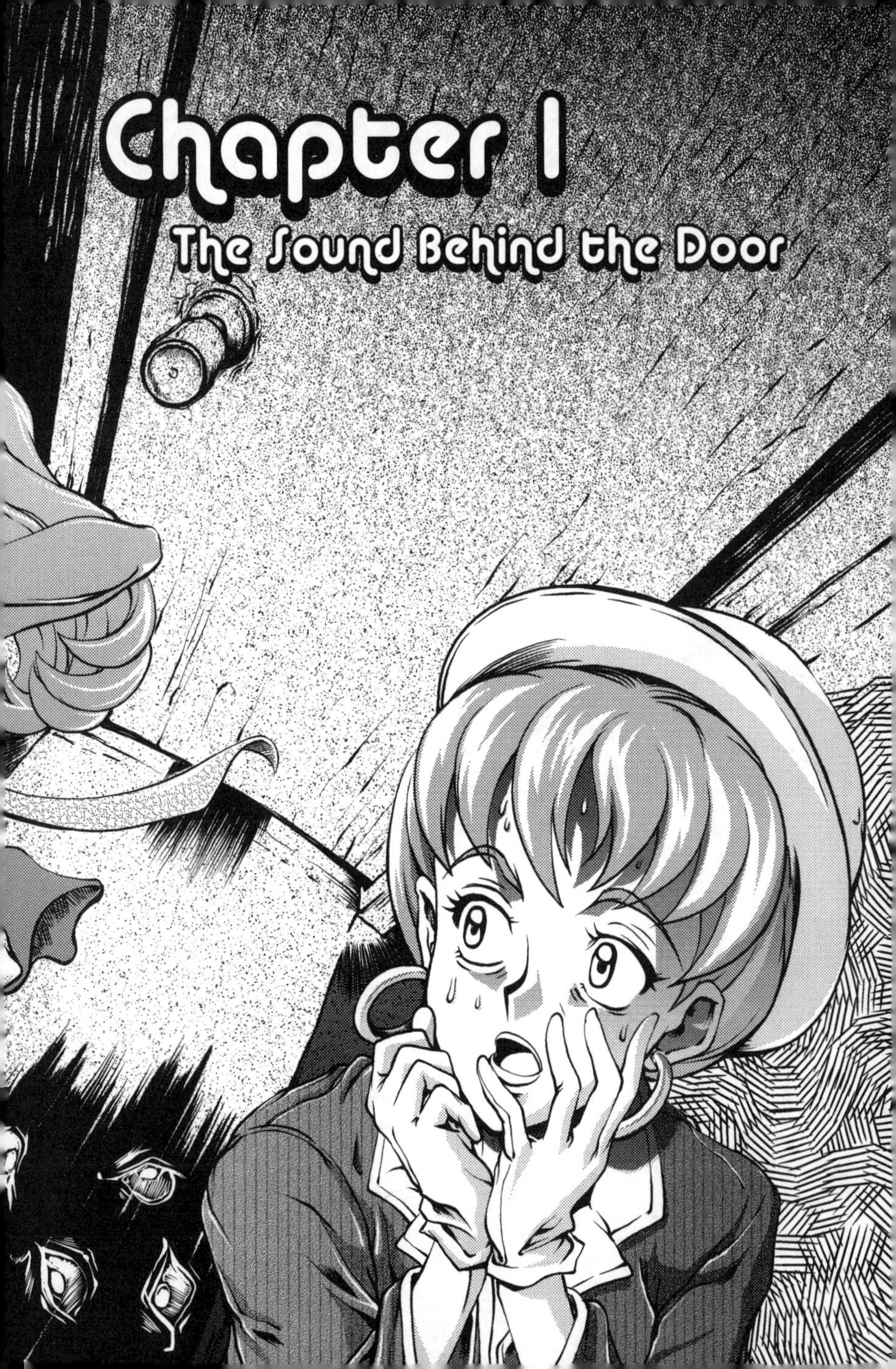
Chapter 1
The Sound Behind the Door

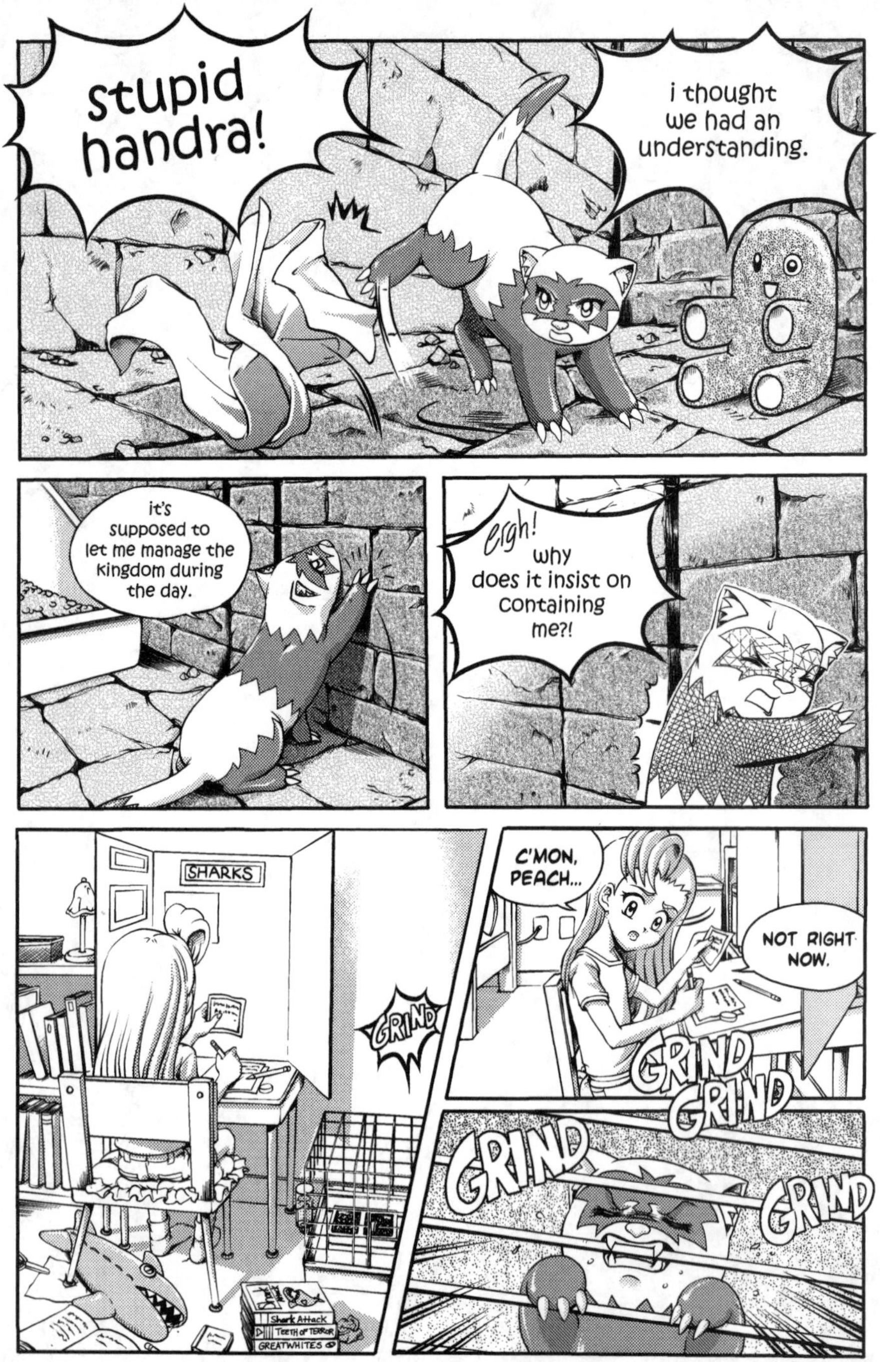
stupid handra!
VVM
i thought we had an understanding.
it's supposed to let me manage the kingdom during the day.
ergh!
why does it insist on containing me?!
SHARKS
GRIND
C'MON, PEACH...
NOT RIGHT NOW.
GRIND GRIND
GRIND
GRIND
Shark Attack
TEETH OF TERROR
GREATWHITES

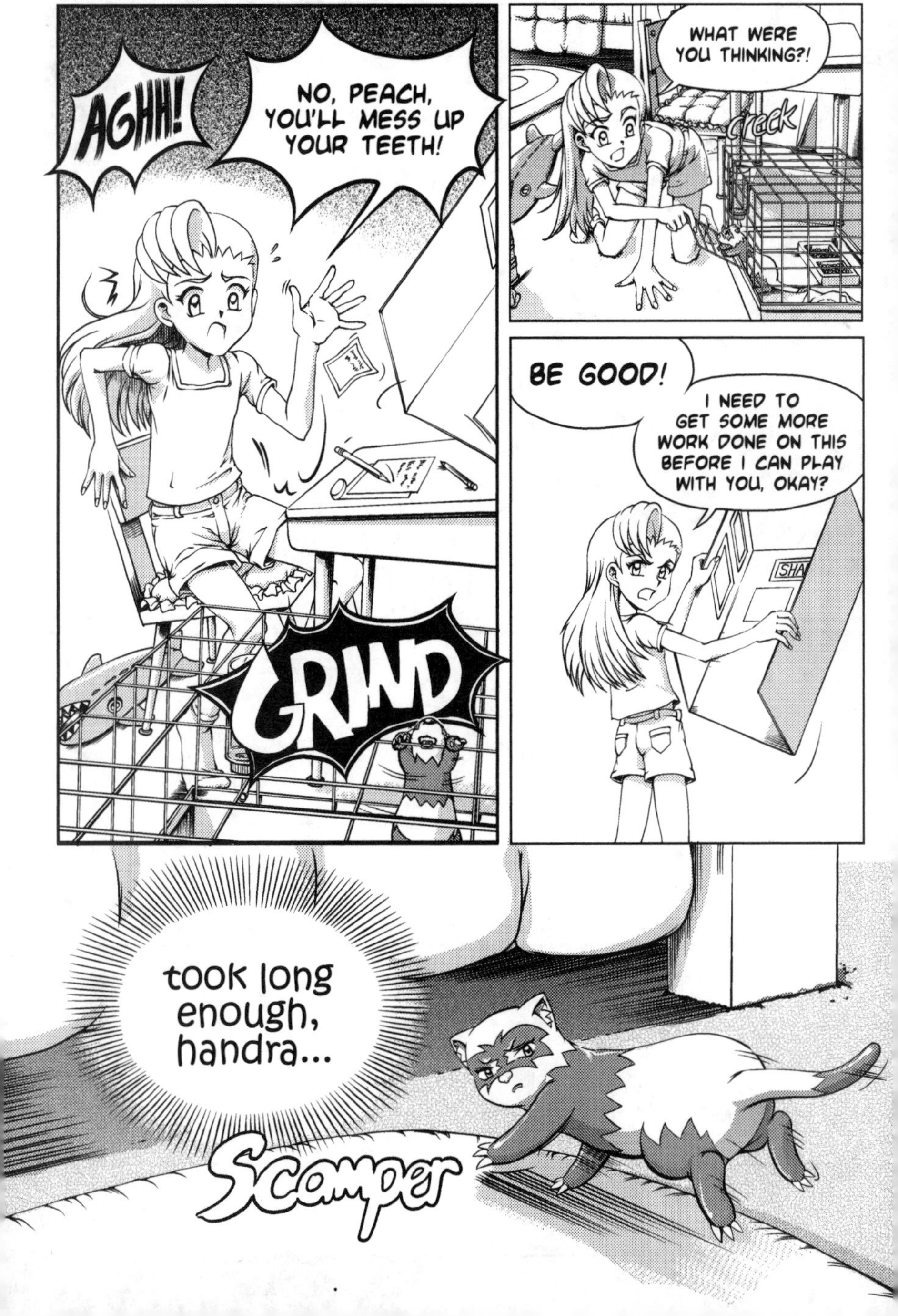
AGHH!
NO, PEACH, YOU'LL MESS UP YOUR TEETH!
GRIND
WHAT WERE YOU THINKING?!
creak
BE GOOD!
I NEED TO GET SOME MORE WORK DONE ON THIS BEFORE I CAN PLAY WITH YOU, OKAY?
took long enough, handra...
Scamper

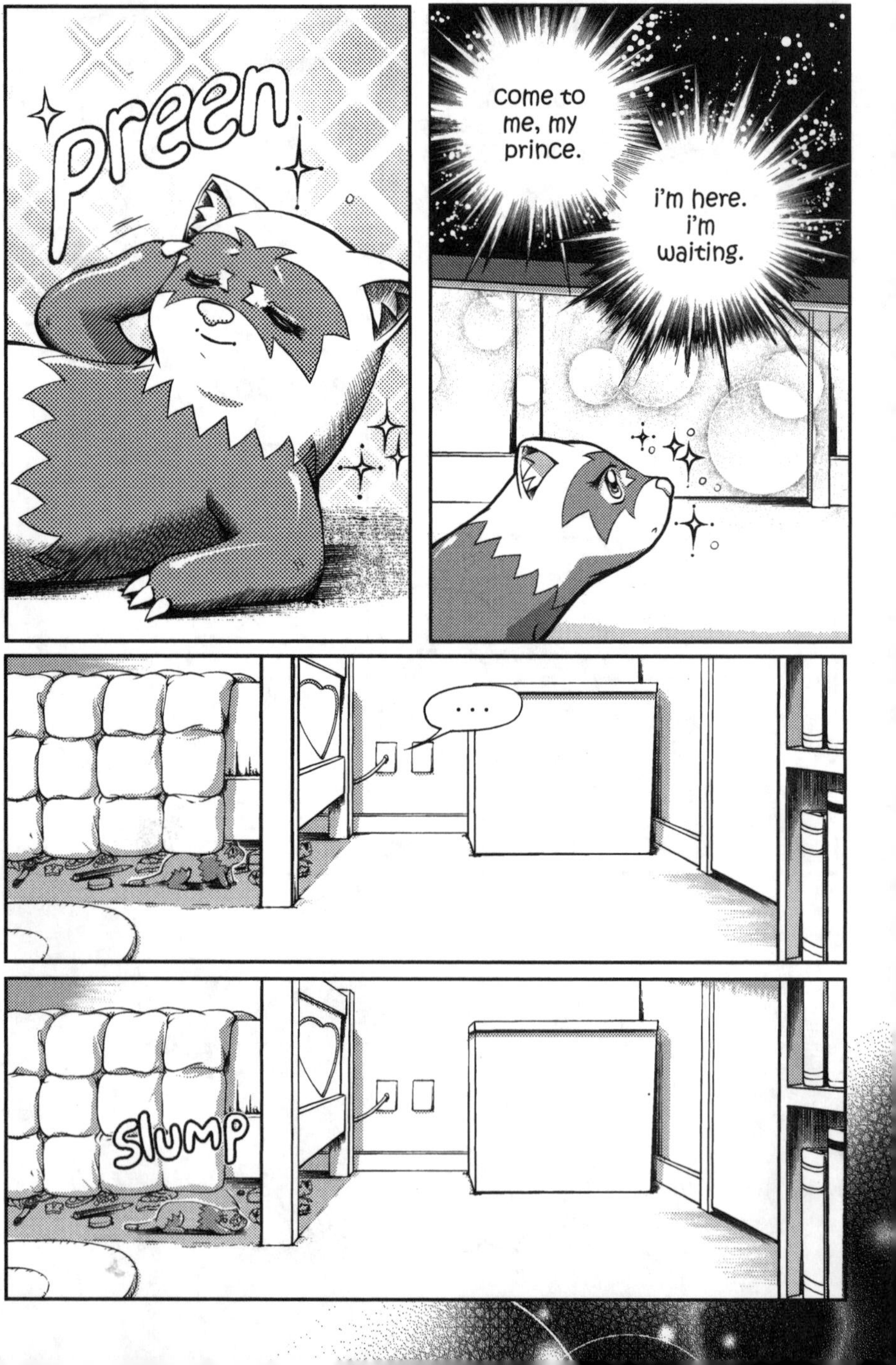
preen
come to me, my prince.
i'm here. i'm waiting.
...
slump

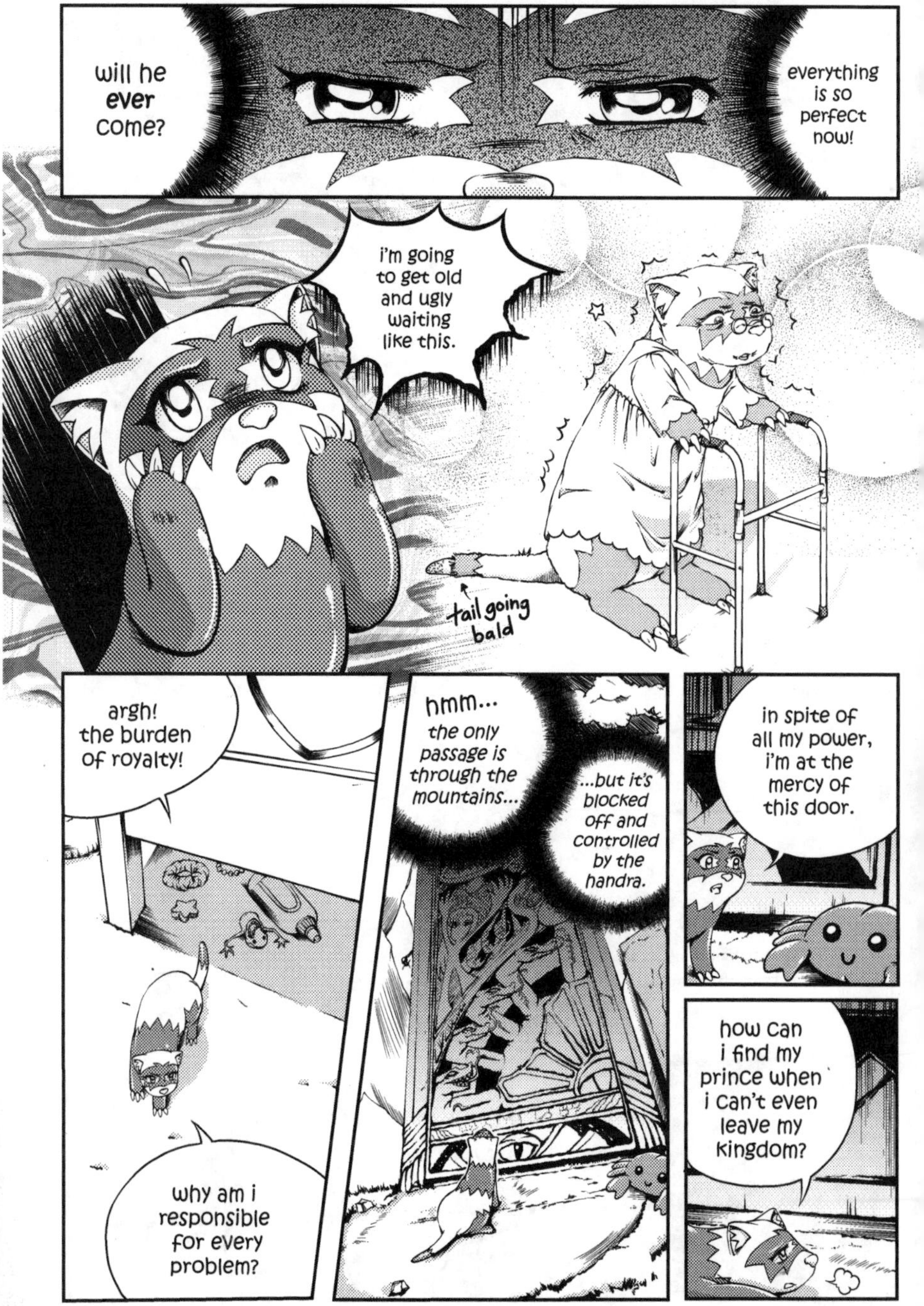
will he ever come?
everything is so perfect now!
i'm going to get old and ugly waiting like this.
tail going bald
argh! the burden of royalty!
why am i responsible for every problem?
hmm... the only passage is through the mountains...
...but it's blocked off and controlled by the handra.
in spite of all my power, i'm at the mercy of this door.
how can i find my prince when i can't even leave my kingdom?

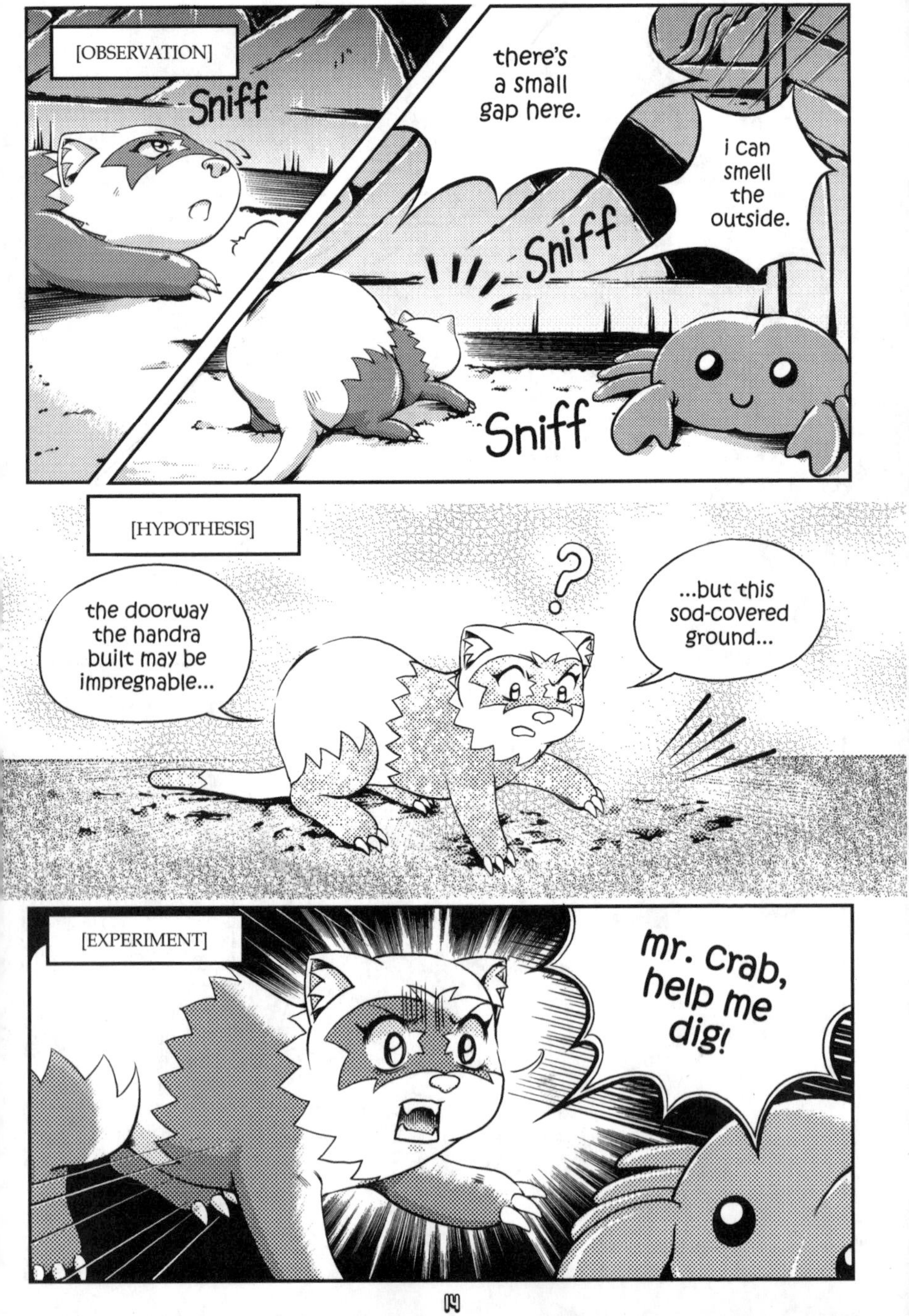
[OBSERVATION]
Sniff
there's a small gap here.
Sniff
i can smell the outside.
Sniff
[HYPOTHESIS]
the doorway the handra built may be impregnable...
?
...but this sod-covered ground...
[EXPERIMENT]
mr. Crab, help me dig!

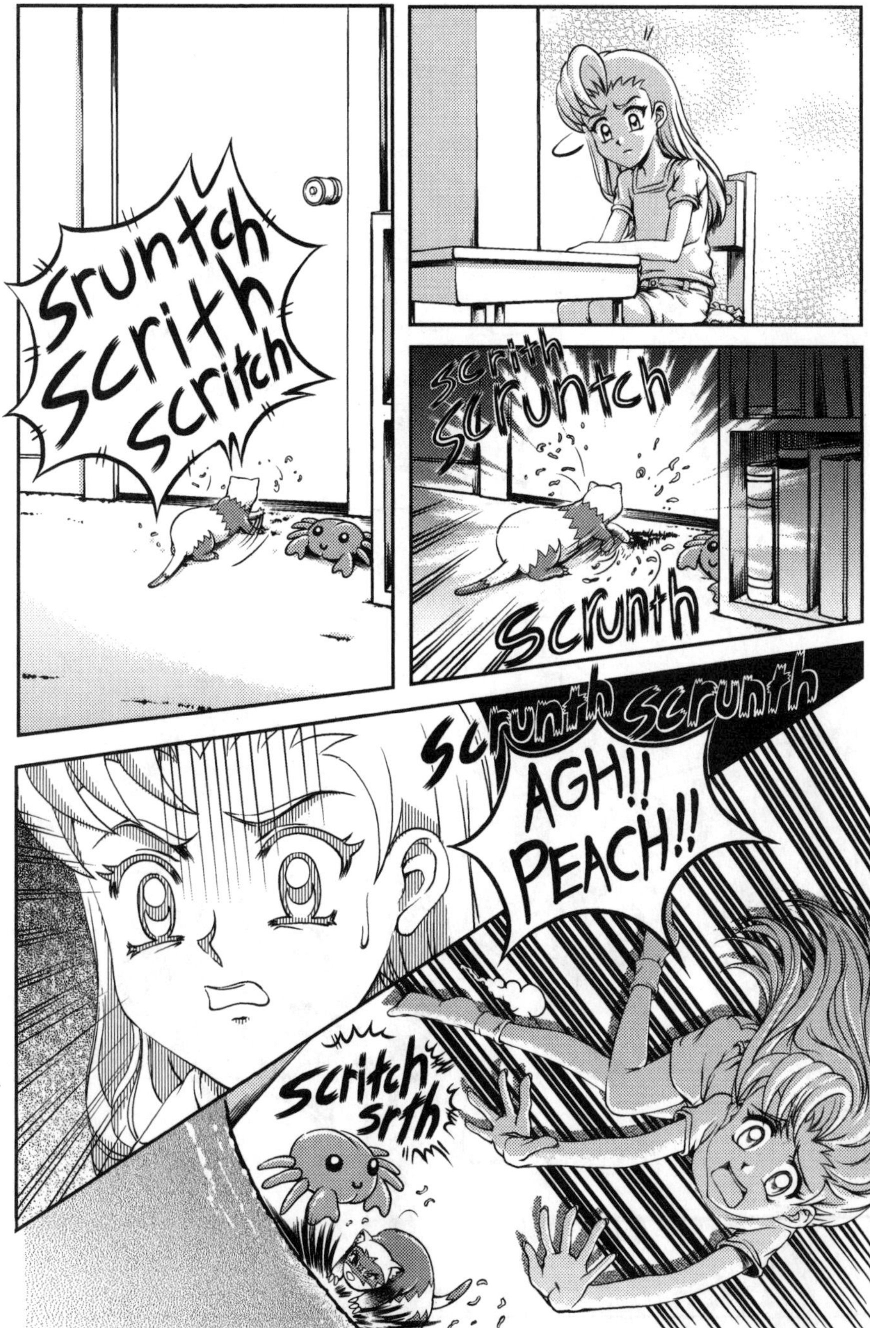
Sruntch
Scrith
scritch
scrith
Scruntch
Scrunth
Scrunth scrunth
AGH!!
PEACH!!
Scritch
srth

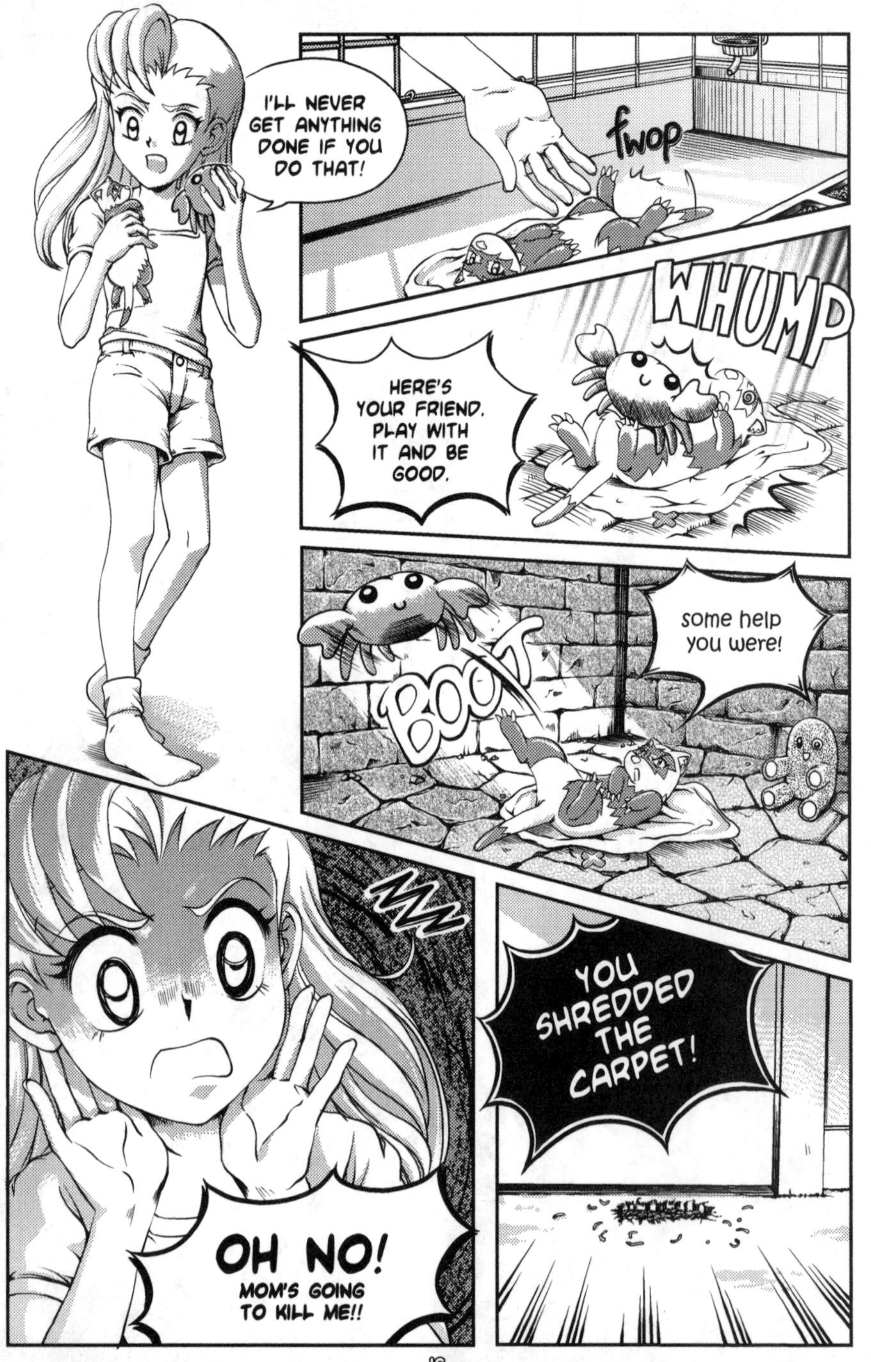
I'LL NEVER GET ANYTHING DONE IF YOU DO THAT!
fwop
WHUMP
HERE'S YOUR FRIEND. PLAY WITH IT AND BE GOOD.
some help you were!
BOOT
YOU SHREDDED THE CARPET!
OH NO! MOM'S GOING TO KILL ME!!

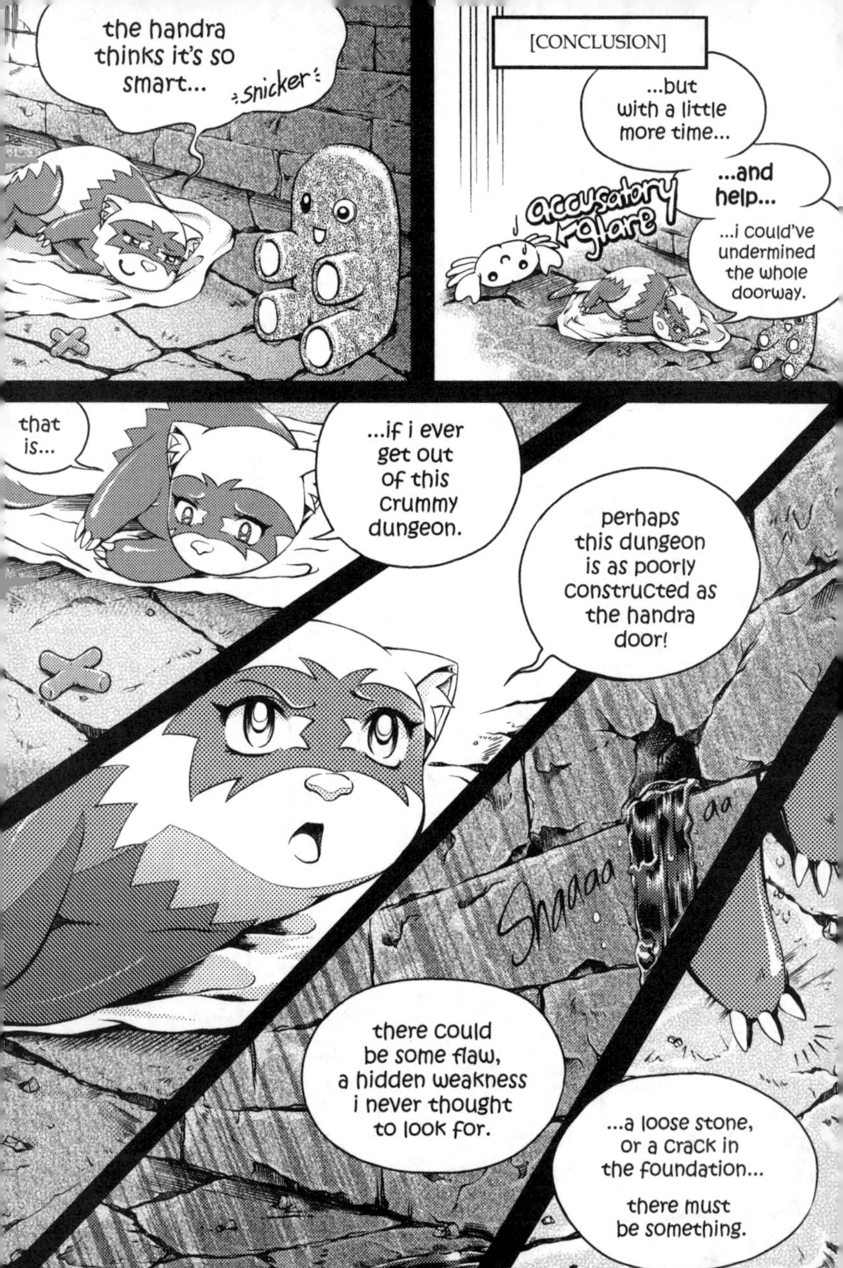

the handra thinks it's so smart...
snicker
[CONCLUSION]
...but with a little more time...
...and help...
...i could've undermined the whole doorway.
accusatory glare
that is...
...if i ever get out of this crummy dungeon.
perhaps this dungeon is as poorly constructed as the handra door!
Shaaaa aa
there could be some flaw, a hidden weakness i never thought to look for.
...a loose stone, or a crack in the foundation...
there must be something.

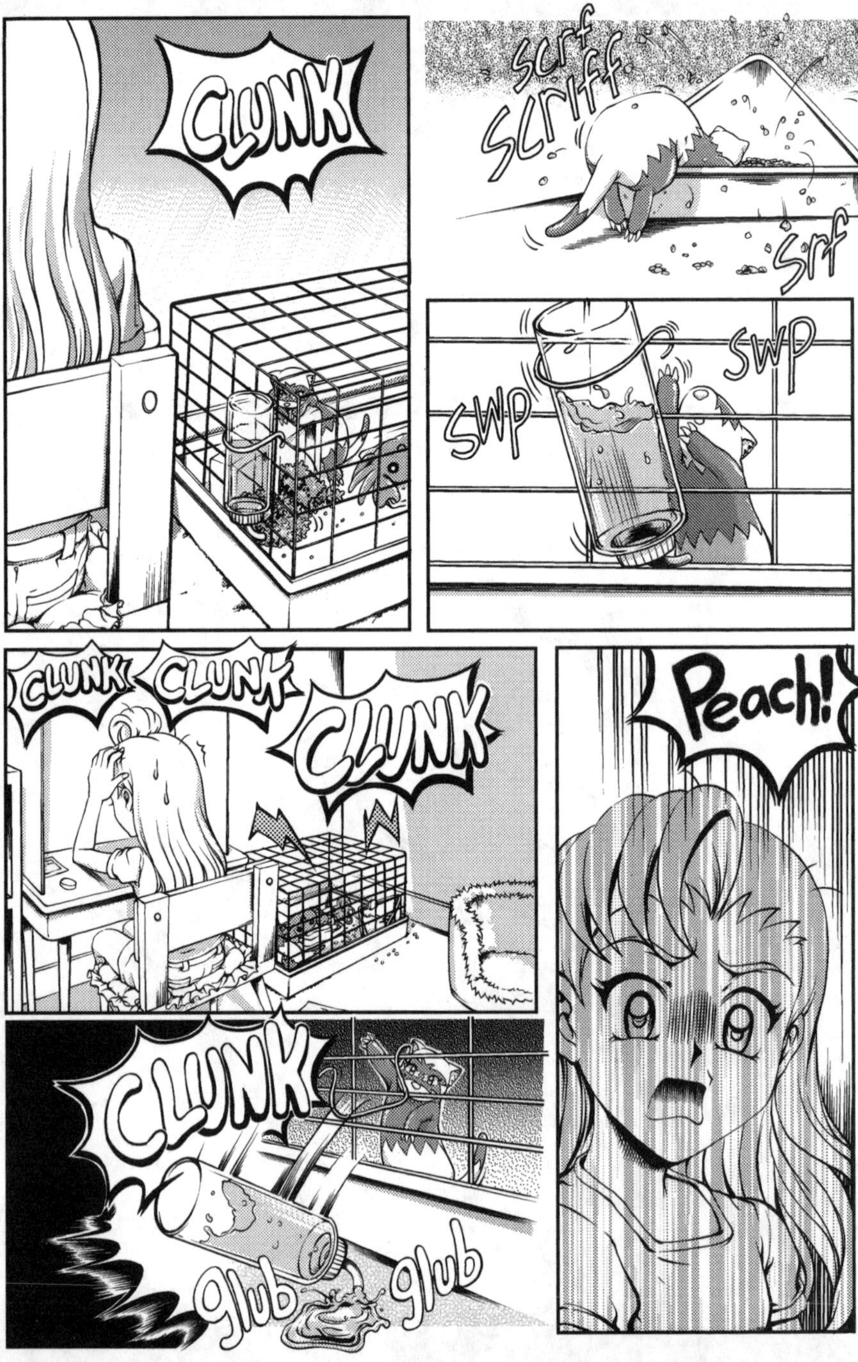
CLUNK
scrf
scriff
srf
swp
swp
CLUNK! CLUNK
CLUNK
CLUNK
glub glub
Peach!

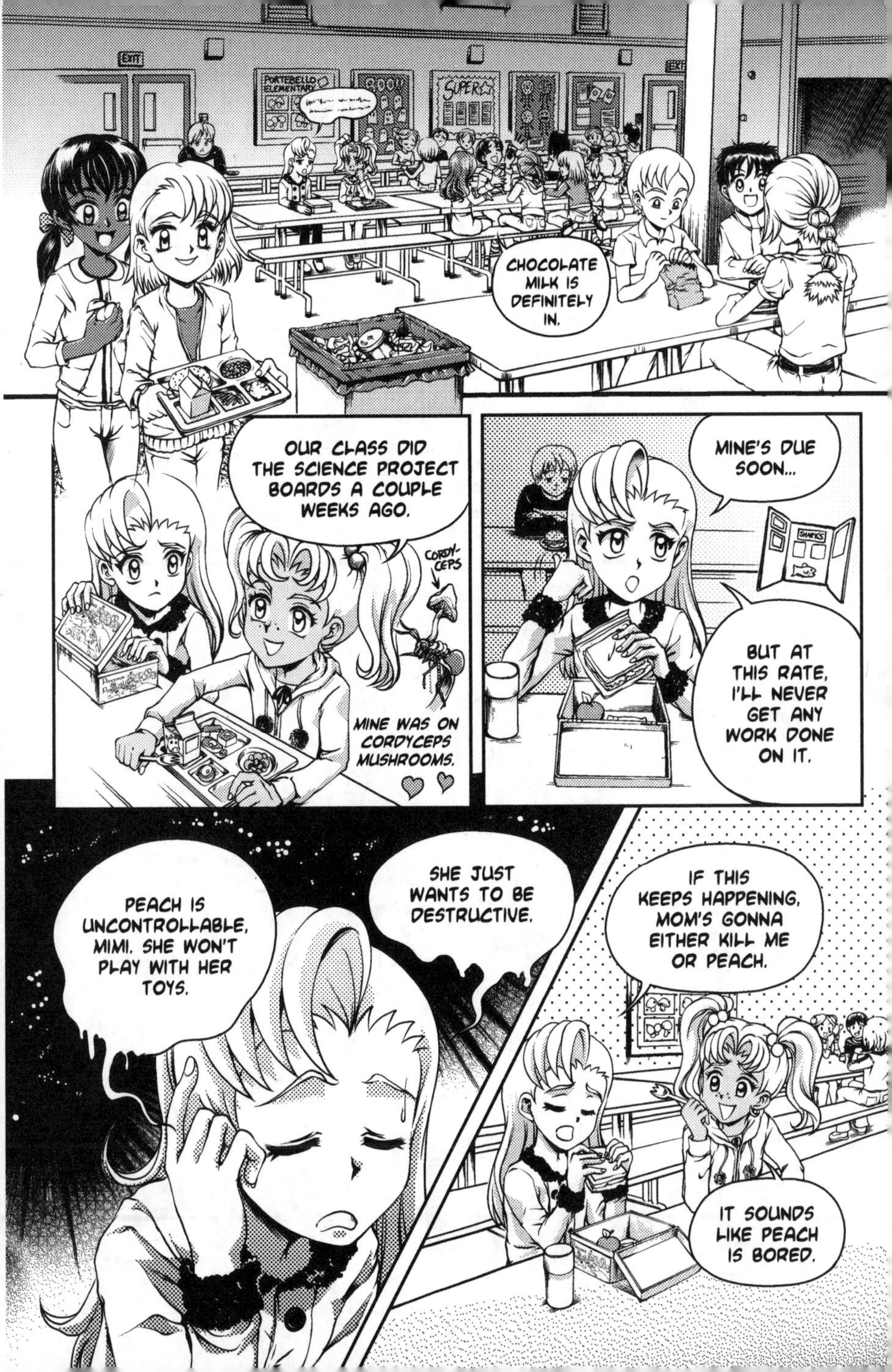
PORTEBELLO ELEMENTARY
SUPER
CHOCOLATE MILK IS DEFINITELY IN.
OUR CLASS DID THE SCIENCE PROJECT BOARDS A COUPLE WEEKS AGO.
CORDY-CEPS
MINE WAS ON CORDYCEPS MUSHROOMS.
MINE'S DUE SOON...
SHARKS
BUT AT THIS RATE, I'LL NEVER GET ANY WORK DONE ON IT.
PEACH IS UNCONTROLLABLE, MIMI. SHE WON'T PLAY WITH HER TOYS.
SHE JUST WANTS TO BE DESTRUCTIVE.
IF THIS KEEPS HAPPENING, MOM'S GONNA EITHER KILL ME OR PEACH.
IT SOUNDS LIKE PEACH IS BORED.

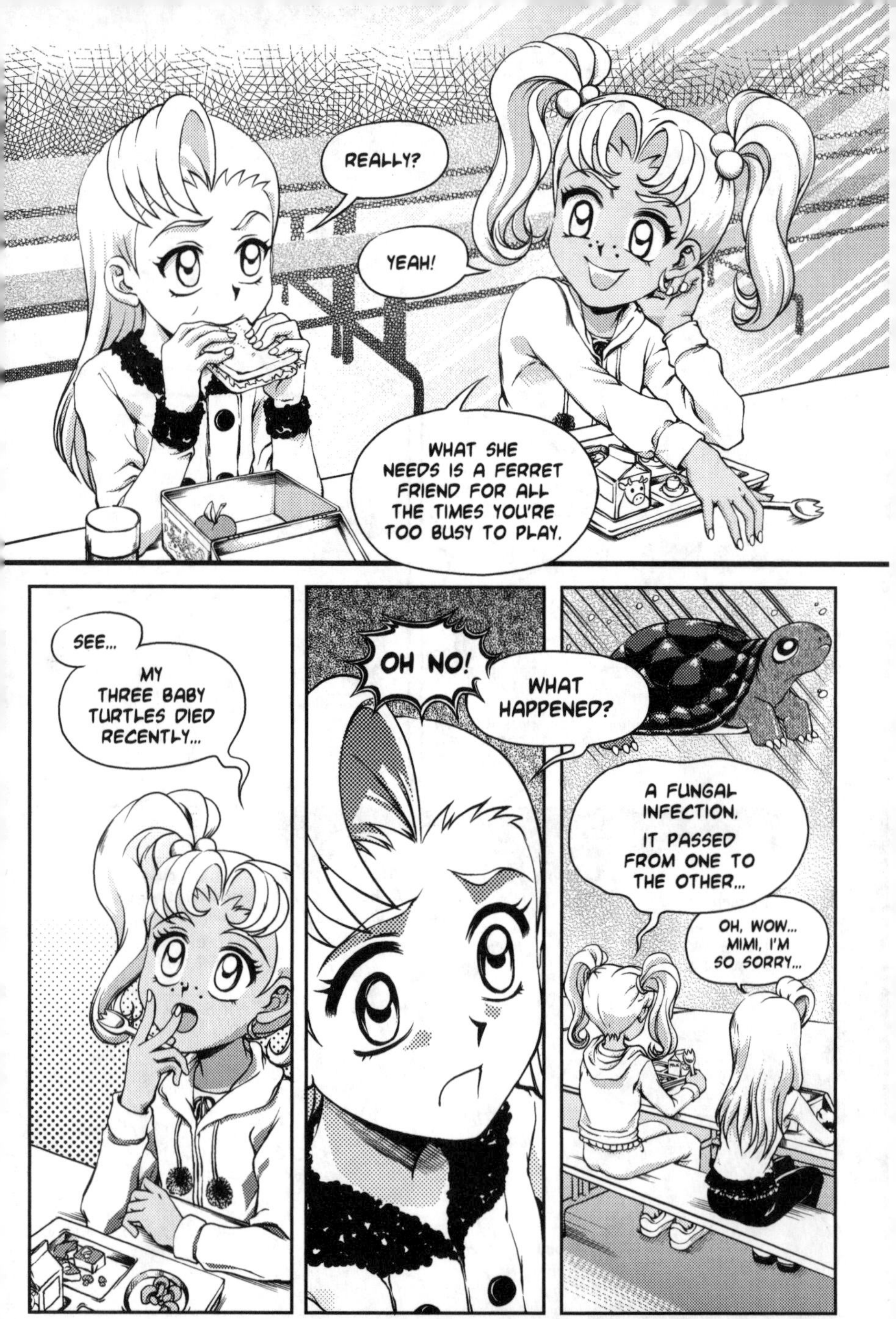
REALLY?
YEAH!
WHAT SHE NEEDS IS A FERRET FRIEND FOR ALL THE TIMES YOU'RE TOO BUSY TO PLAY.
SEE...
MY THREE BABY TURTLES DIED RECENTLY...
OH NO!
WHAT HAPPENED?
A FUNGAL INFECTION.
IT PASSED FROM ONE TO THE OTHER...
OH, WOW... MIMI, I'M SO SORRY...

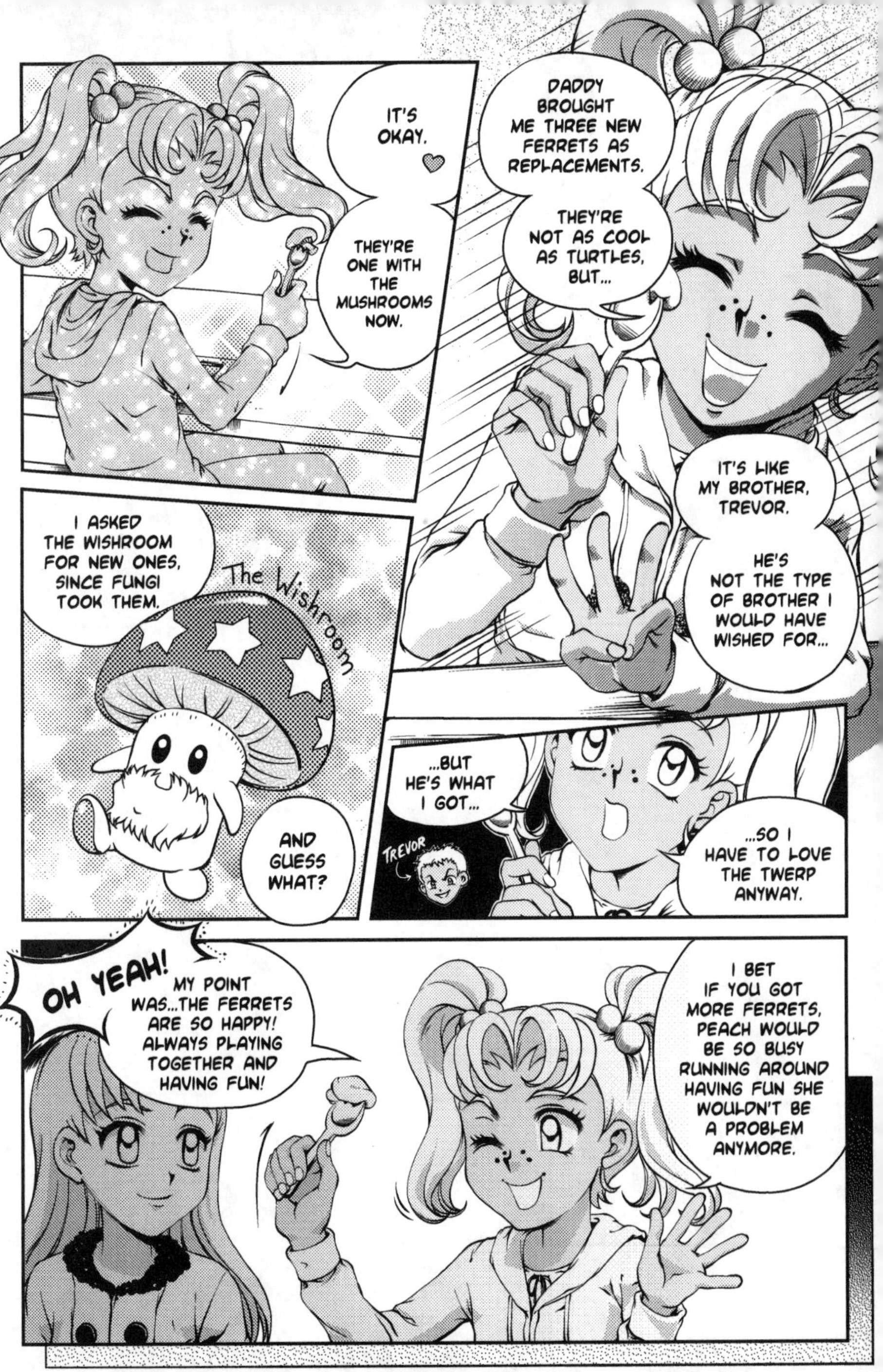
IT'S OKAY.
THEY'RE ONE WITH THE MUSHROOMS NOW.
DADDY BROUGHT ME THREE NEW FERRETS AS REPLACEMENTS.
THEY'RE NOT AS COOL AS TURTLES, BUT...
I ASKED THE WISHROOM FOR NEW ONES, SINCE FUNGI TOOK THEM.
The Wishroom
AND GUESS WHAT?
IT'S LIKE MY BROTHER, TREVOR.
HE'S NOT THE TYPE OF BROTHER I WOULD HAVE WISHED FOR...
...BUT HE'S WHAT I GOT...
TREVOR
...SO I HAVE TO LOVE THE TWERP ANYWAY.
OH YEAH!
MY POINT WAS...THE FERRETS ARE SO HAPPY! ALWAYS PLAYING TOGETHER AND HAVING FUN!
I BET IF YOU GOT MORE FERRETS, PEACH WOULD BE SO BUSY RUNNING AROUND HAVING FUN SHE WOULDN'T BE A PROBLEM ANYMORE.

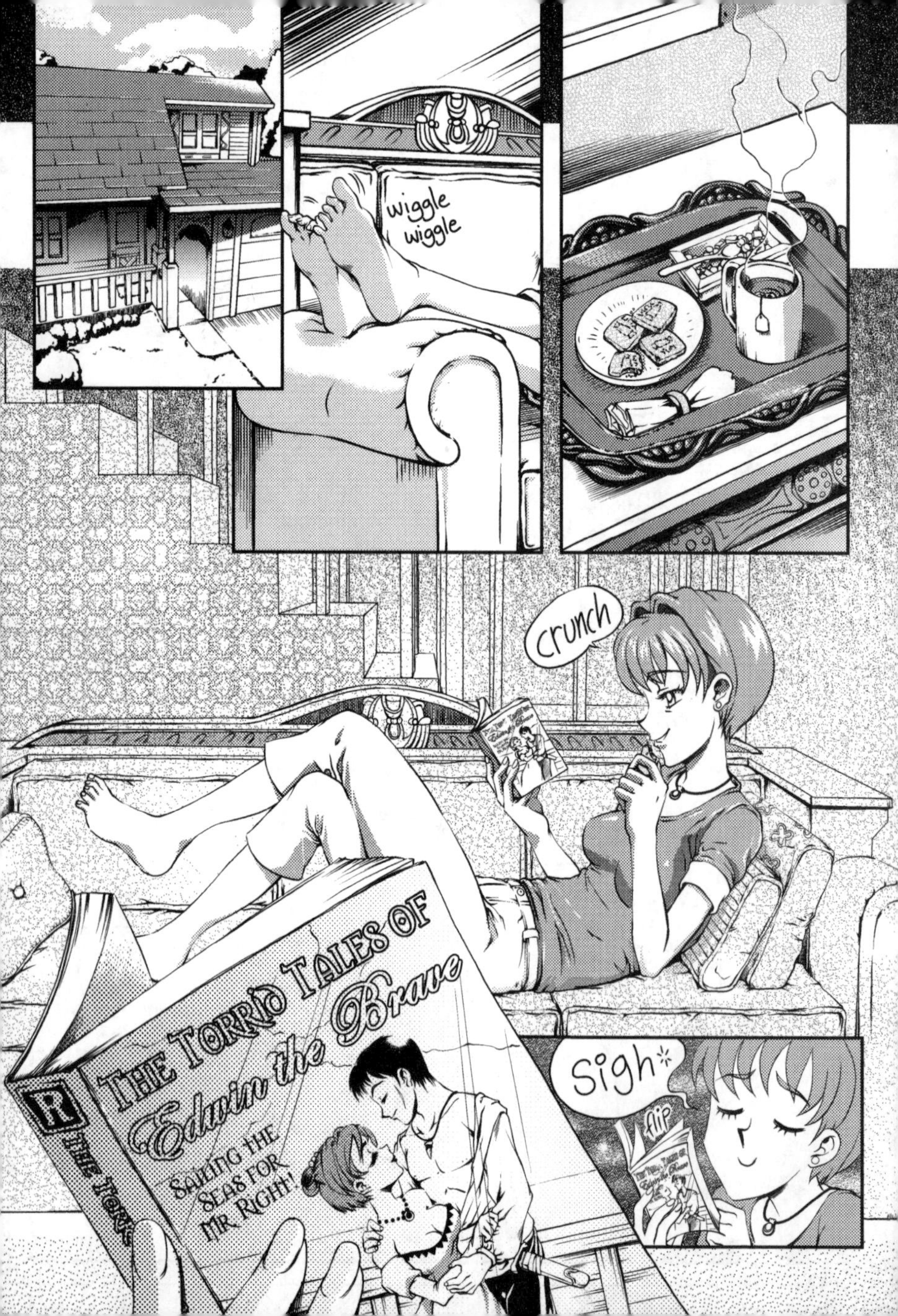
wiggle wiggle
crunch
THE TORRID TALES OF
Edwin the Brave
SAILING THE SEAS FOR MR RIGHT!
R
Sigh
flip

His eyes sparkled brilliantly, like diamonds in the soft flickering lamplight of the lower decks. Fresh blood dripped from his brow, staining what remained of his fancy attire. His black hair was matted with sweat and blood, but he didn't care. He smiled as he swaggered toward the ship's hold, thinking of the treasure awaiting him there.

Edwin threw open the doors, moving like a man possessed, but it wasn't ale that intoxicated the Sea Wolf. The thrill of piracy, the excess of plunder drove him. It drove him here, below decks, to the hold, where Meg hid in the shadows.

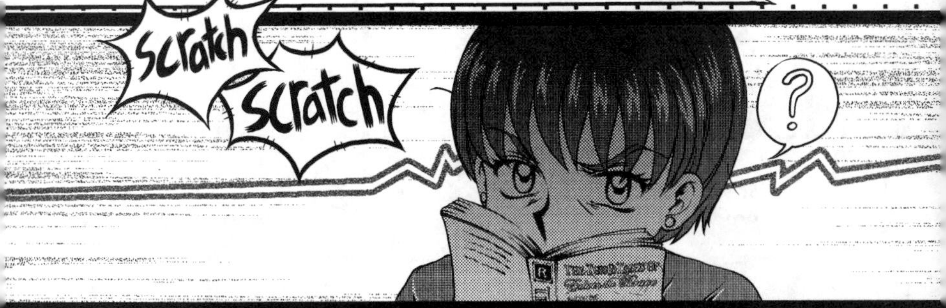
Scratch
Scratch
?

"You're right milady." A wry smile graced the Sea Wolf's face. "I am a scoundrel. But it's thanks to me that you are safe now."

He moved closer to Meg, pressing up against her. She stumbled back, resistant to his touch, even as she felt herself strangely attracted.

"I could plunder any treasure on the ocean, but only this treasure will do..."

His li... This ... word m...

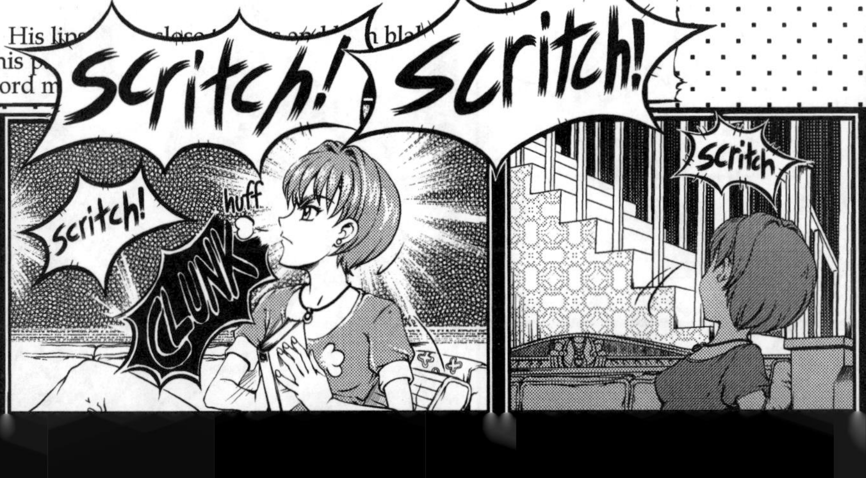
Scritch!
Scritch!
Scritch!
huff
CLUNK
Scritch

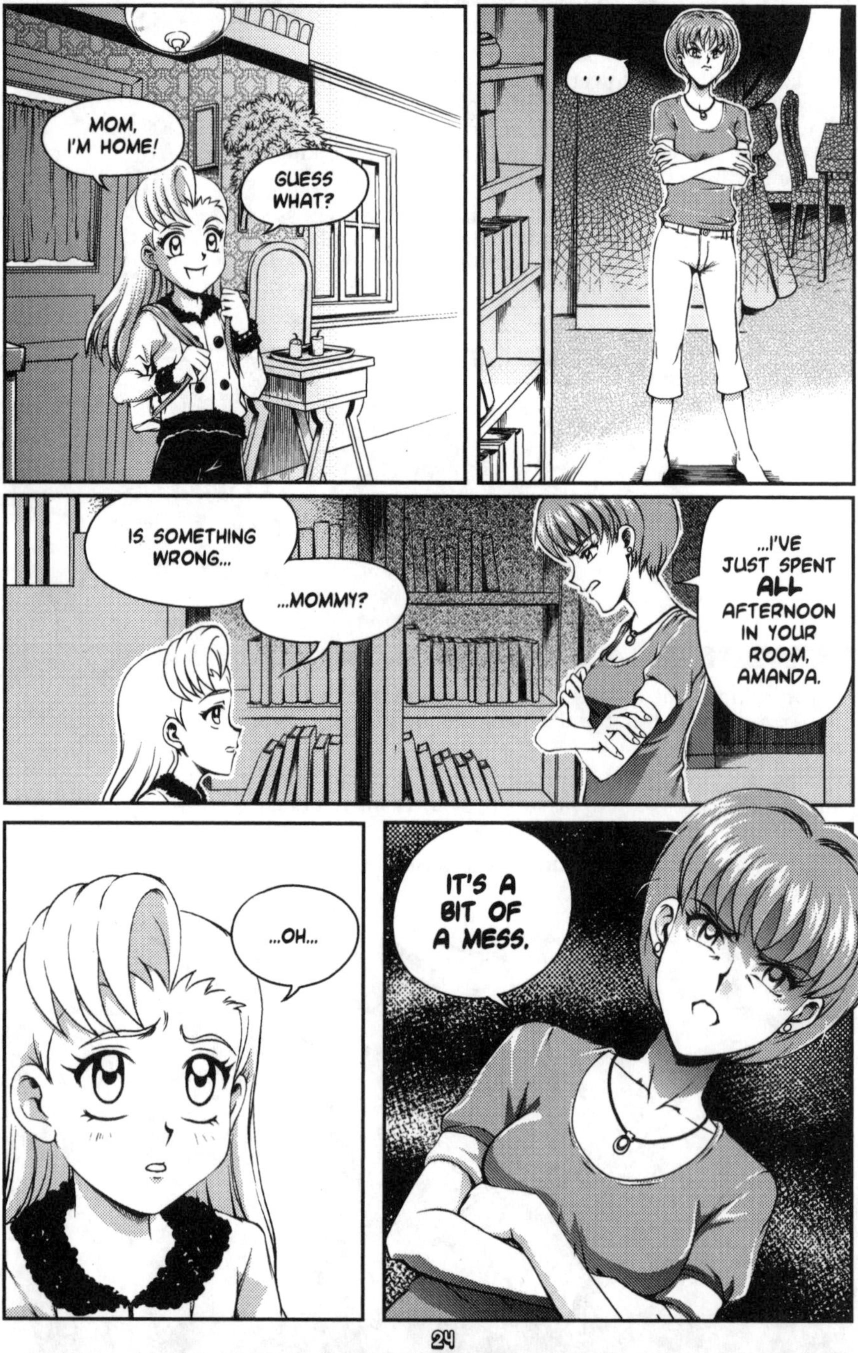
MOM, I'M HOME!
GUESS WHAT?
...
IS SOMETHING WRONG...
...MOMMY?
...I'VE JUST SPENT ALL AFTERNOON IN YOUR ROOM, AMANDA.
...OH...
IT'S A BIT OF A MESS.

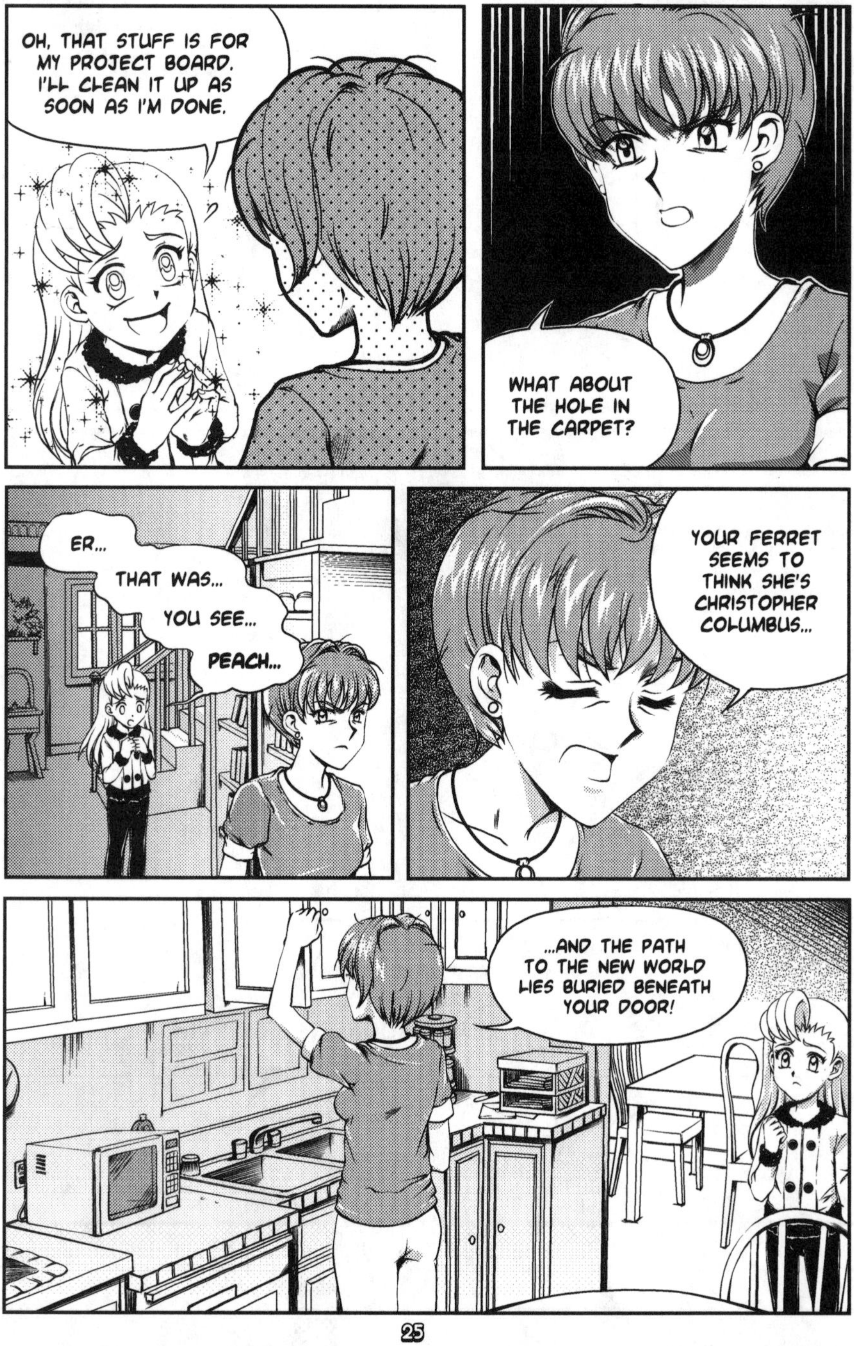
OH, THAT STUFF IS FOR MY PROJECT BOARD. I'LL CLEAN IT UP AS SOON AS I'M DONE.
WHAT ABOUT THE HOLE IN THE CARPET?
ER...
THAT WAS...
YOU SEE...
PEACH...
YOUR FERRET SEEMS TO THINK SHE'S CHRISTOPHER COLUMBUS...
...AND THE PATH TO THE NEW WORLD LIES BURIED BENEATH YOUR DOOR!

MIMI SAYS--

I CALLED AROUND TO A COUPLE OF VETS TODAY.

I FOUND A VET THAT SPECIALIZES IN FERRETS.

Shaaa

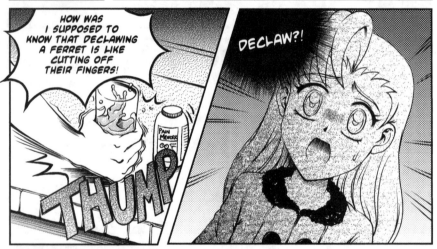

HOW WAS I SUPPOSED TO KNOW THAT DECLAWING A FERRET IS LIKE CUTTING OFF THEIR FINGERS!

PAIN MENDER

THUMP

DECLAW?!

THEY'LL DECLAW CATS!

IT SEEMED LIKE A PRACTICAL SUGGESTION!

Shaka Shaka

gulp!

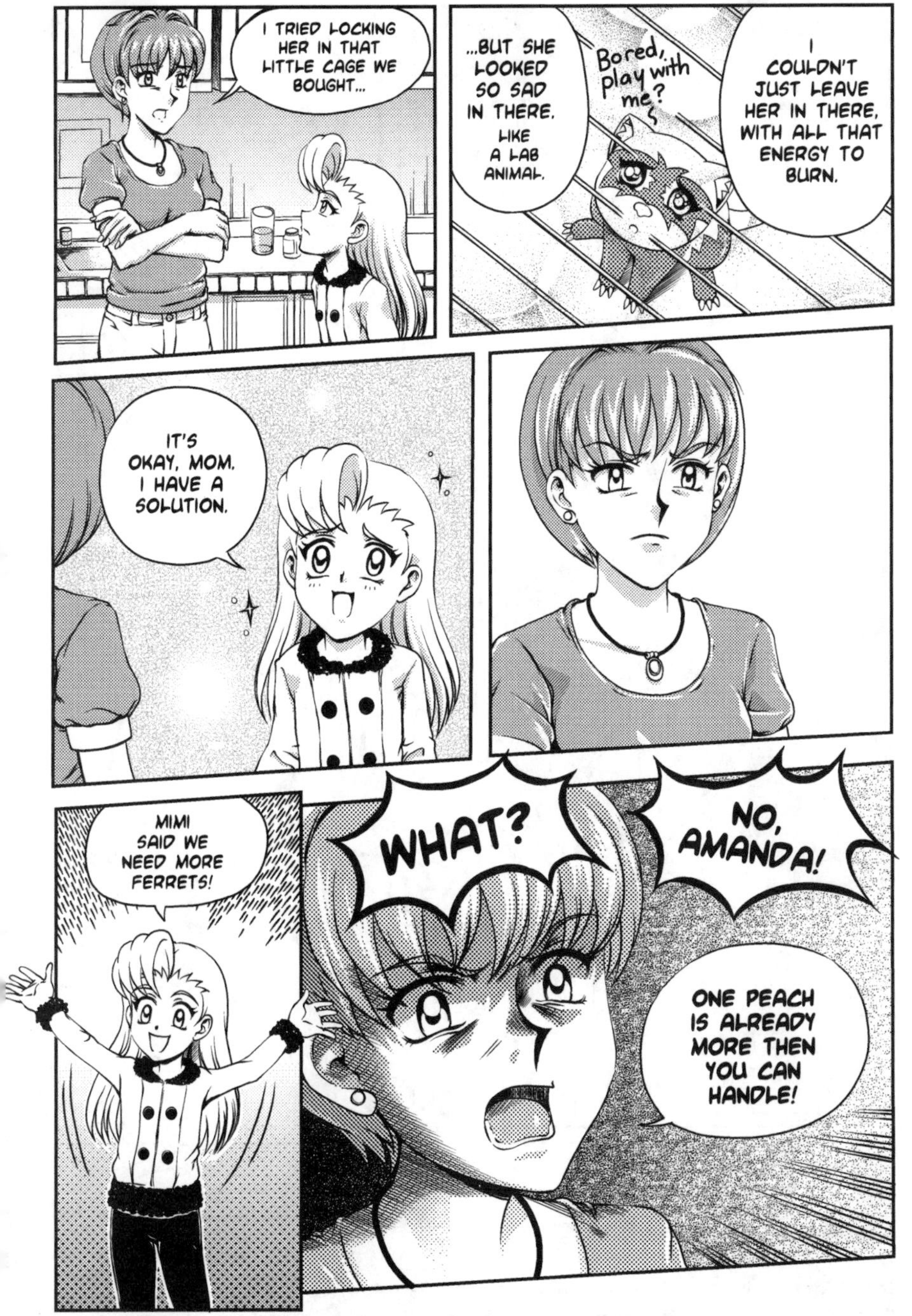
I TRIED LOCKING HER IN THAT LITTLE CAGE WE BOUGHT...
...BUT SHE LOOKED SO SAD IN THERE.
LIKE A LAB ANIMAL.
Bored, play with me?
I COULDN'T JUST LEAVE HER IN THERE, WITH ALL THAT ENERGY TO BURN.
IT'S OKAY, MOM. I HAVE A SOLUTION.
MIMI SAID WE NEED MORE FERRETS!
WHAT?
NO, AMANDA!
ONE PEACH IS ALREADY MORE THEN YOU CAN HANDLE!

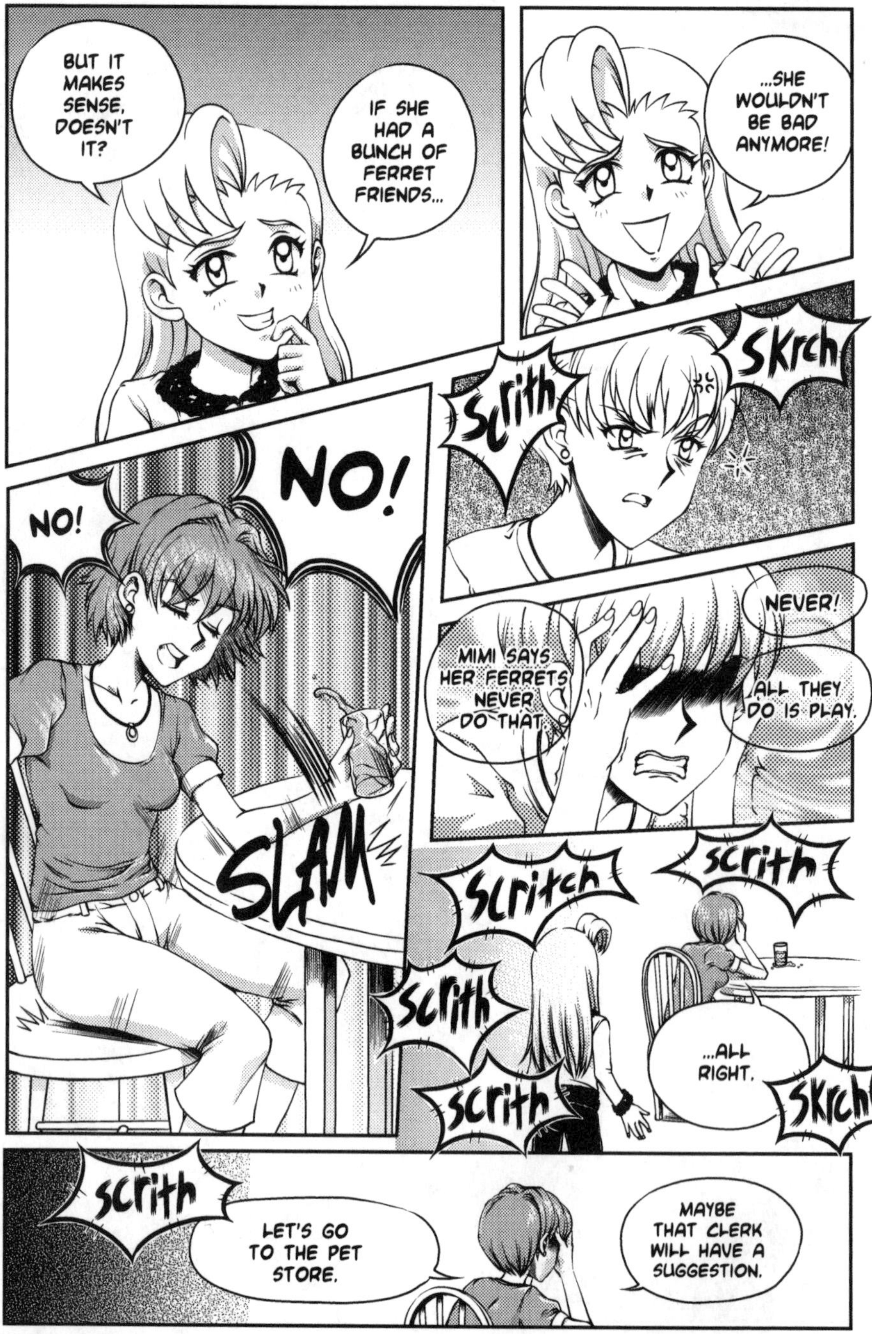
BUT IT MAKES SENSE, DOESN'T IT?
IF SHE HAD A BUNCH OF FERRET FRIENDS...
...SHE WOULDN'T BE BAD ANYMORE!
Scrith
Skrch
NO!
NO!
SLAM
MIMI SAYS HER FERRETS NEVER DO THAT.
NEVER!
ALL THEY DO IS PLAY.
Scritch
scrith
Scrith
scrith
...ALL RIGHT.
Skrch
scrith
LET'S GO TO THE PET STORE.
MAYBE THAT CLERK WILL HAVE A SUGGESTION.

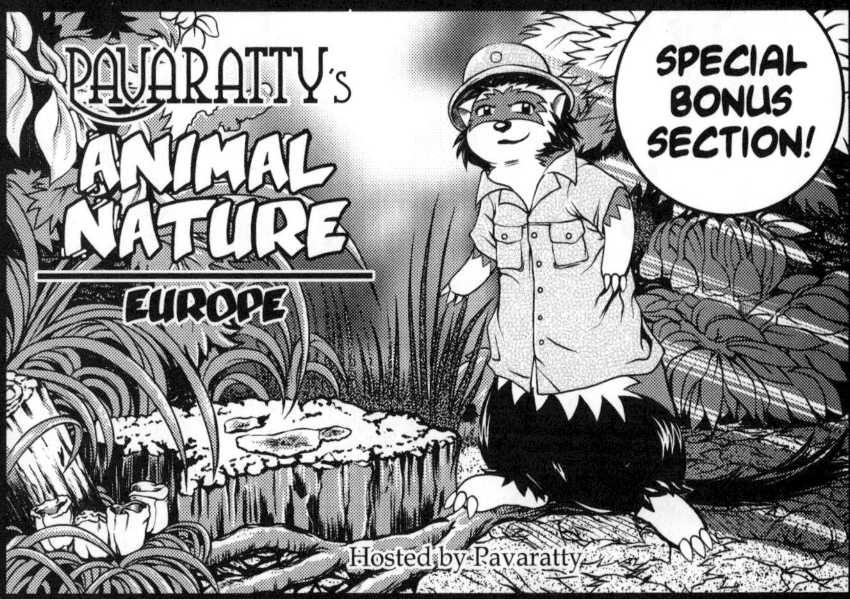
PAVARATTY's
ANIMAL NATURE
EUROPE
SPECIAL BONUS SECTION!
Hosted by Pavaratty

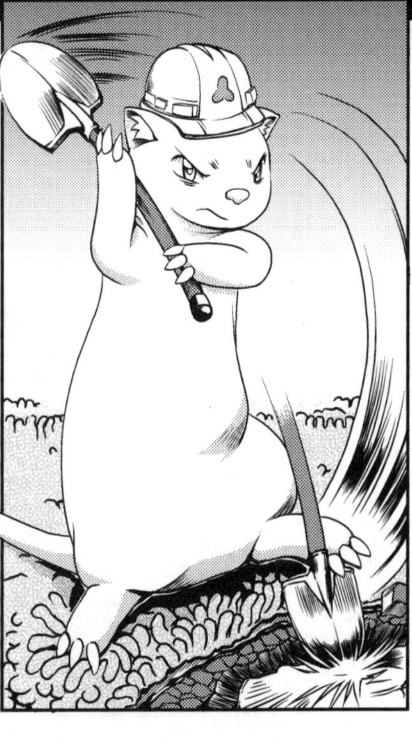

Episode 1: The Digging Ferret

Ferrets have a predilection towards burrowing—a trait passed down from our ill-mannered ancestor, the forest-dwelling European Polecat. Using their claws as excavating tools, these feral ferret cousins can scoot out tremendous amounts of dirt to build dens and find prey. Unlike the polecat, rarely do we ferrets need to use digging for hunting or building—enjoying instead the plush surroundings and free meals provided by our handlers. But our inherited capacity for digging isn't wasted. It comes in quite handy for exploring.

Cracks, holes, gaps, and tunnels entice us with the promise of new sights and smells. When the path is blocked, our claws can be employed to rend all but the hardest substances. Alas, some handlers see digging as an act of desecration and reprimand us. They do not understand that ferrets are simply compelled to dig our way into these new worlds of discovery.

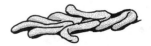

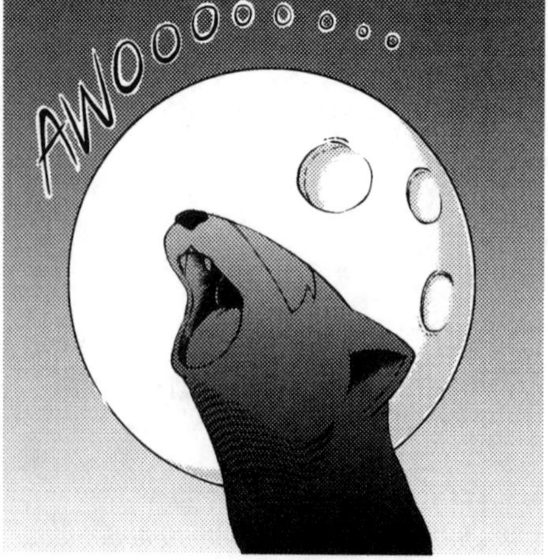
AWOOOOOOO...

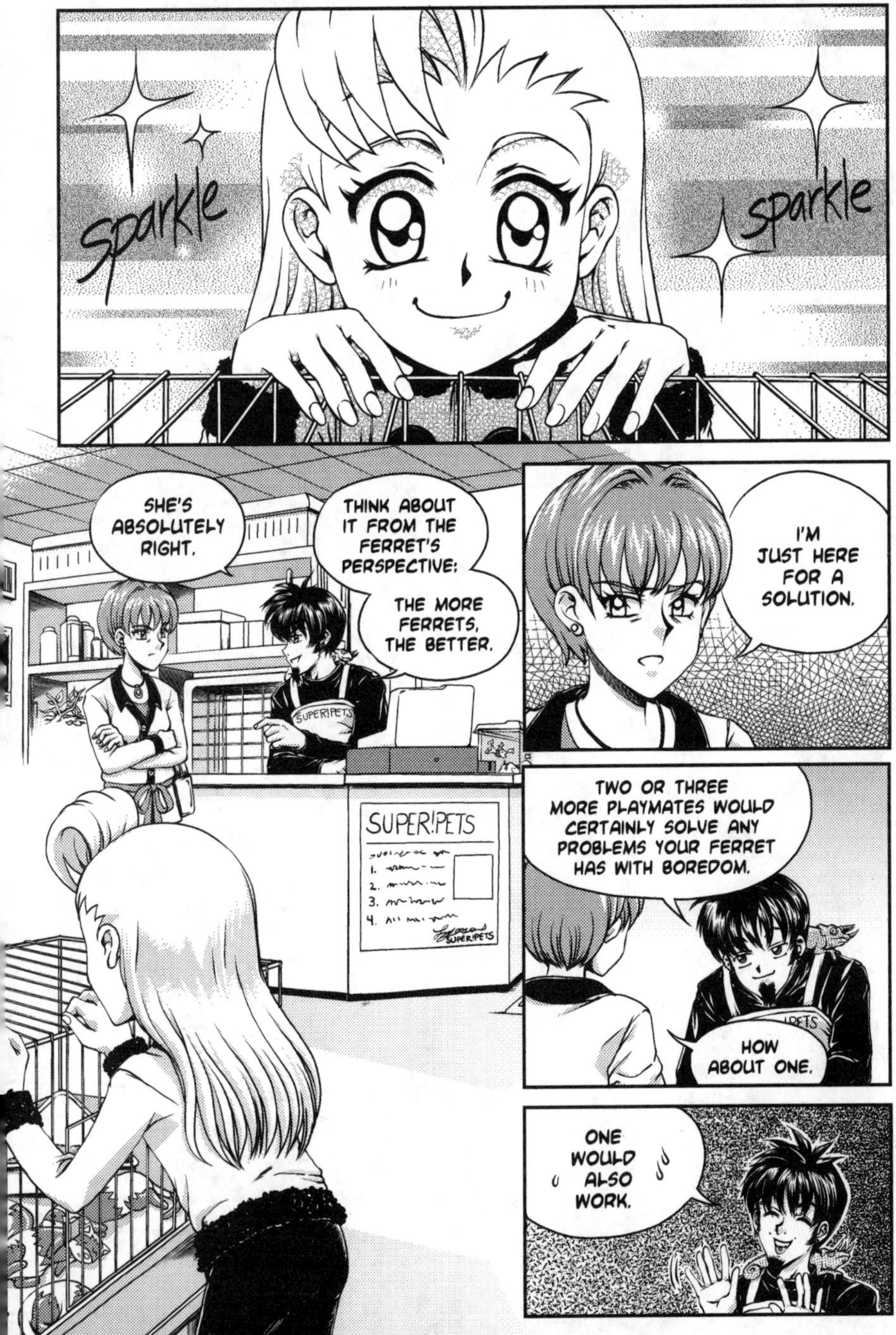
sparkle
sparkle
SHE'S ABSOLUTELY RIGHT.
THINK ABOUT IT FROM THE FERRET'S PERSPECTIVE:
THE MORE FERRETS, THE BETTER.
SUPER!PETS
SUPER!PETS
I'M JUST HERE FOR A SOLUTION.
TWO OR THREE MORE PLAYMATES WOULD CERTAINLY SOLVE ANY PROBLEMS YOUR FERRET HAS WITH BOREDOM.
HOW ABOUT ONE.
ONE WOULD ALSO WORK.

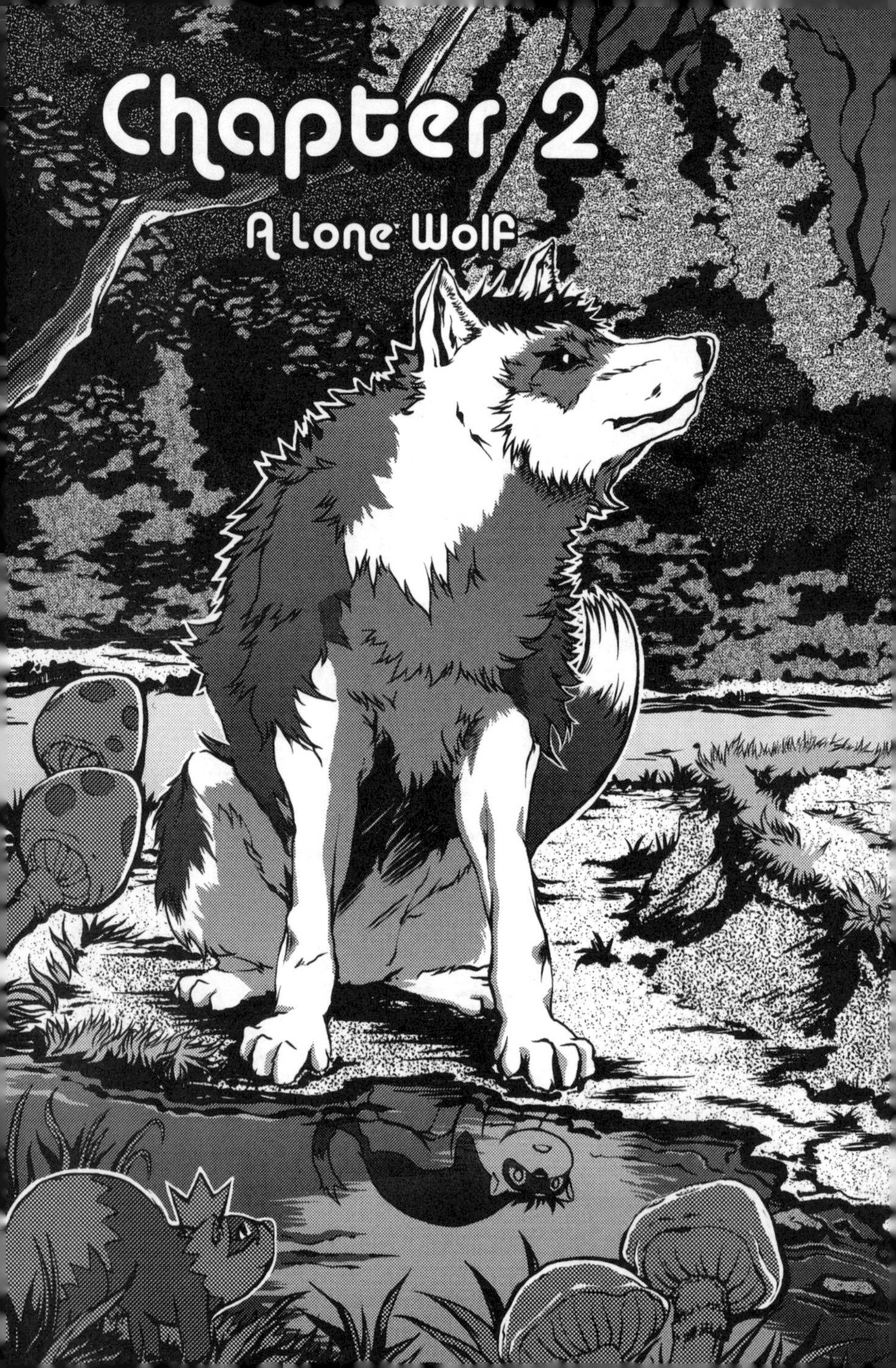
Chapter 2
A Lone Wolf

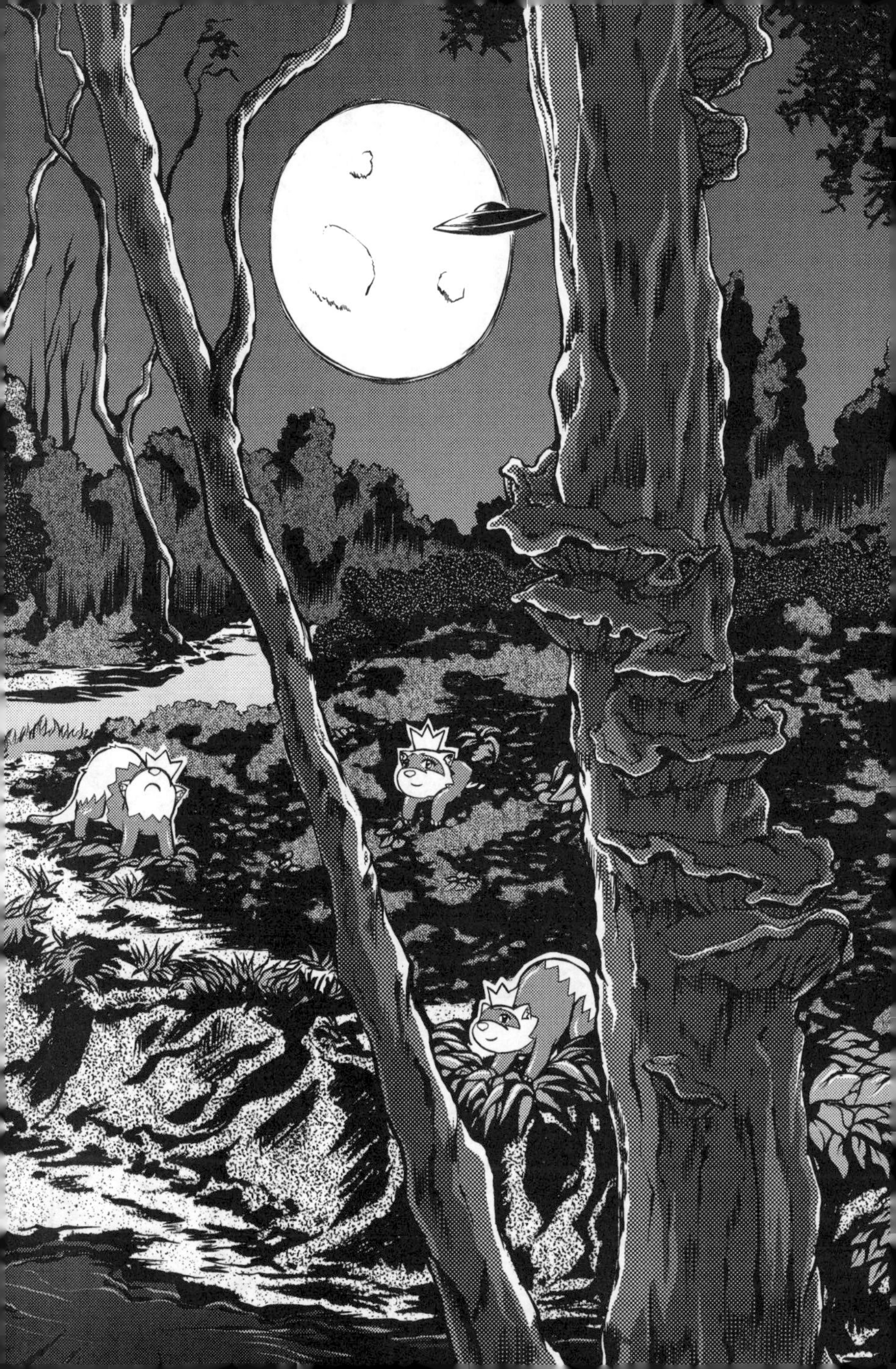

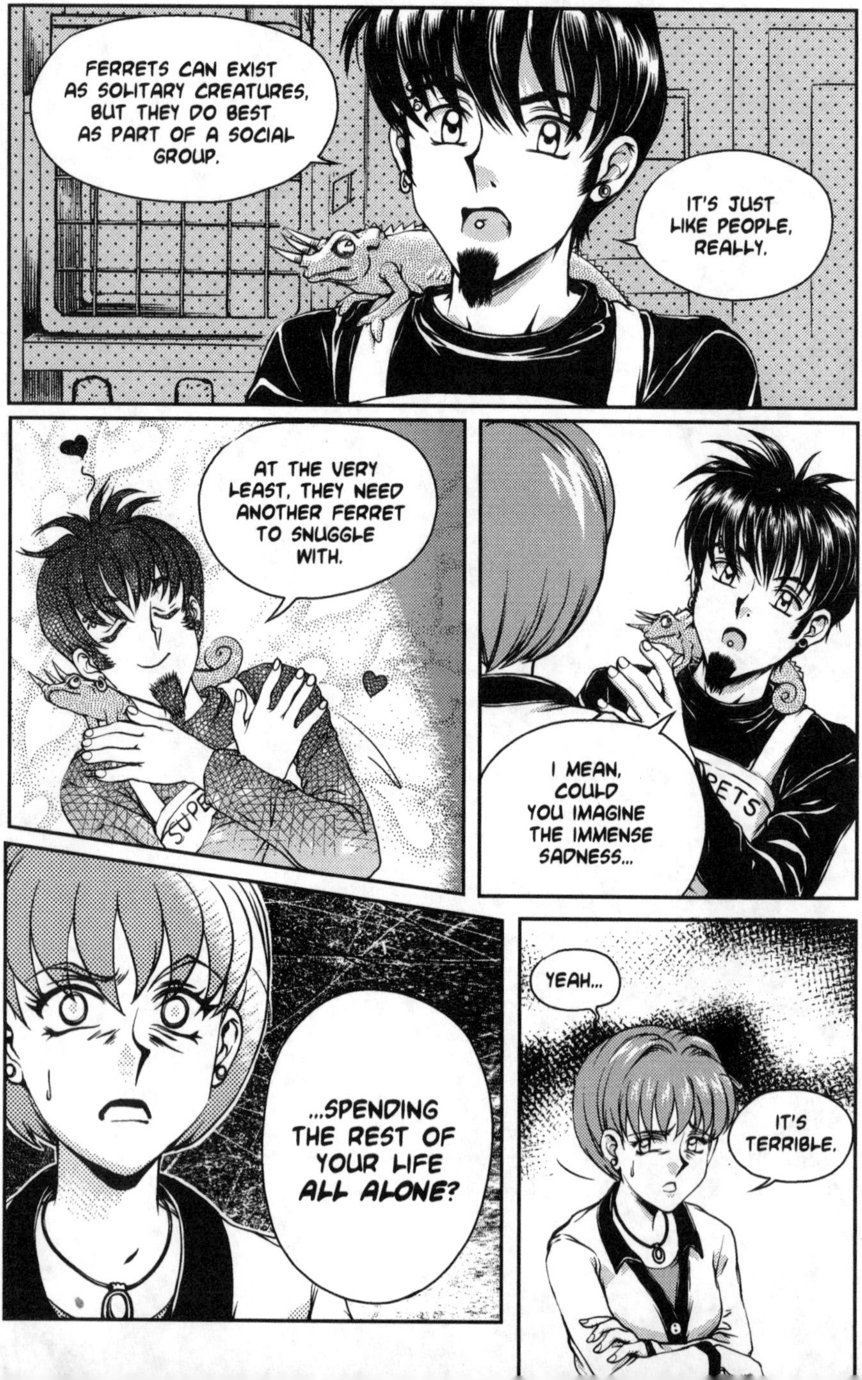
FERRETS CAN EXIST AS SOLITARY CREATURES, BUT THEY DO BEST AS PART OF A SOCIAL GROUP.
IT'S JUST LIKE PEOPLE, REALLY.
AT THE VERY LEAST, THEY NEED ANOTHER FERRET TO SNUGGLE WITH.
I MEAN, COULD YOU IMAGINE THE IMMENSE SADNESS...
...SPENDING THE REST OF YOUR LIFE ALL ALONE?
YEAH...
IT'S TERRIBLE.

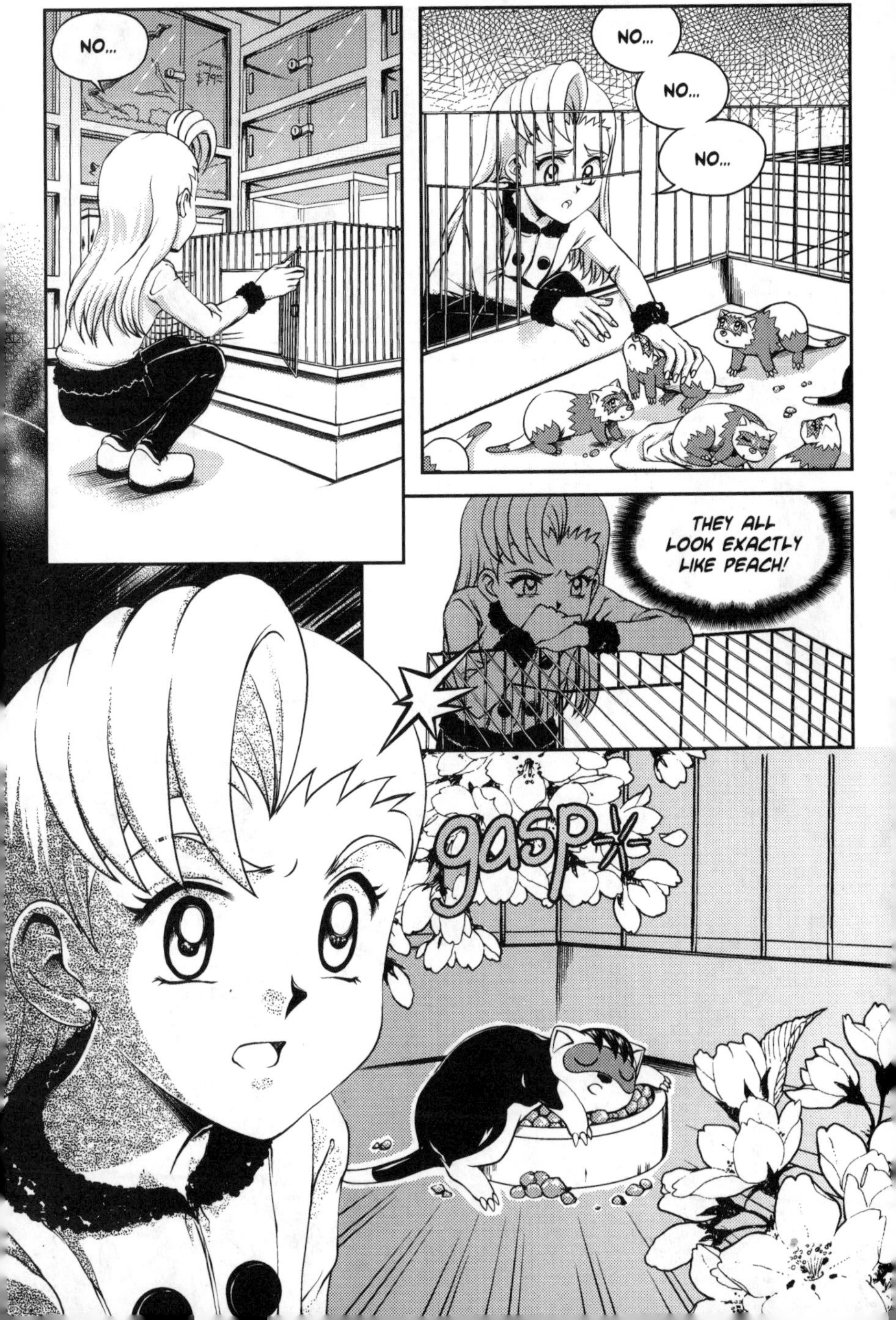
NO...
NO...
NO...
NO...
THEY ALL LOOK EXACTLY LIKE PEACH!
gasp

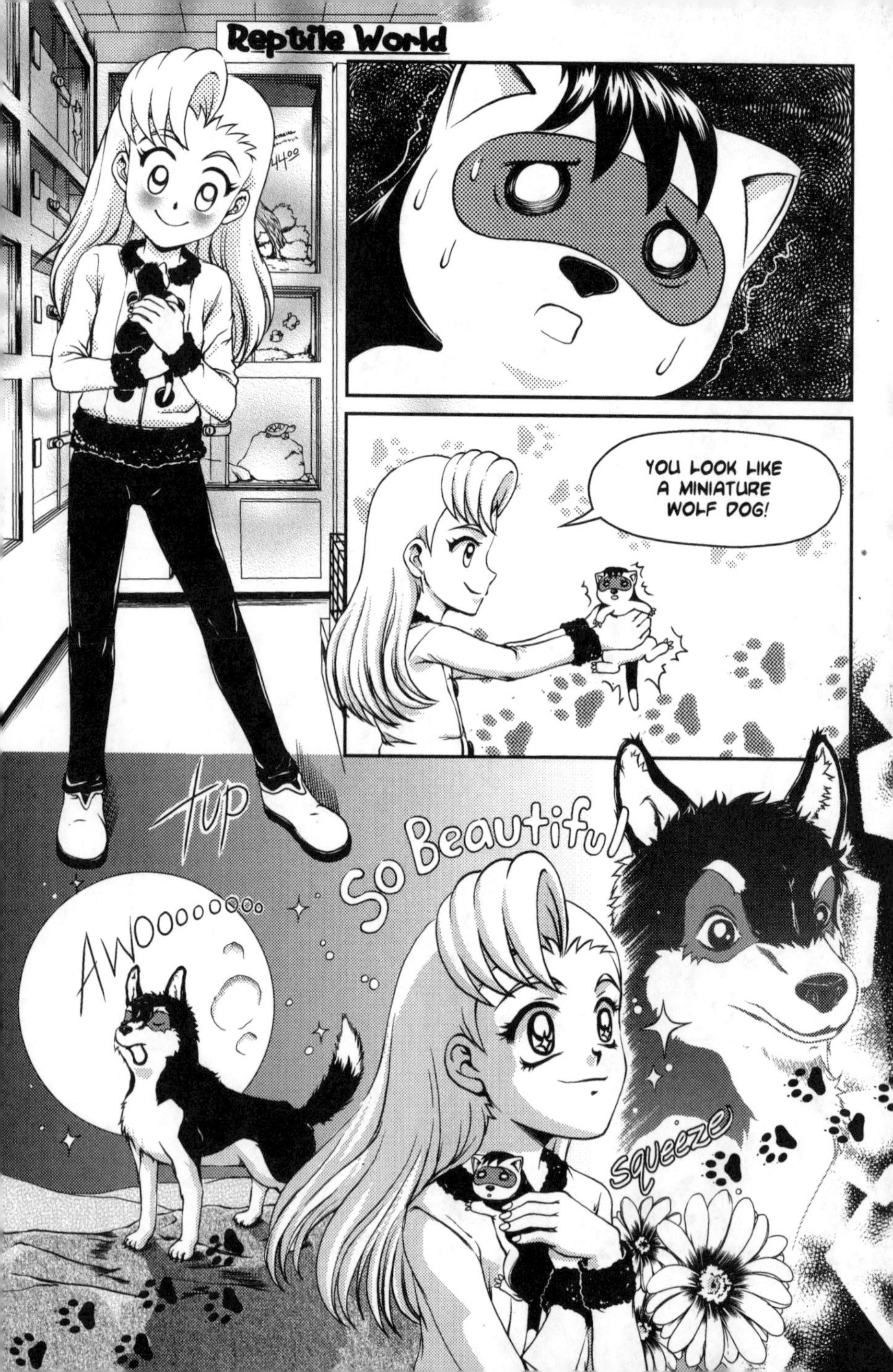
Reptile World
YOU LOOK LIKE A MINIATURE WOLF DOG!
Hup
So Beautiful
AWOooooooo
squeeze

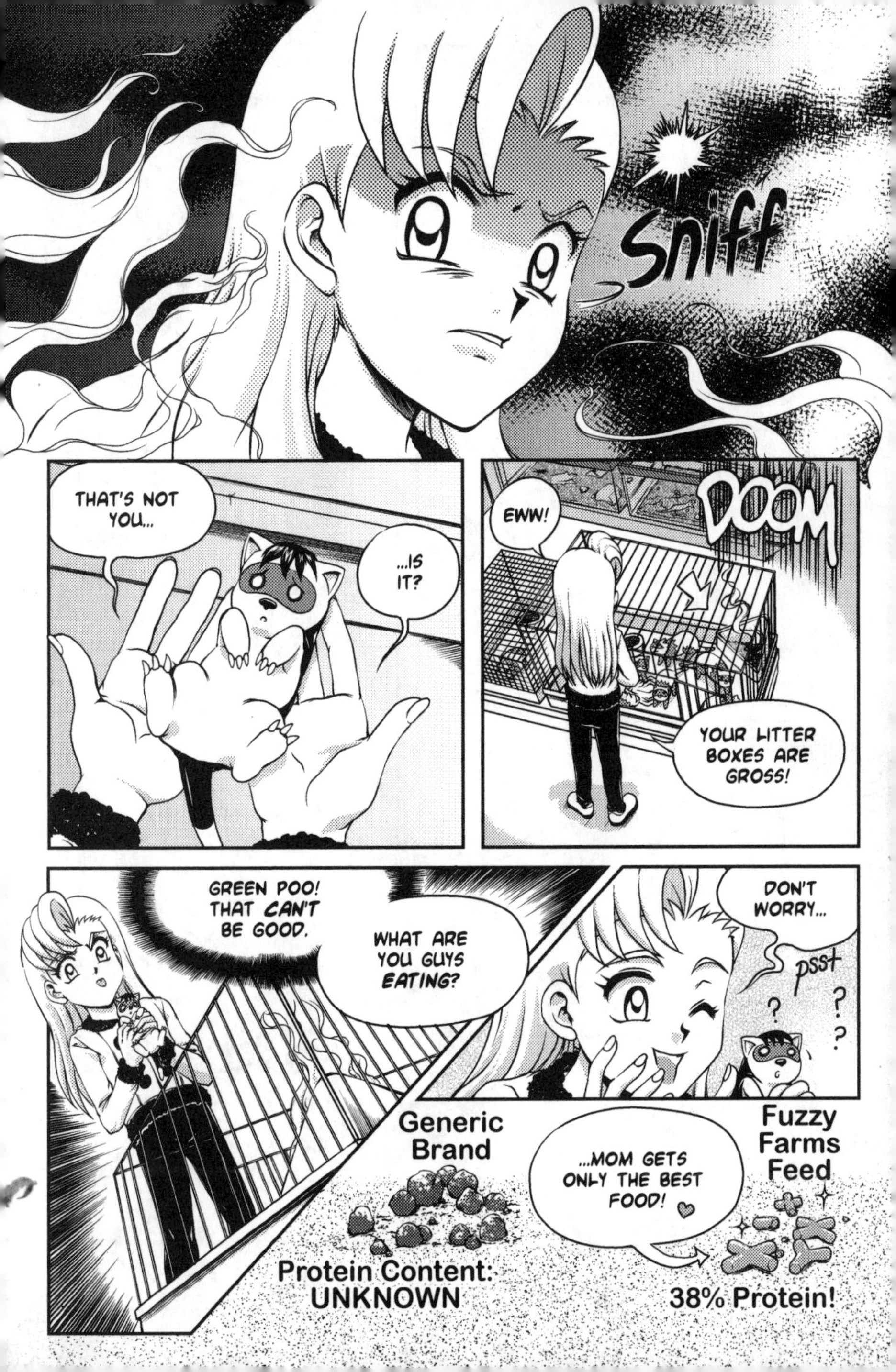
Sniff
THAT'S NOT YOU...
...IS IT?
EWW!
DOOM
YOUR LITTER BOXES ARE GROSS!
GREEN POO! THAT CAN'T BE GOOD.
WHAT ARE YOU GUYS EATING?
DON'T WORRY...
PSST
? ? ? ?
Generic Brand
Protein Content: UNKNOWN
...MOM GETS ONLY THE BEST FOOD!
Fuzzy Farms Feed
38% Protein!

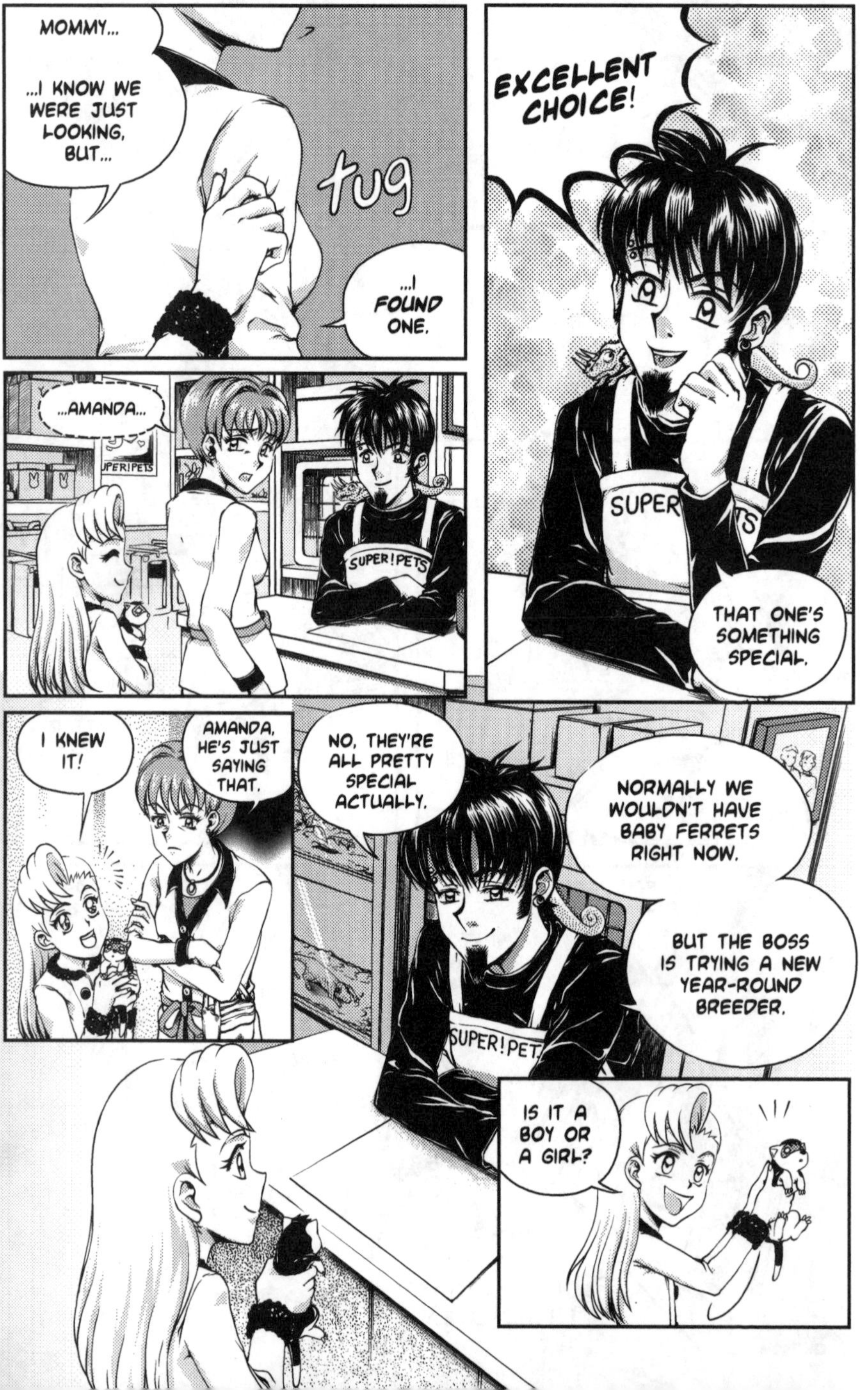

MOMMY...
...I KNOW WE WERE JUST LOOKING, BUT...
tug
...I FOUND ONE.
EXCELLENT CHOICE!
...AMANDA...
SUPER!PETS
SUPER!PETS
SUPER!PETS
THAT ONE'S SOMETHING SPECIAL.
I KNEW IT!
AMANDA, HE'S JUST SAYING THAT.
NO, THEY'RE ALL PRETTY SPECIAL ACTUALLY.
NORMALLY WE WOULDN'T HAVE BABY FERRETS RIGHT NOW.
BUT THE BOSS IS TRYING A NEW YEAR-ROUND BREEDER.
SUPER!PETS
IS IT A BOY OR A GIRL?

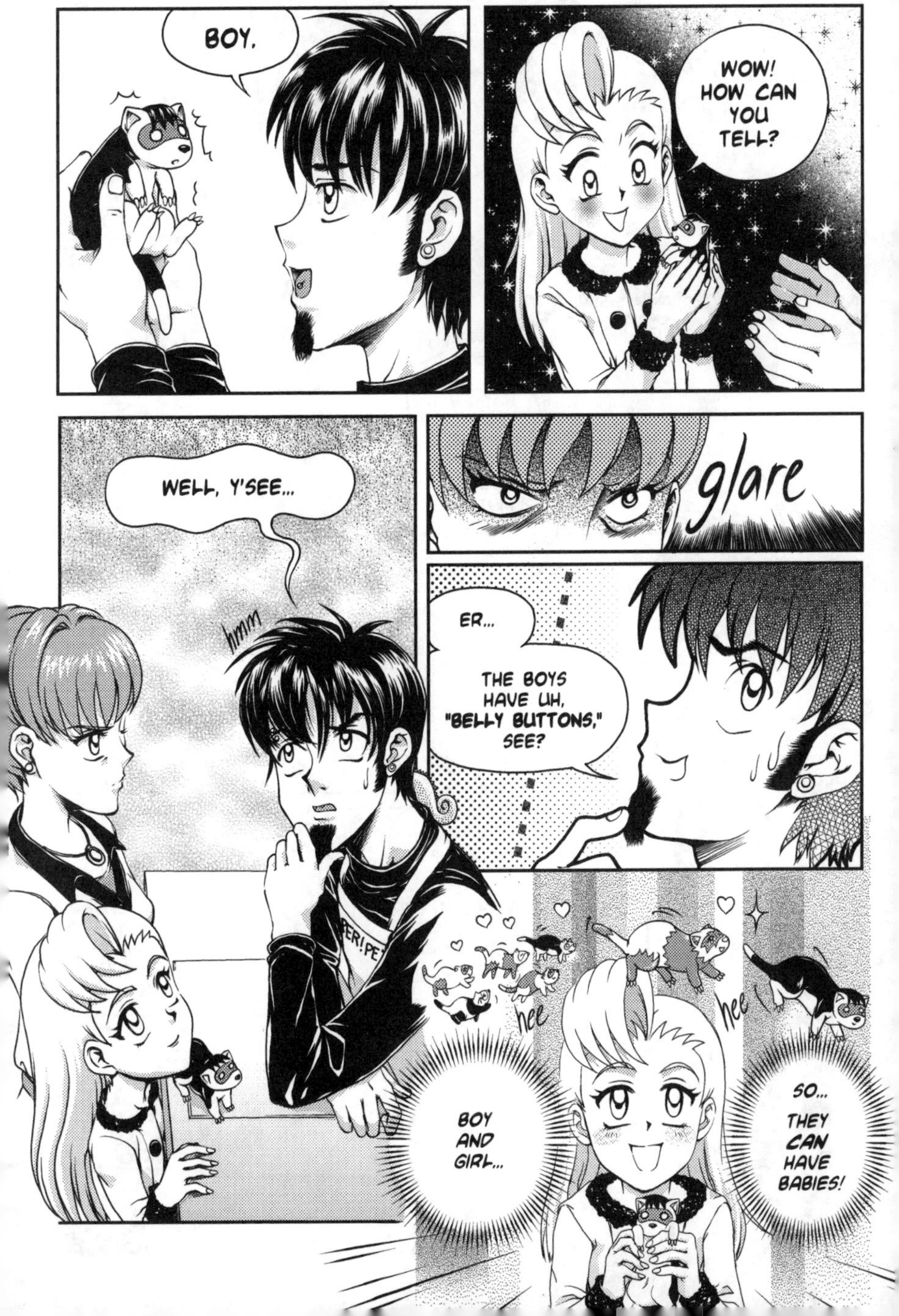
BOY.
WOW! HOW CAN YOU TELL?
WELL, Y'SEE...
hmm
glare
ER...
THE BOYS HAVE UH, "BELLY BUTTONS," SEE?
hee
hee
BOY AND GIRL...
SO... THEY CAN HAVE BABIES!

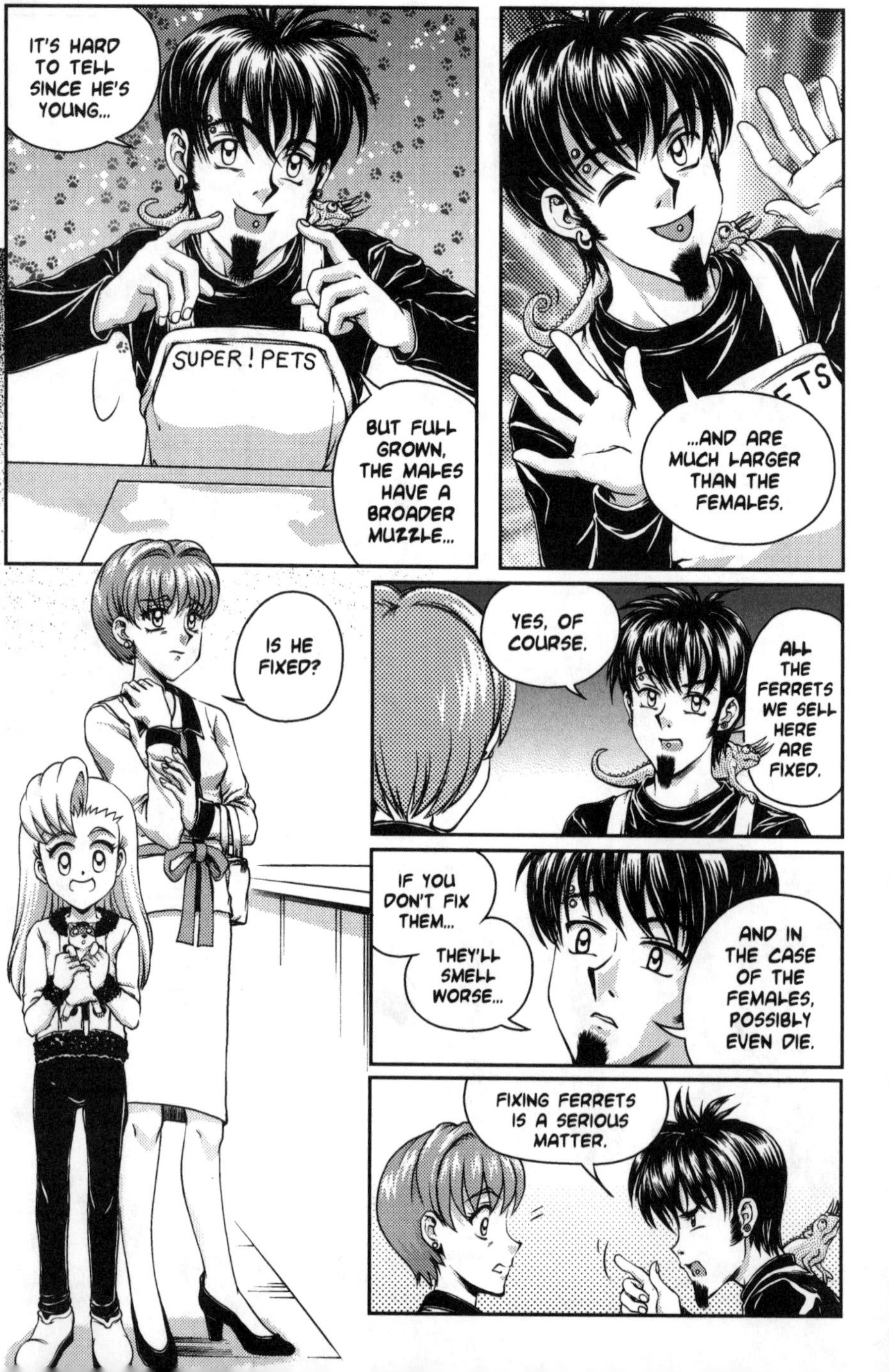
IT'S HARD TO TELL SINCE HE'S YOUNG...
SUPER ! PETS
BUT FULL GROWN, THE MALES HAVE A BROADER MUZZLE...
...AND ARE MUCH LARGER THAN THE FEMALES.
IS HE FIXED?
YES, OF COURSE.
ALL THE FERRETS WE SELL HERE ARE FIXED.
IF YOU DON'T FIX THEM...
THEY'LL SMELL WORSE...
AND IN THE CASE OF THE FEMALES, POSSIBLY EVEN DIE.
FIXING FERRETS IS A SERIOUS MATTER.

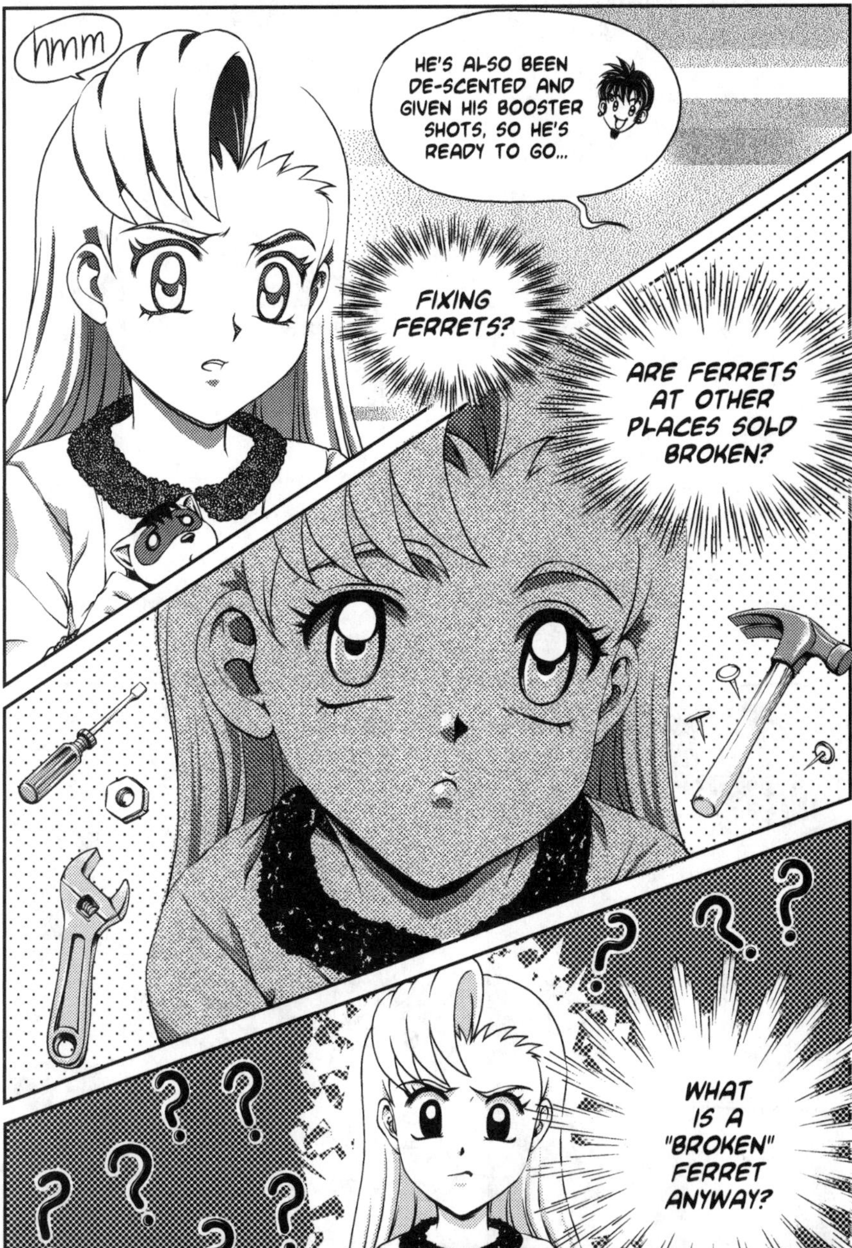
hmm
HE'S ALSO BEEN DE-SCENTED AND GIVEN HIS BOOSTER SHOTS, SO HE'S READY TO GO...
FIXING FERRETS?
ARE FERRETS AT OTHER PLACES SOLD BROKEN?
WHAT IS A "BROKEN" FERRET ANYWAY?

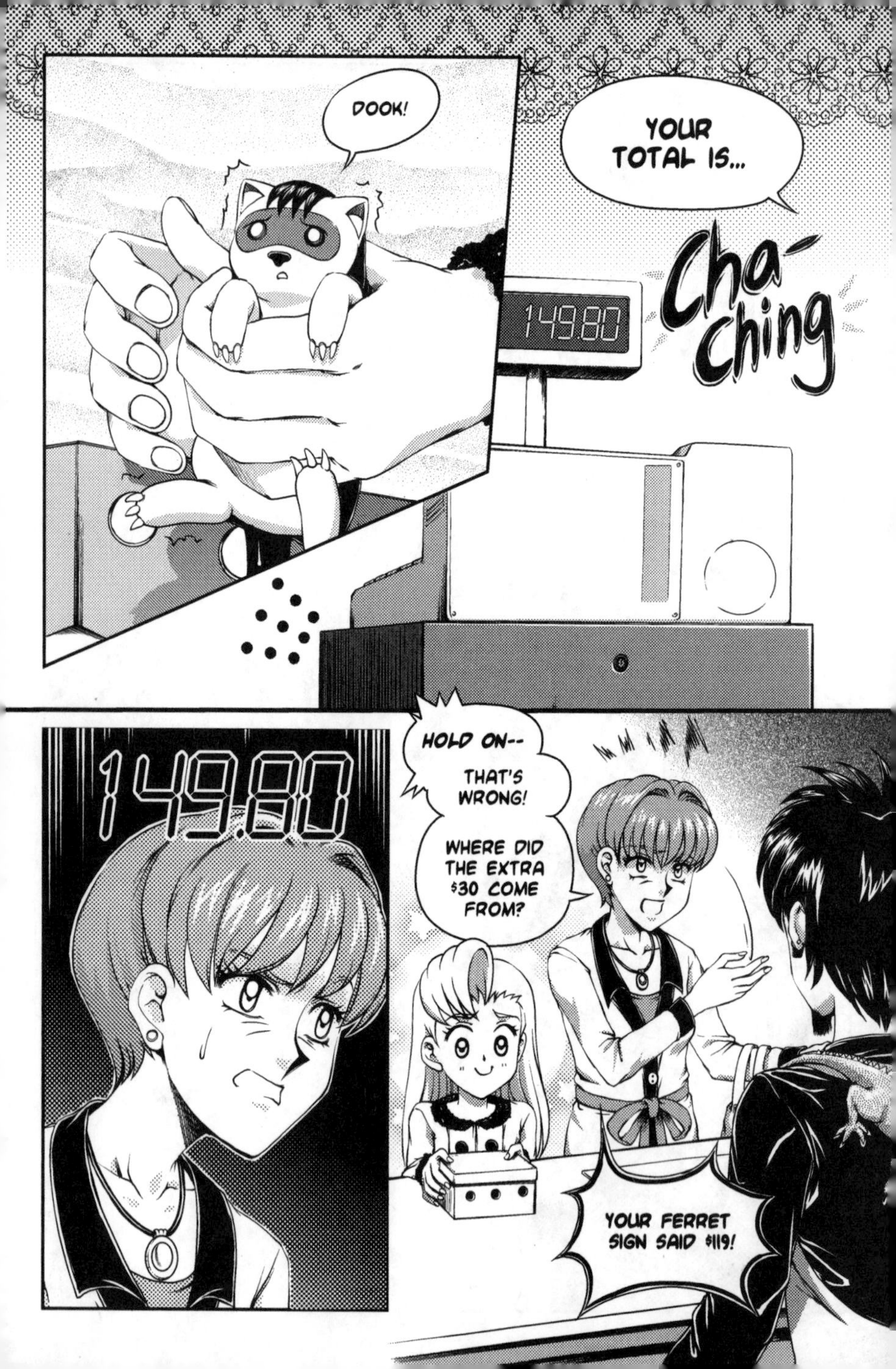
DOOK!
YOUR TOTAL IS...
149.80
Cha-Ching
149.80
HOLD ON--
THAT'S WRONG!
WHERE DID THE EXTRA $30 COME FROM?
YOUR FERRET SIGN SAID $119!

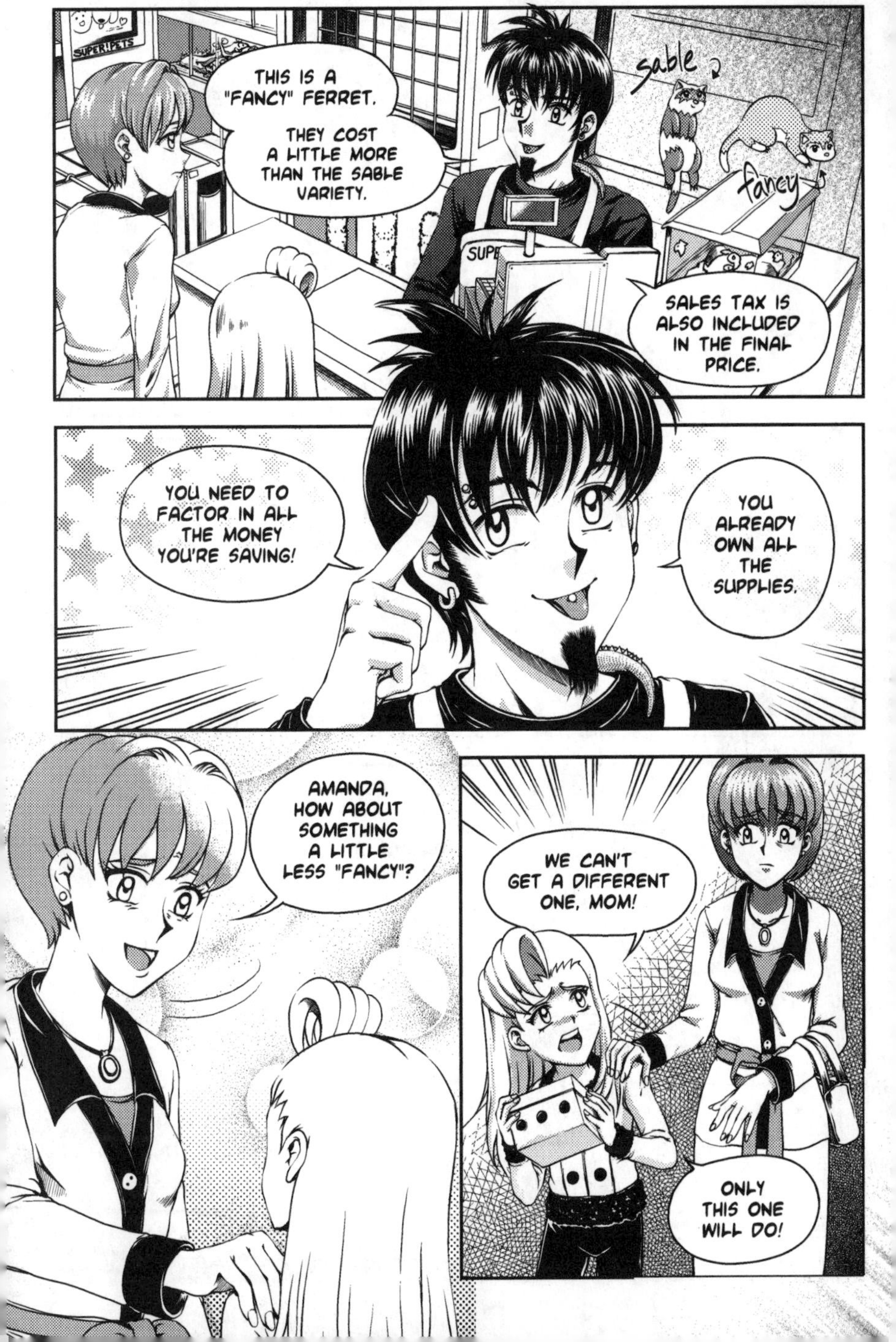
SUPER!PETS
THIS IS A "FANCY" FERRET.
THEY COST A LITTLE MORE THAN THE SABLE VARIETY.
sable
fancy
SALES TAX IS ALSO INCLUDED IN THE FINAL PRICE.
YOU ALREADY OWN ALL THE SUPPLIES.
YOU NEED TO FACTOR IN ALL THE MONEY YOU'RE SAVING!
AMANDA, HOW ABOUT SOMETHING A LITTLE LESS "FANCY"?
WE CAN'T GET A DIFFERENT ONE, MOM!
ONLY THIS ONE WILL DO!

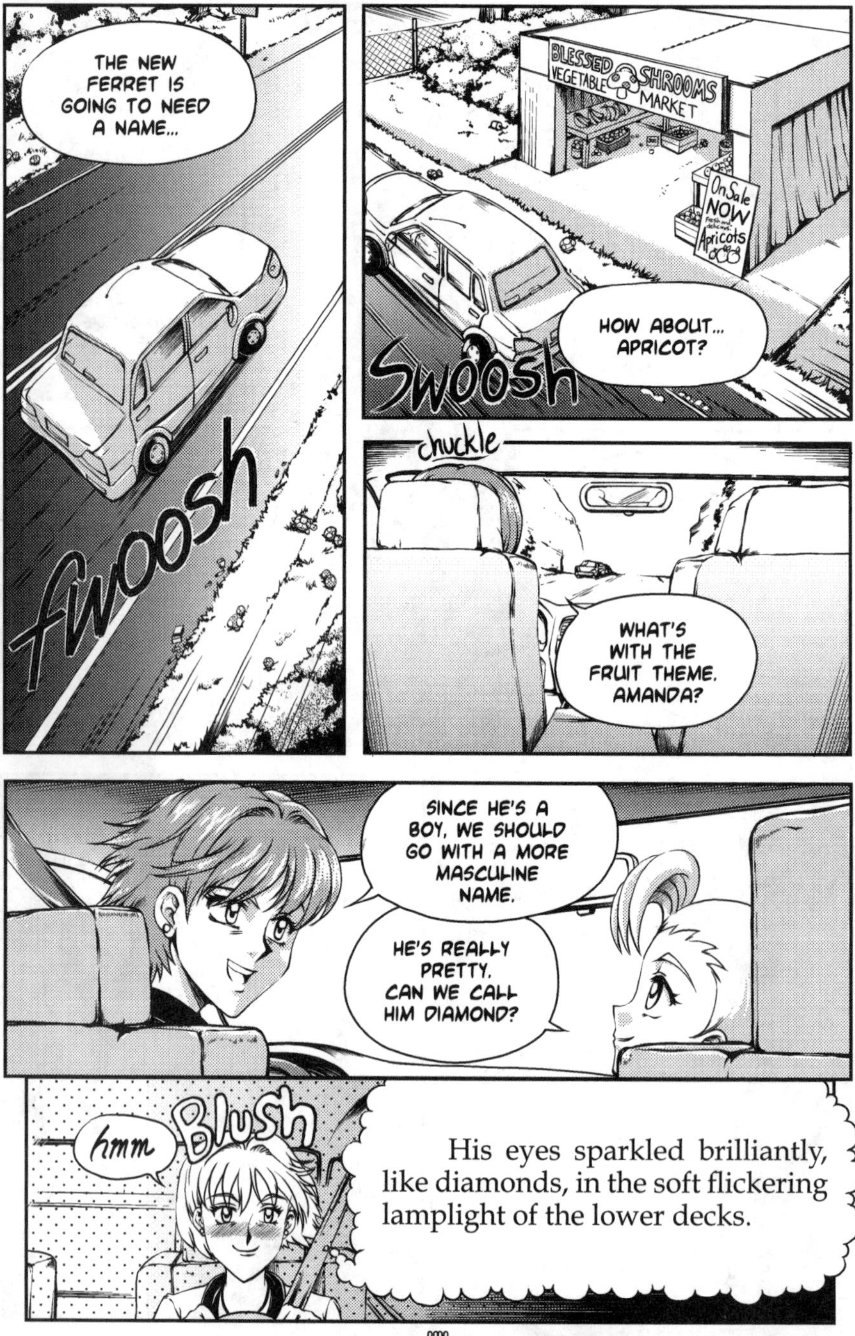
THE NEW FERRET IS GOING TO NEED A NAME...
fwoosh
BLESSED SHROOMS VEGETABLE MARKET
On Sale NOW
Apricots
Swoosh
HOW ABOUT... APRICOT?
chuckle
WHAT'S WITH THE FRUIT THEME. AMANDA?
SINCE HE'S A BOY, WE SHOULD GO WITH A MORE MASCULINE NAME.
HE'S REALLY PRETTY. CAN WE CALL HIM DIAMOND?
hmm
Blush
His eyes sparkled brilliantly, like diamonds, in the soft flickering lamplight of the lower decks.

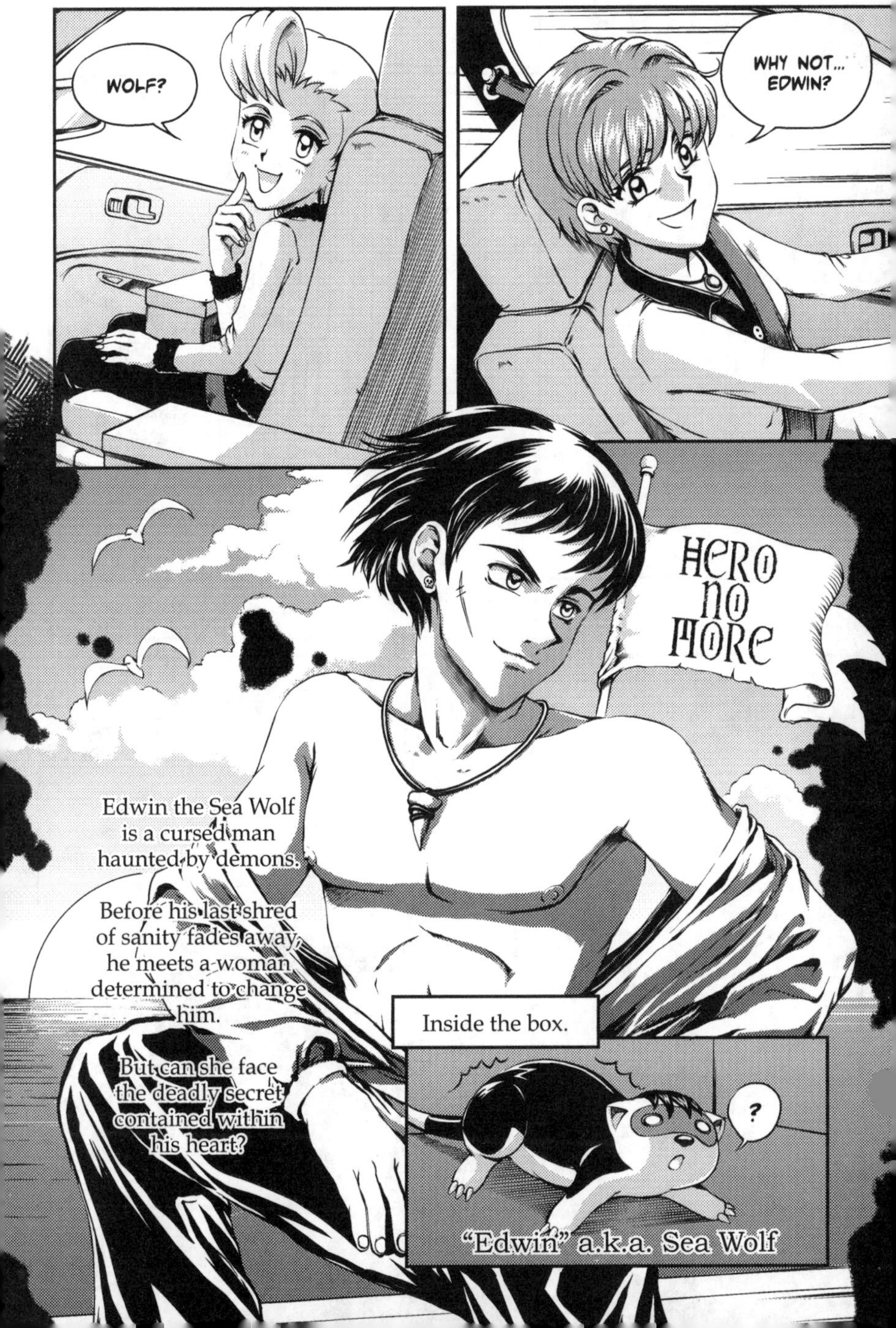
WOLF?
WHY NOT... EDWIN?
HERO NO MORE
Edwin the Sea Wolf is a cursed man haunted by demons.
Before his last shred of sanity fades away, he meets a woman determined to change him.
But can she face the deadly secret contained within his heart?
Inside the box.
?
"Edwin" a.k.a. Sea Wolf

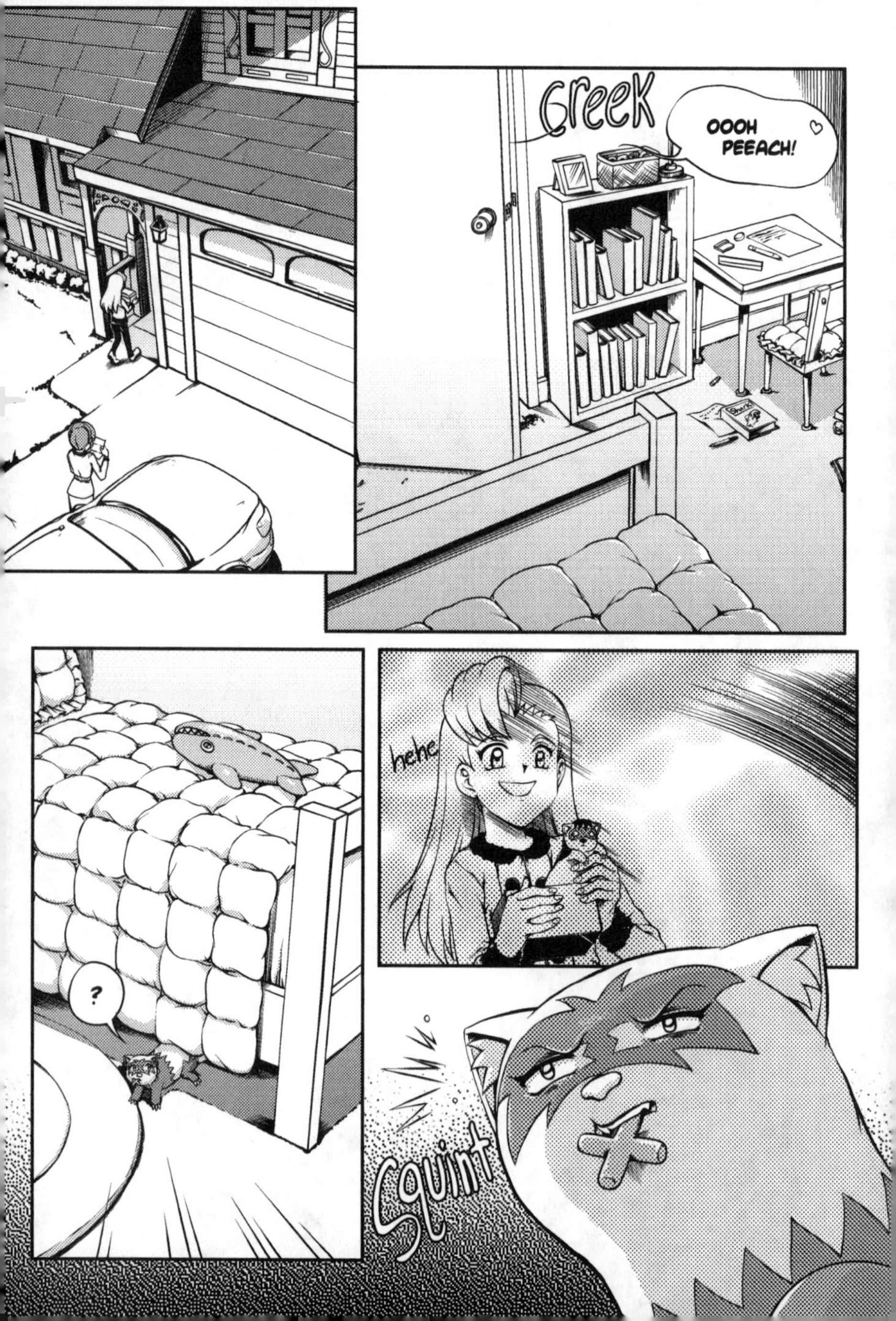
CREEK
OOOH PEEACH!
?
hehe
Squint

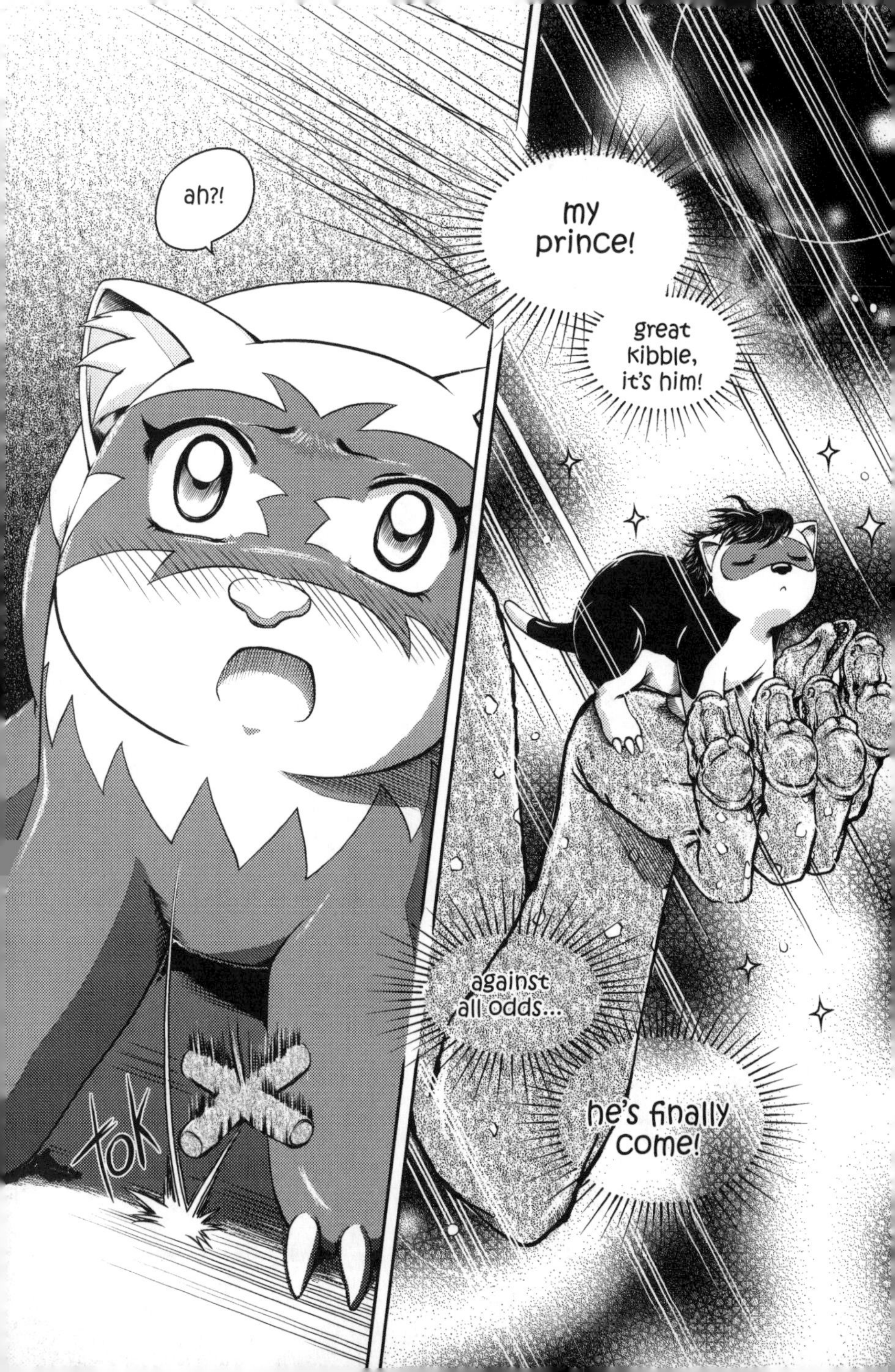
ah?!
my prince!
great kibble, it's him!
against all odds...
he's finally come!
TOK

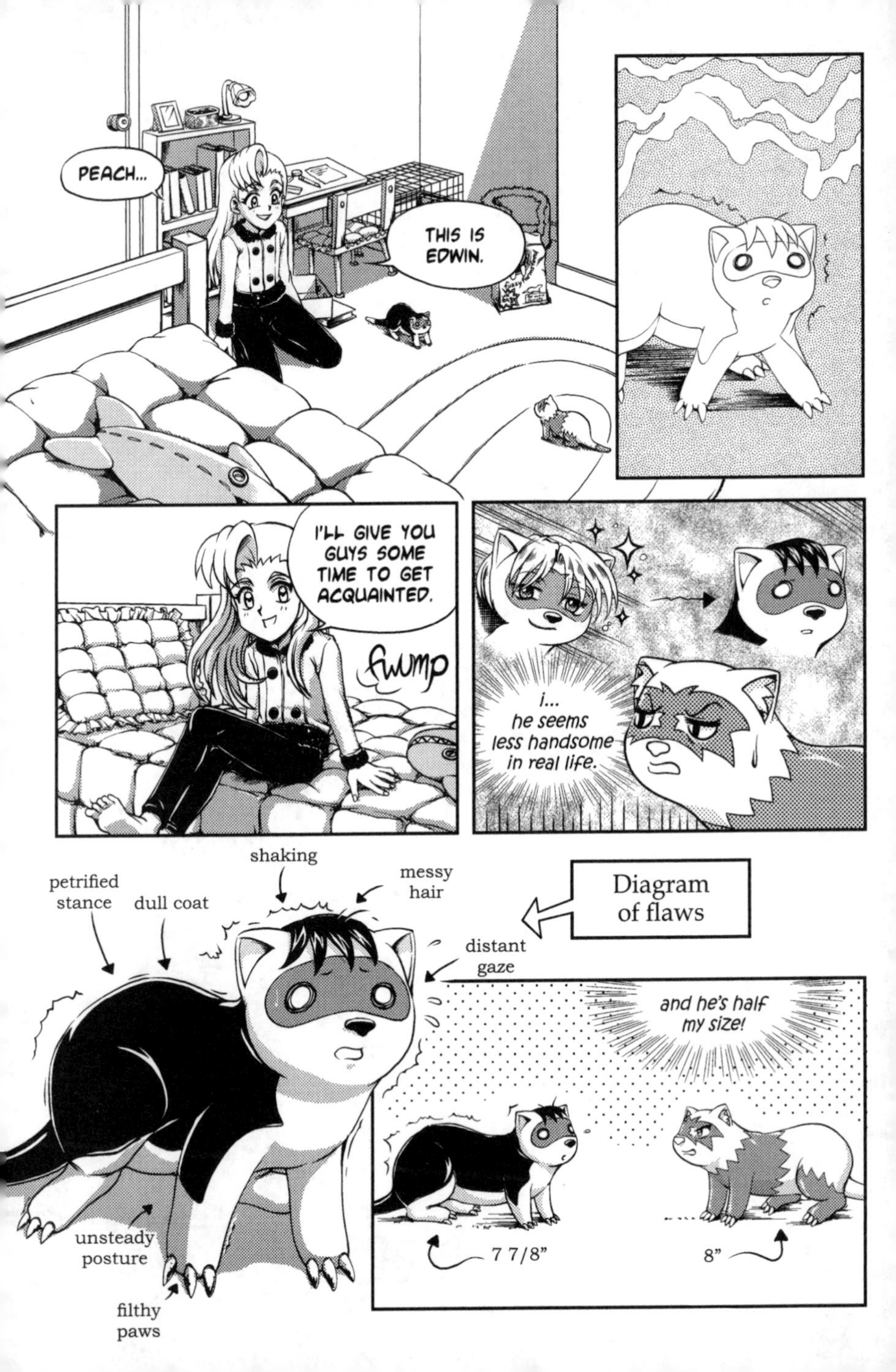
PEACH...
THIS IS EDWIN.
I'LL GIVE YOU GUYS SOME TIME TO GET ACQUAINTED.
fwump
i... he seems less handsome in real life.
shaking
petrified stance
dull coat
messy hair
Diagram of flaws
distant gaze
unsteady posture
filthy paws
and he's half my size!
7 7/8"
8"

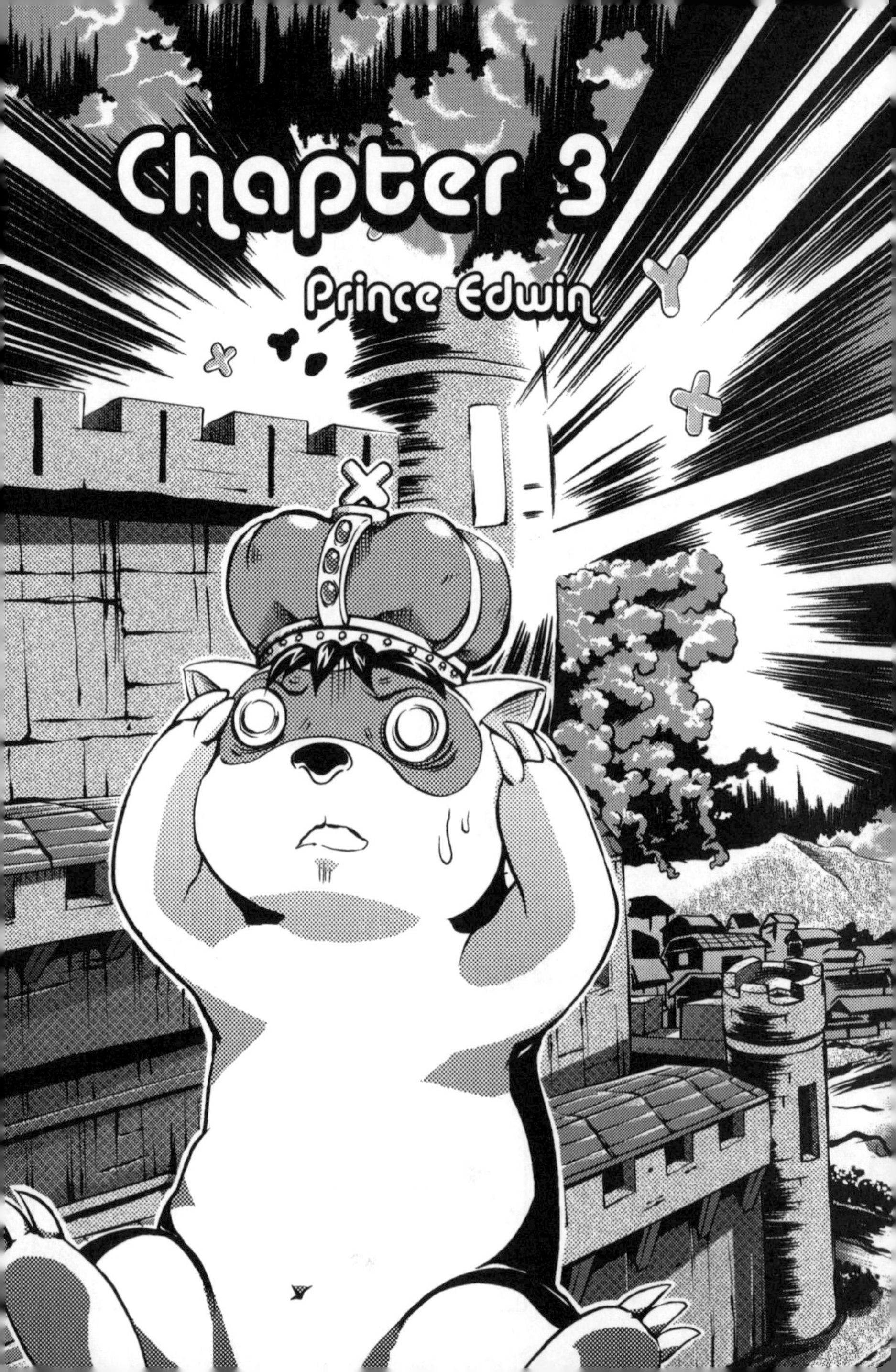

Chapter 3
Prince Edwin

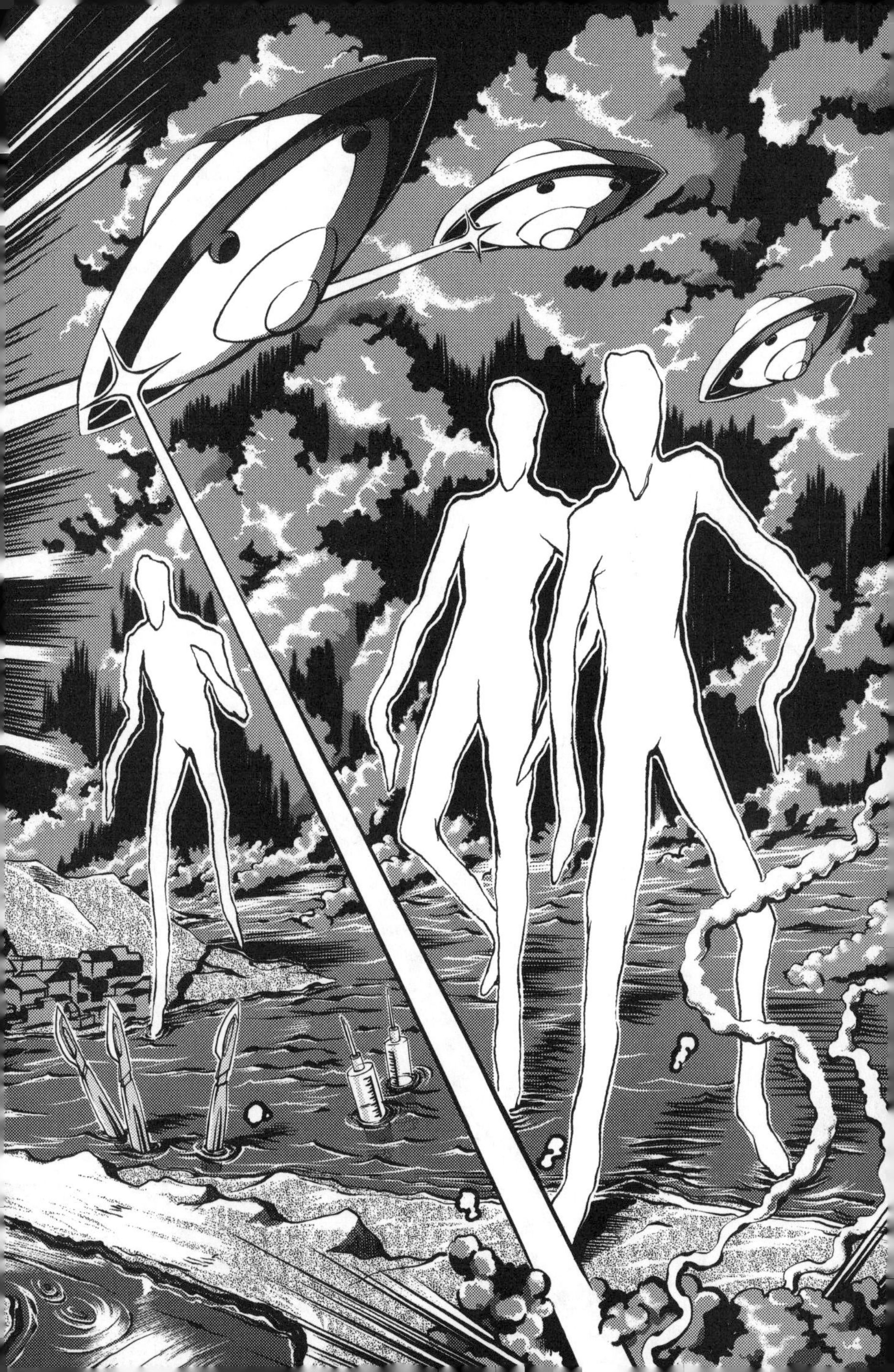

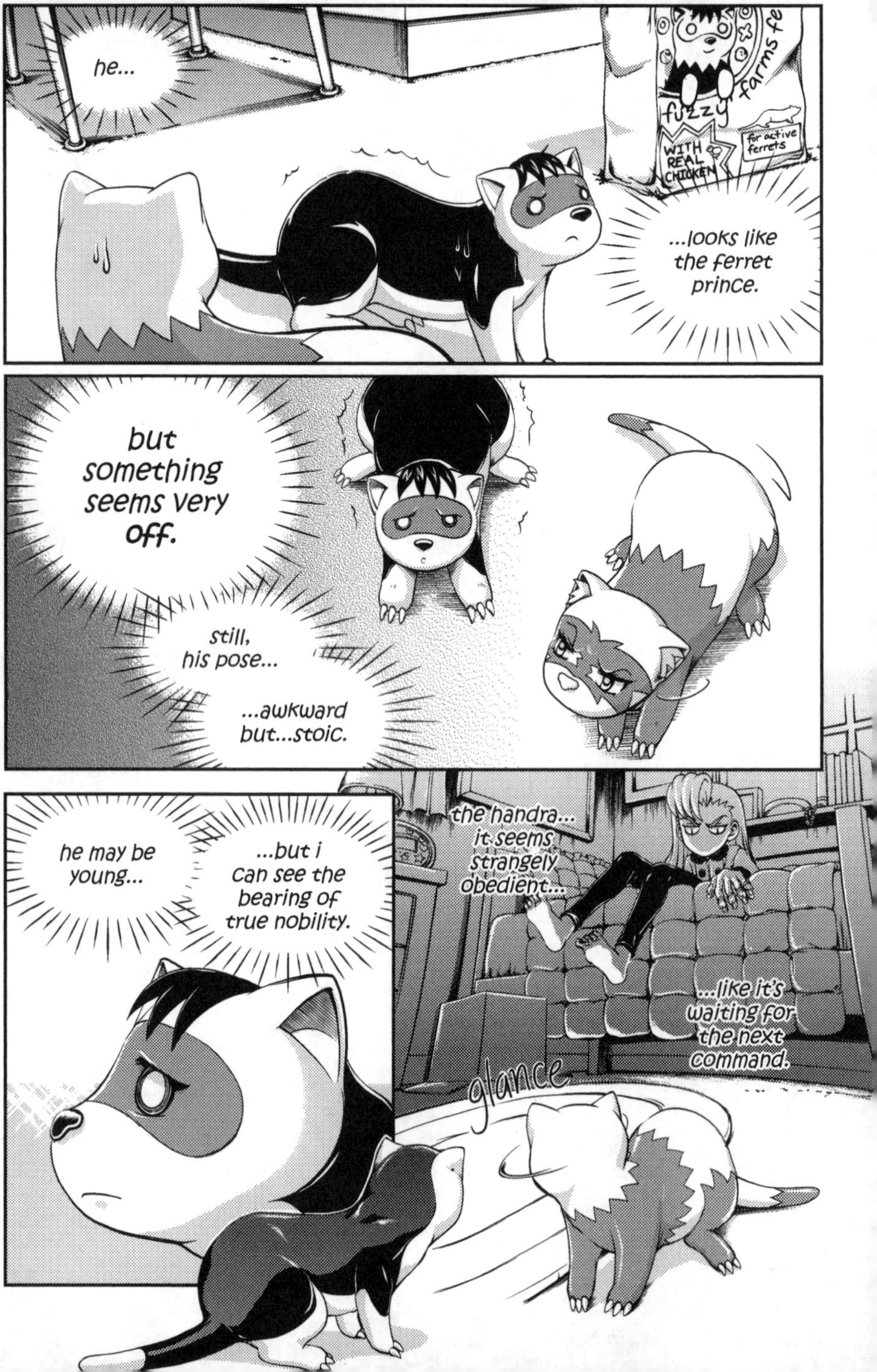
he...
fuzzy farms
WITH REAL CHICKEN
for active ferrets
...looks like the ferret prince.
but something seems very off.
still, his pose...
...awkward but...stoic.
the handra... it seems strangely obedient...
...like it's waiting for the next command.
he may be young...
...but i can see the bearing of true nobility.
glance

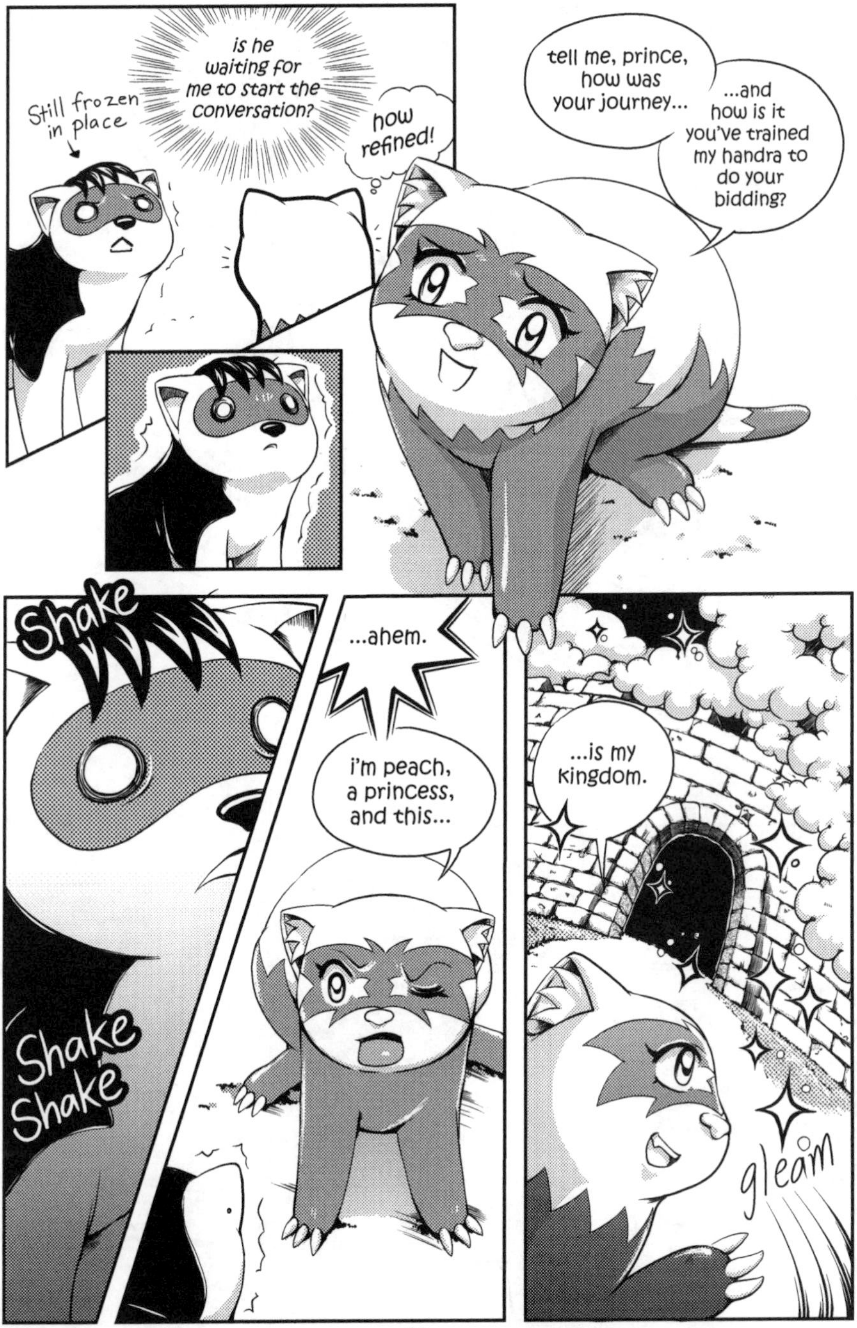
Still frozen in place
is he waiting for me to start the conversation?
how refined!
tell me, prince, how was your journey...
...and how is it you've trained my handra to do your bidding?
Shake
Shake Shake
...ahem.
i'm peach, a princess, and this...
...is my kingdom.
gleam

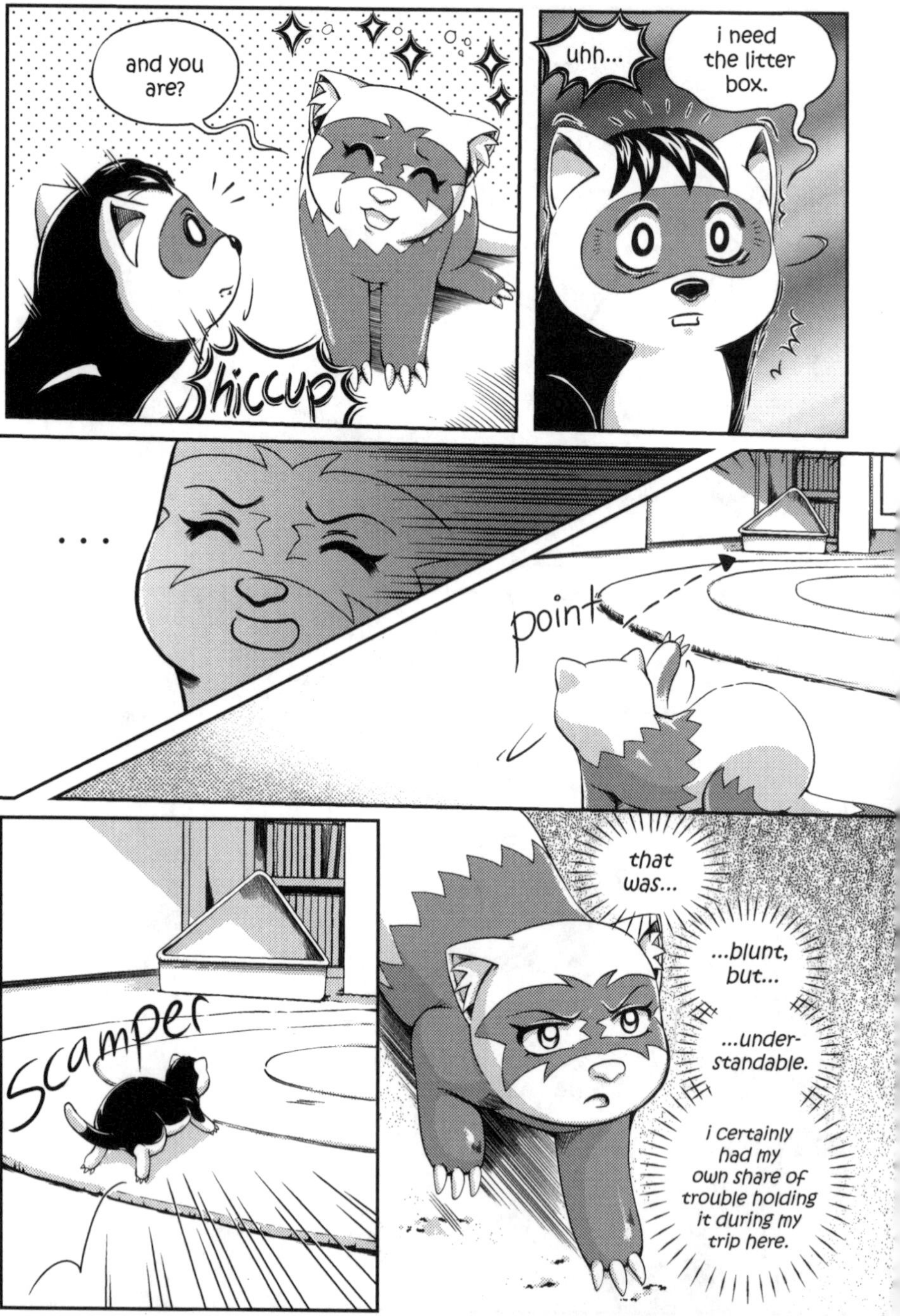
and you are?
hiccup
uhh...
i need the litter box.
...
point
scamper
that was...
...blunt, but...
...under-standable.
i certainly had my own share of trouble holding it during my trip here.

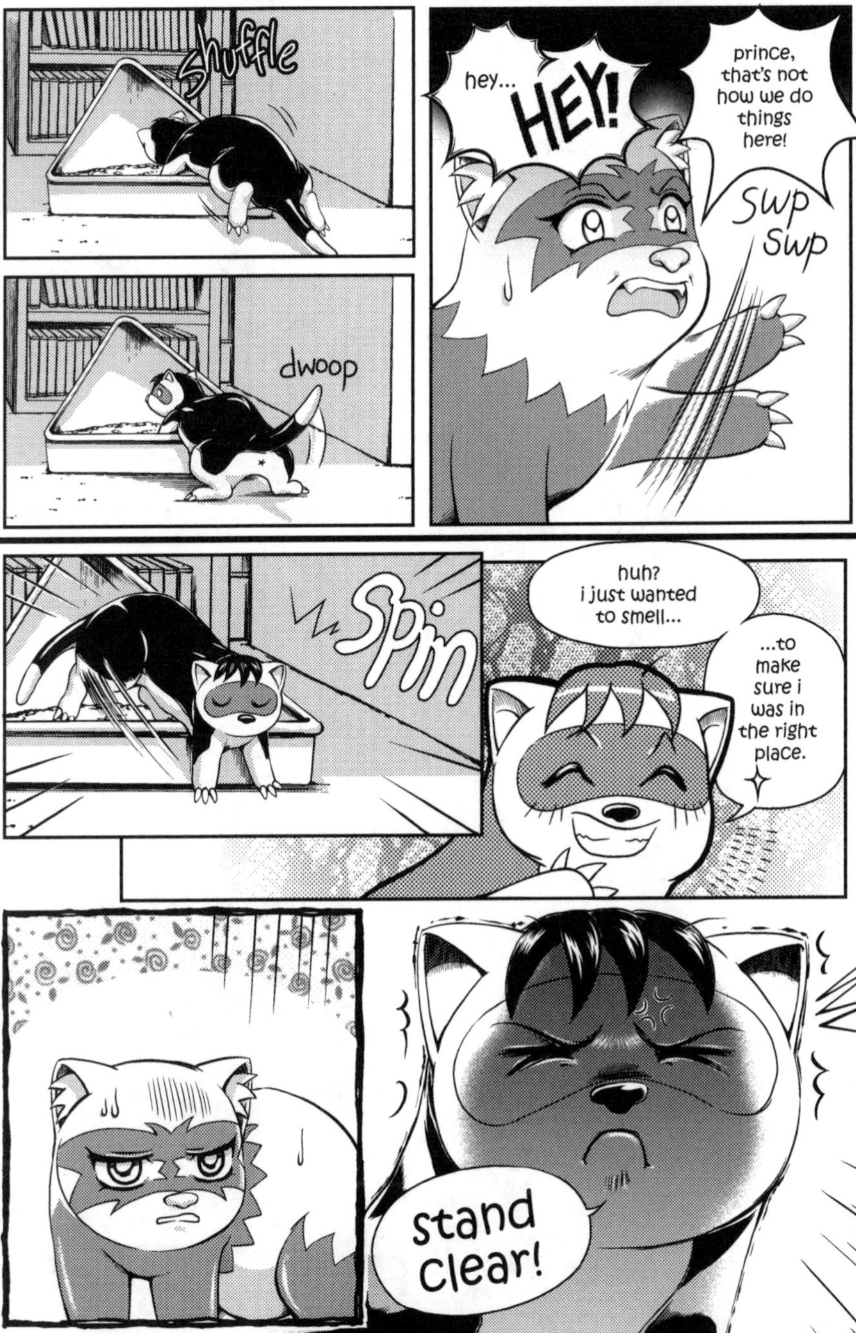
shuffle
dwoop
hey... HEY!
prince, that's not how we do things here!
swp swp
Spin
huh? i just wanted to smell...
...to make sure i was in the right place.
stand clear!

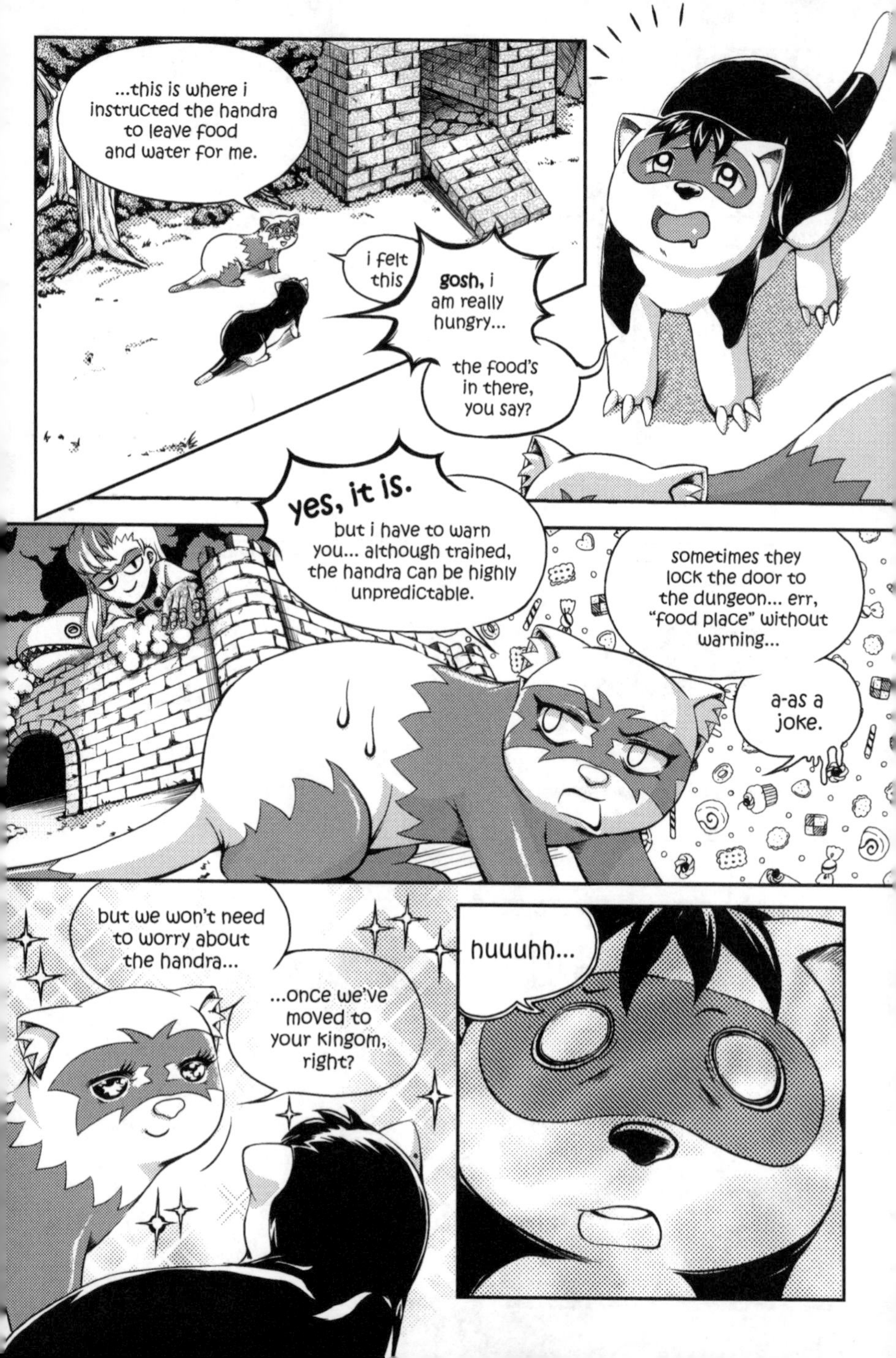
...this is where i instructed the handra to leave food and water for me.
i felt this
gosh, i am really hungry...
the food's in there, you say?
yes, it is.
but i have to warn you... although trained, the handra can be highly unpredictable.
sometimes they lock the door to the dungeon... err, "food place" without warning...
a-as a joke.
but we won't need to worry about the handra...
...once we've moved to your kingom, right?
huuuhh...

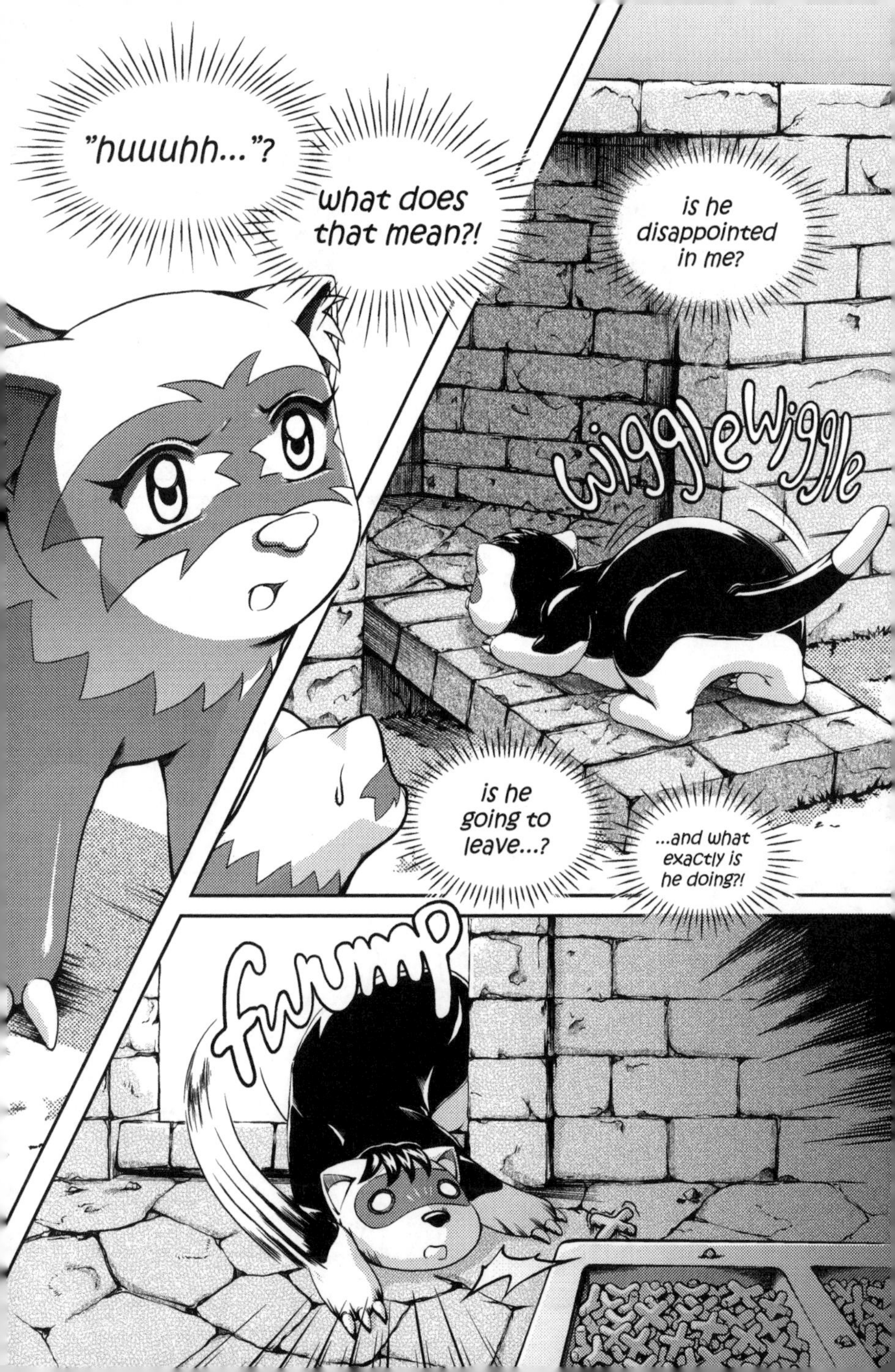
"huuuhh..."?
what does that mean?!
is he disappointed in me?
wigglewiggle
is he going to leave...?
...and what exactly is he doing?!
fwump

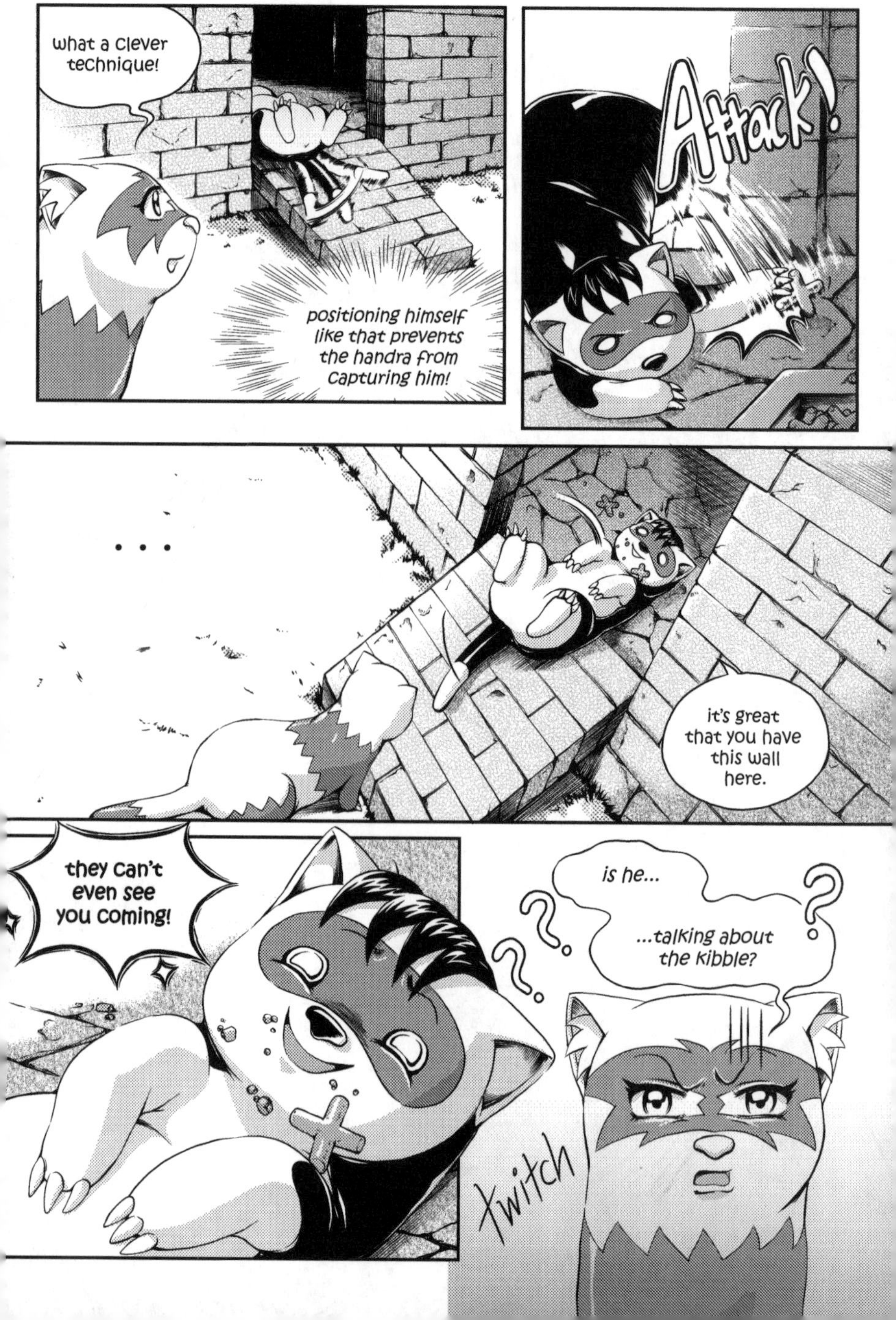
what a clever technique!
positioning himself like that prevents the handra from capturing him!
Attack!
...
it's great that you have this wall here.
they can't even see you coming!
is he...
...talking about the kibble?
twitch

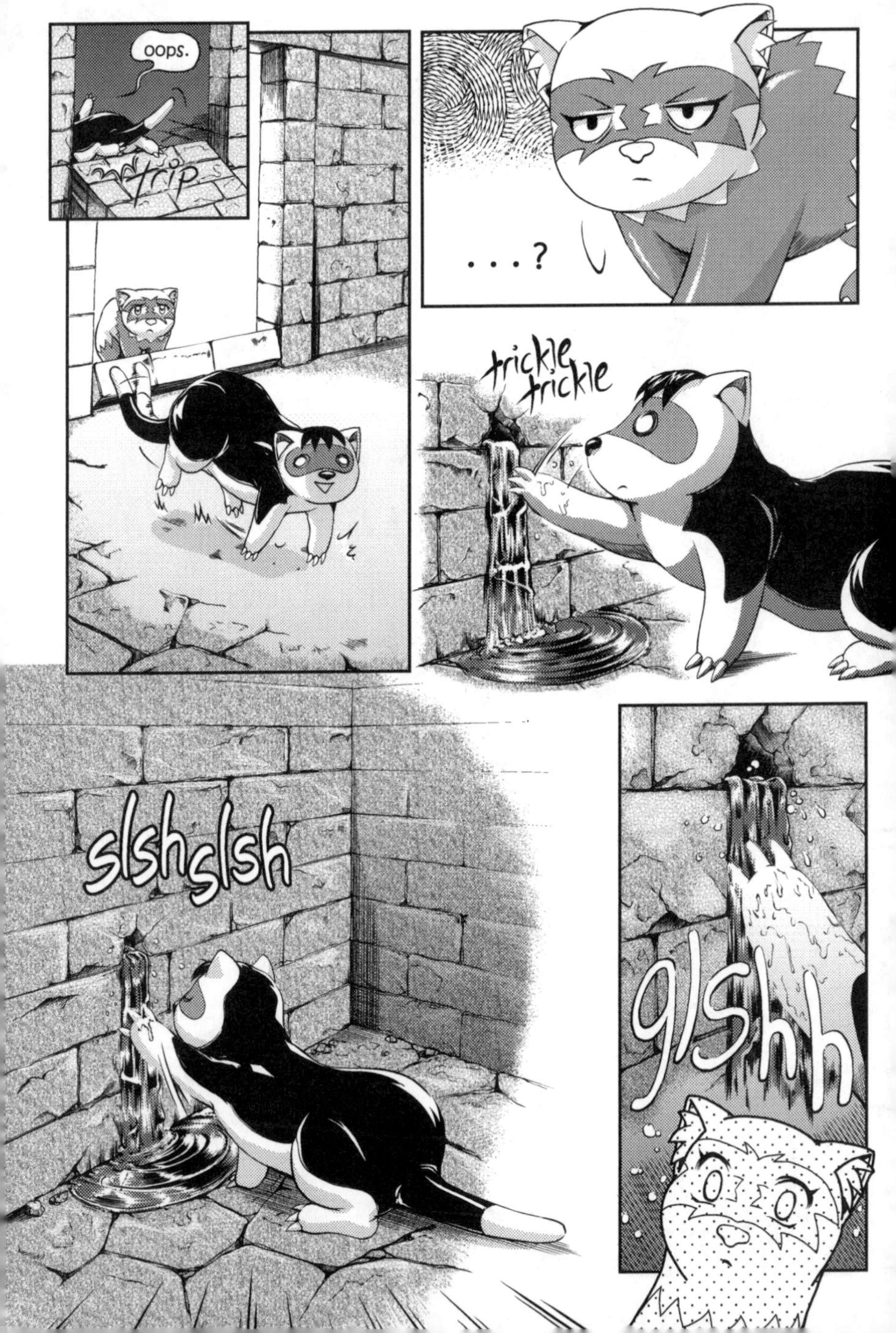
oops.
trip
. . . ?
trickle trickle
slshslsh
glShh

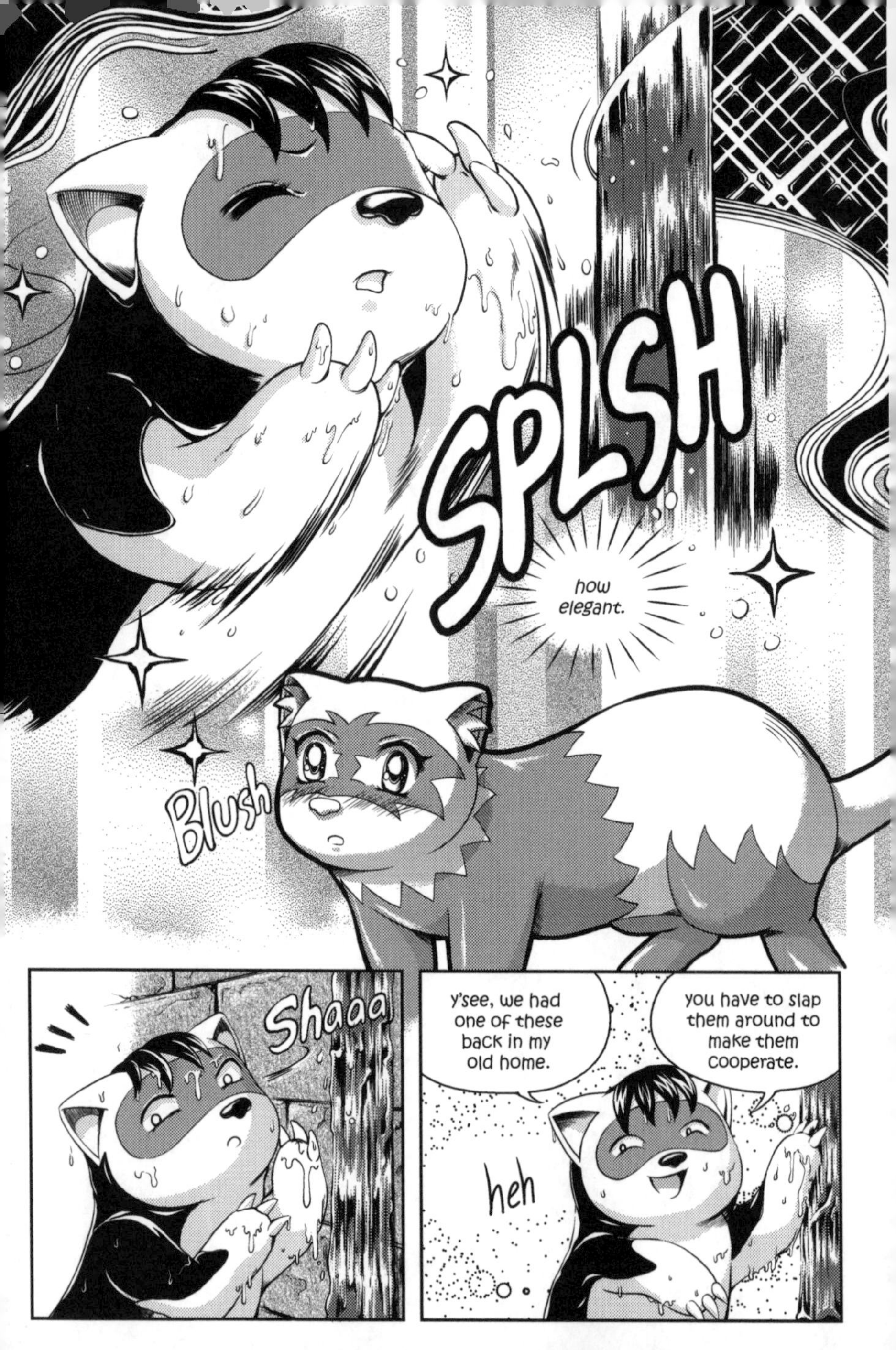
SPLSH
how elegant.
Blush
Shaaa
y'see, we had one of these back in my old home.
you have to slap them around to make them cooperate.
heh

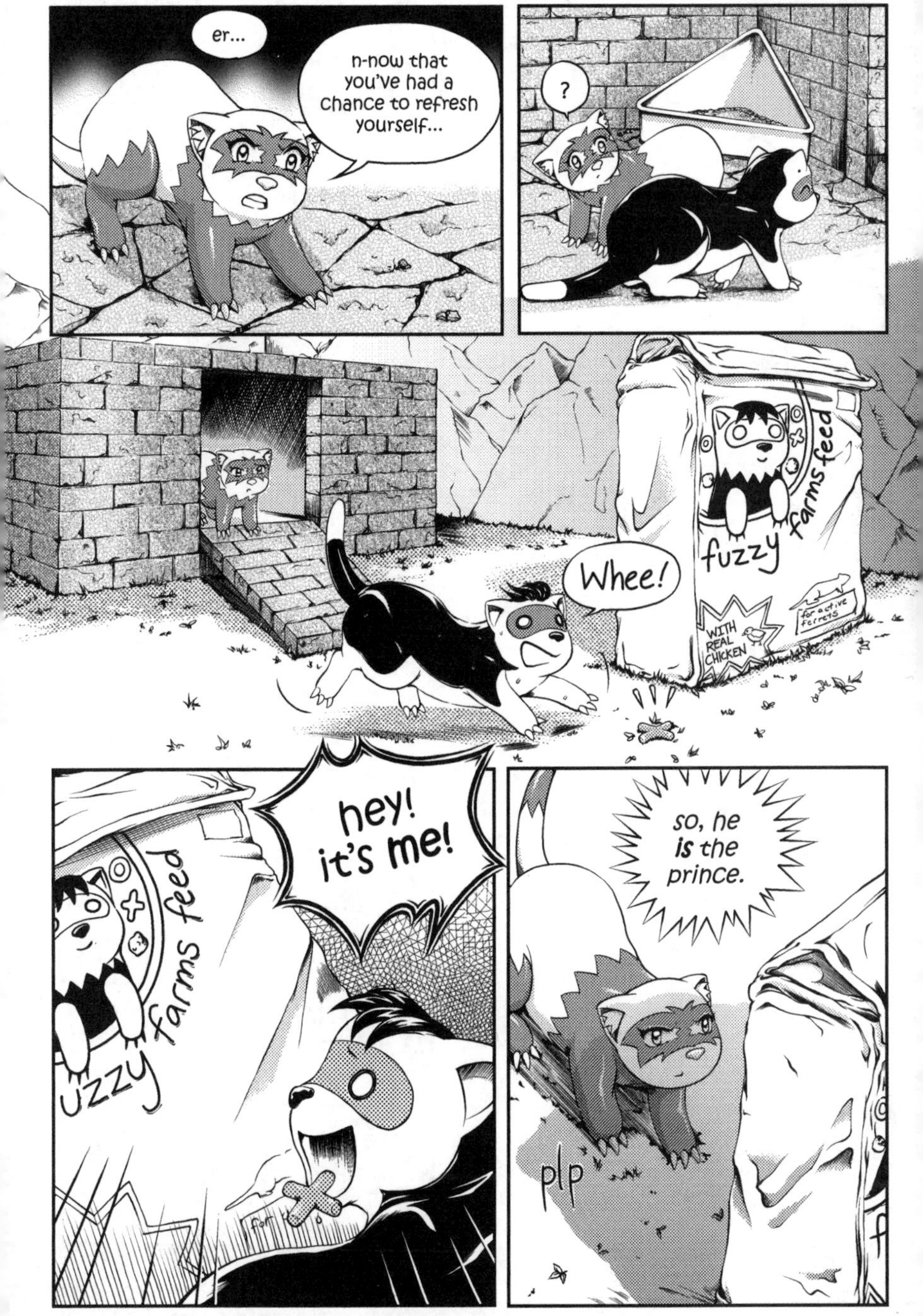
er...
n-now that you've had a chance to refresh yourself...
?
fuzzy farms feed
for active ferrets
WITH REAL CHICKEN
Whee!
hey! it's me!
so, he **is** the prince.
plp

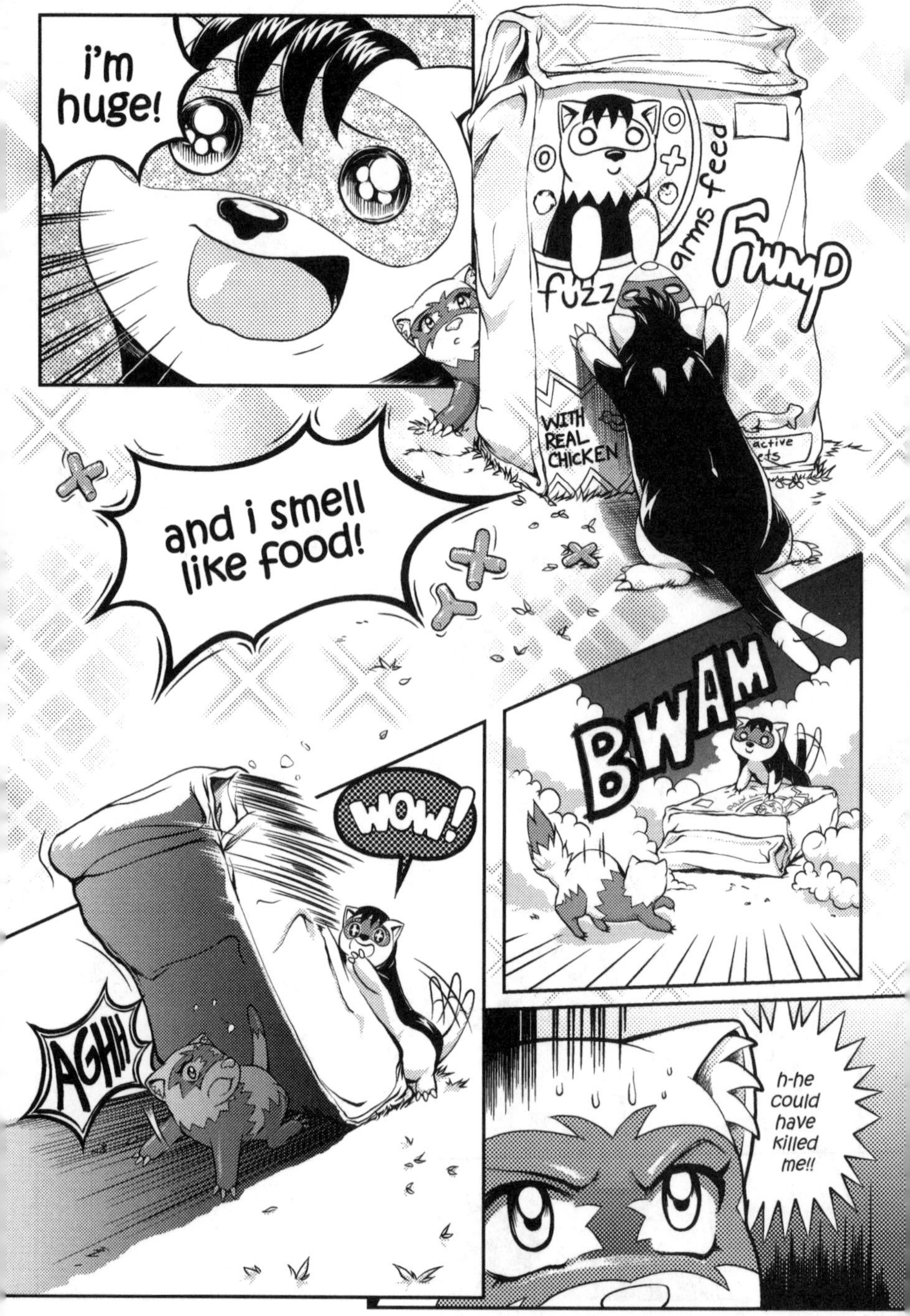
i'm huge!
and i smell like food!
fuzz arms feed
WITH REAL CHICKEN
FWUMP
BWAM
WOW!
AGHH
h-he could have killed me!!

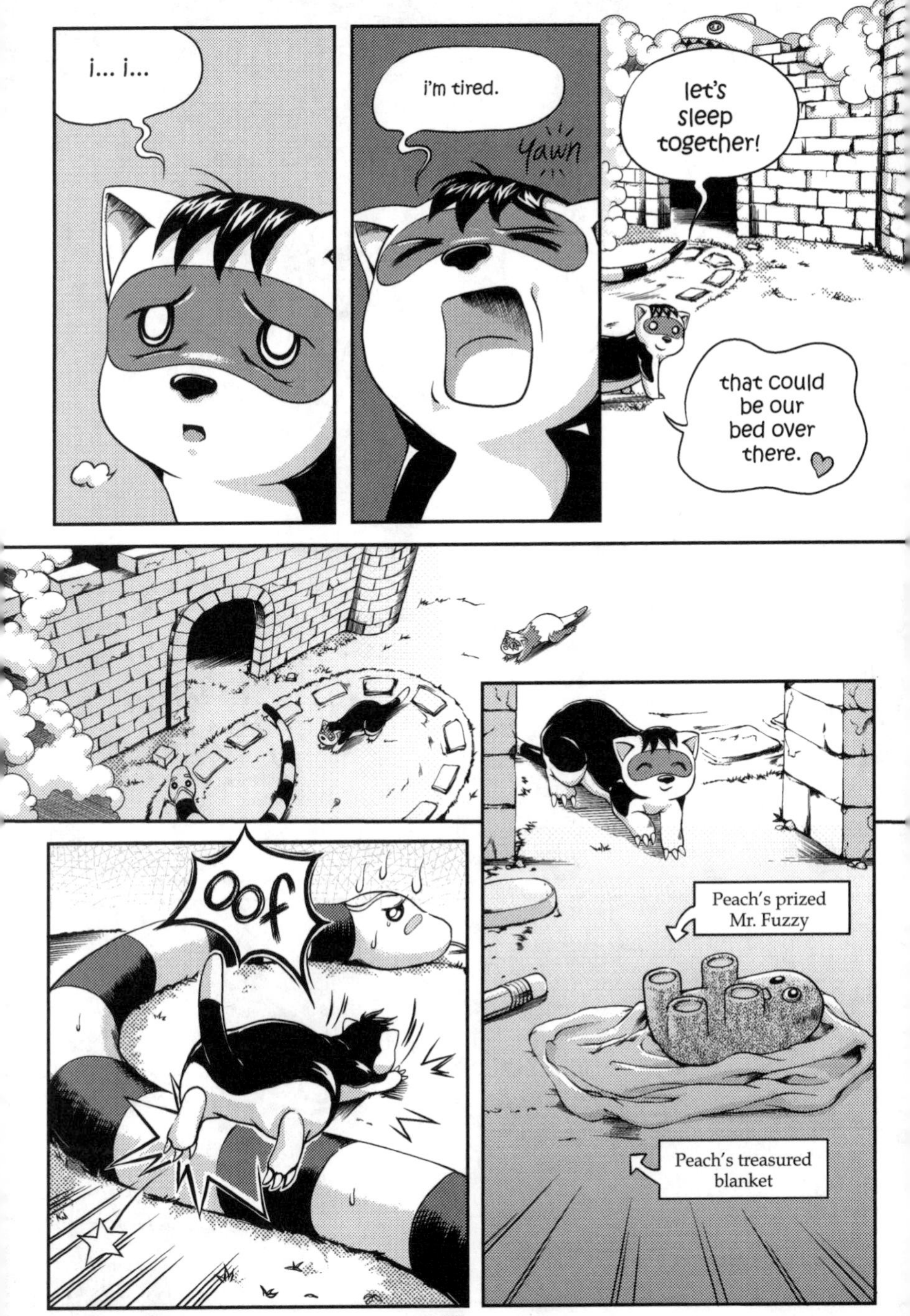
i... i...
i'm tired.
yawn
let's sleep together!
that could be our bed over there.
Peach's prized Mr. Fuzzy
Peach's treasured blanket
oof

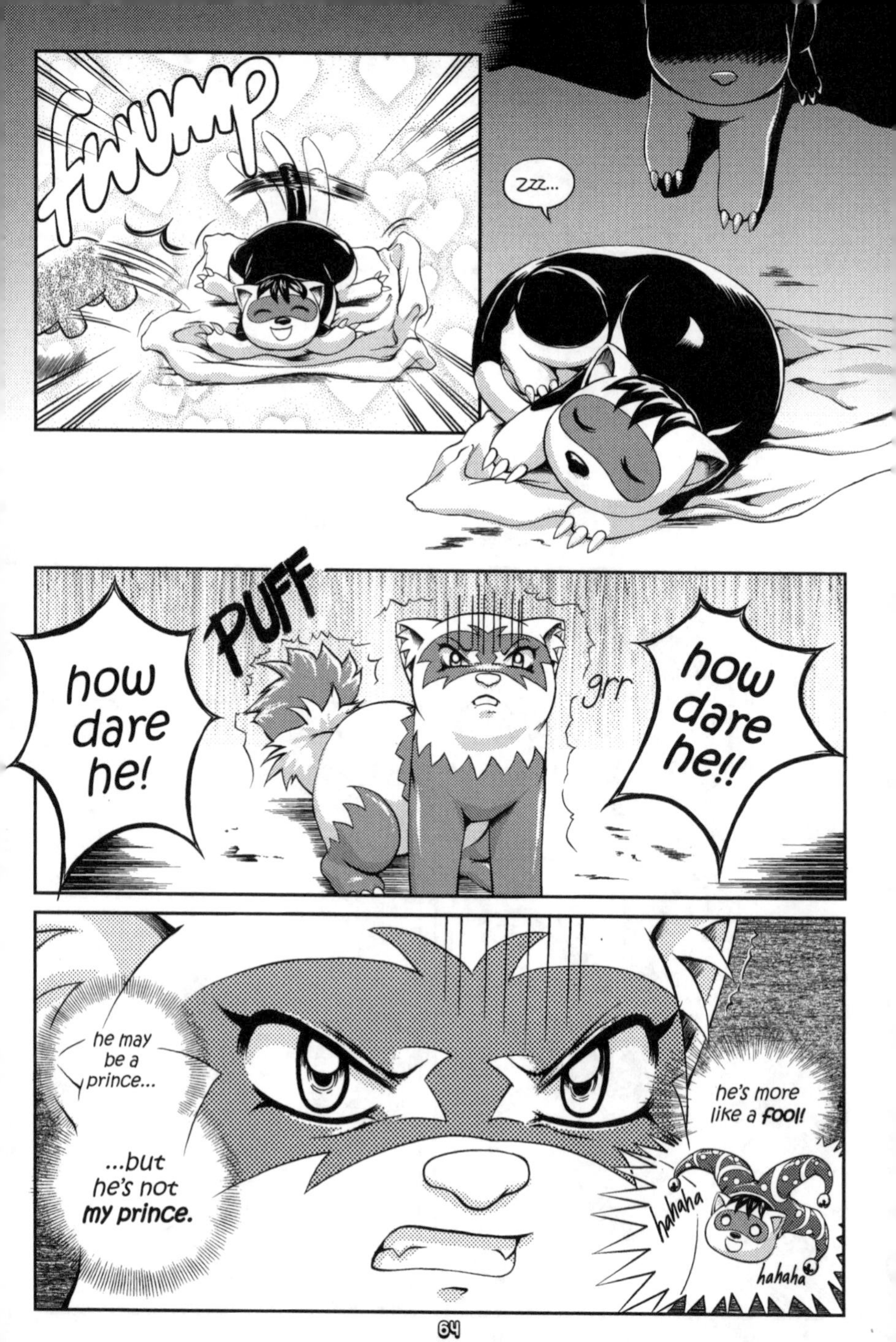
fwump
zzz...
PUFF
how dare he!
grr
how dare he!!
he may be a prince...
...but he's not my prince.
he's more like a fool!
hahaha
hahaha

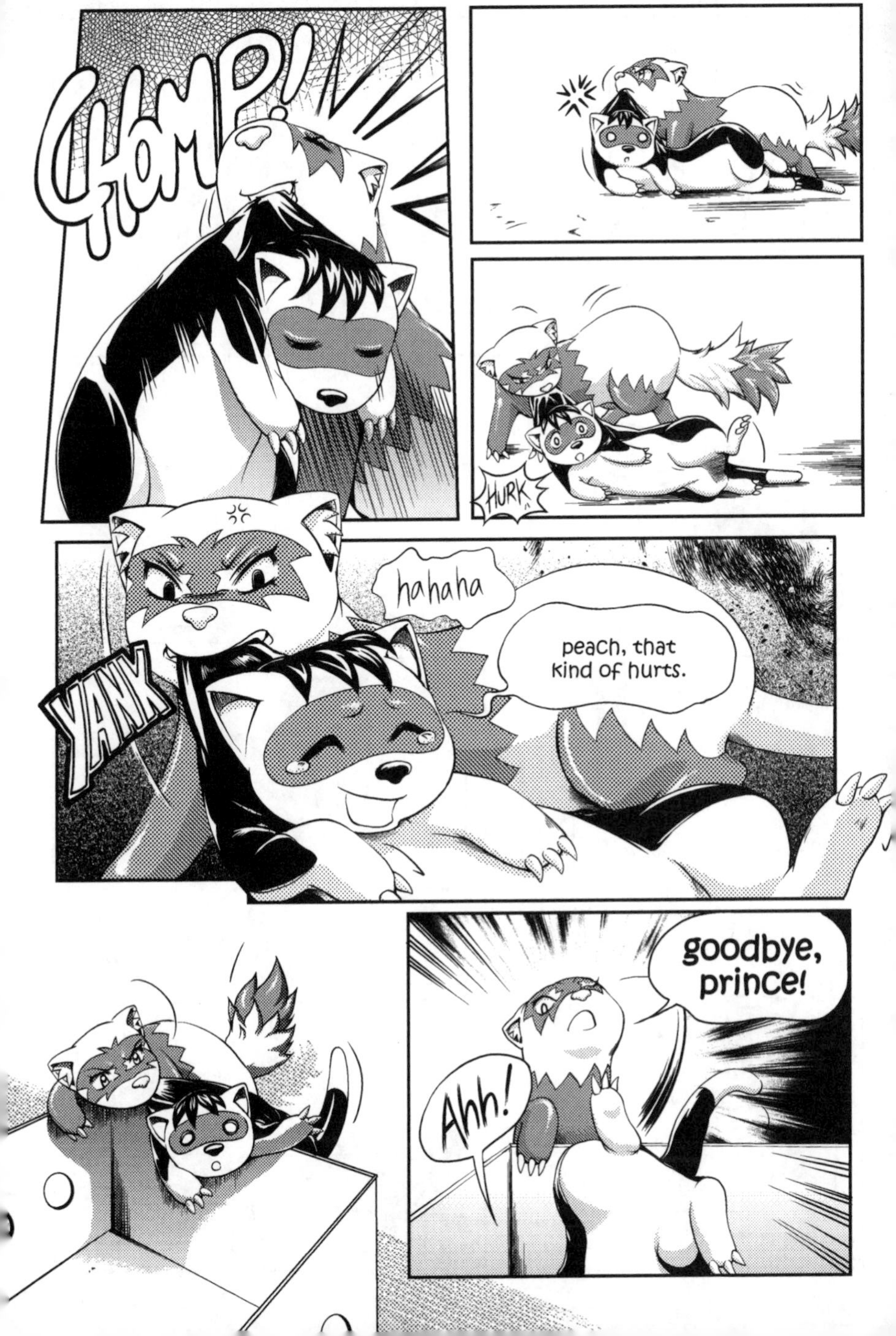
CHOMP!
HURK
hahaha
YANK
peach, that kind of hurts.
goodbye, prince!
Ahh!

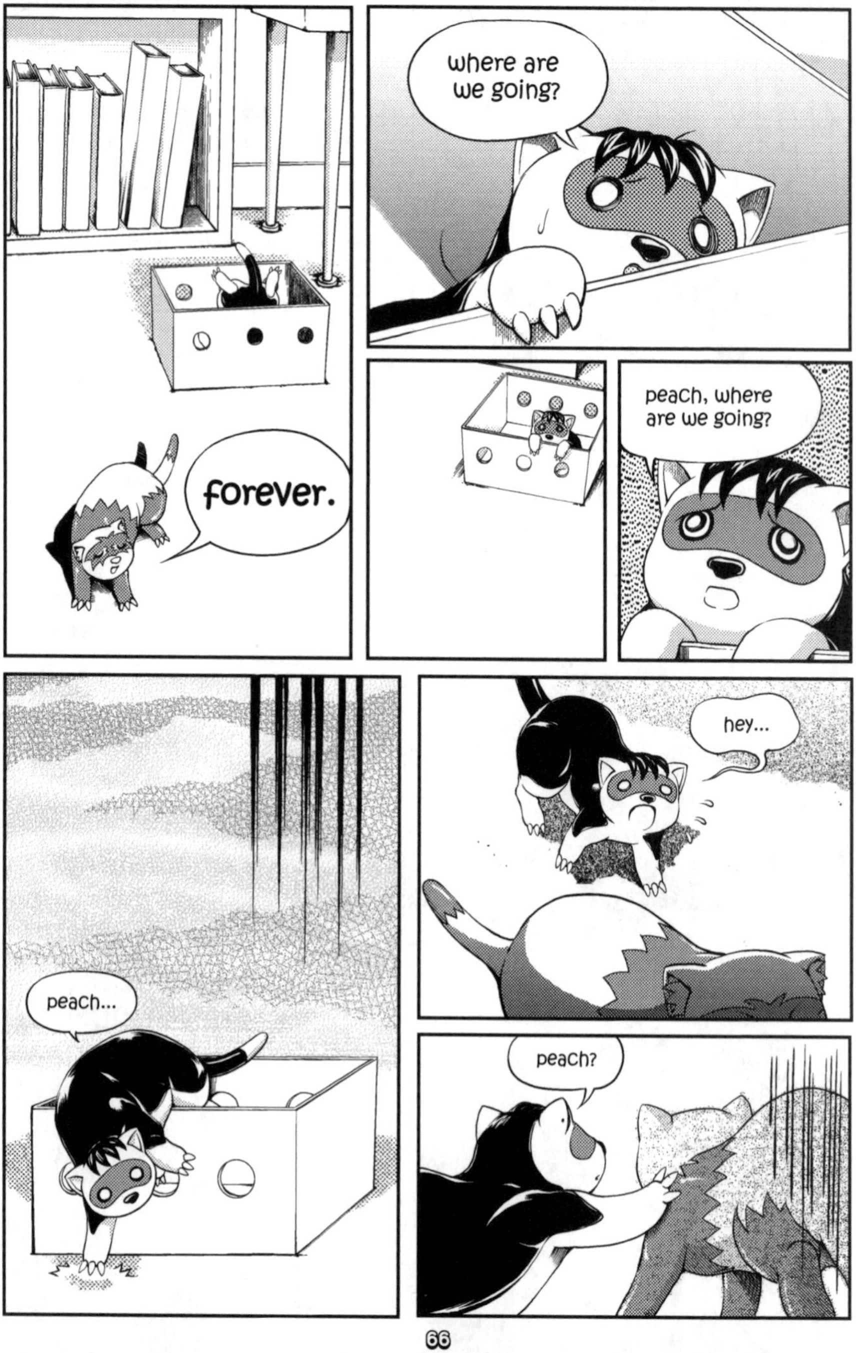
forever.
where are we going?
peach, where are we going?
peach...
hey...
peach?

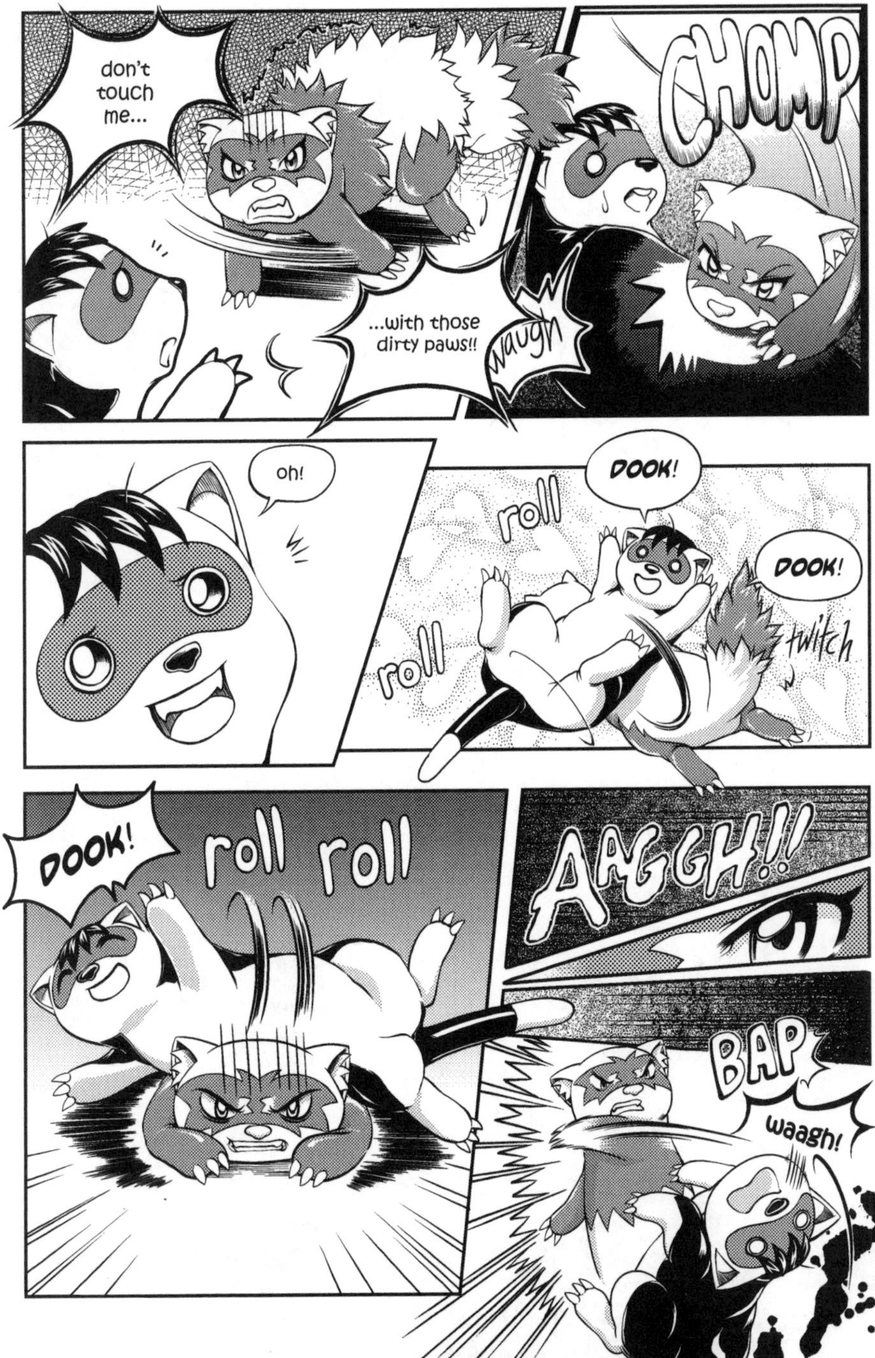
don't touch me...
...with those dirty paws!!
CHOMP
waugh
oh!
DOOK!
roll
roll
DOOK!
twitch
DOOK!
roll roll
AAGGH!!
BAP
waagh!

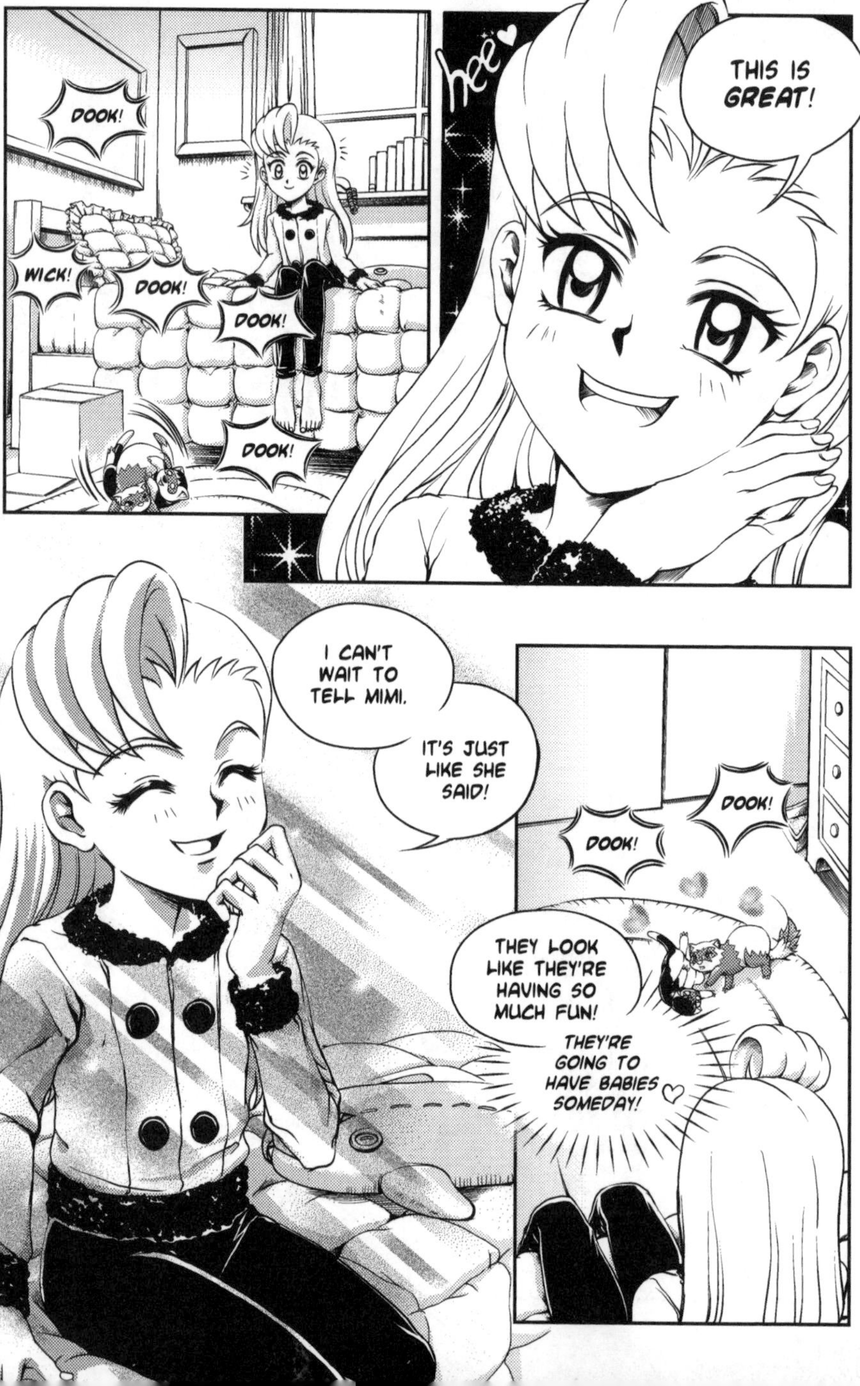
DOOK!
WICK!
DOOK!
DOOK!
DOOK!
hee
THIS IS GREAT!
I CAN'T WAIT TO TELL MIMI.
IT'S JUST LIKE SHE SAID!
DOOK!
DOOK!
THEY LOOK LIKE THEY'RE HAVING SO MUCH FUN!
THEY'RE GOING TO HAVE BABIES SOMEDAY!

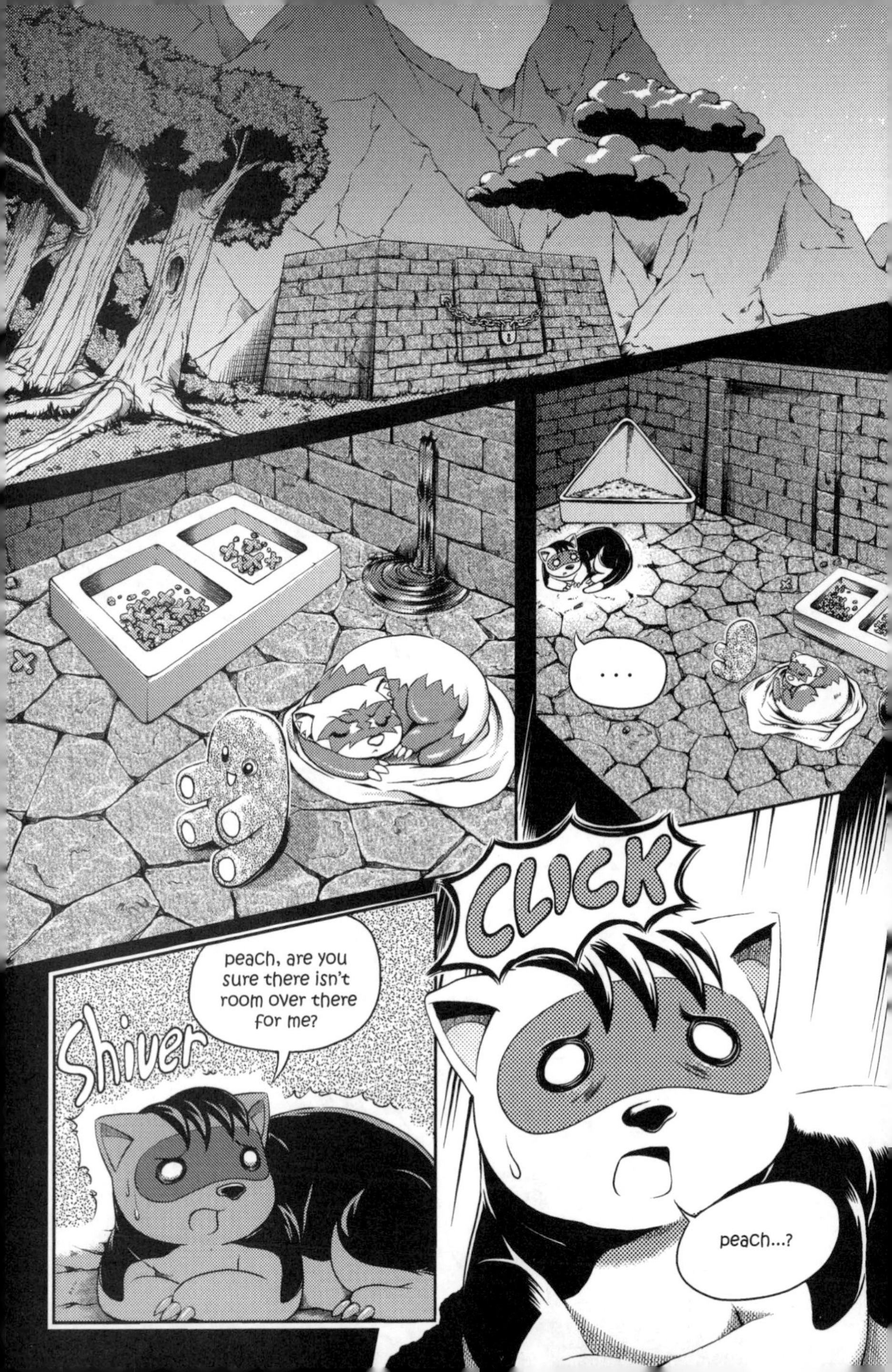

...
CLICK
peach, are you sure there isn't room over there for me?
Shiver
peach...?

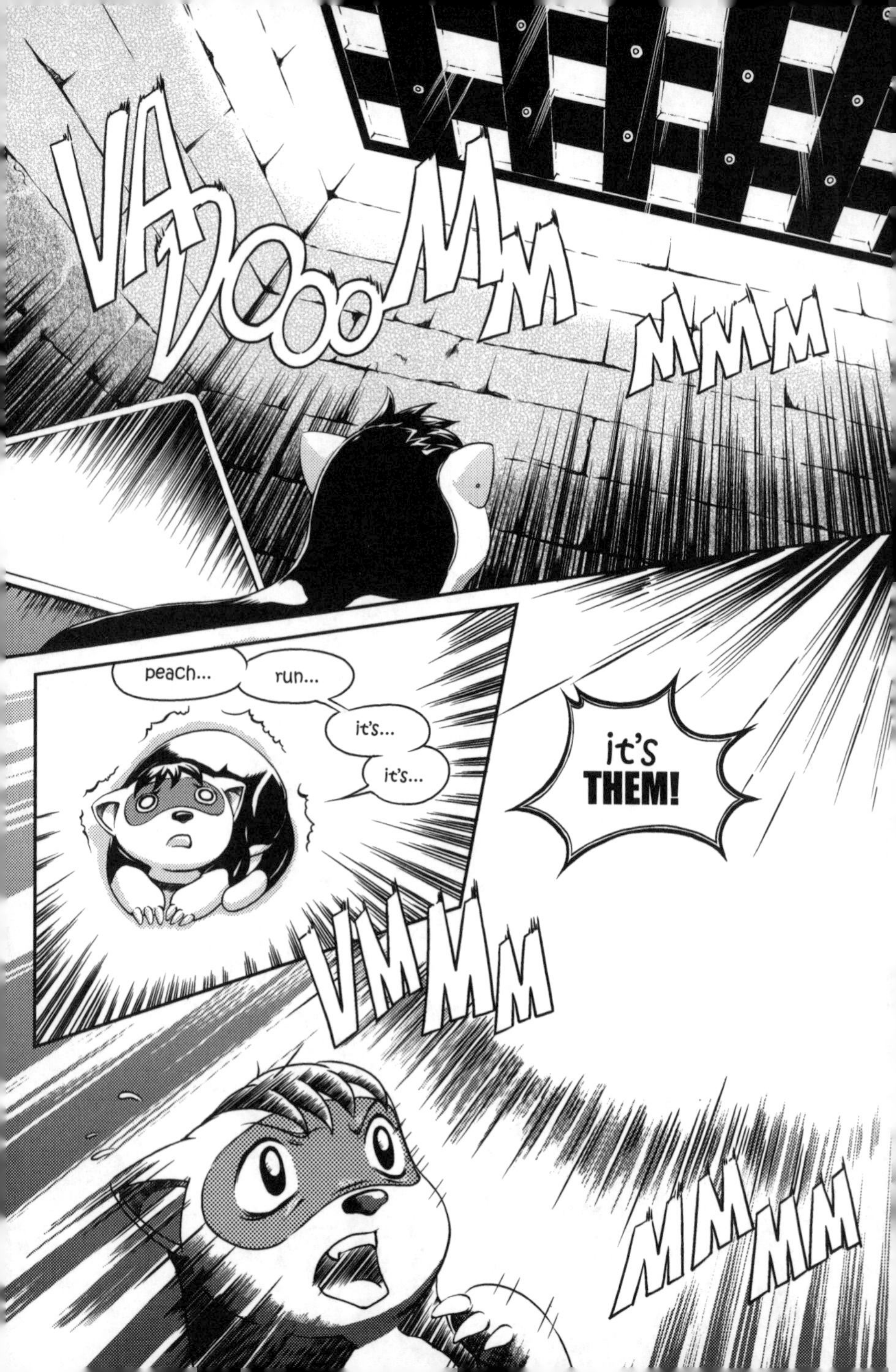
VADOOOMM
MMM
peach...
run...
it's...
it's...
it's THEM!
VMMM
MMMM

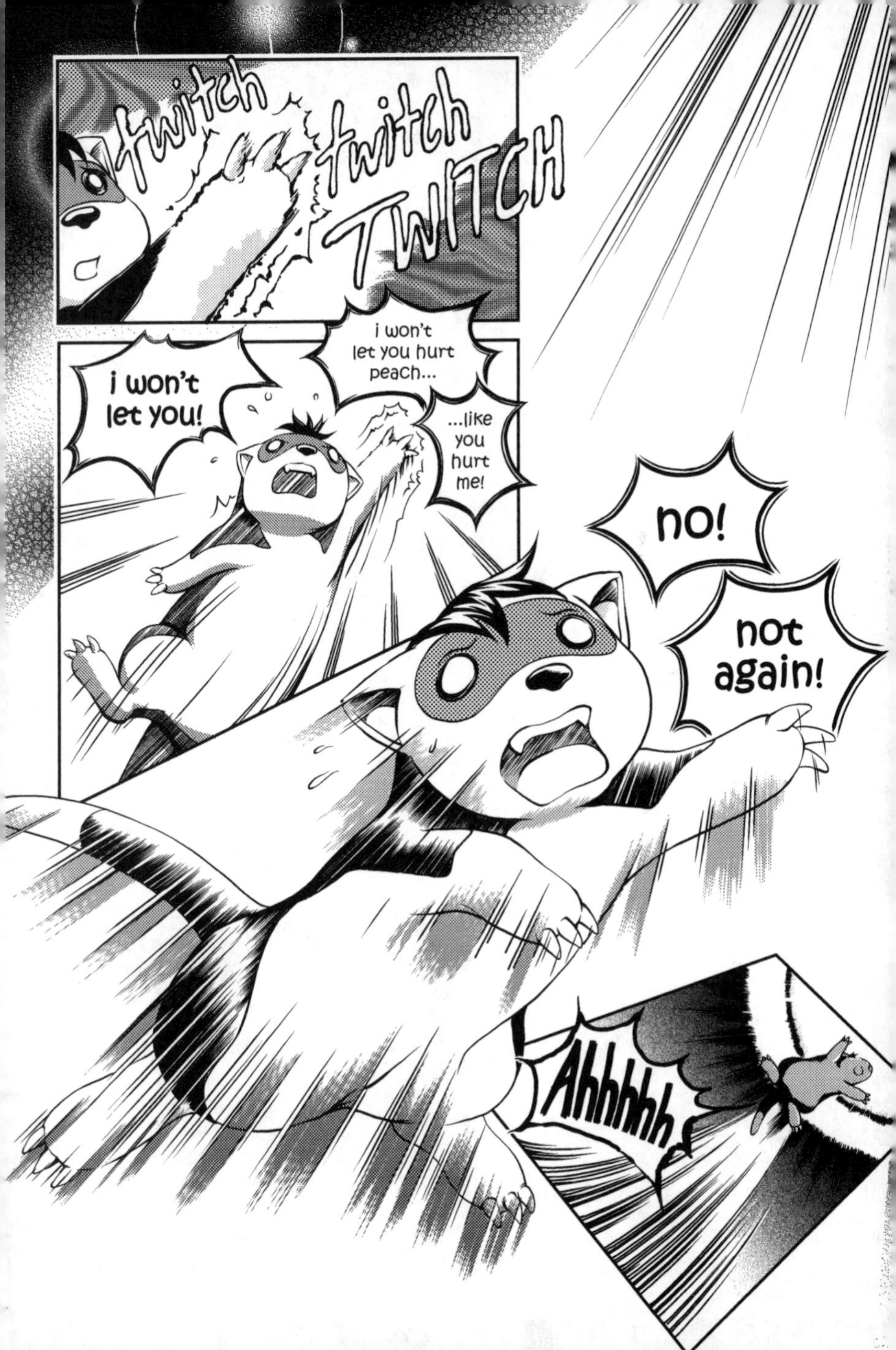
twitch
twitch
TWITCH
i won't let you!
i won't let you hurt peach...
...like you hurt me!
no!
not again!
Ahhhhh

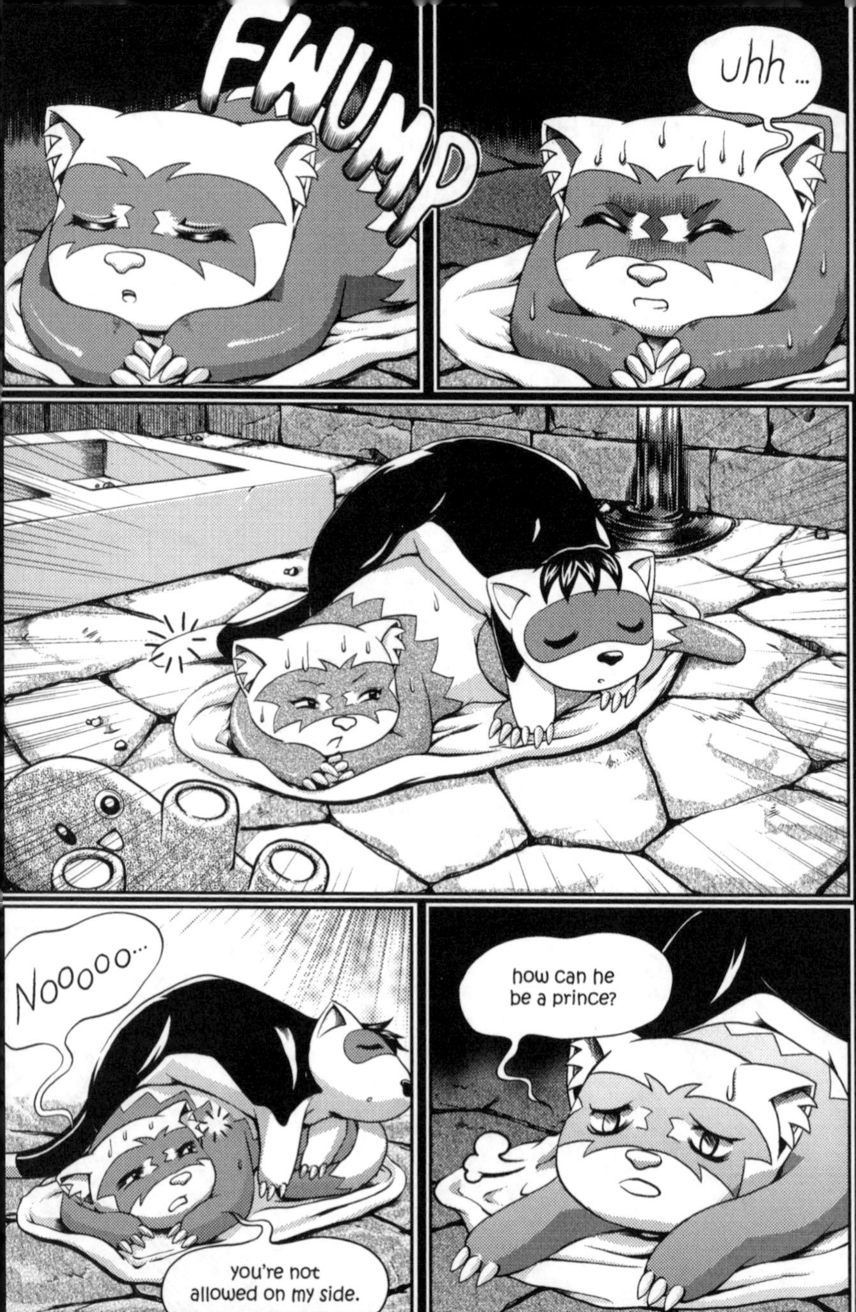
FWUMP
uhh...
Nooooo...
you're not allowed on my side.
how can he be a prince?

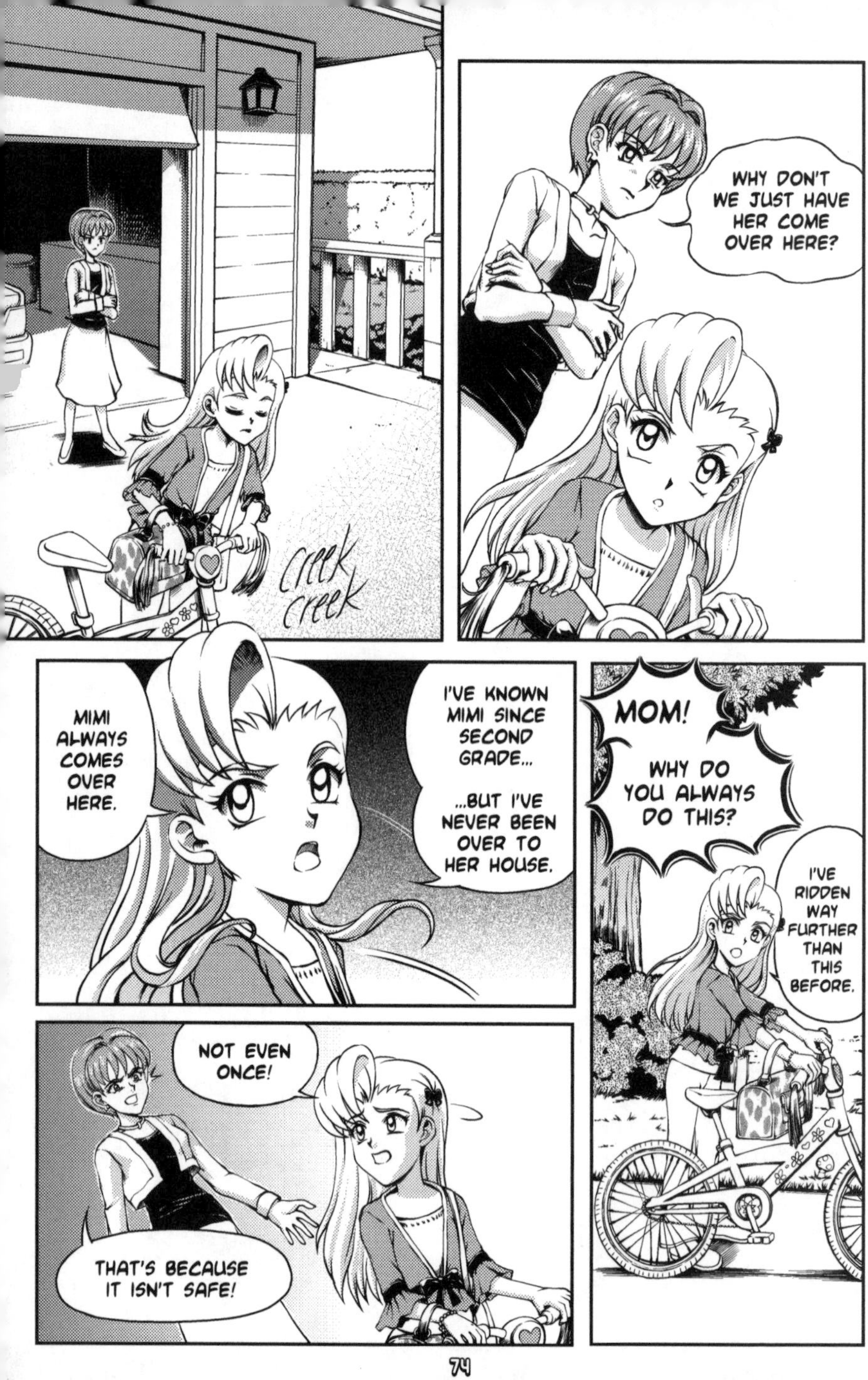
creek creek
WHY DON'T WE JUST HAVE HER COME OVER HERE?
MIMI ALWAYS COMES OVER HERE.
I'VE KNOWN MIMI SINCE SECOND GRADE...
...BUT I'VE NEVER BEEN OVER TO HER HOUSE.
NOT EVEN ONCE!
THAT'S BECAUSE IT ISN'T SAFE!
MOM!
WHY DO YOU ALWAYS DO THIS?
I'VE RIDDEN WAY FURTHER THAN THIS BEFORE.

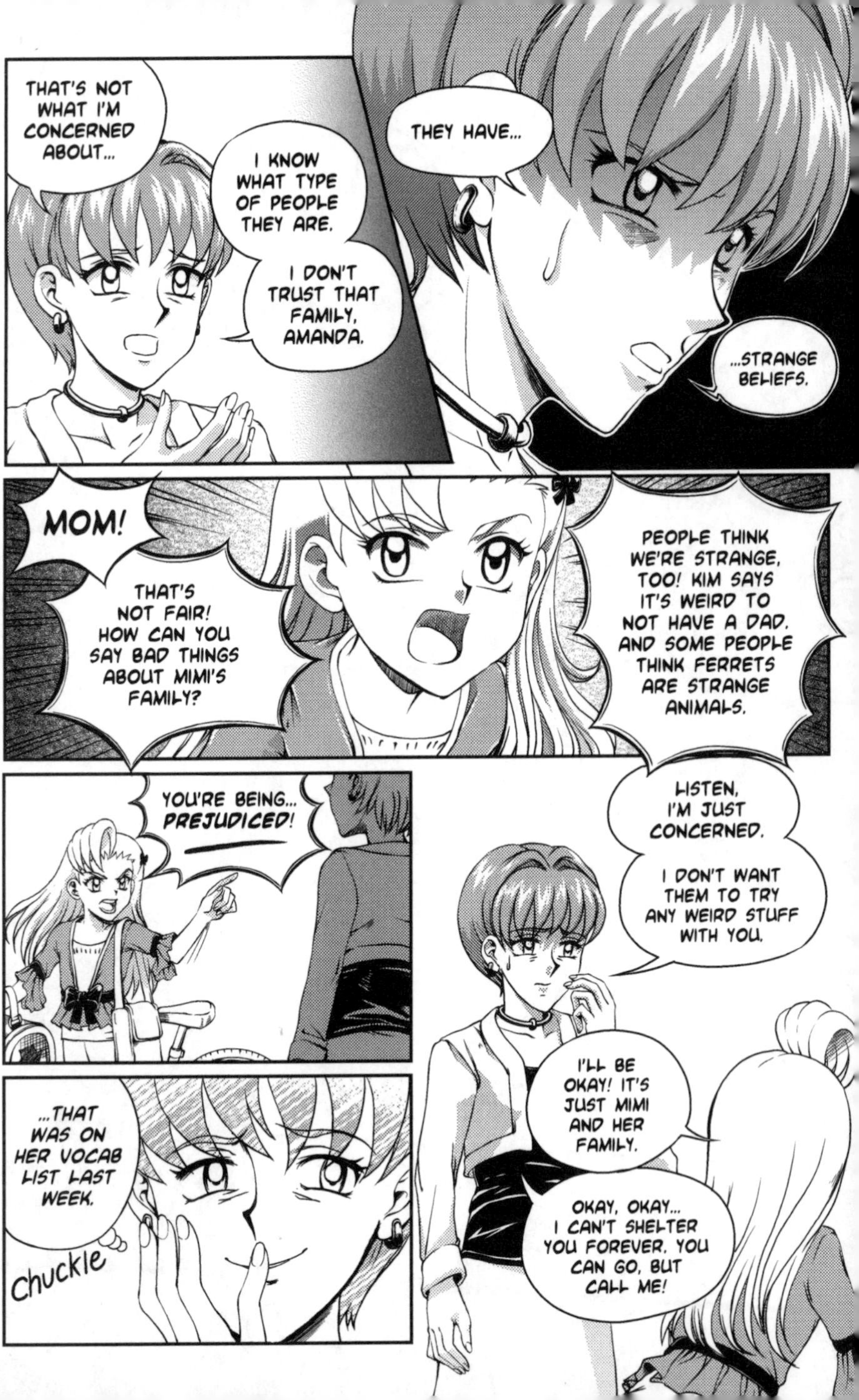
THAT'S NOT WHAT I'M CONCERNED ABOUT...
I KNOW WHAT TYPE OF PEOPLE THEY ARE.
I DON'T TRUST THAT FAMILY, AMANDA.
THEY HAVE...
...STRANGE BELIEFS.
MOM!
THAT'S NOT FAIR! HOW CAN YOU SAY BAD THINGS ABOUT MIMI'S FAMILY?
PEOPLE THINK WE'RE STRANGE, TOO! KIM SAYS IT'S WEIRD TO NOT HAVE A DAD. AND SOME PEOPLE THINK FERRETS ARE STRANGE ANIMALS.
YOU'RE BEING... *PREJUDICED*!
LISTEN, I'M JUST CONCERNED.
I DON'T WANT THEM TO TRY ANY WEIRD STUFF WITH YOU.
...THAT WAS ON HER VOCAB LIST LAST WEEK.
Chuckle
I'LL BE OKAY! IT'S JUST MIMI AND HER FAMILY.
OKAY, OKAY... I CAN'T SHELTER YOU FOREVER. YOU CAN GO, BUT CALL ME!

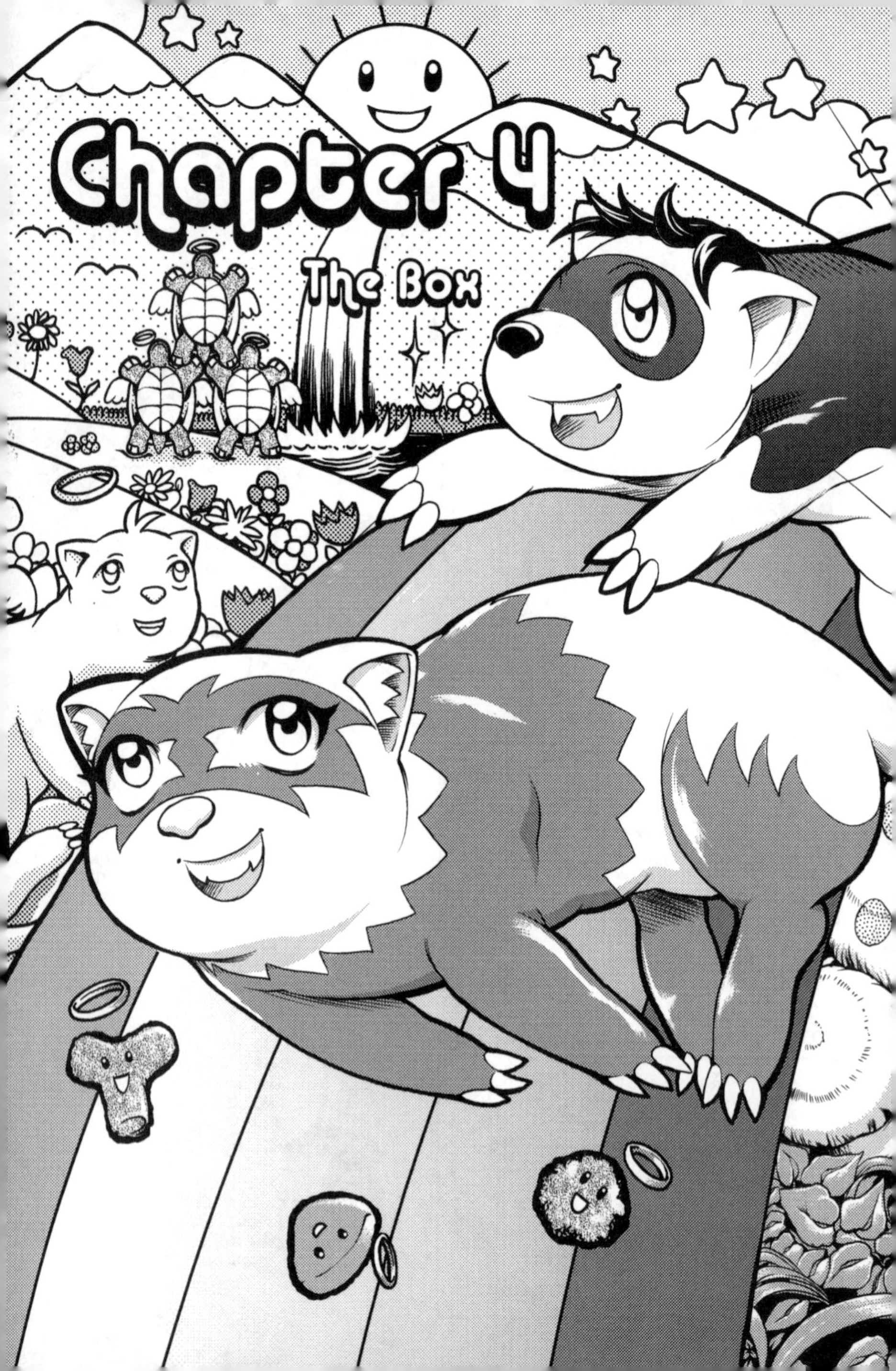
Chapter 4
The Box

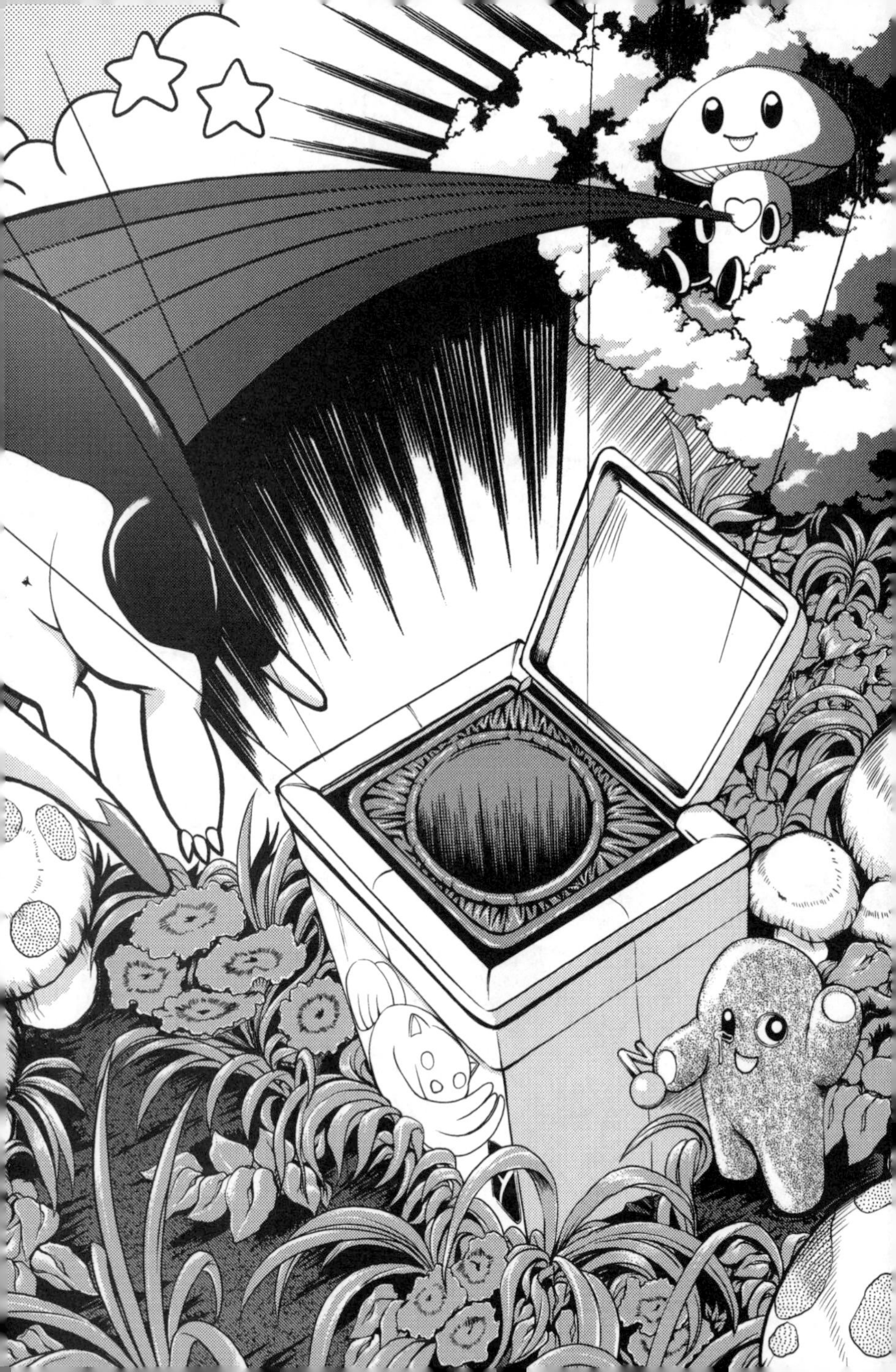

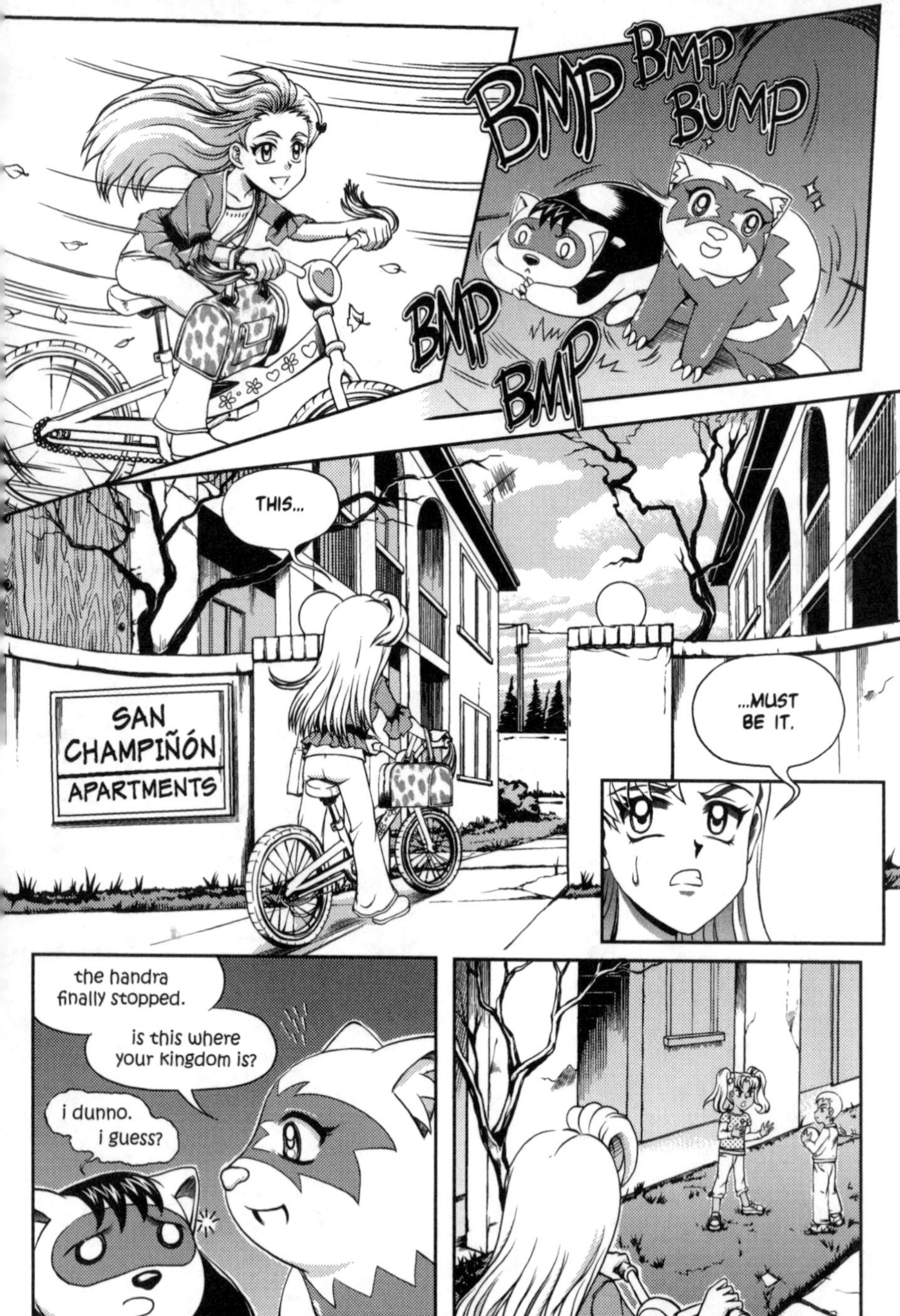
BMP BMP BUMP
BMP
BMP
THIS...
SAN CHAMPIÑÓN APARTMENTS
...MUST BE IT.
the handra finally stopped.
is this where your kingdom is?
i dunno. i guess?

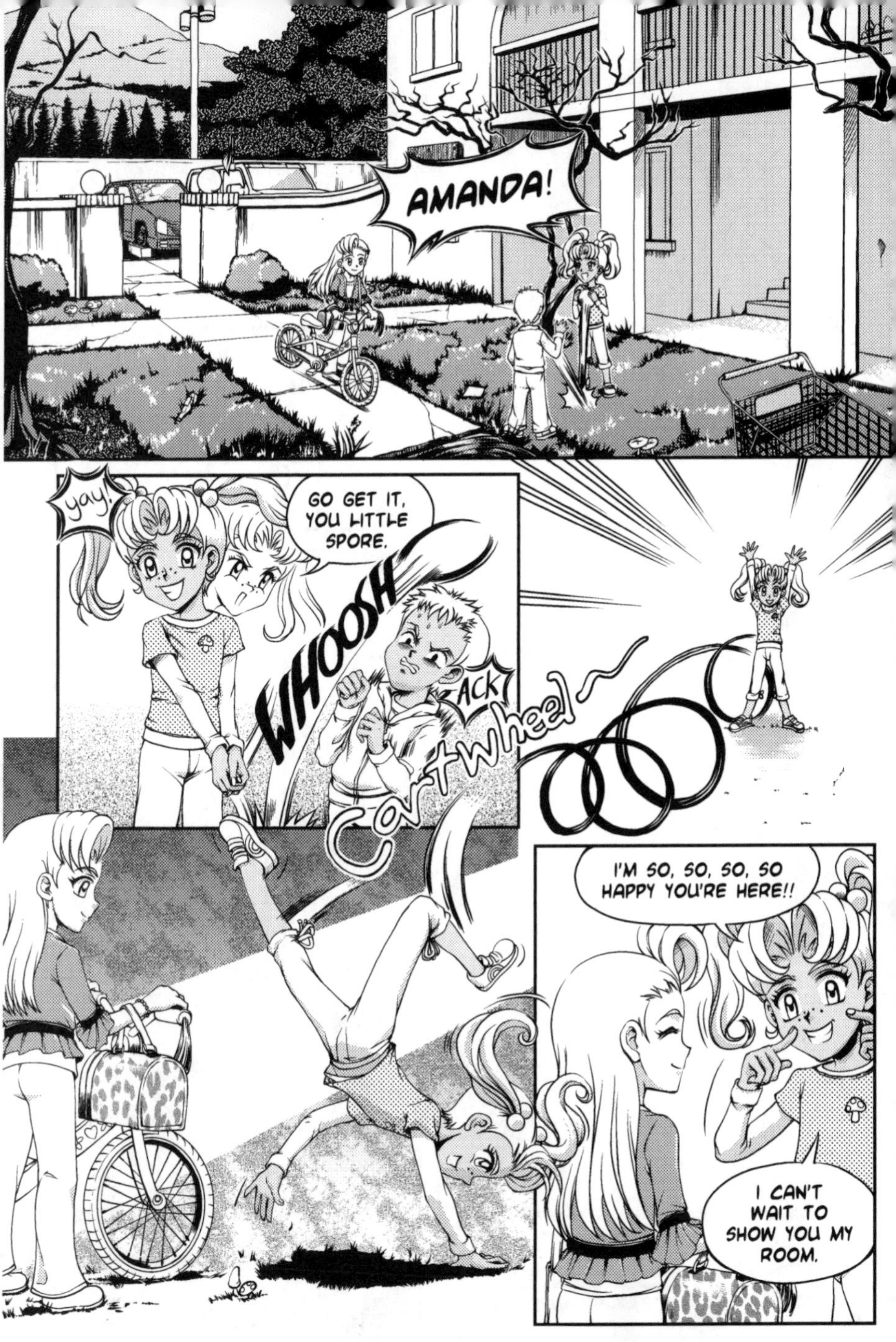
AMANDA!
yay!
GO GET IT, YOU LITTLE SPORE.
WHOOSH
ACK
Cartwheel
I'M SO, SO, SO, SO HAPPY YOU'RE HERE!!
I CAN'T WAIT TO SHOW YOU MY ROOM.

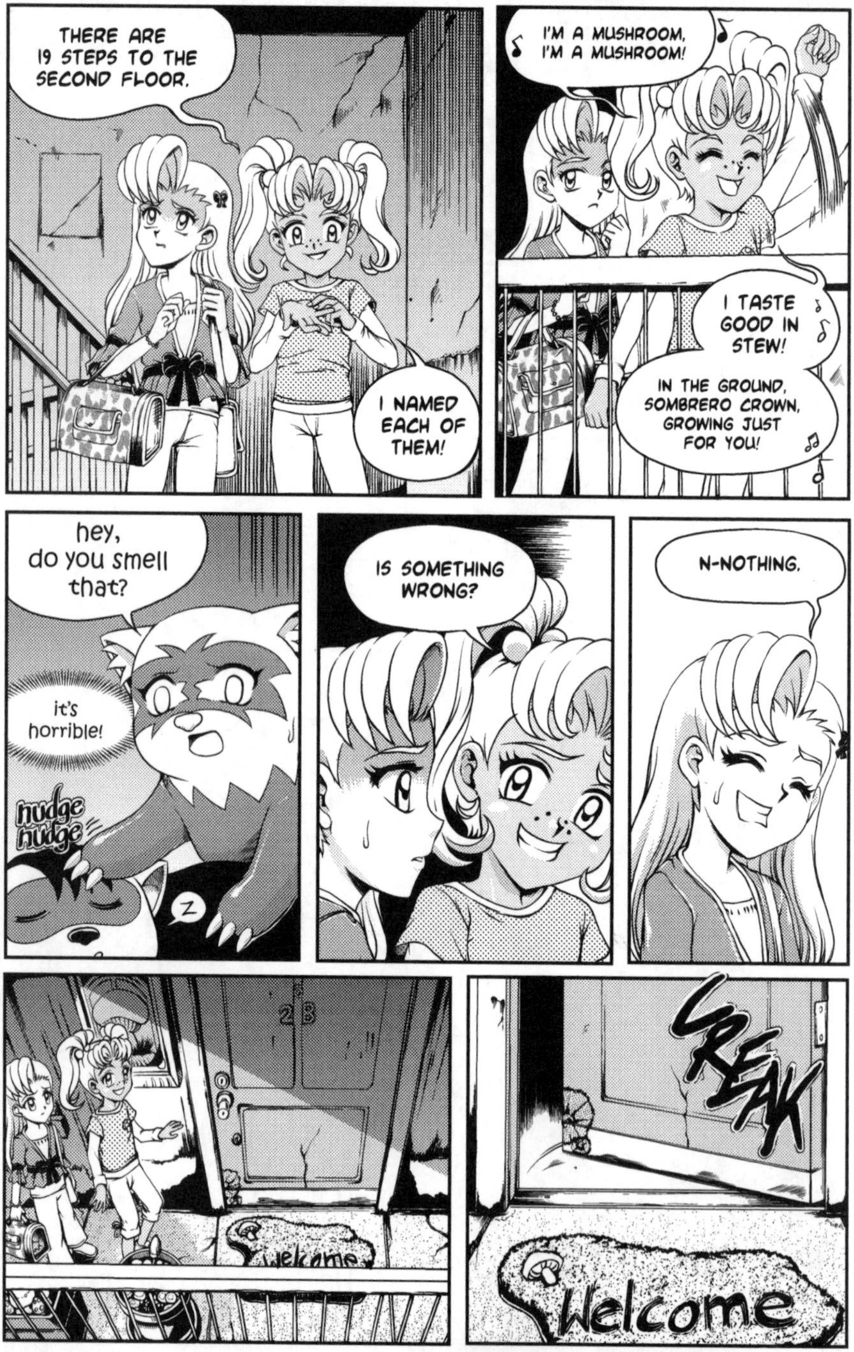
THERE ARE 19 STEPS TO THE SECOND FLOOR.
I NAMED EACH OF THEM!
I'M A MUSHROOM, I'M A MUSHROOM!
I TASTE GOOD IN STEW!
IN THE GROUND, SOMBRERO CROWN, GROWING JUST FOR YOU!
hey, do you smell that?
it's horrible!
nudge nudge
Z
IS SOMETHING WRONG?
N-NOTHING.
2B
welcome
CREAK
Welcome

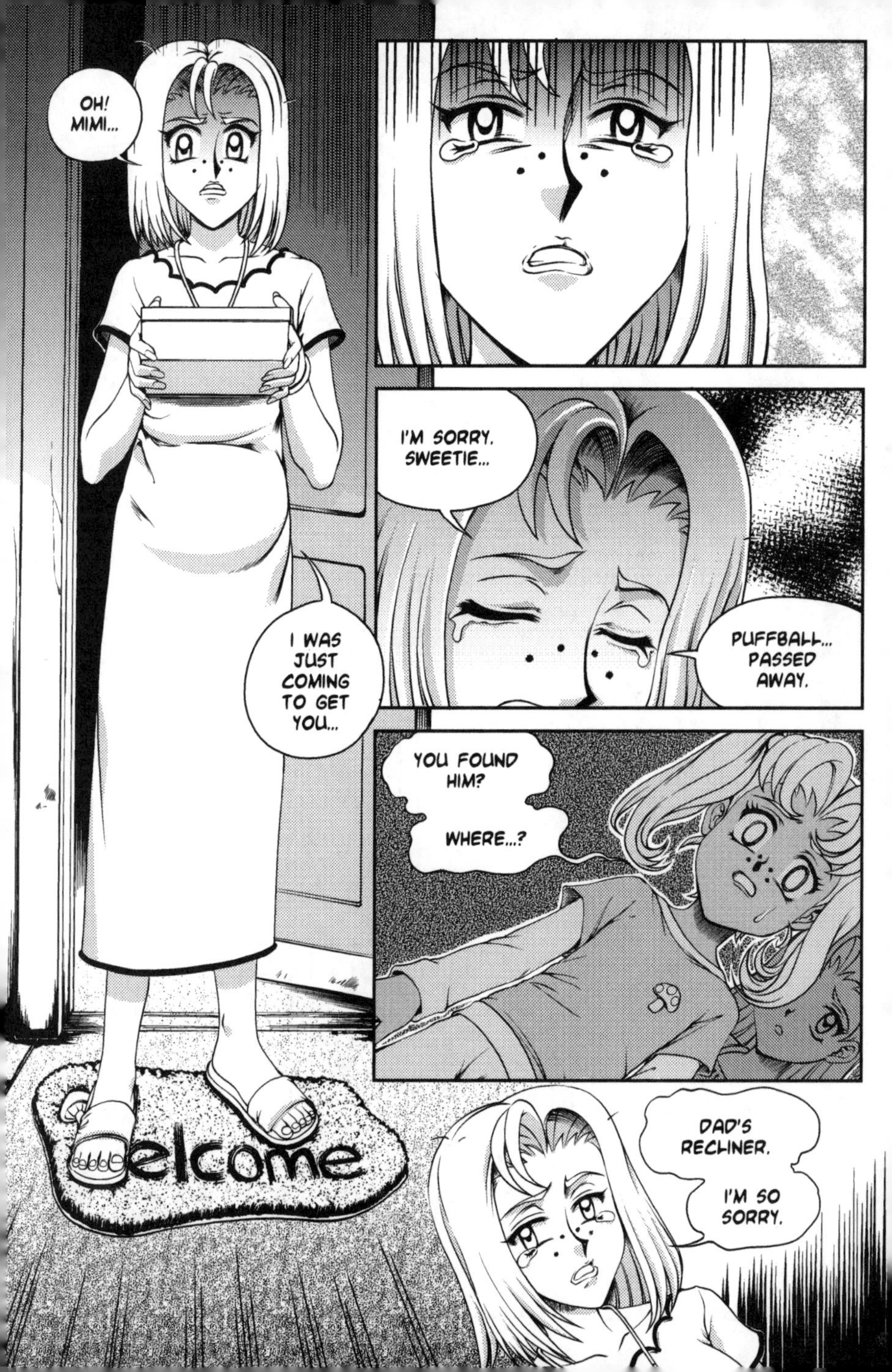
OH! MIMI...
I'M SORRY. SWEETIE...
I WAS JUST COMING TO GET YOU...
PUFFBALL... PASSED AWAY.
YOU FOUND HIM?
WHERE...?
DAD'S RECLINER.
I'M SO SORRY.
elcome

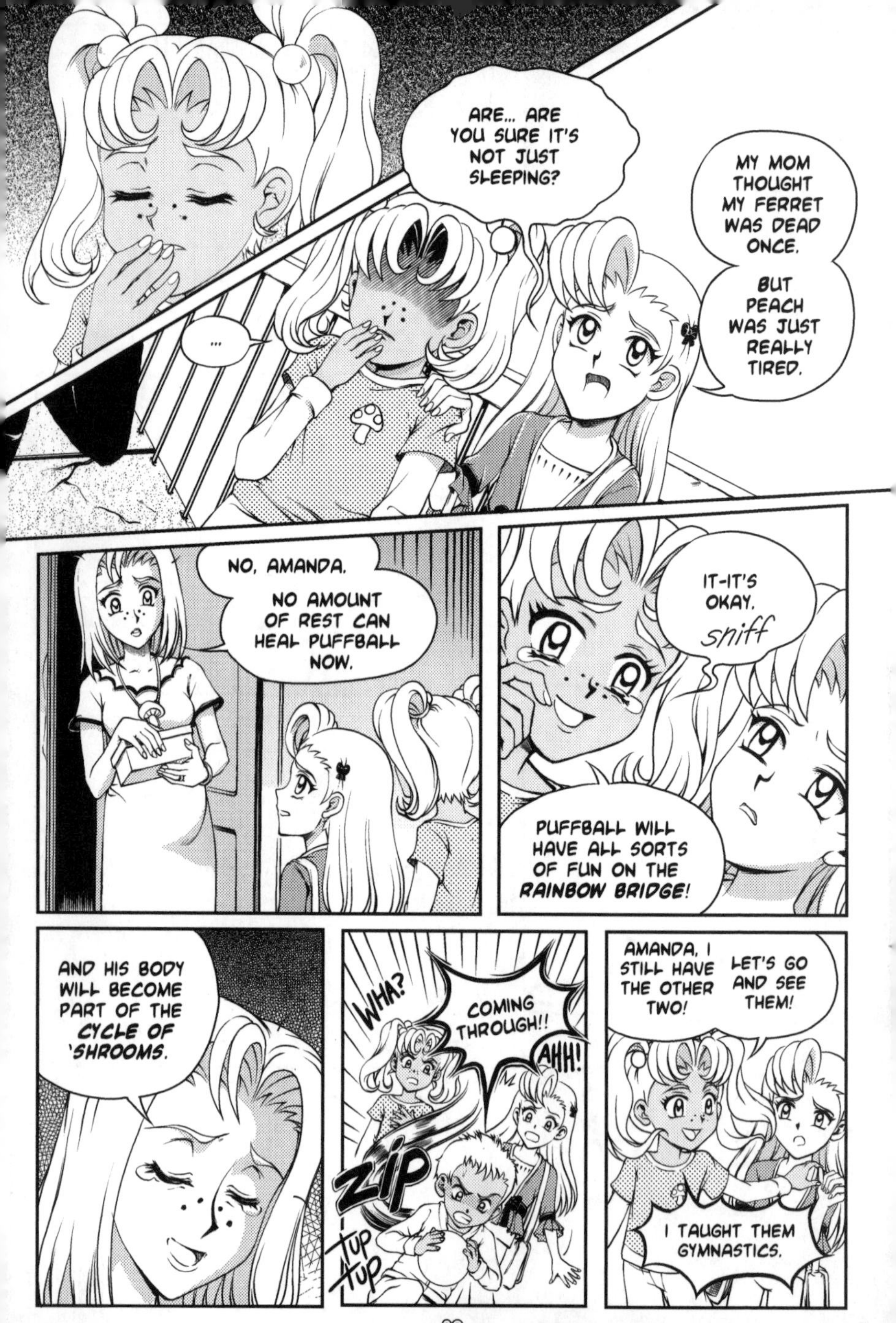

ARE... ARE YOU SURE IT'S NOT JUST SLEEPING?
...
MY MOM THOUGHT MY FERRET WAS DEAD ONCE.
BUT PEACH WAS JUST REALLY TIRED.
NO, AMANDA.
NO AMOUNT OF REST CAN HEAL PUFFBALL NOW.
IT-IT'S OKAY.
sniff
PUFFBALL WILL HAVE ALL SORTS OF FUN ON THE RAINBOW BRIDGE!
AND HIS BODY WILL BECOME PART OF THE CYCLE OF 'SHROOMS.
WHA?
COMING THROUGH!!
AHH!
ZIP
TUP TUP
AMANDA, I STILL HAVE THE OTHER TWO!
LET'S GO AND SEE THEM!
I TAUGHT THEM GYMNASTICS.

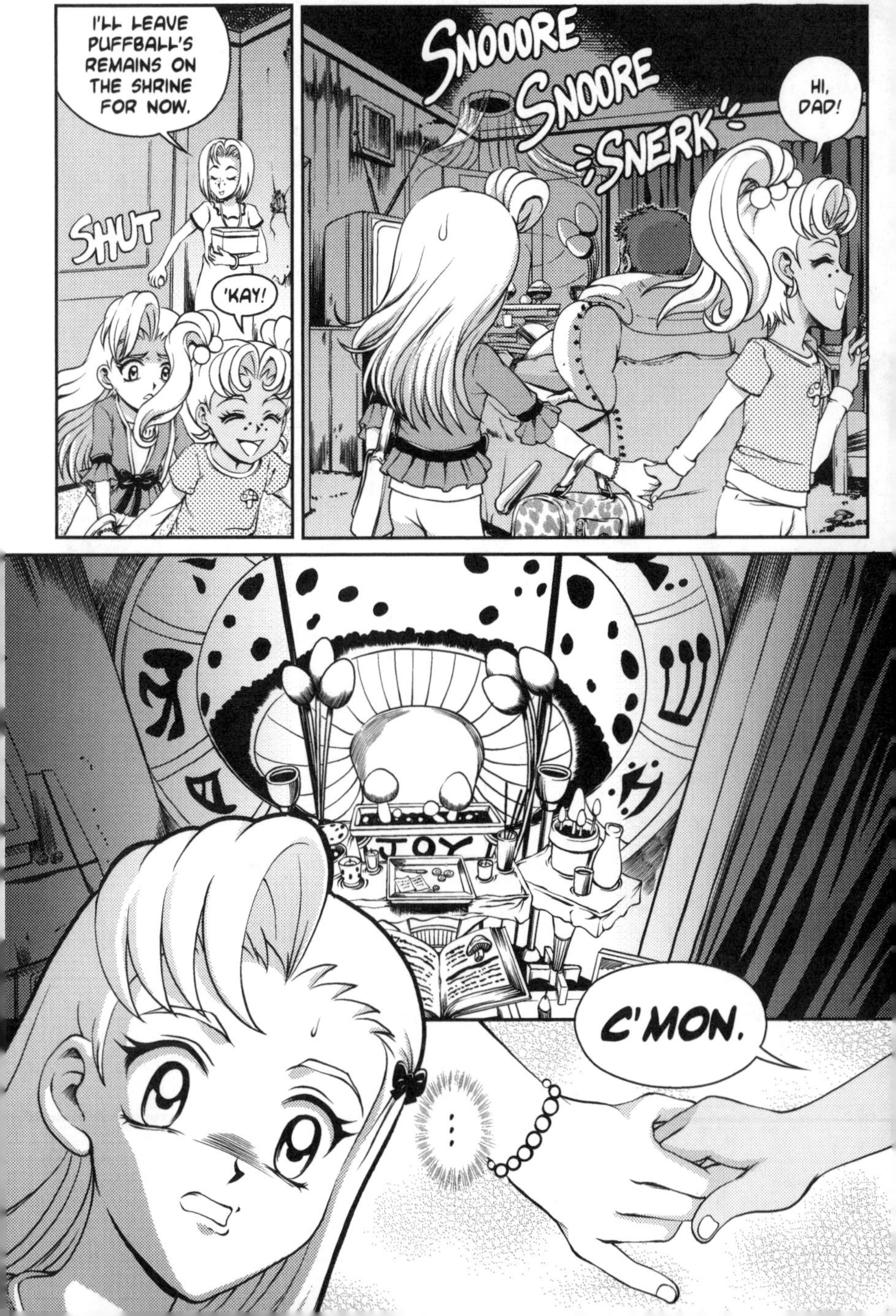
I'LL LEAVE PUFFBALL'S REMAINS ON THE SHRINE FOR NOW.
SHUT
'KAY!
SNOOORE
SNOORE
SNERK
HI, DAD!
JOY
C'MON.
. . .

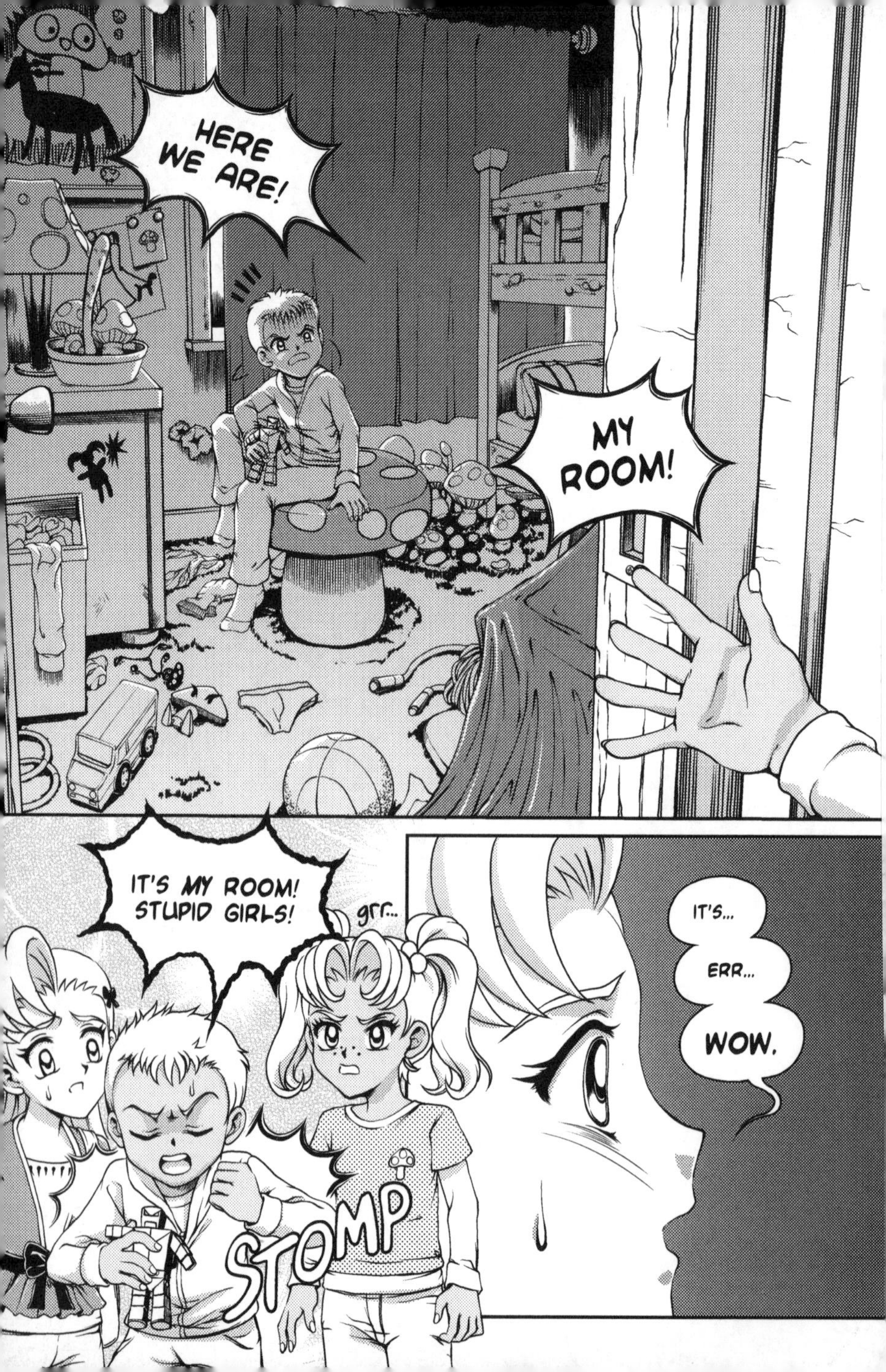
HERE WE ARE!
MY ROOM!
IT'S MY ROOM! STUPID GIRLS!
grr...
STOMP
IT'S...
ERR...
WOW.

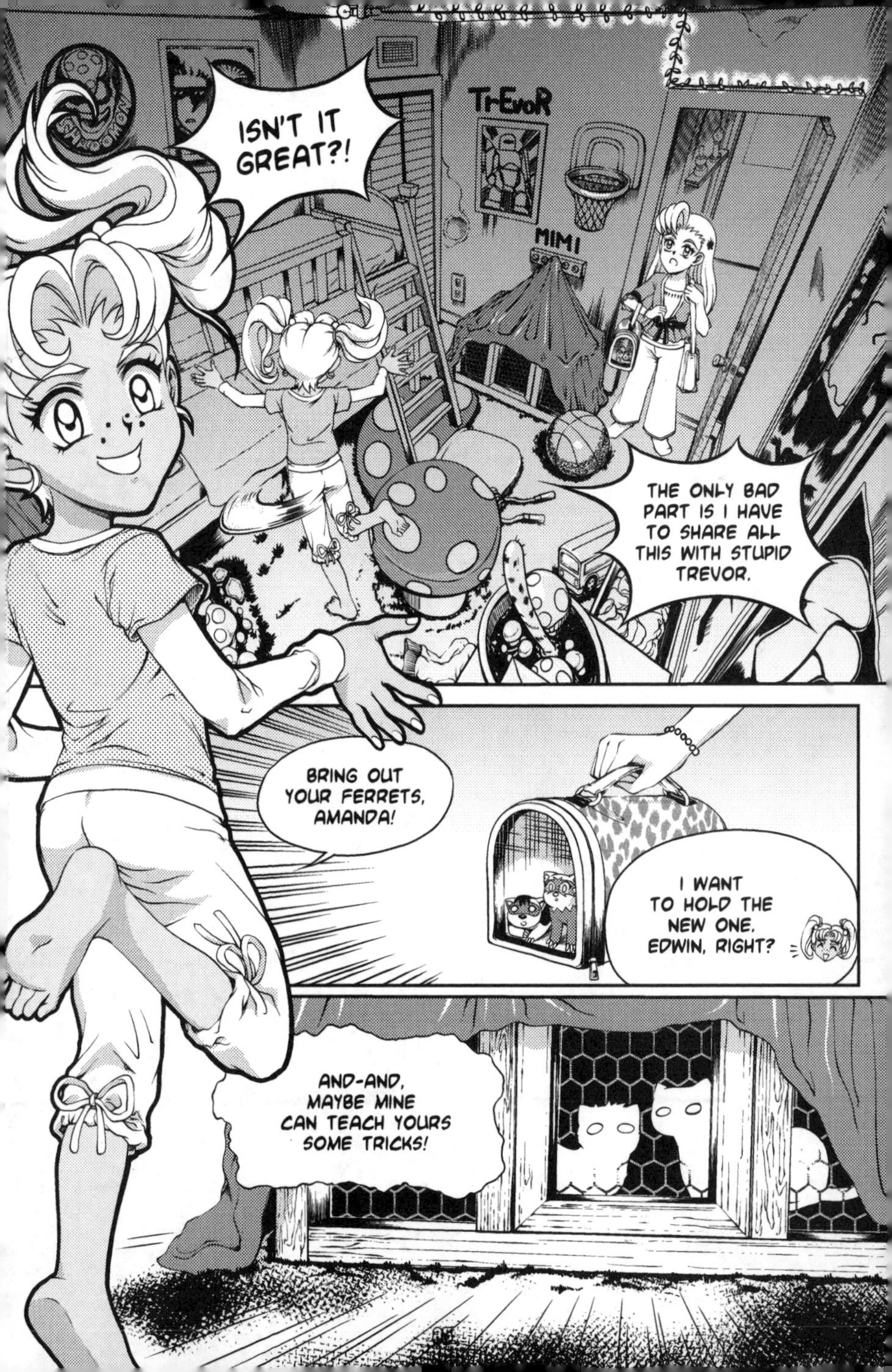
ISN'T IT GREAT?!
TrEvoR
MIMI
THE ONLY BAD PART IS I HAVE TO SHARE ALL THIS WITH STUPID TREVOR.
BRING OUT YOUR FERRETS, AMANDA!
I WANT TO HOLD THE NEW ONE. EDWIN, RIGHT?
AND-AND, MAYBE MINE CAN TEACH YOURS SOME TRICKS!

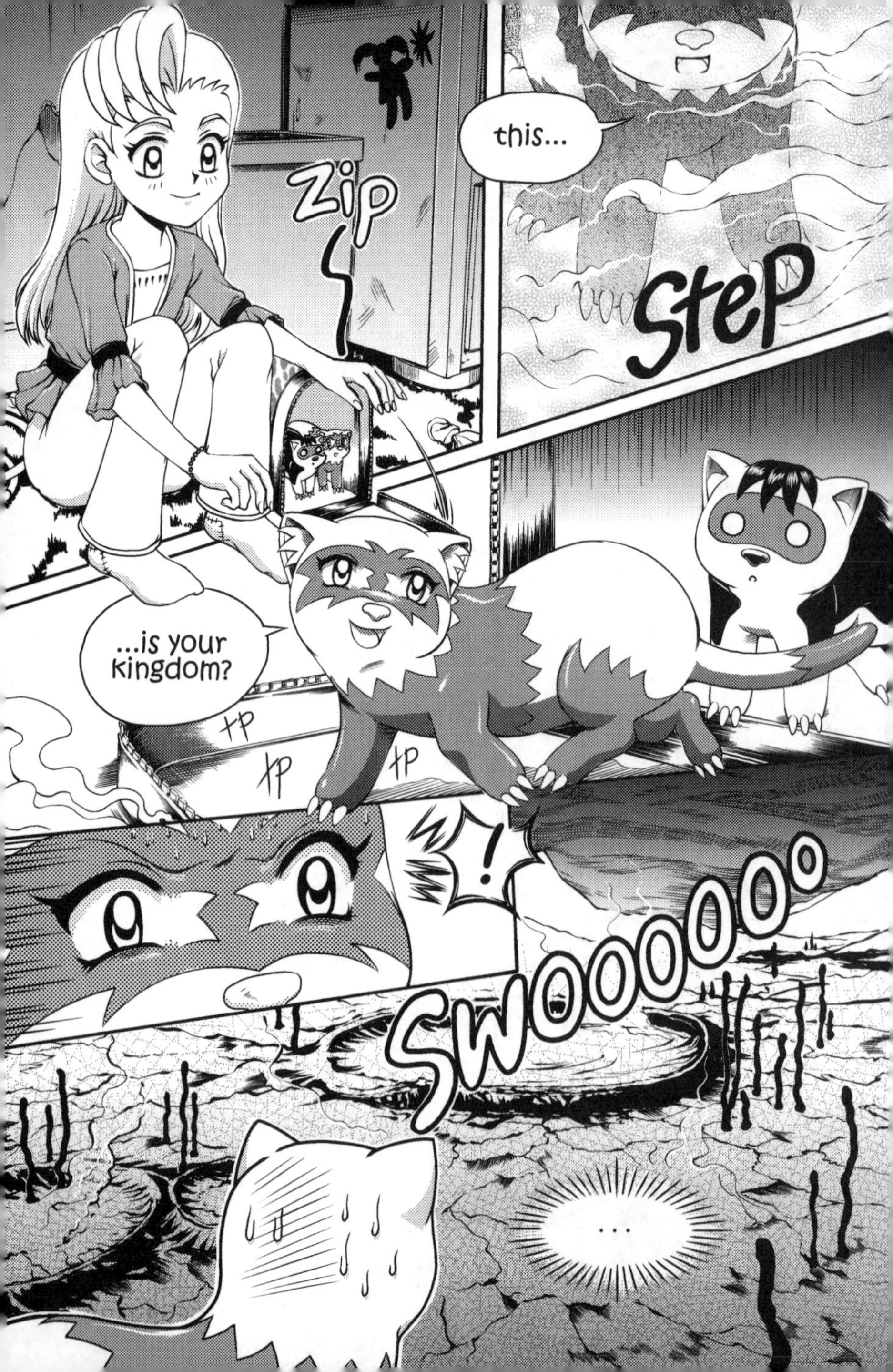

this...
Zip
Step
...is your kingdom?
tp
tp
tp
!
SWOOOOOO
...

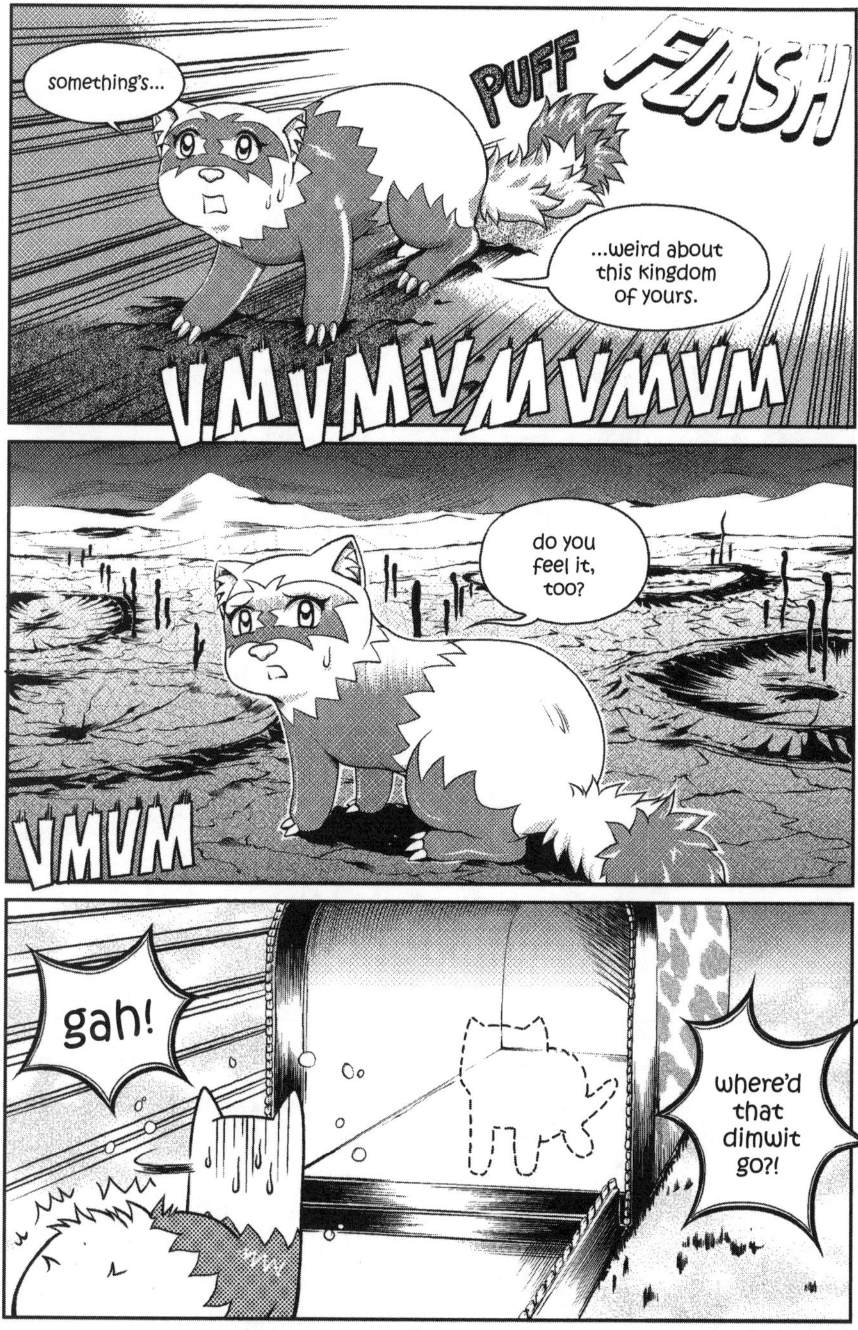
something's...
PUFF
FLASH
...weird about this kingdom of yours.
VMVMVMMVMVM
do you feel it, too?
VMVM
gah!
where'd that dimwit go?!

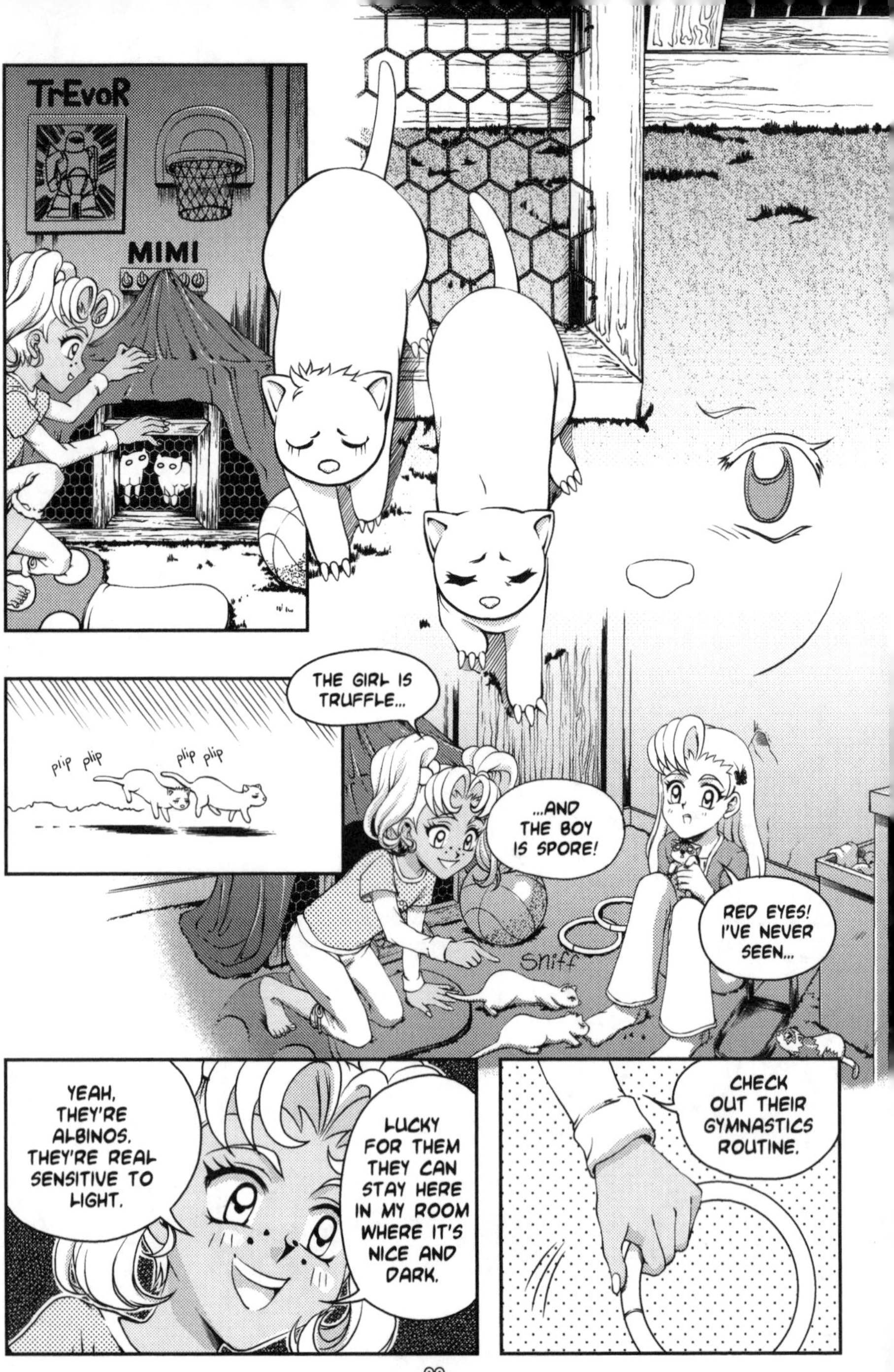
TrEvoR
MIMI
plip plip
plip plip
THE GIRL IS TRUFFLE...
...AND THE BOY IS SPORE!
RED EYES! I'VE NEVER SEEN...
Sniff
YEAH, THEY'RE ALBINOS. THEY'RE REAL SENSITIVE TO LIGHT.
LUCKY FOR THEM THEY CAN STAY HERE IN MY ROOM WHERE IT'S NICE AND DARK.
CHECK OUT THEIR GYMNASTICS ROUTINE.

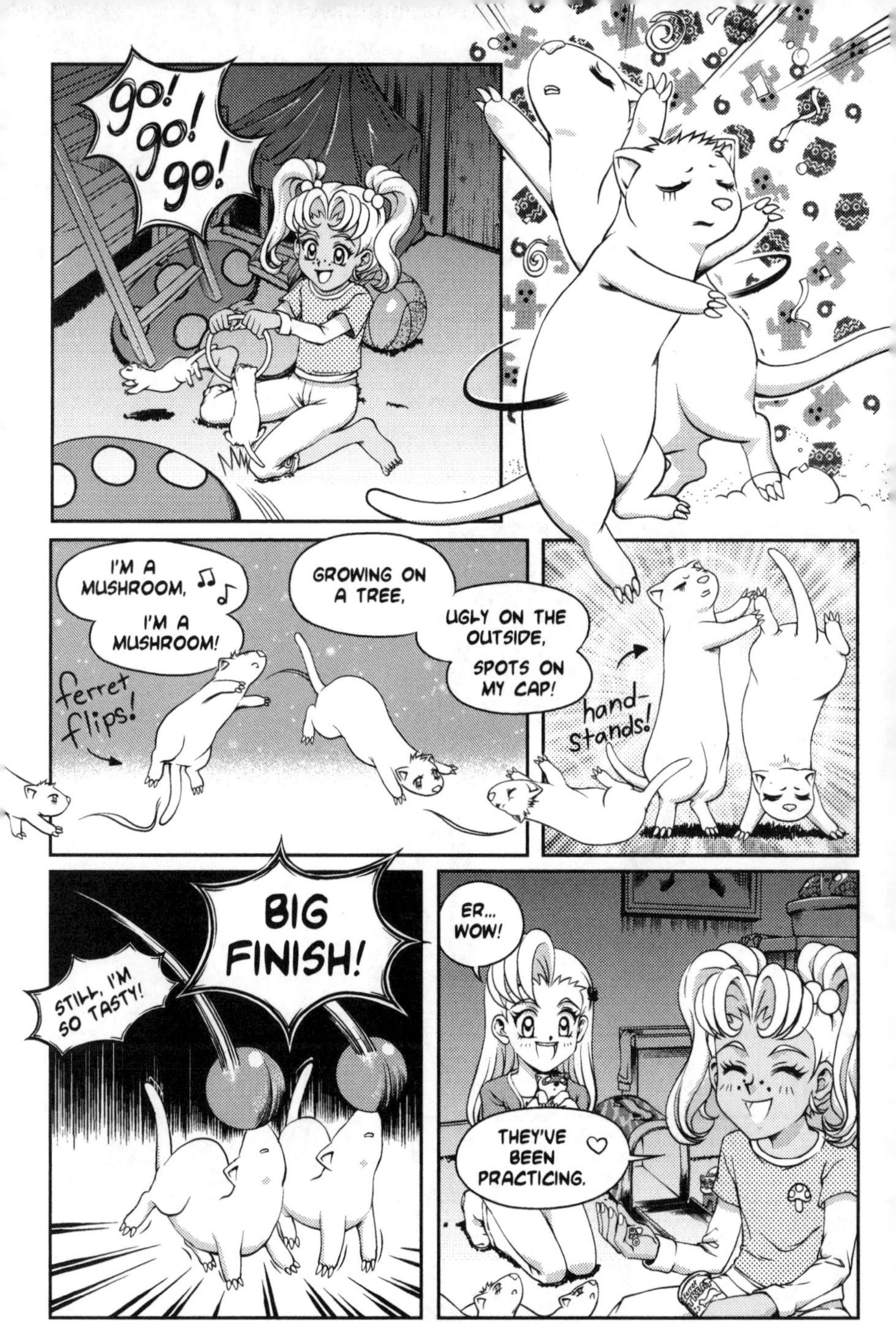
go! go! go!
I'M A MUSHROOM, I'M A MUSHROOM!
GROWING ON A TREE,
UGLY ON THE OUTSIDE, SPOTS ON MY CAP!
ferret flips!
hand-stands!
BIG FINISH!
STILL, I'M SO TASTY!
ER... WOW!
THEY'VE BEEN PRACTICING.

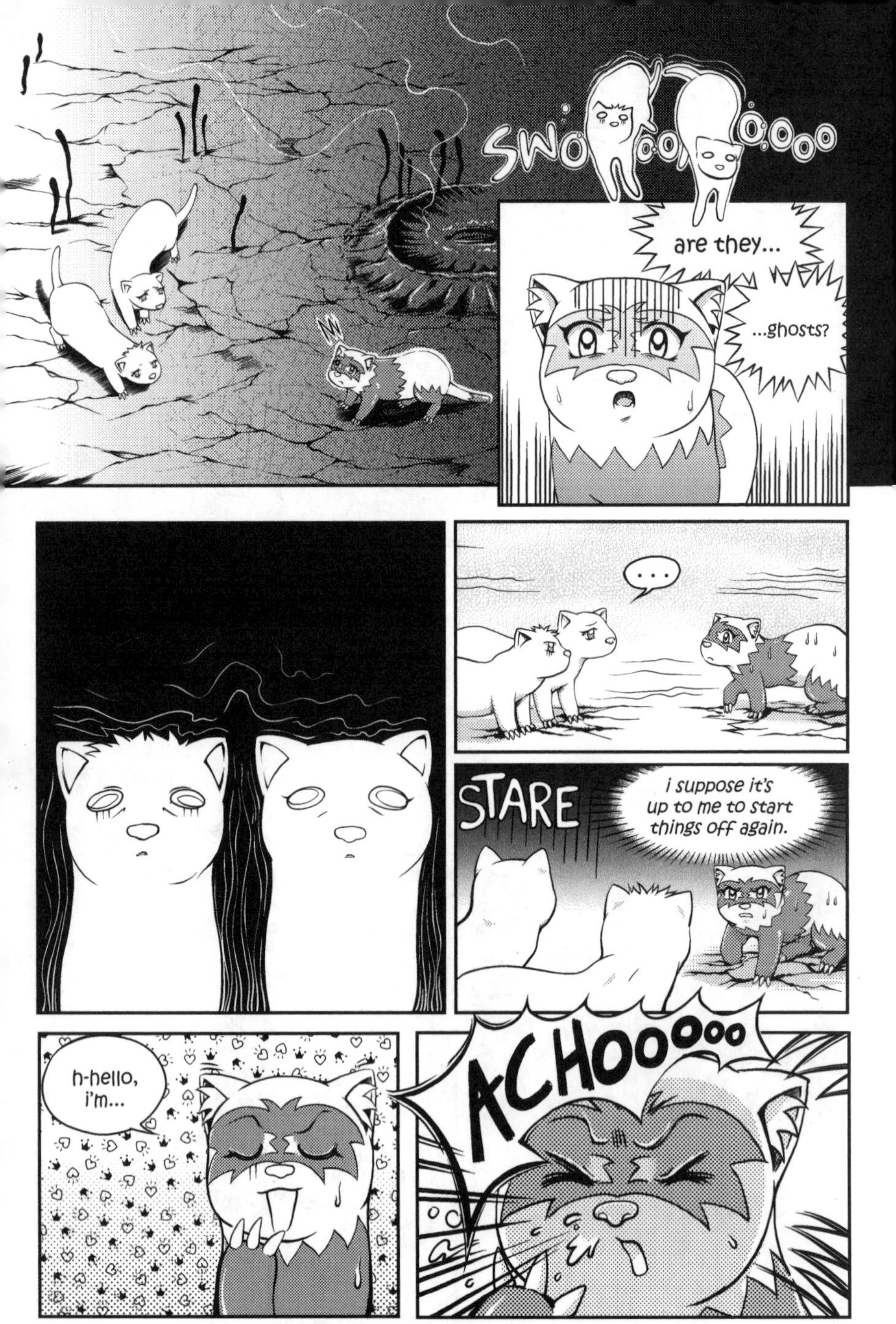
SWOOOOOOOOO
are they...
...ghosts?
. . .
STARE
i suppose it's up to me to start things off again.
h-hello, i'm...
ACHOOOOO

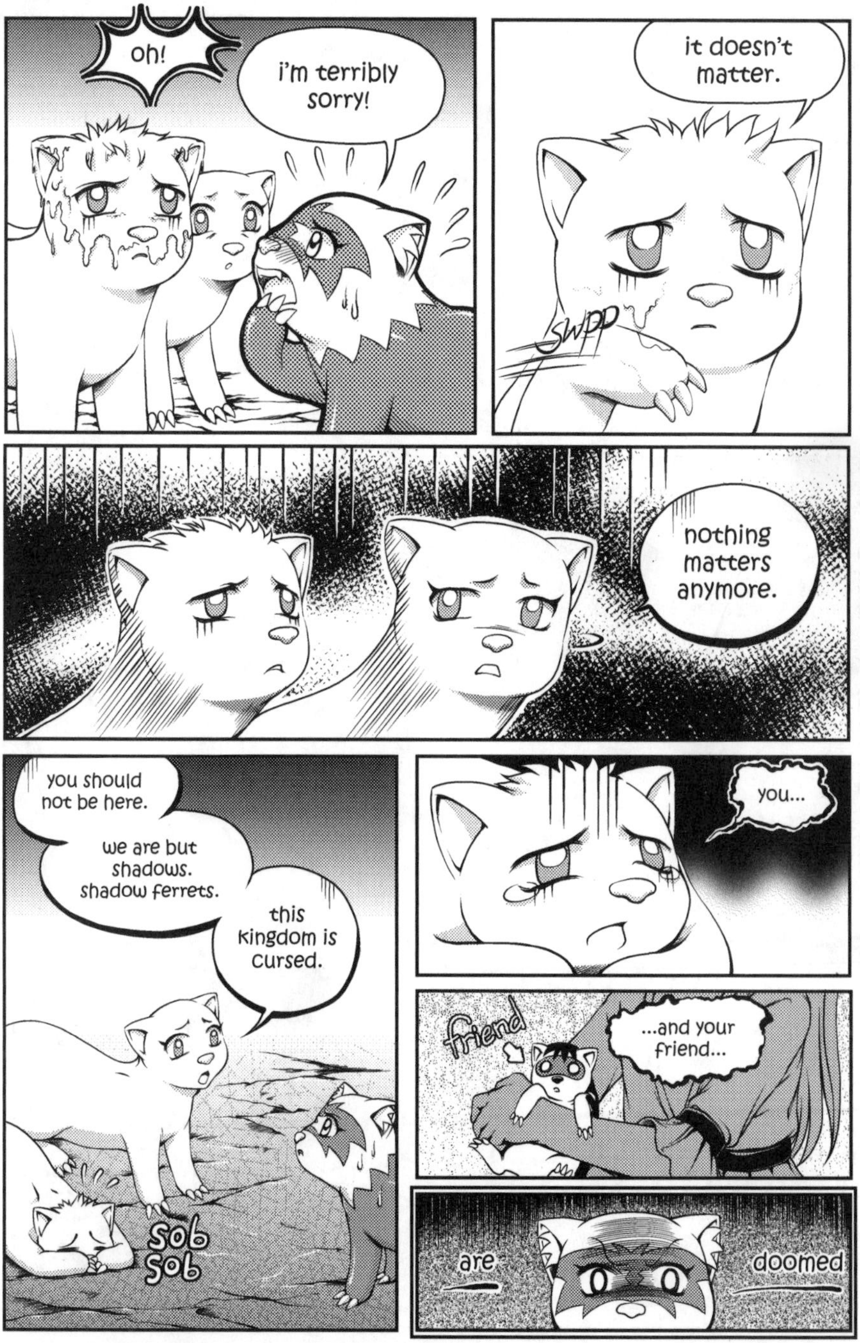
oh!
i'm terribly sorry!
it doesn't matter.
SWPP
nothing matters anymore.
you should not be here.
we are but shadows. shadow ferrets.
this kingdom is cursed.
sob sob
you...
friend
...and your friend...
are
doomed

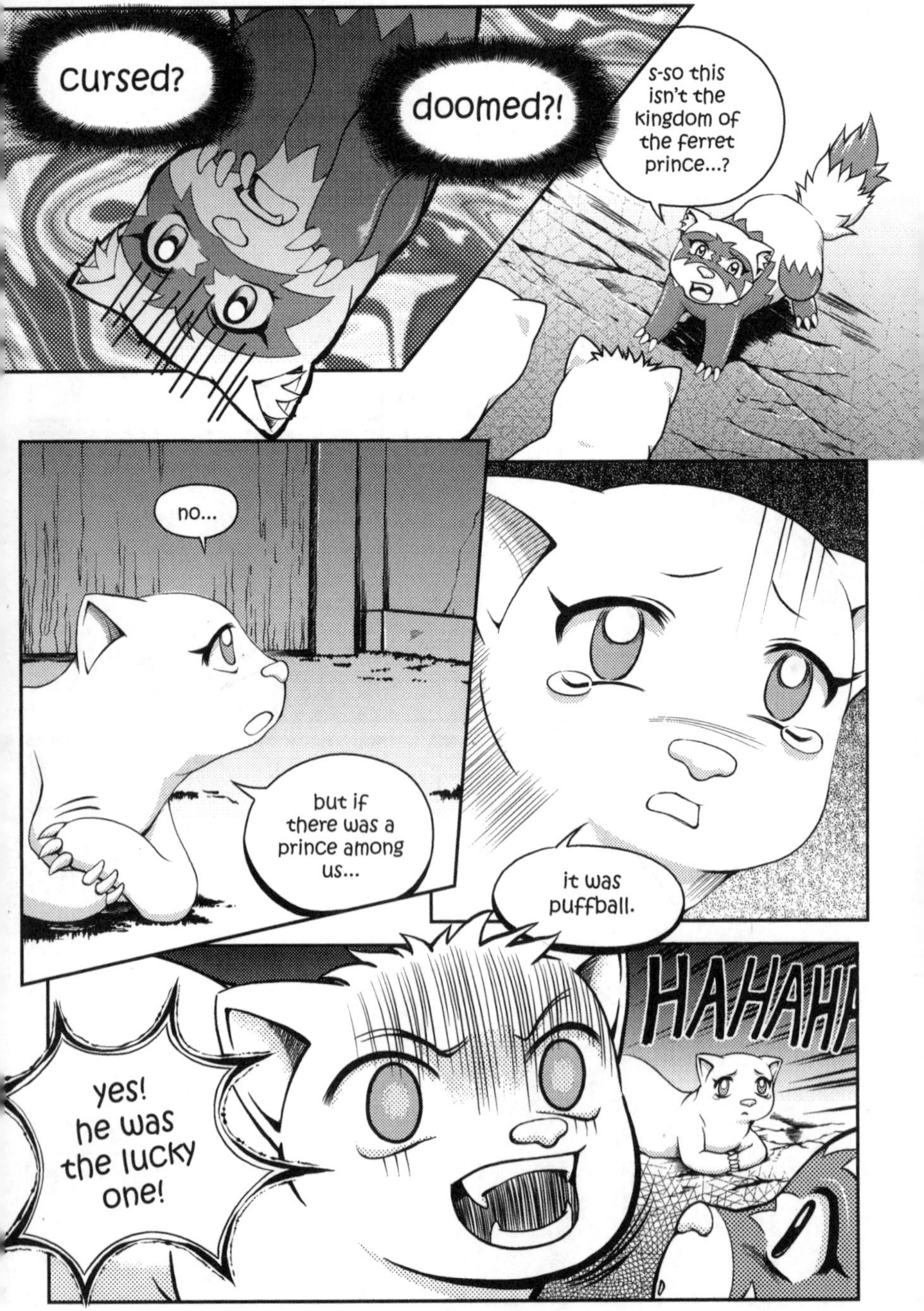
cursed?
doomed?!
s-so this isn't the kingdom of the ferret prince...?
no...
but if there was a prince among us...
it was puffball.
HAHAHA
yes! he was the lucky one!

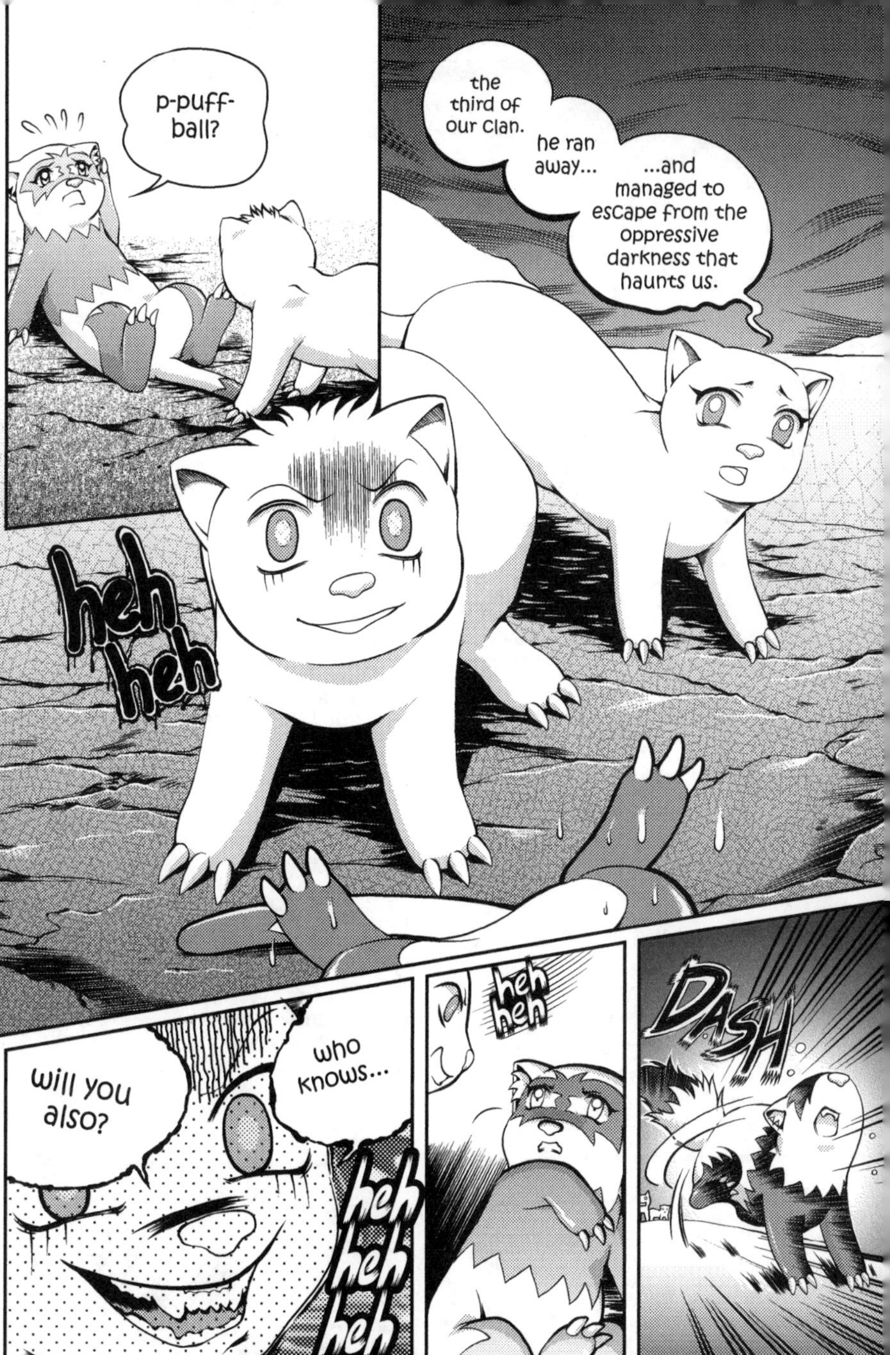
p-puff-ball?
the third of our clan.
he ran away...
...and managed to escape from the oppressive darkness that haunts us.
heh heh
will you also?
who knows...
heh heh heh
heh heh
DASH

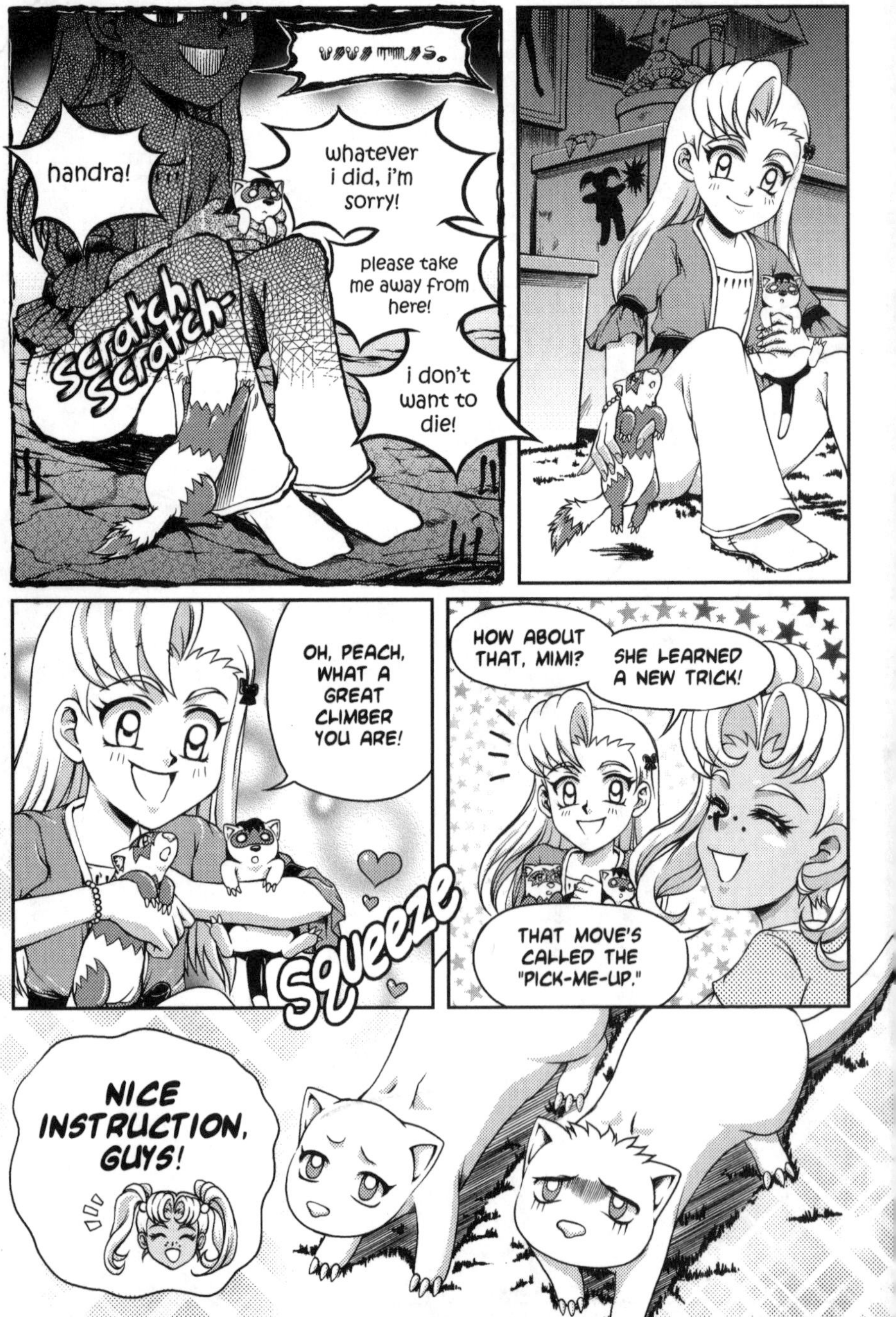
handra!
whatever i did, i'm sorry!
please take me away from here!
i don't want to die!
scratch-scratch-
OH, PEACH, WHAT A GREAT CLIMBER YOU ARE!
Squeeze
HOW ABOUT THAT, MIMI?
SHE LEARNED A NEW TRICK!
THAT MOVE'S CALLED THE "PICK-ME-UP."
NICE INSTRUCTION, GUYS!

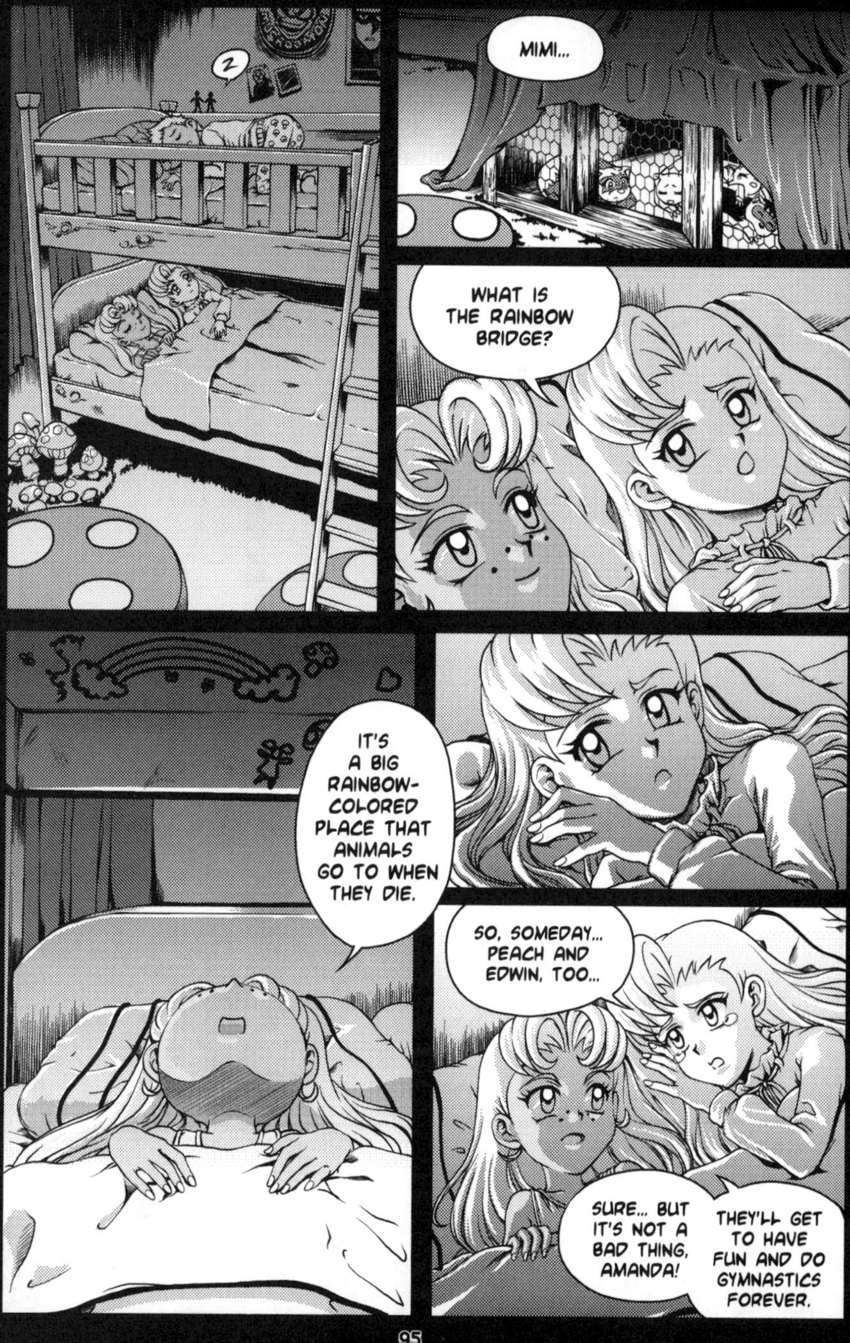
Z
MIMI...
WHAT IS THE RAINBOW BRIDGE?
IT'S A BIG RAINBOW-COLORED PLACE THAT ANIMALS GO TO WHEN THEY DIE.
SO, SOMEDAY... PEACH AND EDWIN, TOO...
SURE... BUT IT'S NOT A BAD THING, AMANDA!
THEY'LL GET TO HAVE FUN AND DO GYMNASTICS FOREVER.

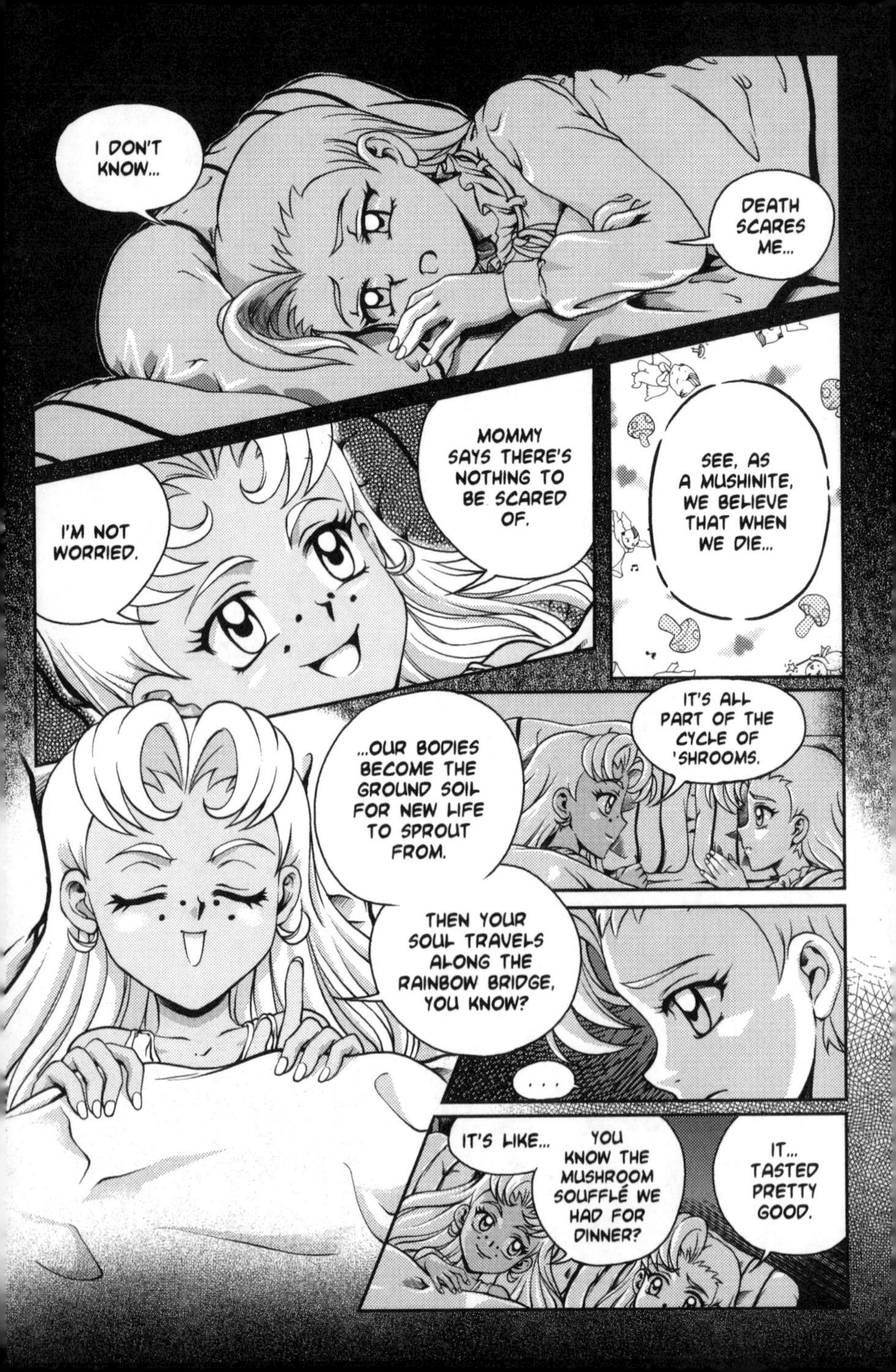
I DON'T KNOW...
DEATH SCARES ME...
MOMMY SAYS THERE'S NOTHING TO BE SCARED OF.
I'M NOT WORRIED.
SEE, AS A MUSHINITE, WE BELIEVE THAT WHEN WE DIE...
...OUR BODIES BECOME THE GROUND SOIL FOR NEW LIFE TO SPROUT FROM.
IT'S ALL PART OF THE CYCLE OF 'SHROOMS.
THEN YOUR SOUL TRAVELS ALONG THE RAINBOW BRIDGE, YOU KNOW?
. . .
IT'S LIKE...
YOU KNOW THE MUSHROOM SOUFFLÉ WE HAD FOR DINNER?
IT... TASTED PRETTY GOOD.

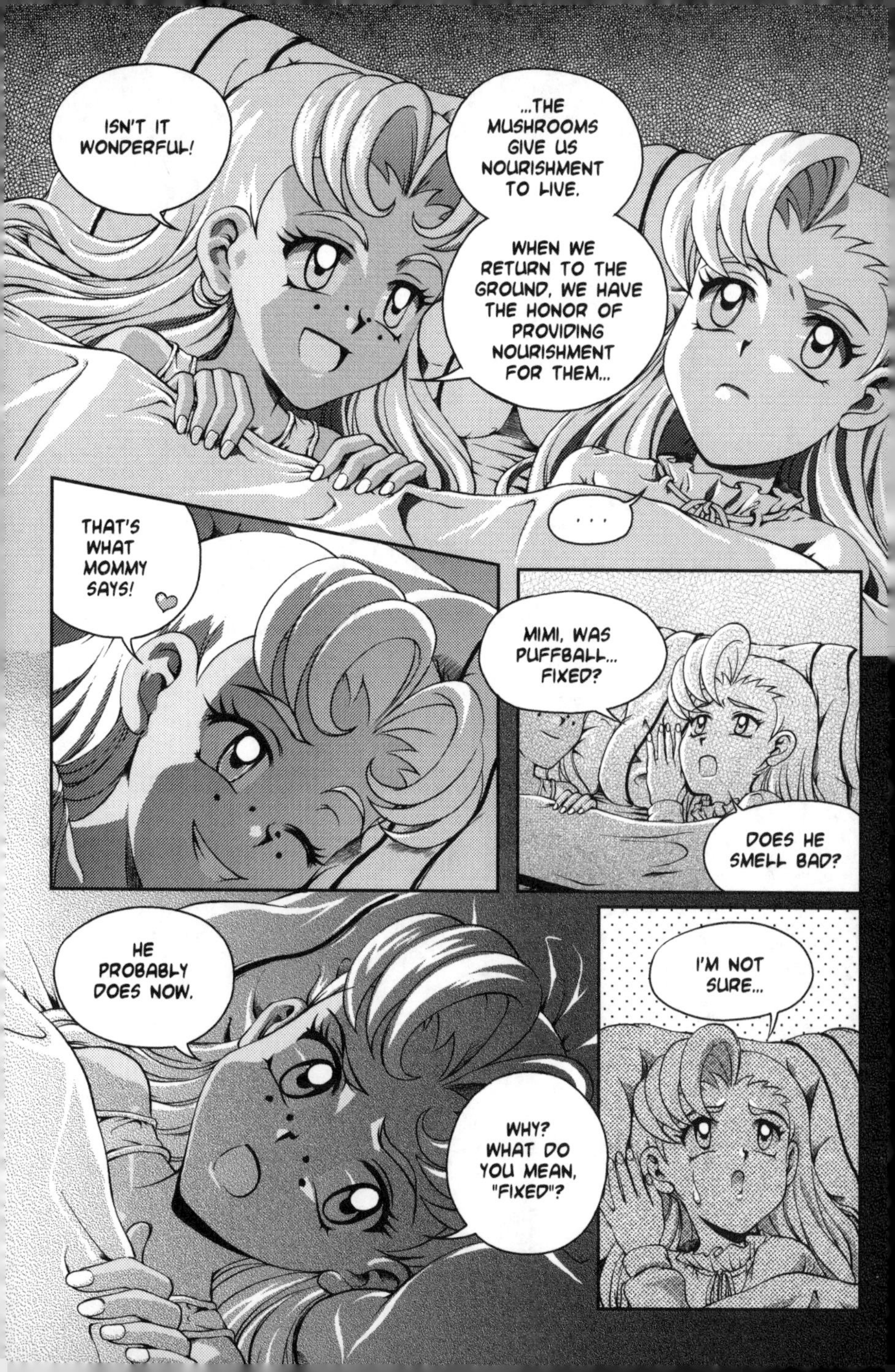
ISN'T IT WONDERFUL!
...THE MUSHROOMS GIVE US NOURISHMENT TO LIVE.
WHEN WE RETURN TO THE GROUND, WE HAVE THE HONOR OF PROVIDING NOURISHMENT FOR THEM...
...
THAT'S WHAT MOMMY SAYS!
MIMI, WAS PUFFBALL... FIXED?
DOES HE SMELL BAD?
HE PROBABLY DOES NOW.
I'M NOT SURE...
WHY? WHAT DO YOU MEAN, "FIXED"?

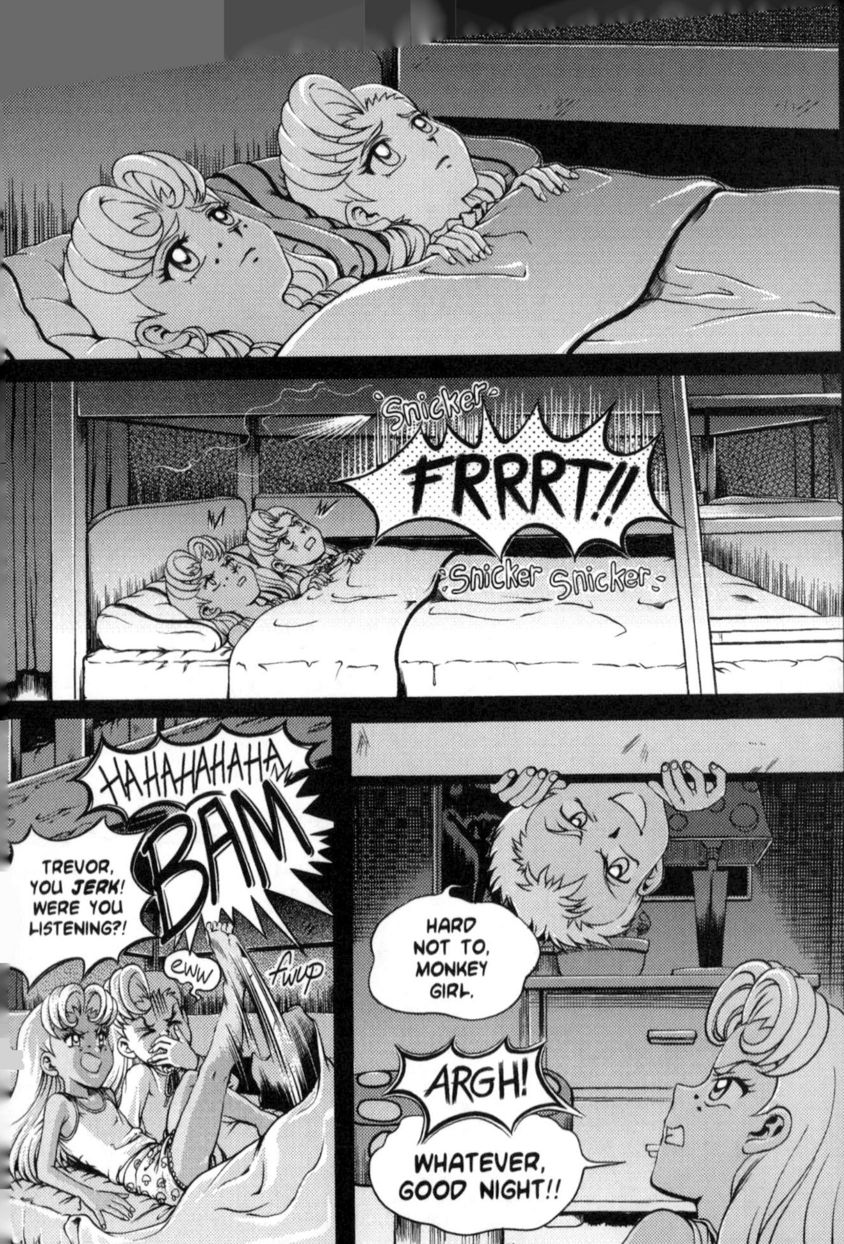
Snicker
FRRRT!!
Snicker Snicker
HAHAHAHAHA
BAM
TREVOR, YOU JERK! WERE YOU LISTENING?!
eww
fwup
HARD NOT TO, MONKEY GIRL.
ARGH!
WHATEVER, GOOD NIGHT!!

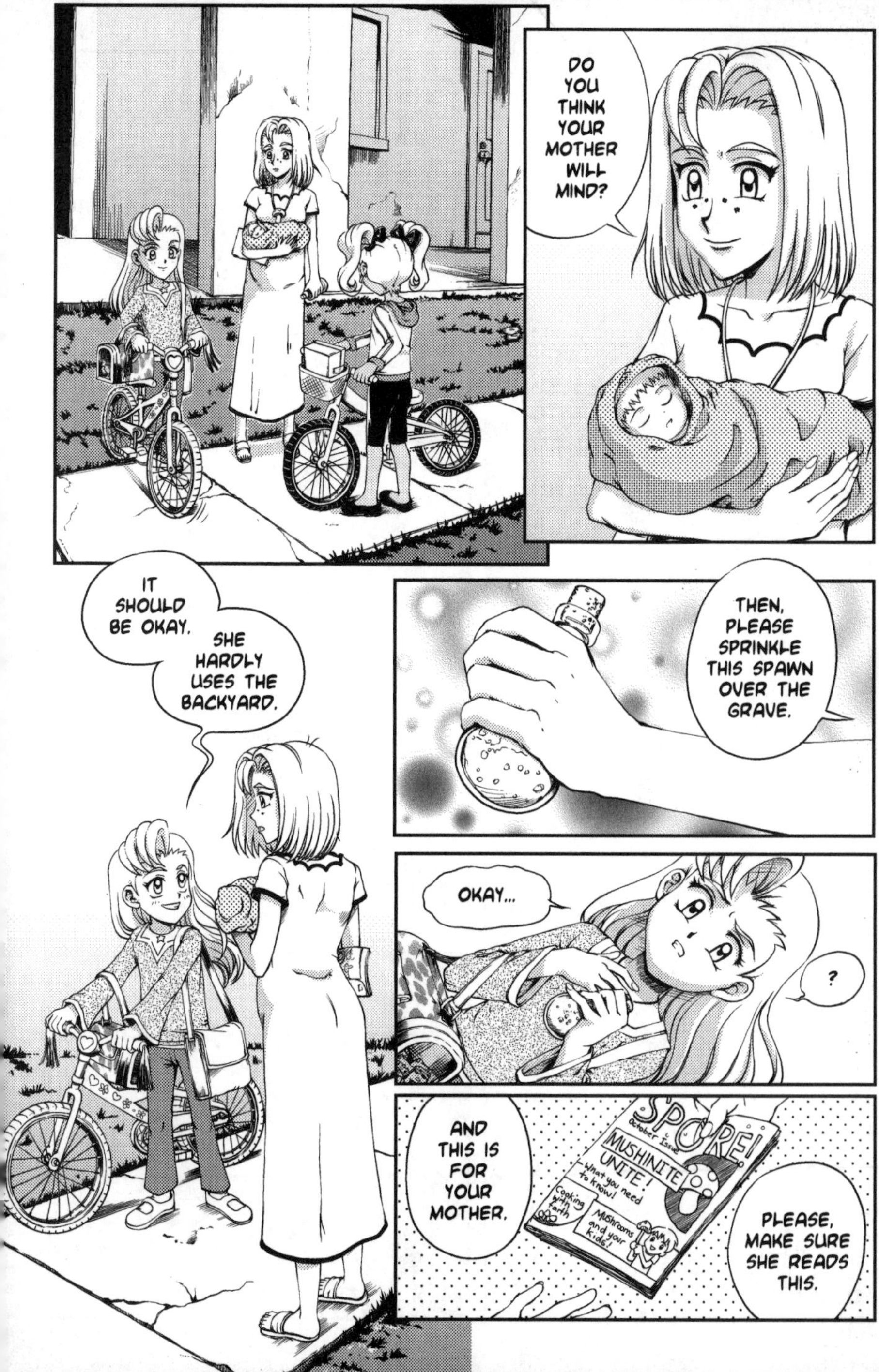
DO YOU THINK YOUR MOTHER WILL MIND?
IT SHOULD BE OKAY.
SHE HARDLY USES THE BACKYARD.
THEN, PLEASE SPRINKLE THIS SPAWN OVER THE GRAVE.
OKAY...
?
AND THIS IS FOR YOUR MOTHER.
SPORE!
October Issue
MUSHINITE UNITE!
-What you need to know!
Mushrooms and your Kids!
PLEASE, MAKE SURE SHE READS THIS.

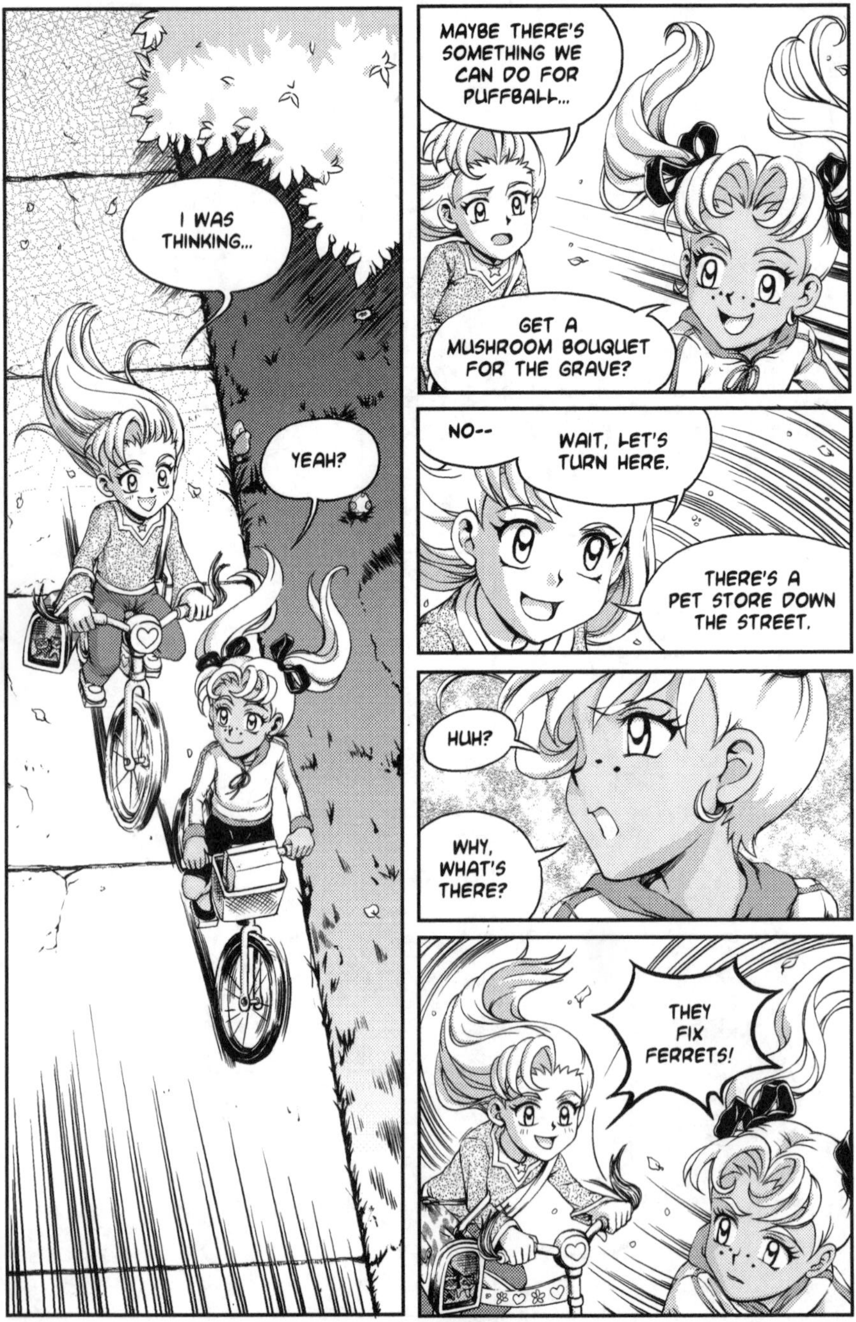
I WAS THINKING...
YEAH?
MAYBE THERE'S SOMETHING WE CAN DO FOR PUFFBALL...
GET A MUSHROOM BOUQUET FOR THE GRAVE?
NO--
WAIT, LET'S TURN HERE.
THERE'S A PET STORE DOWN THE STREET.
HUH?
WHY, WHAT'S THERE?
THEY FIX FERRETS!

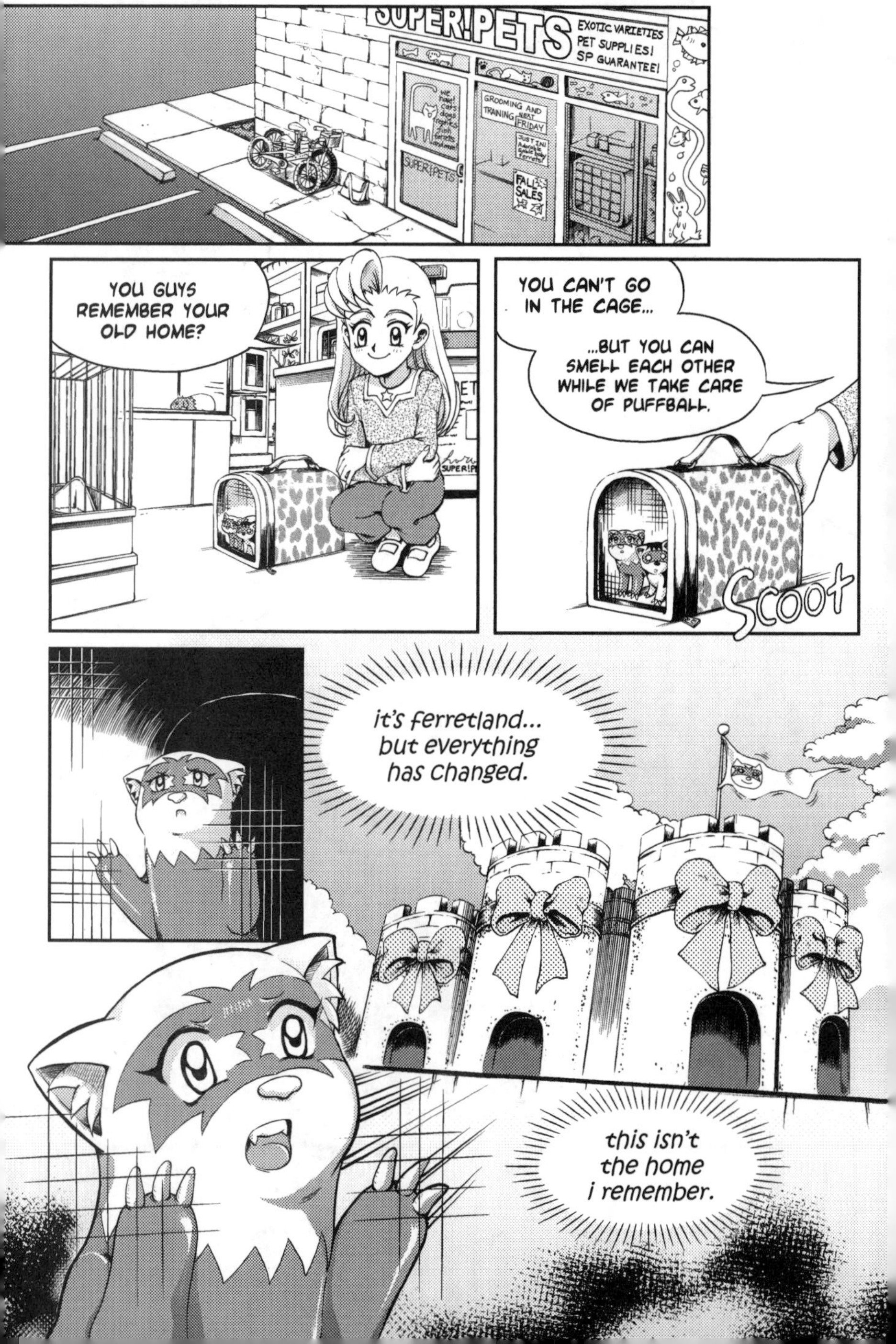
SUPER!PETS
EXOTIC VARIETIES
PET SUPPLIES!
SP GUARANTEE!
GROOMING AND TRANING NEXT FRIDAY
SUPER!PETS
FALL SALES
YOU GUYS REMEMBER YOUR OLD HOME?
YOU CAN'T GO IN THE CAGE...
...BUT YOU CAN SMELL EACH OTHER WHILE WE TAKE CARE OF PUFFBALL.
SCOOT
it's ferretland... but everything has changed.
this isn't the home i remember.

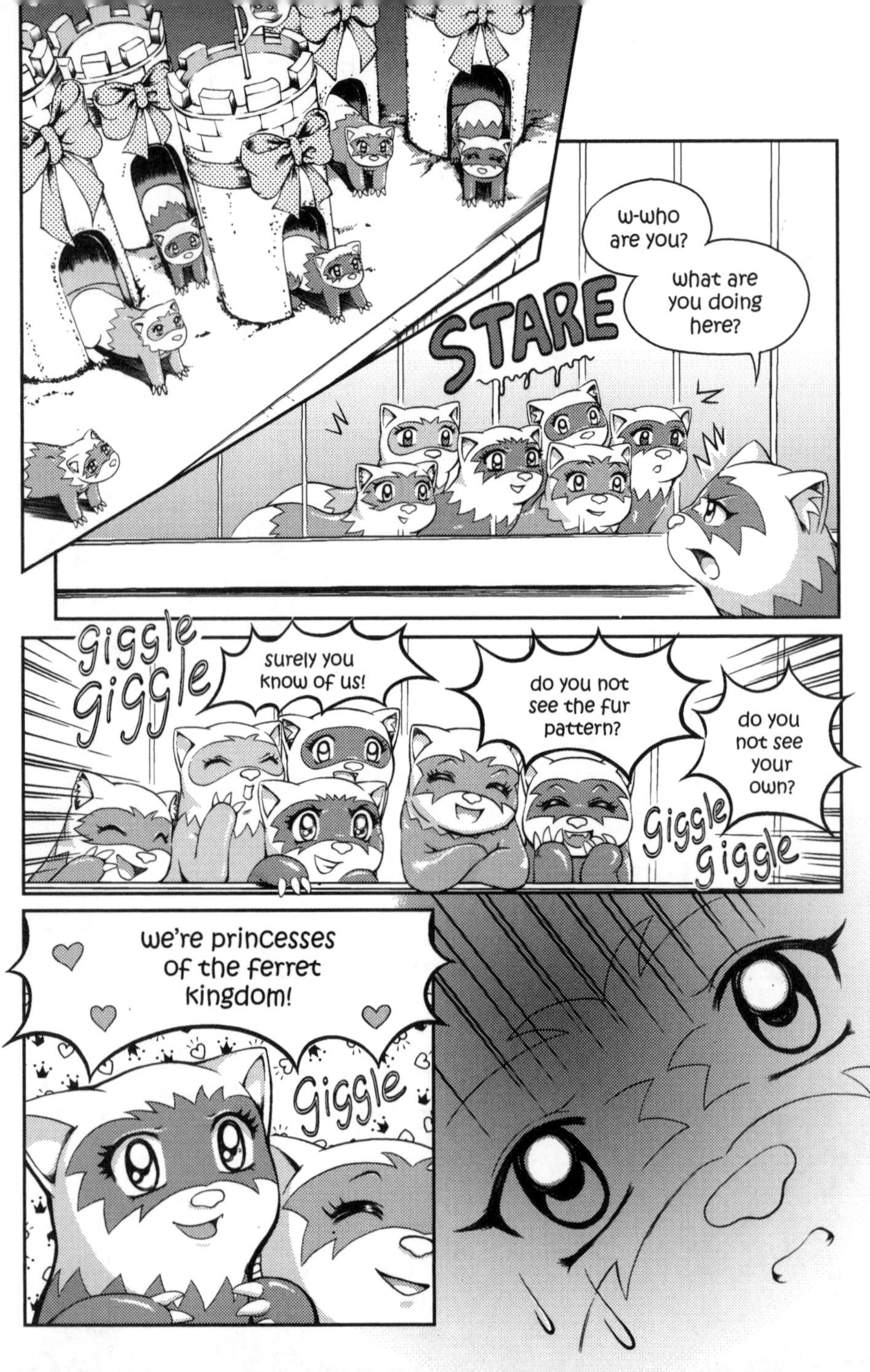
STARE
w-who are you?
what are you doing here?
giggle giggle
surely you know of us!
do you not see the fur pattern?
do you not see your own?
Giggle Giggle
we're princesses of the ferret kingdom!
Giggle

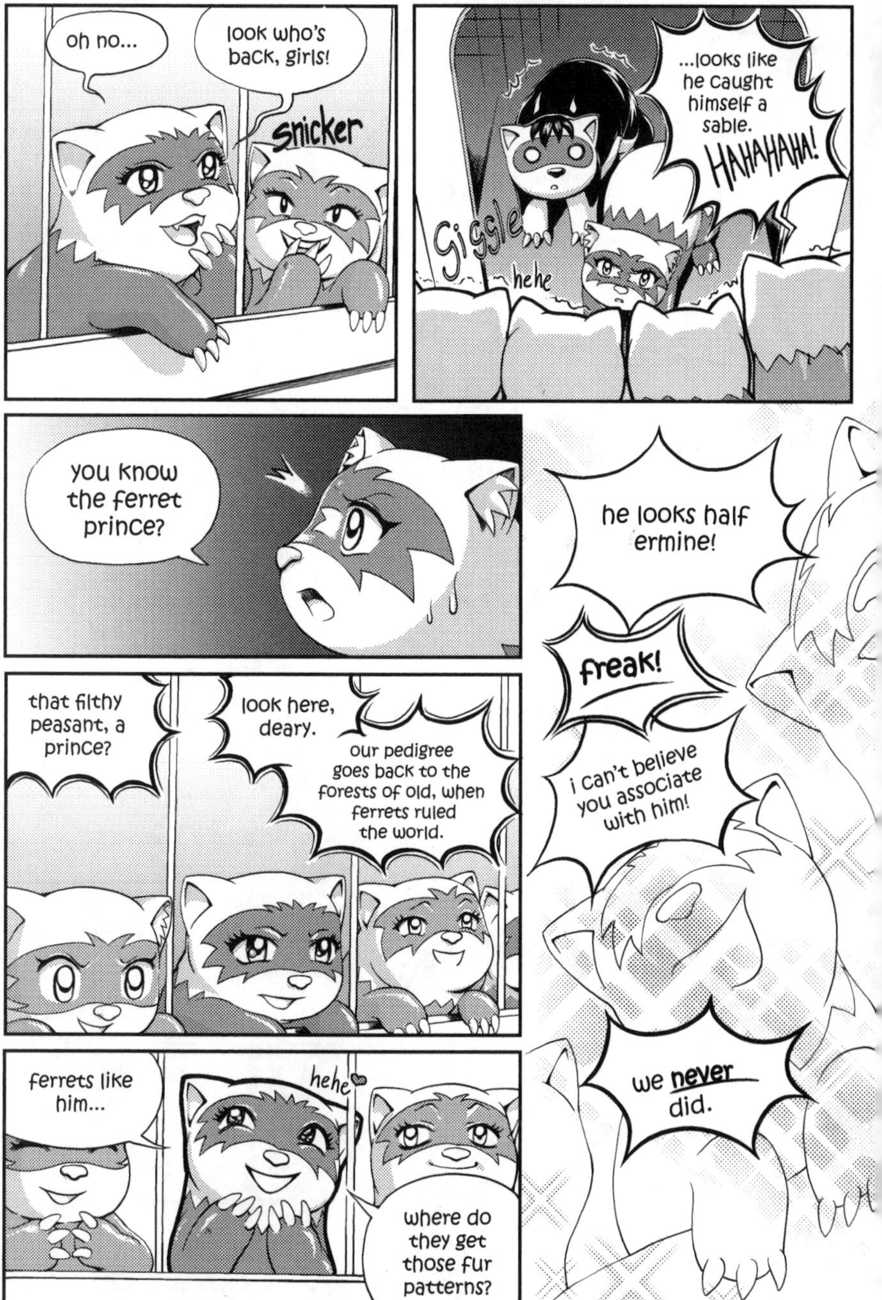

oh no...
look who's back, girls!
Snicker
...looks like he caught himself a sable.
HAHAHAHA!
Giggle
hehe
you know the ferret prince?
that filthy peasant, a prince?
look here, deary.
our pedigree goes back to the forests of old, when ferrets ruled the world.
ferrets like him...
hehe
where do they get those fur patterns?
he looks half ermine!
freak!
i can't believe you associate with him!
we never did.

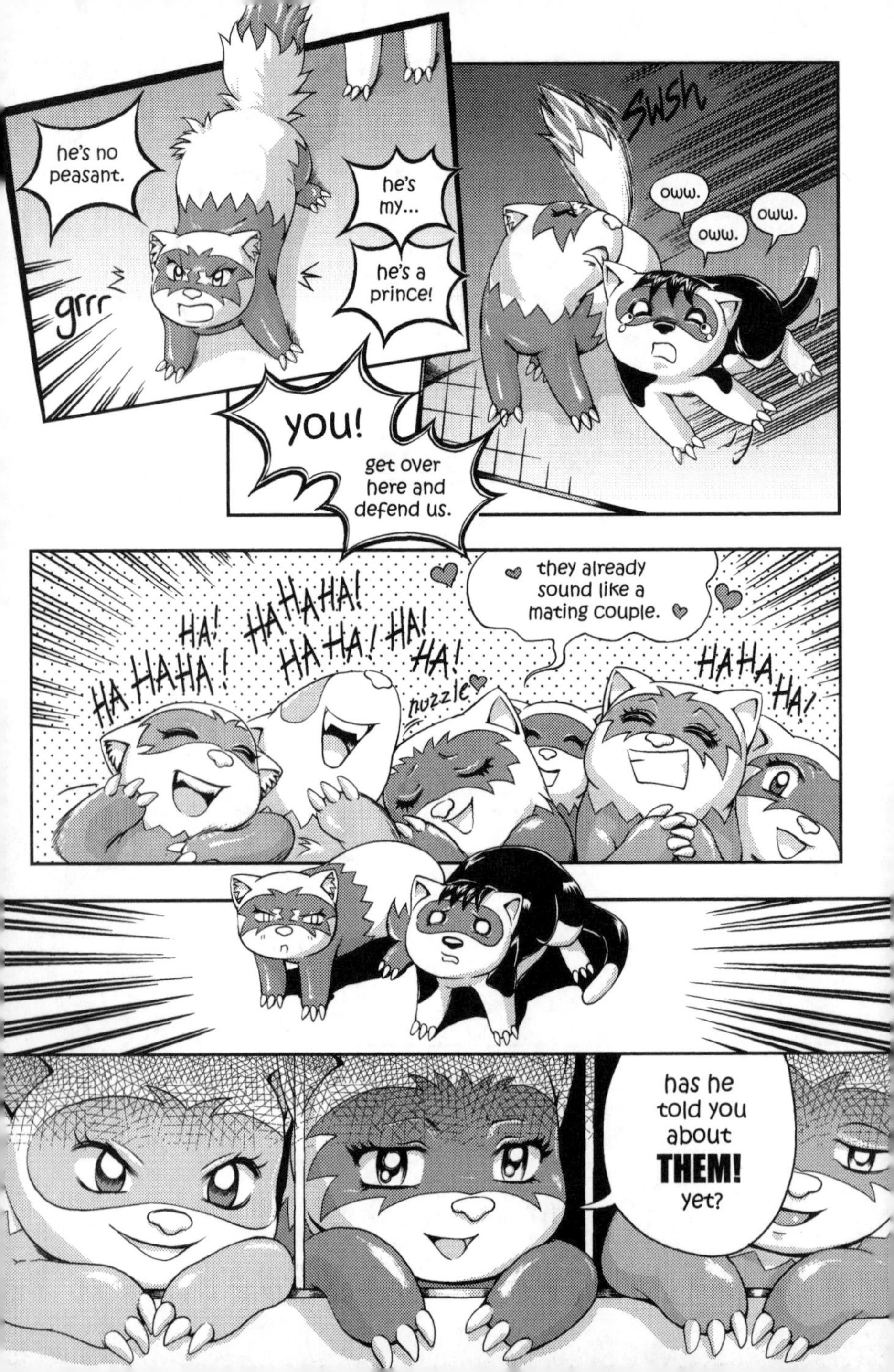
he's no peasant.
grrr
he's my...
he's a prince!
Swsh
oww.
oww.
oww.
YOU!
get over here and defend us.
they already sound like a mating couple.
HA! HAHAHA!
HAHAHA!
HAHA! HA!
HA!
nuzzle
HAHAHA HA!
has he told you about THEM! yet?

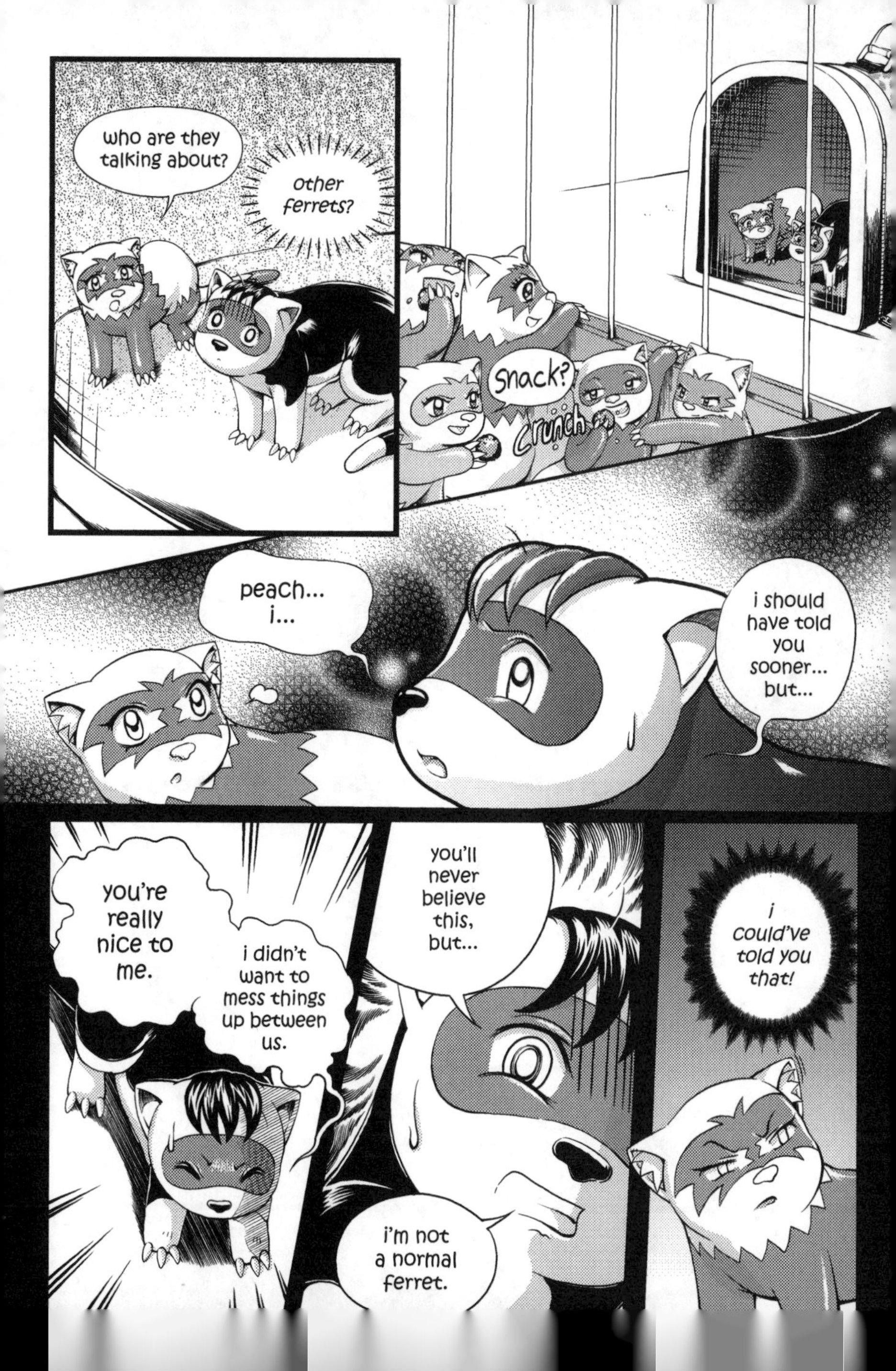
who are they talking about?
other ferrets?
snack?
crunch
peach... i...
i should have told you sooner... but...
you're really nice to me.
i didn't want to mess things up between us.
you'll never believe this, but...
i'm not a normal ferret.
i could've told you that!

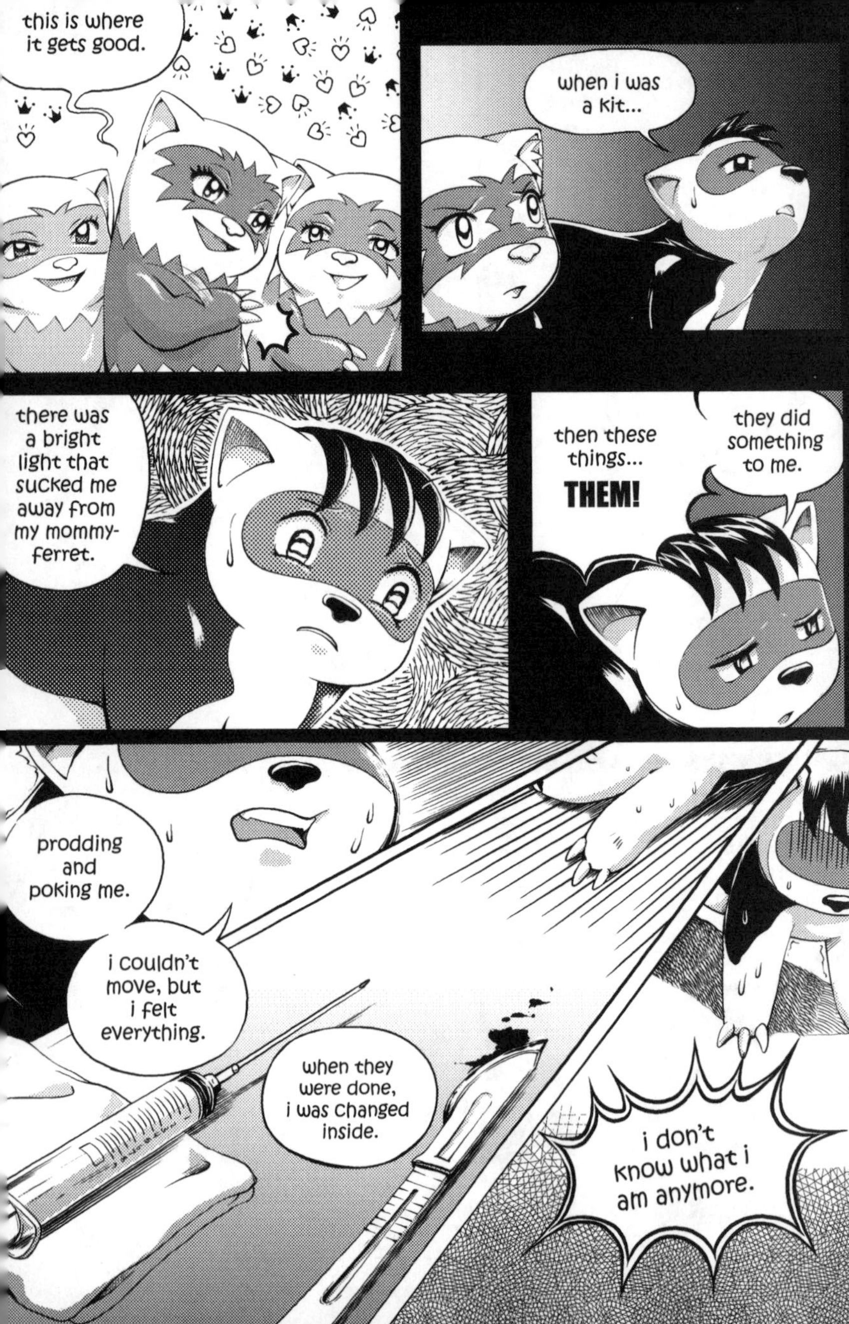
this is where it gets good.
when i was a kit...
there was a bright light that sucked me away from my mommy-ferret.
then these things... THEM!
they did something to me.
prodding and poking me.
i couldn't move, but i felt everything.
when they were done, i was changed inside.
i don't know what i am anymore.

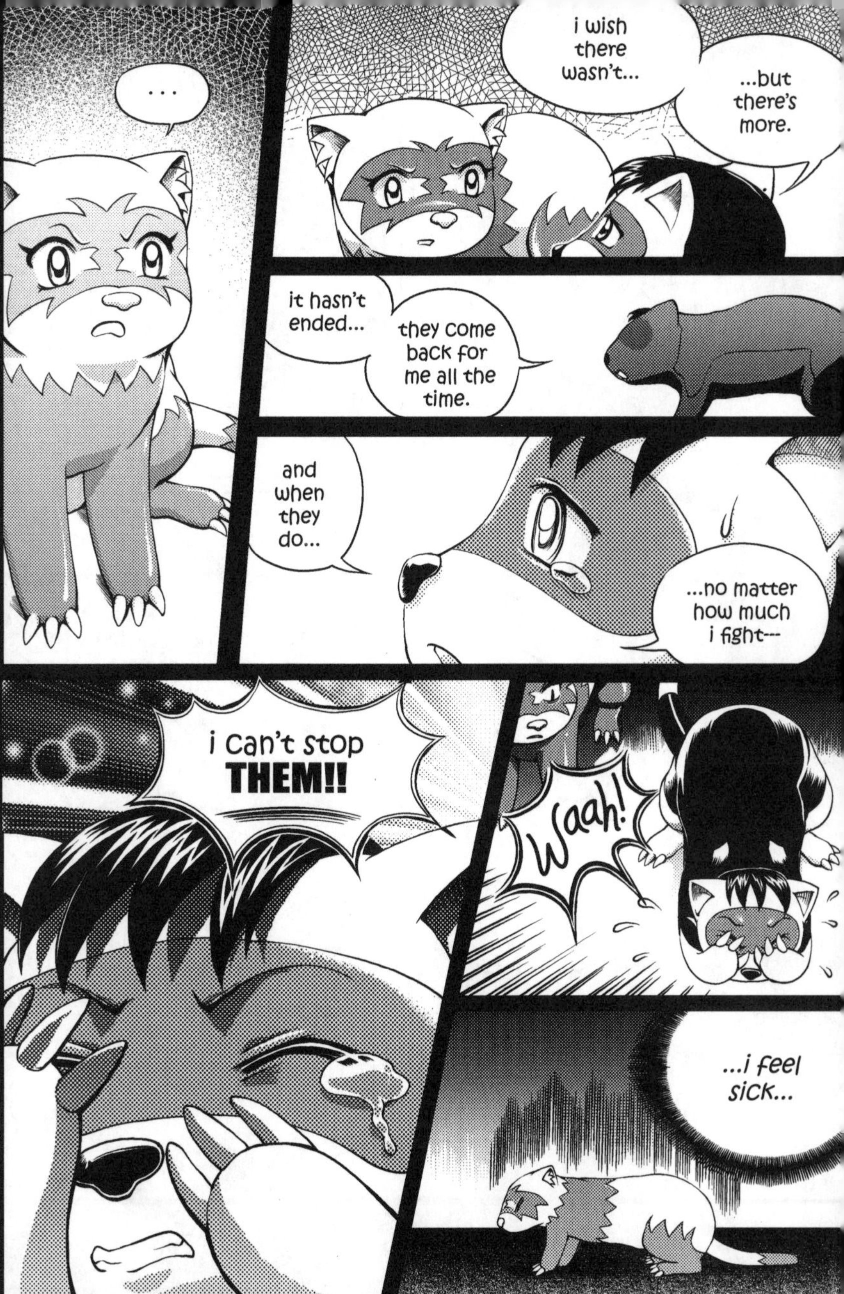
...
i wish there wasn't...
...but there's more.
it hasn't ended...
they come back for me all the time.
and when they do...
...no matter how much i fight---
i can't stop THEM!!
Waah!
...i feel sick...

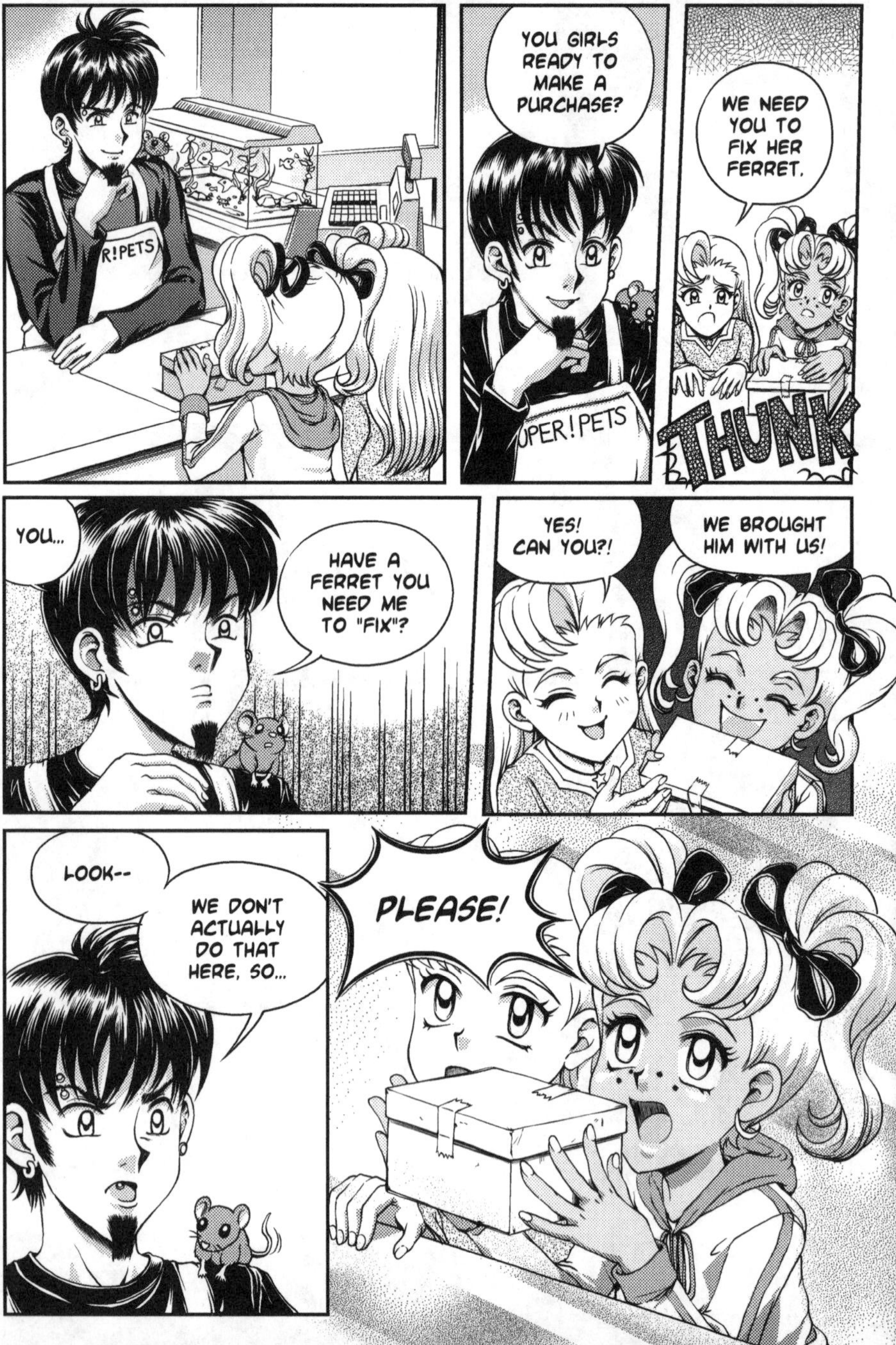
R!PETS
YOU GIRLS READY TO MAKE A PURCHASE?
UPER! PETS
WE NEED YOU TO FIX HER FERRET.
THUNK
YOU...
HAVE A FERRET YOU NEED ME TO "FIX"?
YES! CAN YOU?!
WE BROUGHT HIM WITH US!
LOOK--
WE DON'T ACTUALLY DO THAT HERE, SO...
PLEASE!

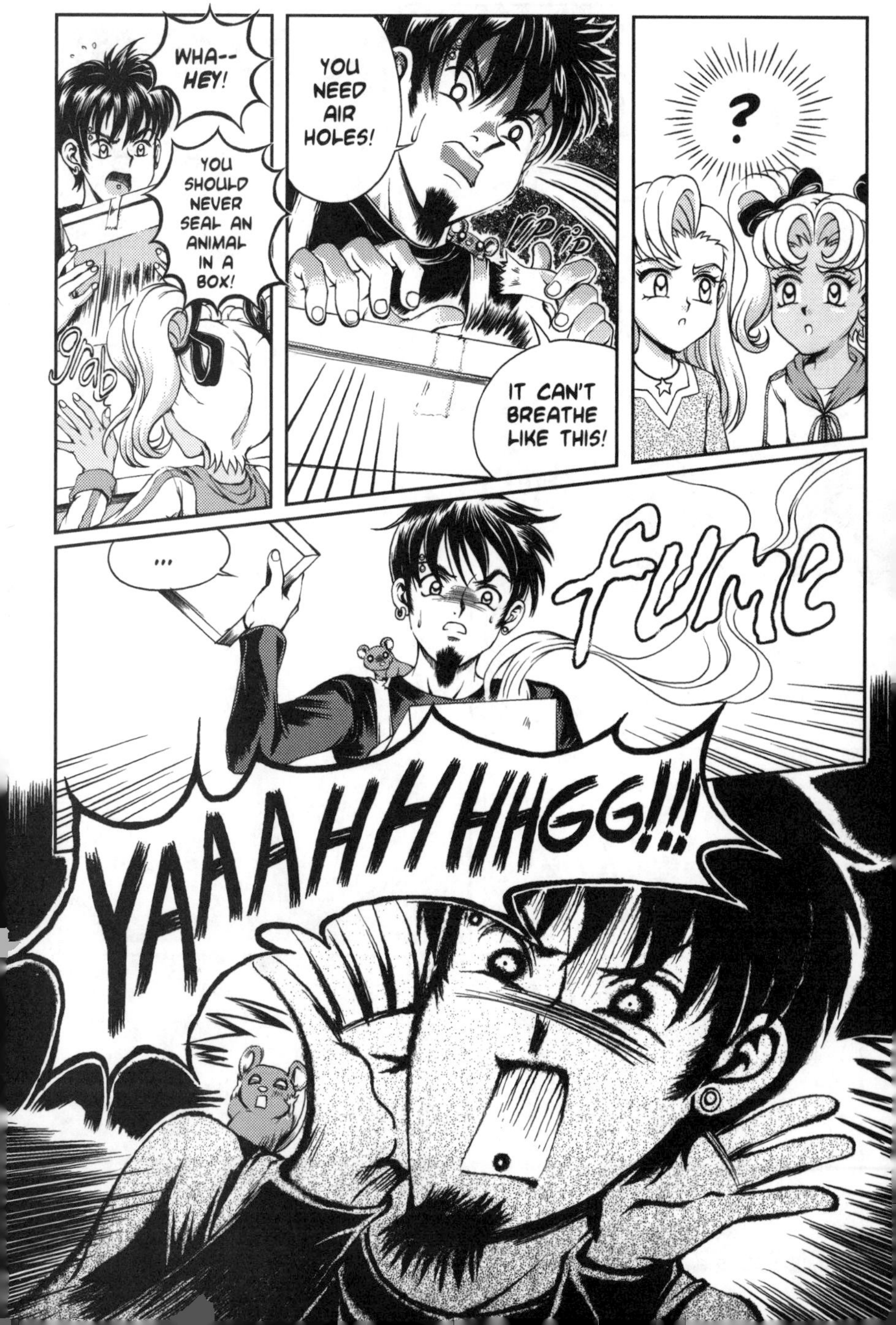
WHA-- HEY!
YOU SHOULD NEVER SEAL AN ANIMAL IN A BOX!
grab
YOU NEED AIR HOLES!
rip rip
IT CAN'T BREATHE LIKE THIS!
?
...
fume
YAAAHHHHGG!!!

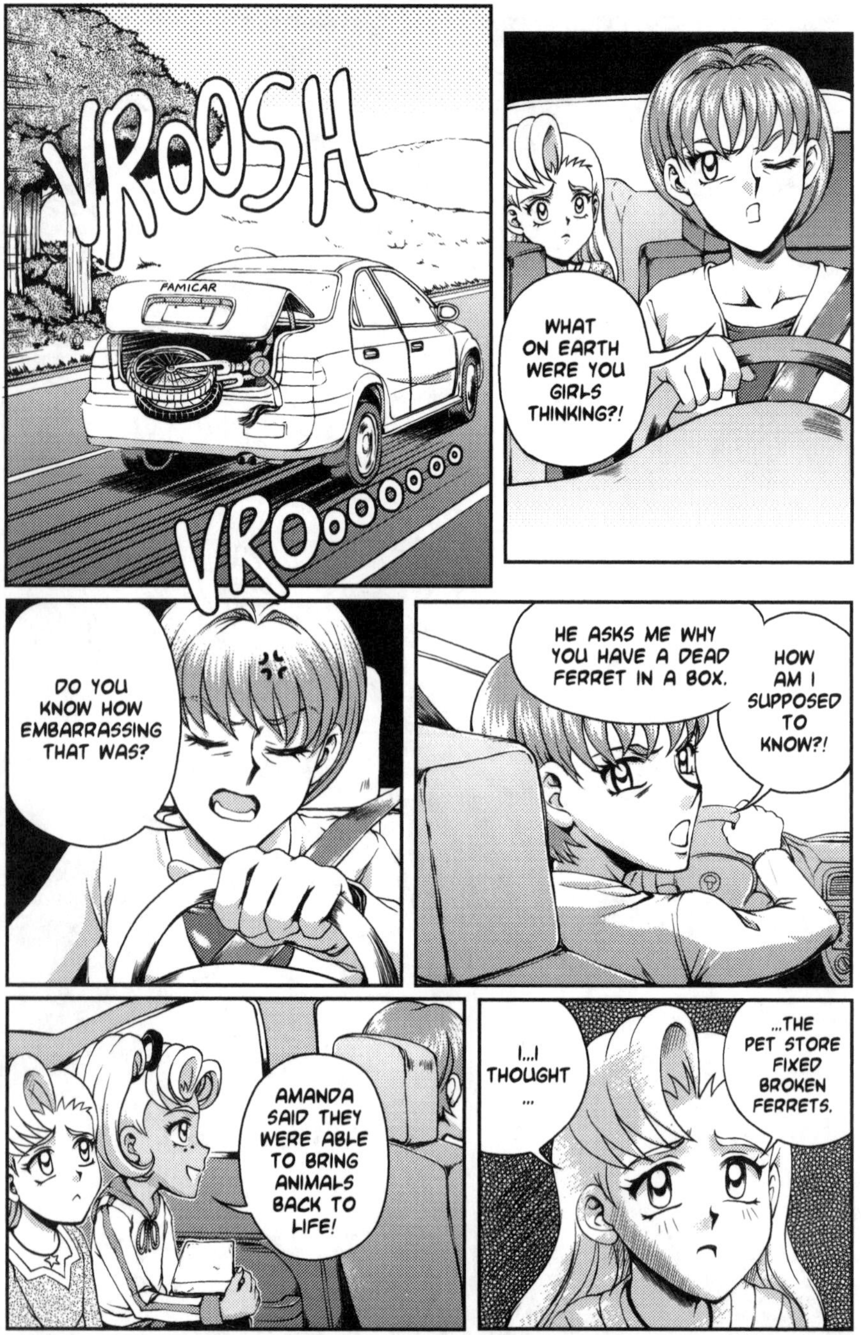
VROOSH
FAMICAR
VROOOOOOO
WHAT ON EARTH WERE YOU GIRLS THINKING?!
DO YOU KNOW HOW EMBARRASSING THAT WAS?
HE ASKS ME WHY YOU HAVE A DEAD FERRET IN A BOX.
HOW AM I SUPPOSED TO KNOW?!
AMANDA SAID THEY WERE ABLE TO BRING ANIMALS BACK TO LIFE!
I...I THOUGHT ...
...THE PET STORE FIXED BROKEN FERRETS.

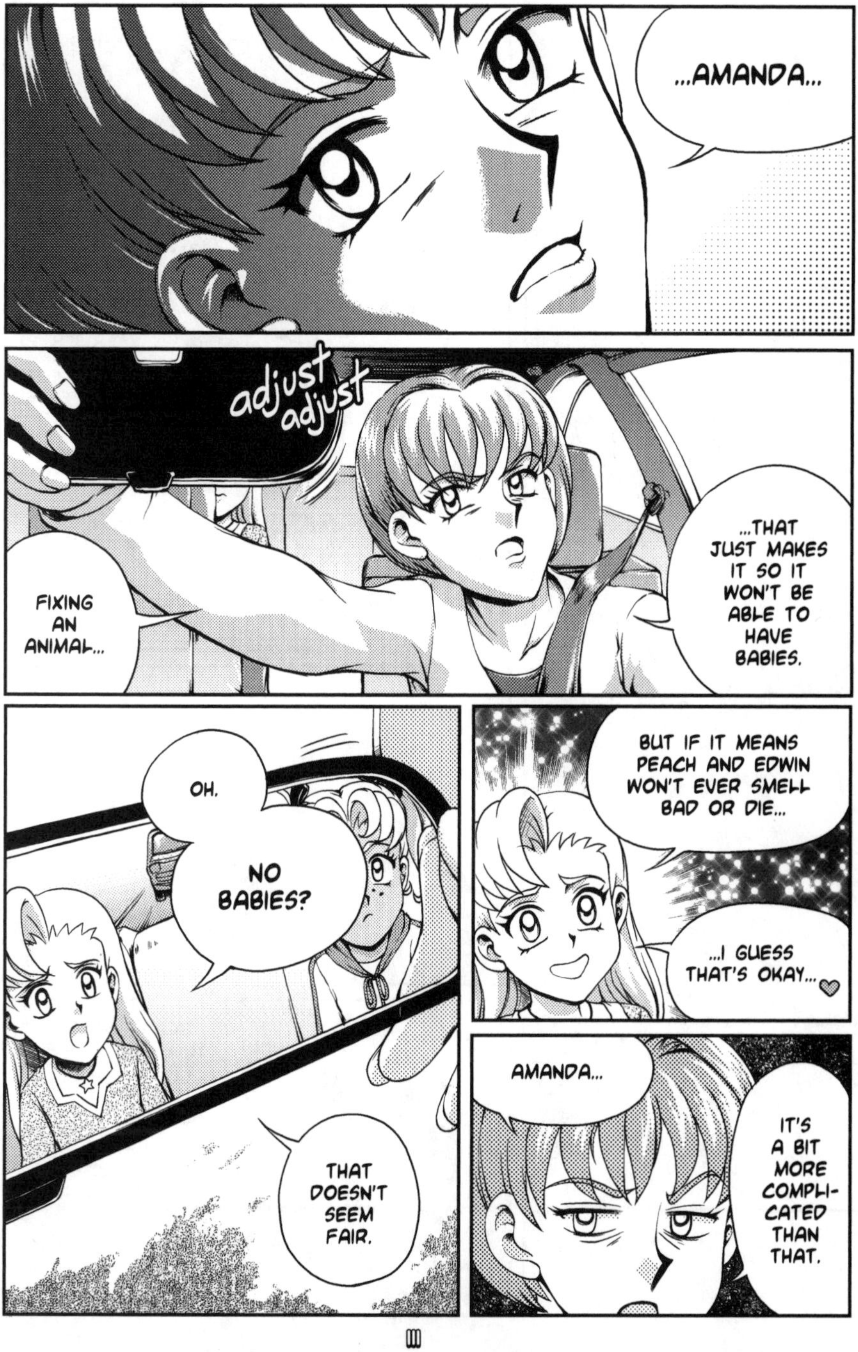
...AMANDA...
adjust adjust
FIXING AN ANIMAL...
...THAT JUST MAKES IT SO IT WON'T BE ABLE TO HAVE BABIES.
OH.
NO BABIES?
THAT DOESN'T SEEM FAIR.
BUT IF IT MEANS PEACH AND EDWIN WON'T EVER SMELL BAD OR DIE...
...I GUESS THAT'S OKAY...
AMANDA...
IT'S A BIT MORE COMPLICATED THAN THAT.

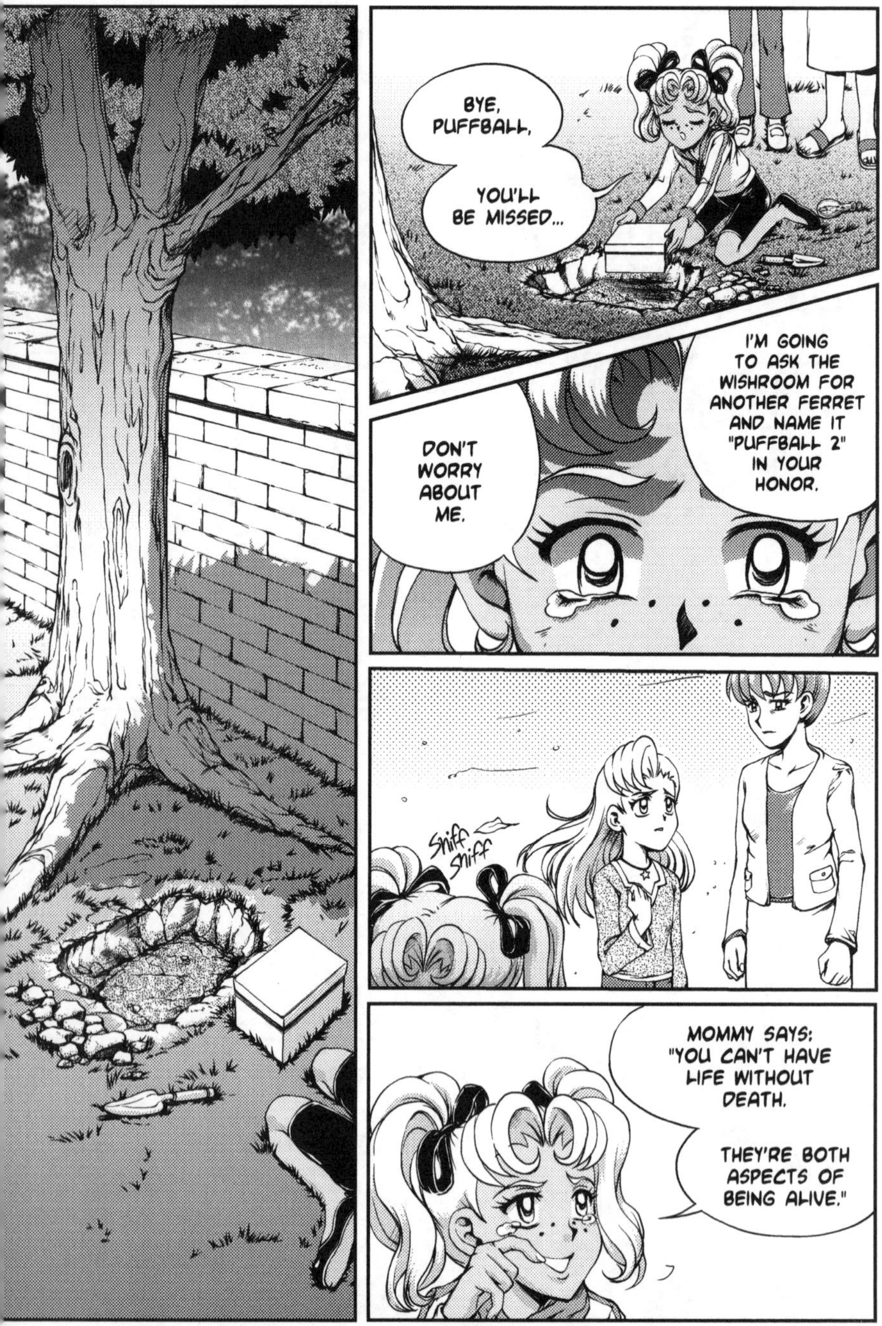
BYE, PUFFBALL,
YOU'LL BE MISSED...
I'M GOING TO ASK THE WISHROOM FOR ANOTHER FERRET AND NAME IT "PUFFBALL 2" IN YOUR HONOR.
DON'T WORRY ABOUT ME.
Sniff Sniff
MOMMY SAYS: "YOU CAN'T HAVE LIFE WITHOUT DEATH.
THEY'RE BOTH ASPECTS OF BEING ALIVE."

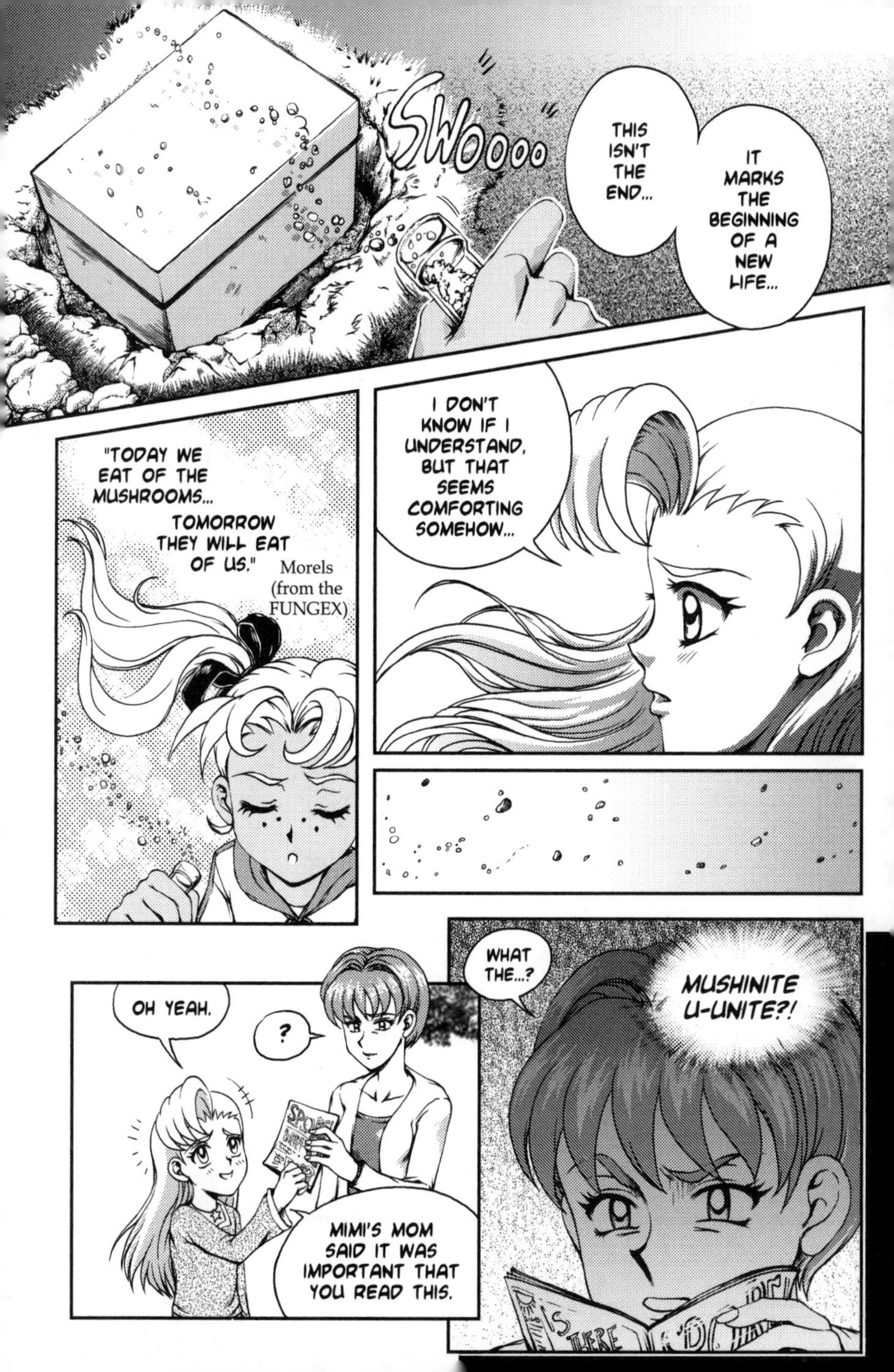
SWOOOO
THIS ISN'T THE END...
IT MARKS THE BEGINNING OF A NEW LIFE...
"TODAY WE EAT OF THE MUSHROOMS... TOMORROW THEY WILL EAT OF US."
Morels (from the FUNGEX)
I DON'T KNOW IF I UNDERSTAND, BUT THAT SEEMS COMFORTING SOMEHOW...
OH YEAH.
?
MIMI'S MOM SAID IT WAS IMPORTANT THAT YOU READ THIS.
WHAT THE...?
MUSHINITE U-UNITE?!

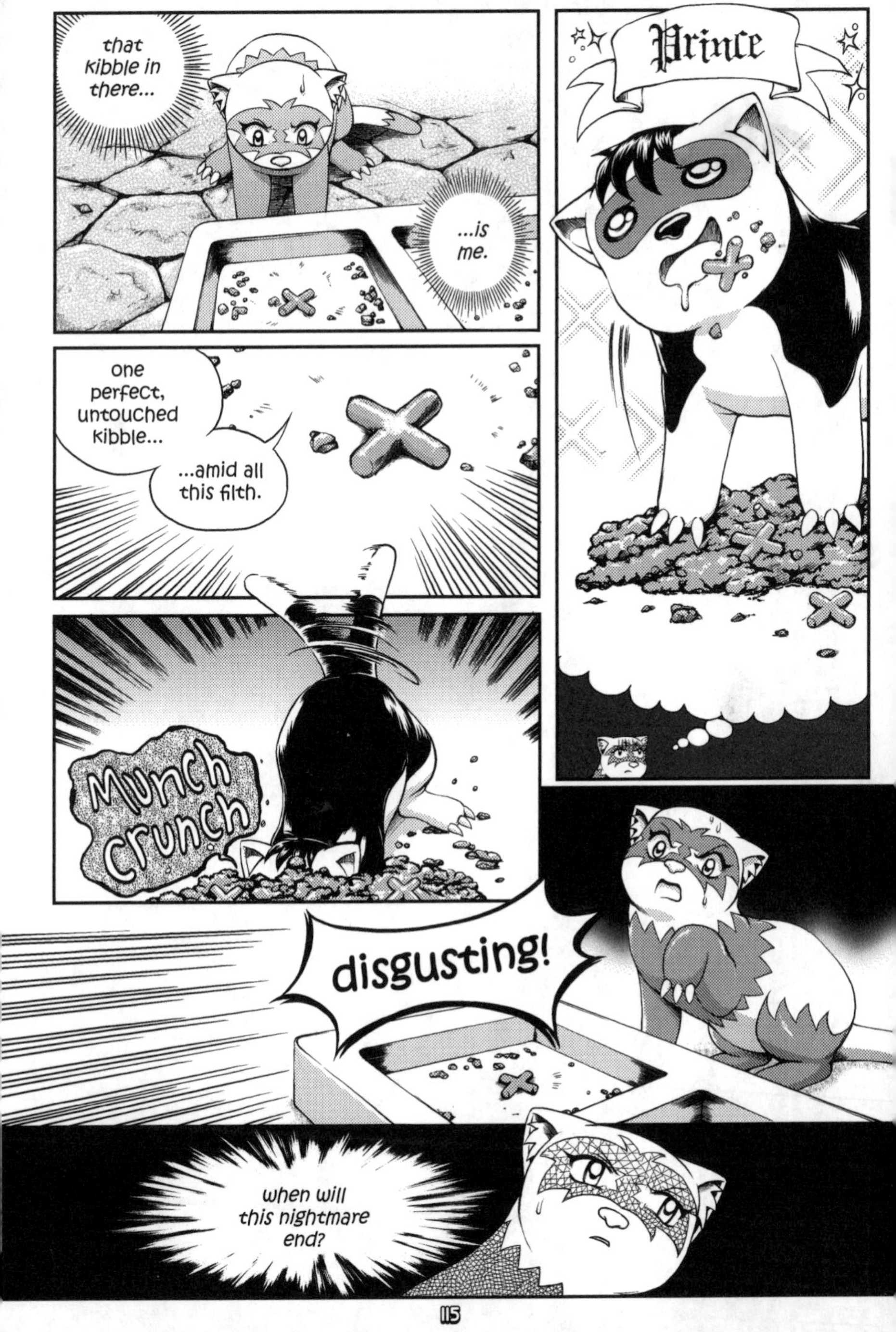

that kibble in there...
...is me.
Prince
one perfect, untouched kibble...
...amid all this filth.
Munch crunch
disgusting!
when will this nightmare end?

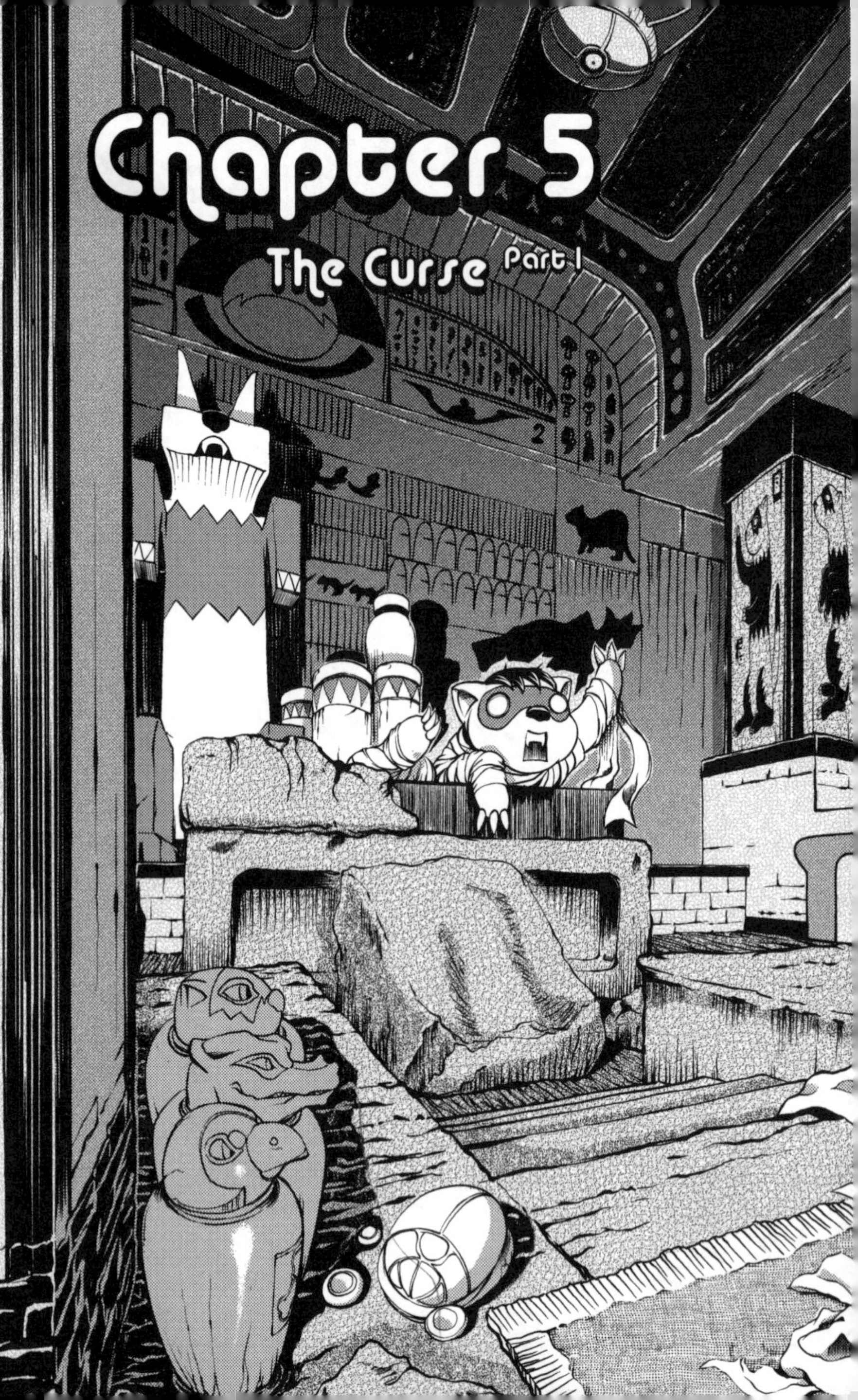
Chapter 5
The Curse Part 1

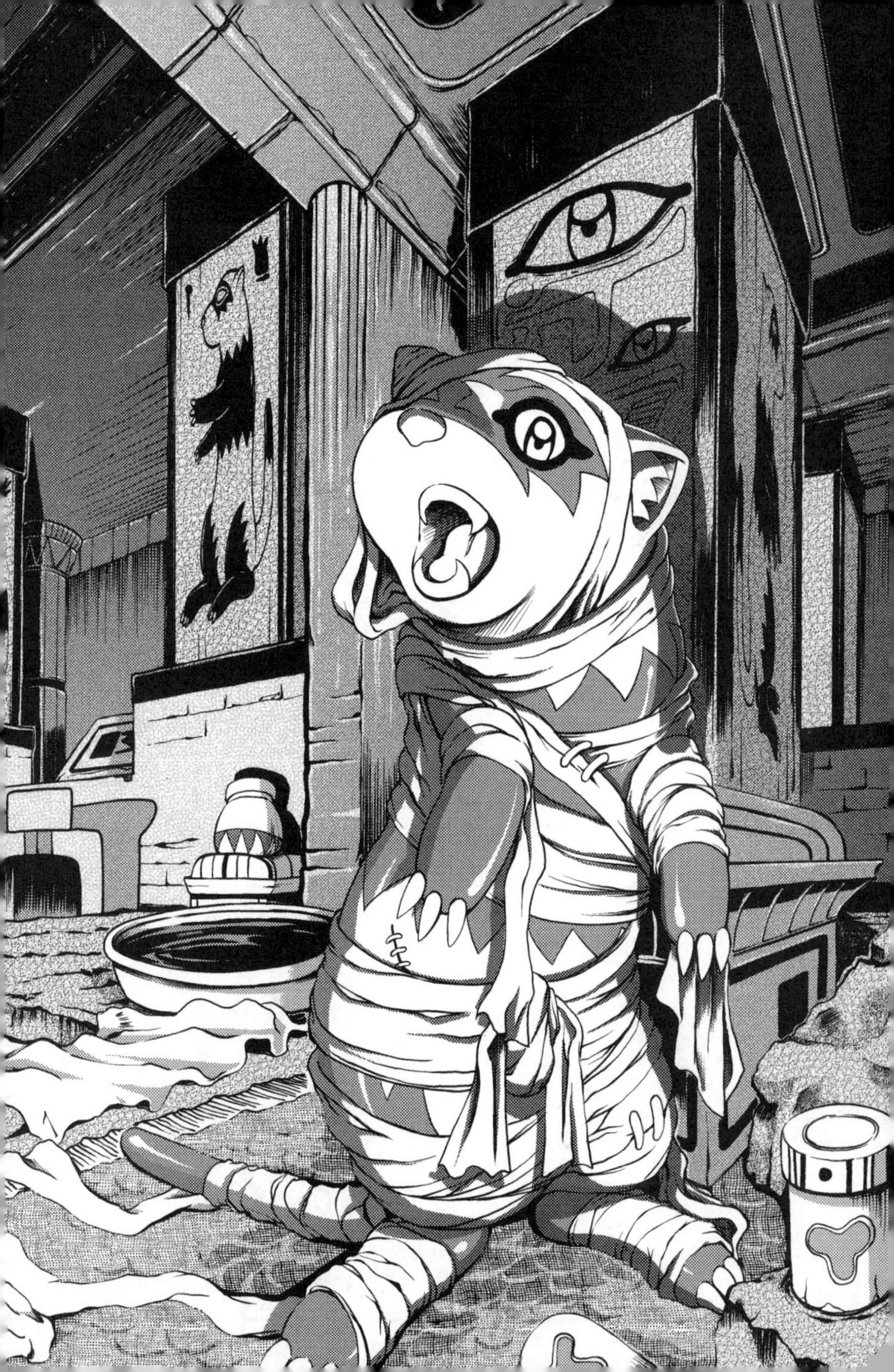

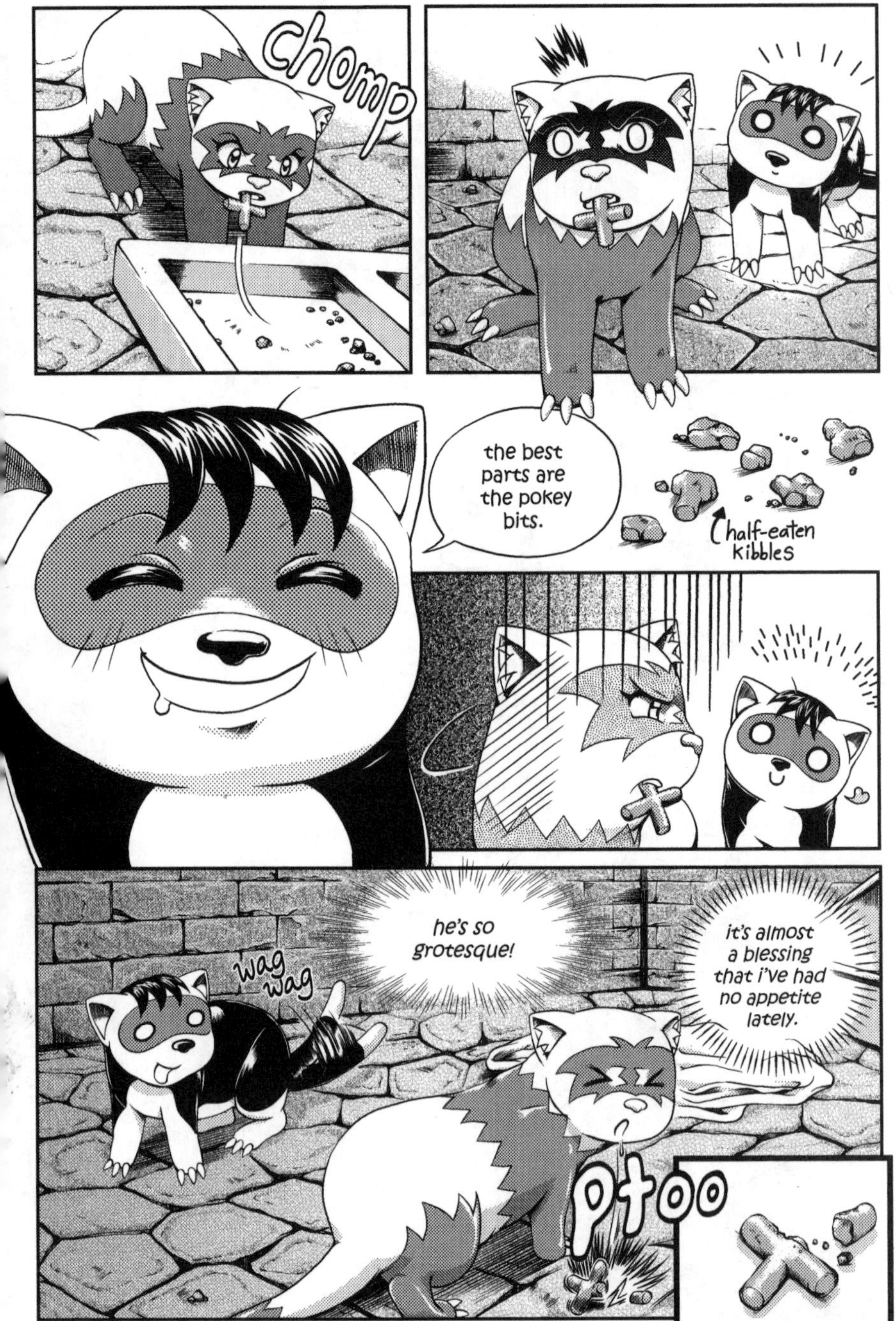
chomp
the best parts are the pokey bits.
half-eaten kibbles
wag wag
he's so grotesque!
it's almost a blessing that i've had no appetite lately.
ptoo

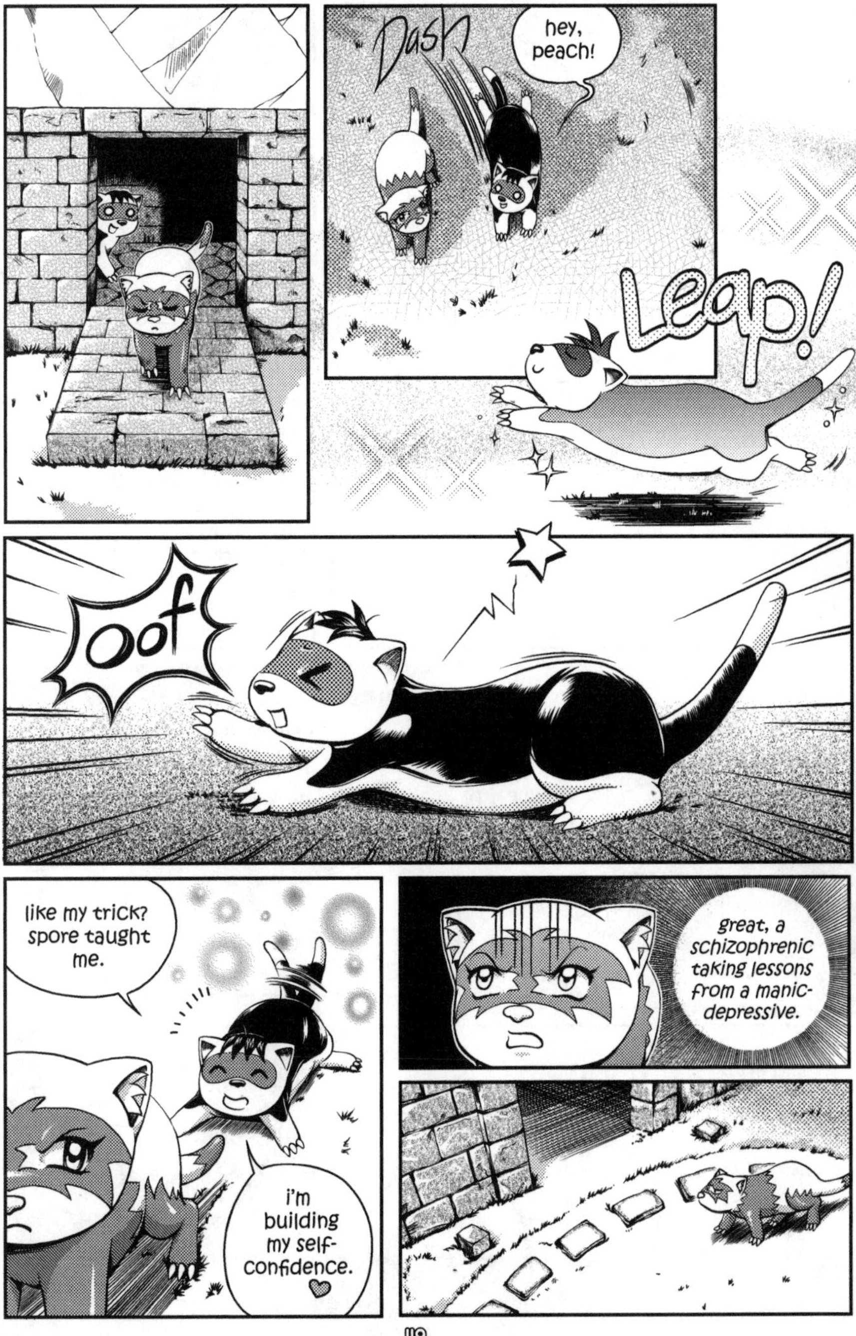
Dash
hey, peach!
Leap!
oof
like my trick? spore taught me.
i'm building my self-confidence.
great, a schizophrenic taking lessons from a manic-depressive.

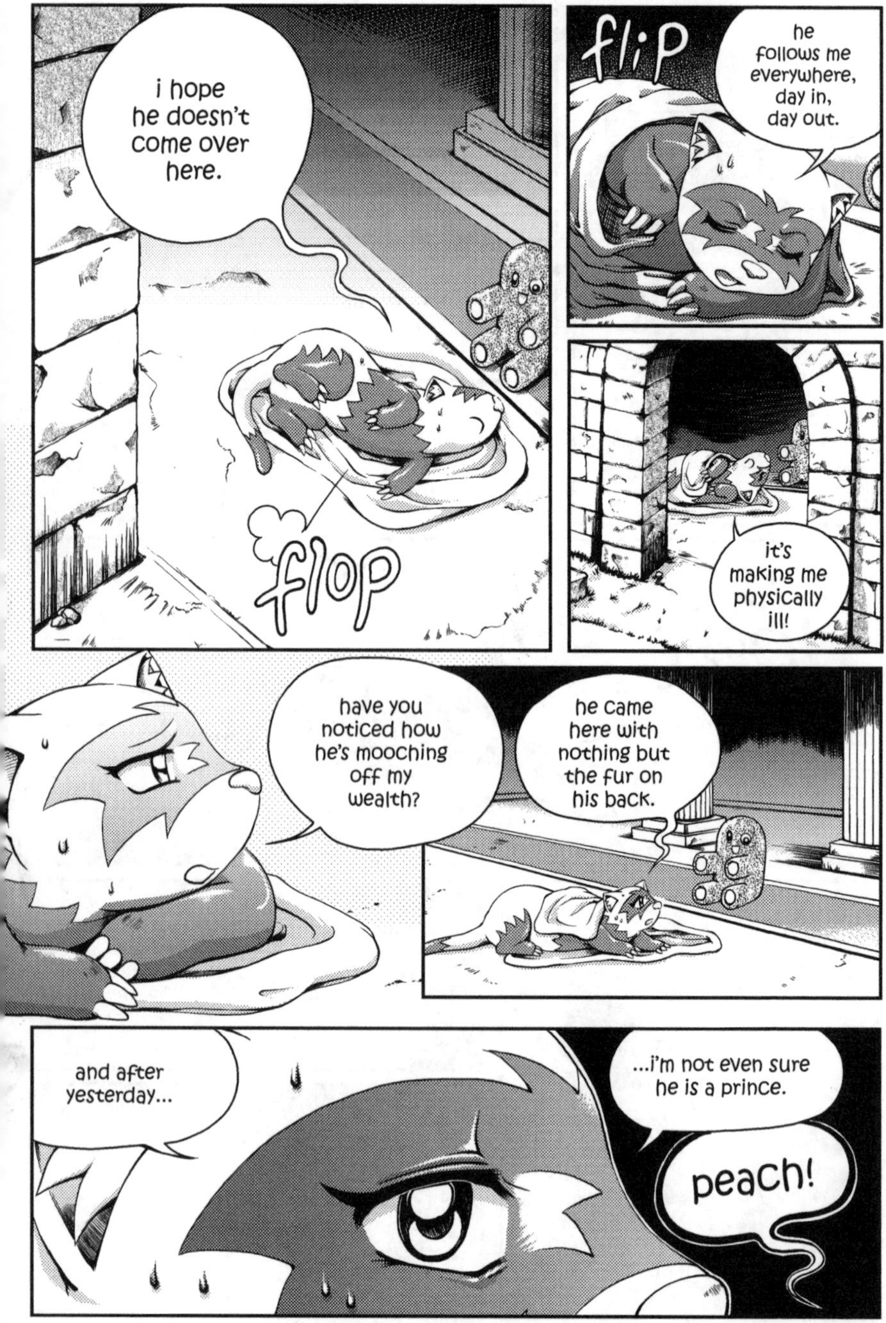
i hope he doesn't come over here.
flop
flip
he follows me everywhere, day in, day out.
it's making me physically ill!
have you noticed how he's mooching off my wealth?
he came here with nothing but the fur on his back.
and after yesterday...
...i'm not even sure he is a prince.
peach!

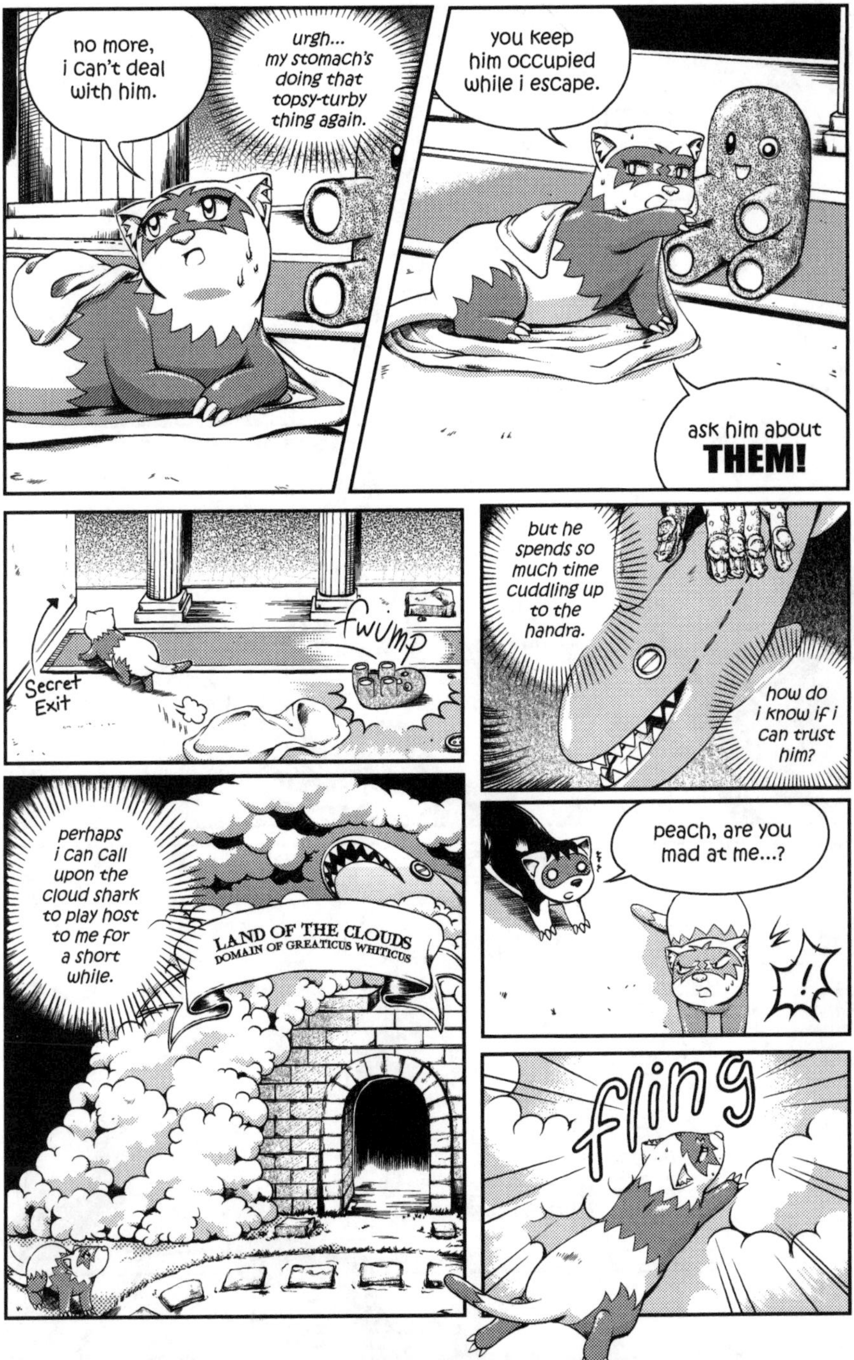
no more, i can't deal with him.
urgh... my stomach's doing that topsy-turby thing again.
you keep him occupied while i escape.
ask him about THEM!
Secret Exit
fwump
but he spends so much time cuddling up to the handra.
how do i know if i can trust him?
perhaps i can call upon the cloud shark to play host to me for a short while.
LAND OF THE CLOUDS
DOMAIN OF GREATICUS WHITICUS
peach, are you mad at me...?
!
fling

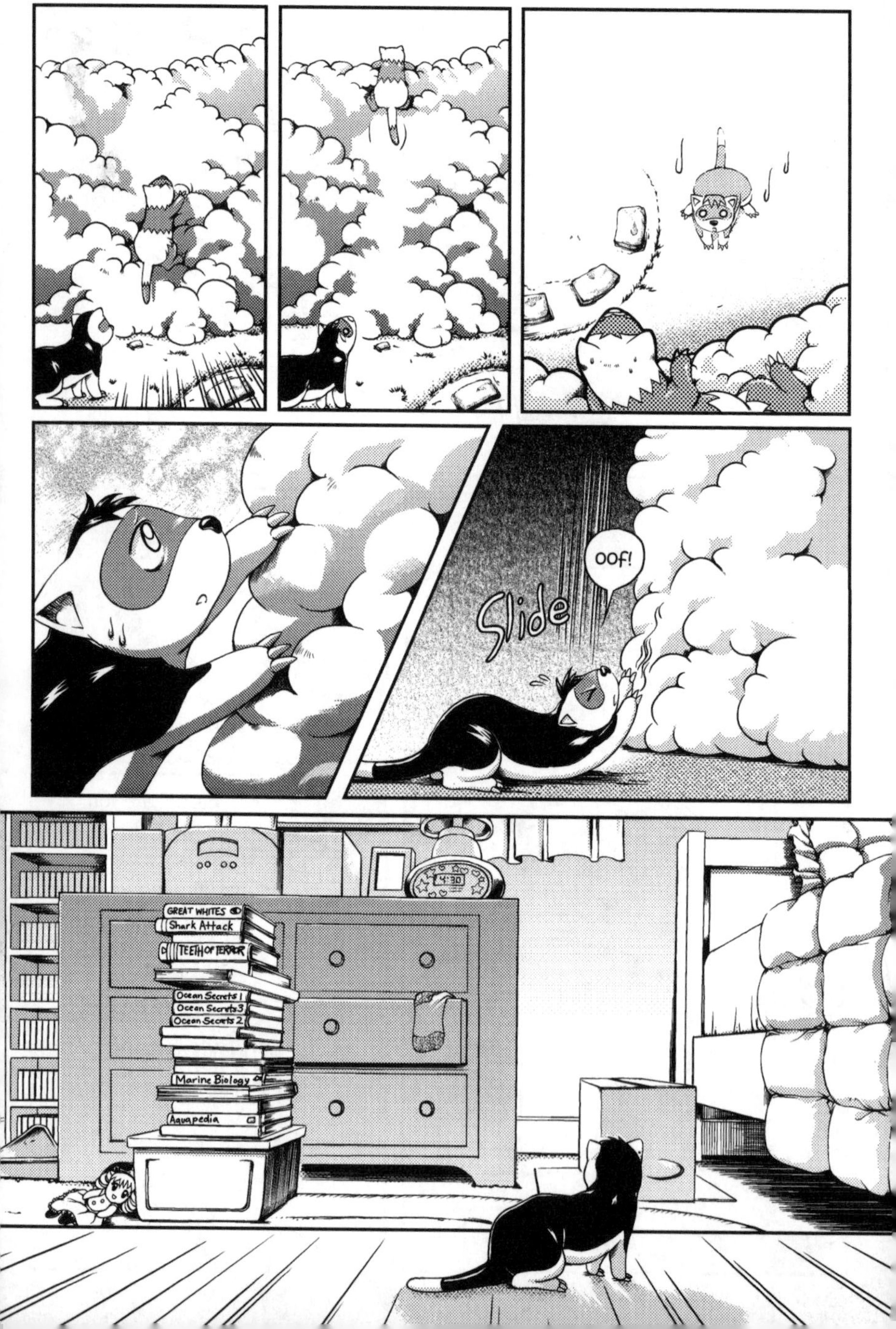

OOF!
Slide
4:30
GREAT WHITES
Shark Attack
TEETH OF TERROR
Ocean Secrets 1
Ocean Secrets 3
Ocean Secrets 2
Marine Biology
Aquapedia

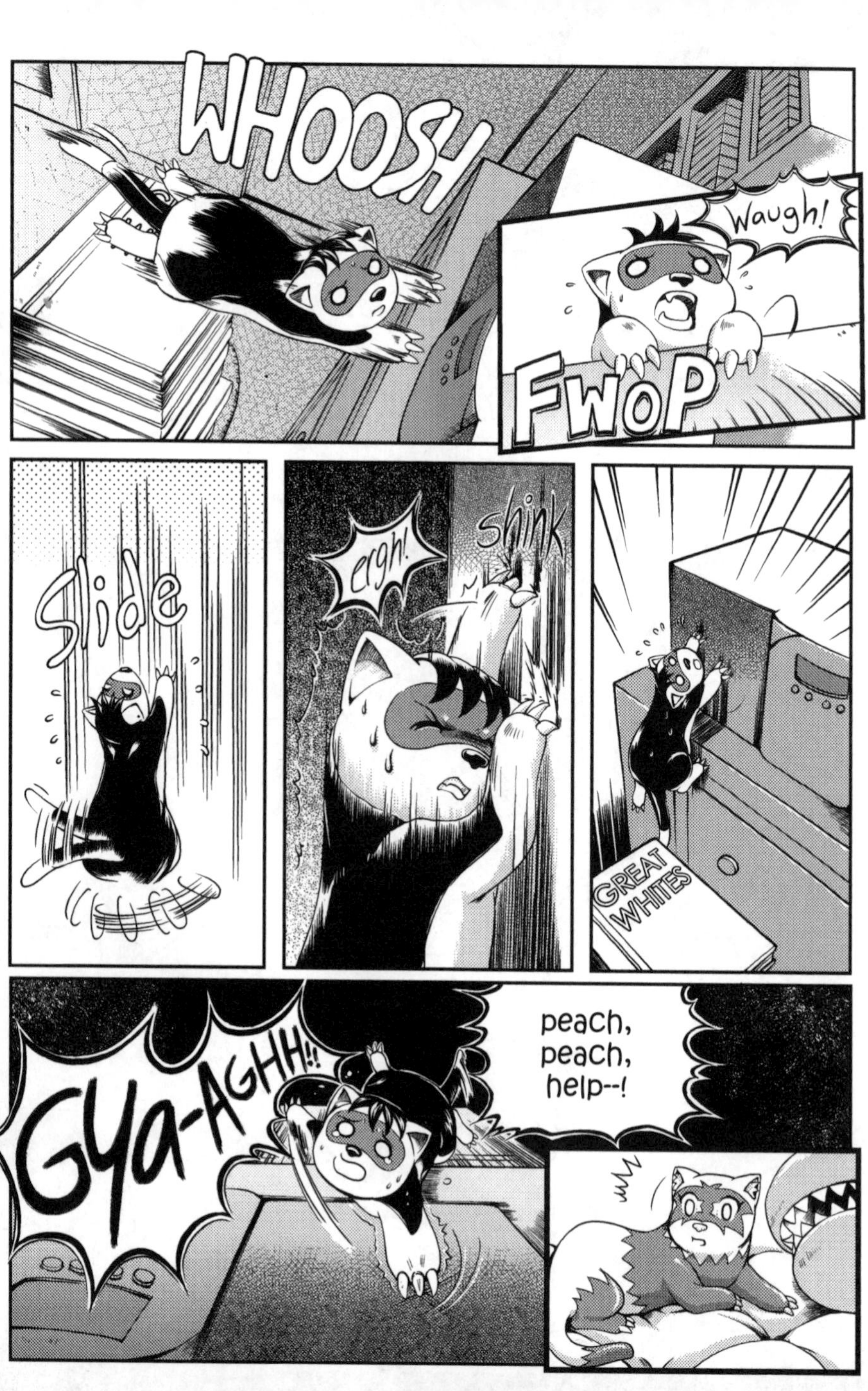
WHOOSH
Waugh!
FWOP
slide
ergh!
shink
GREAT WHITES
GYA-AGHH!!
peach, peach, help--!

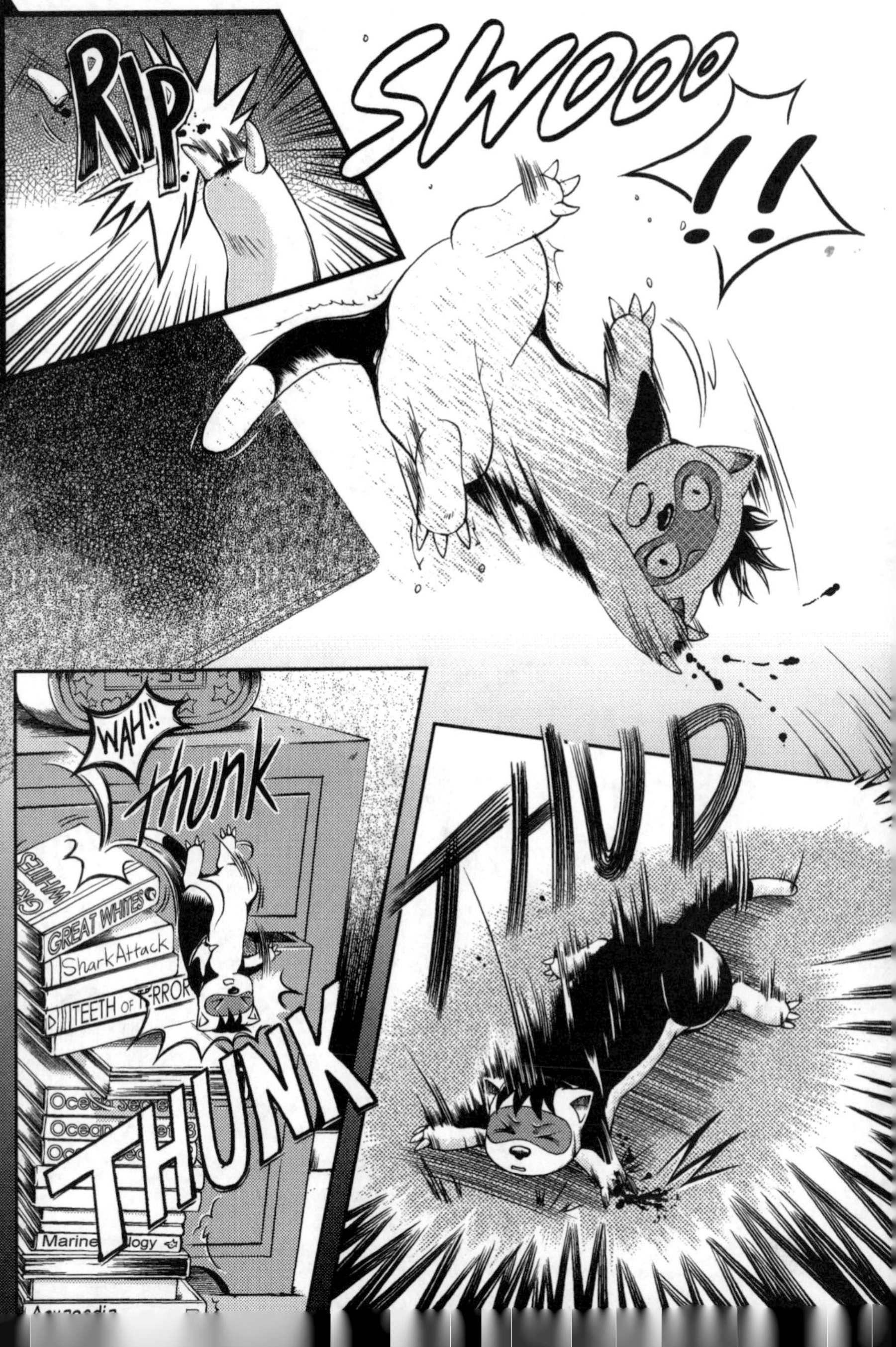
RIP
SWOOO!!
WAH!!
thunk
GREAT WHITES
GREAT WHITES
SharkAttack
THUNK
THUD

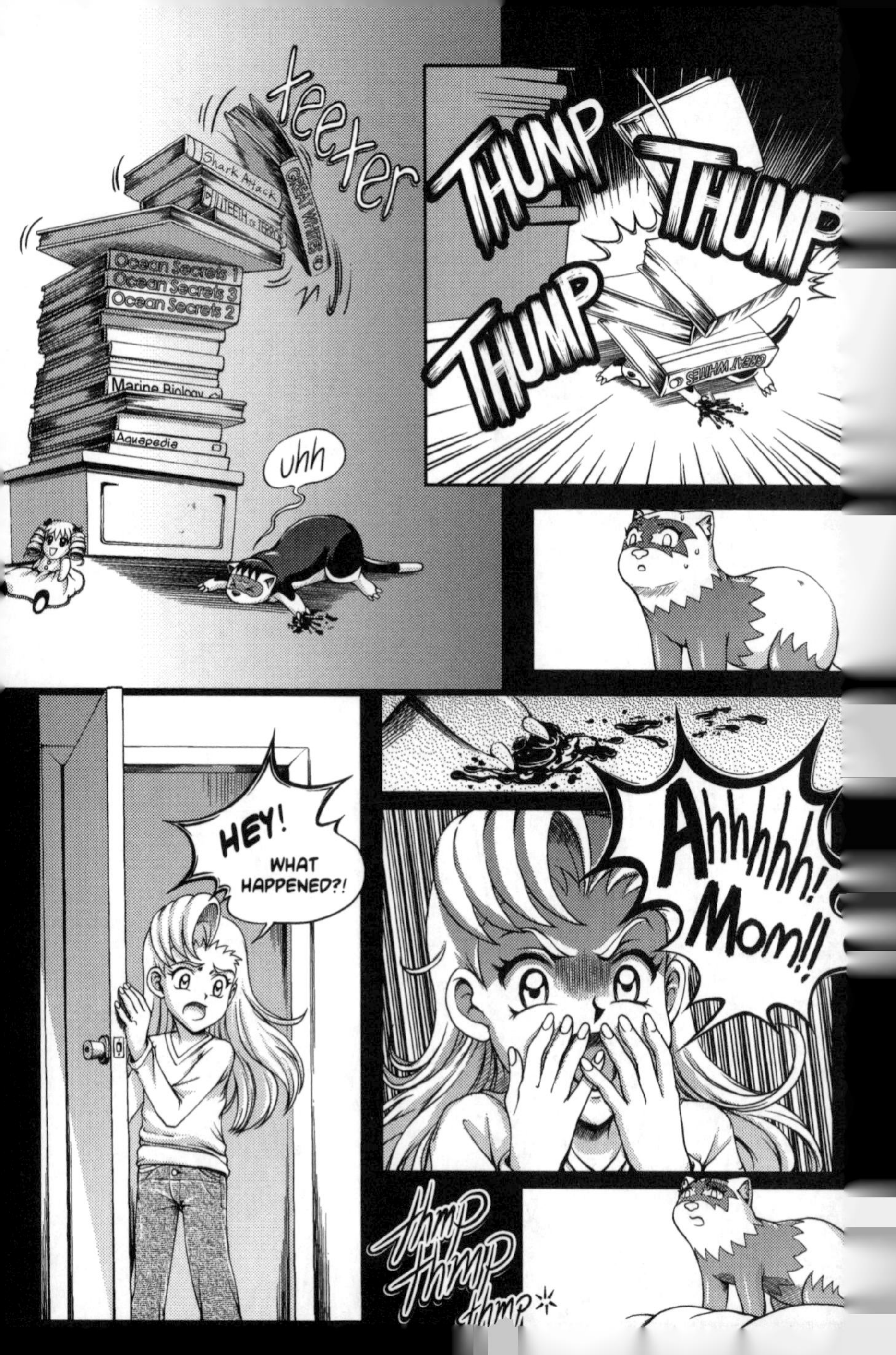
teeter
Shark Attack
GREAT WHITES
TEETH of TERROR
Ocean Secrets 1
Ocean Secrets 3
Ocean Secrets 2
Marine Biology
Aquapedia
uhh
THUMP
THUMP
THUMP
GREAT WHITES
HEY!
WHAT HAPPENED?!
Ahhhhh!
Mom!!
thmp
thmp
thmp

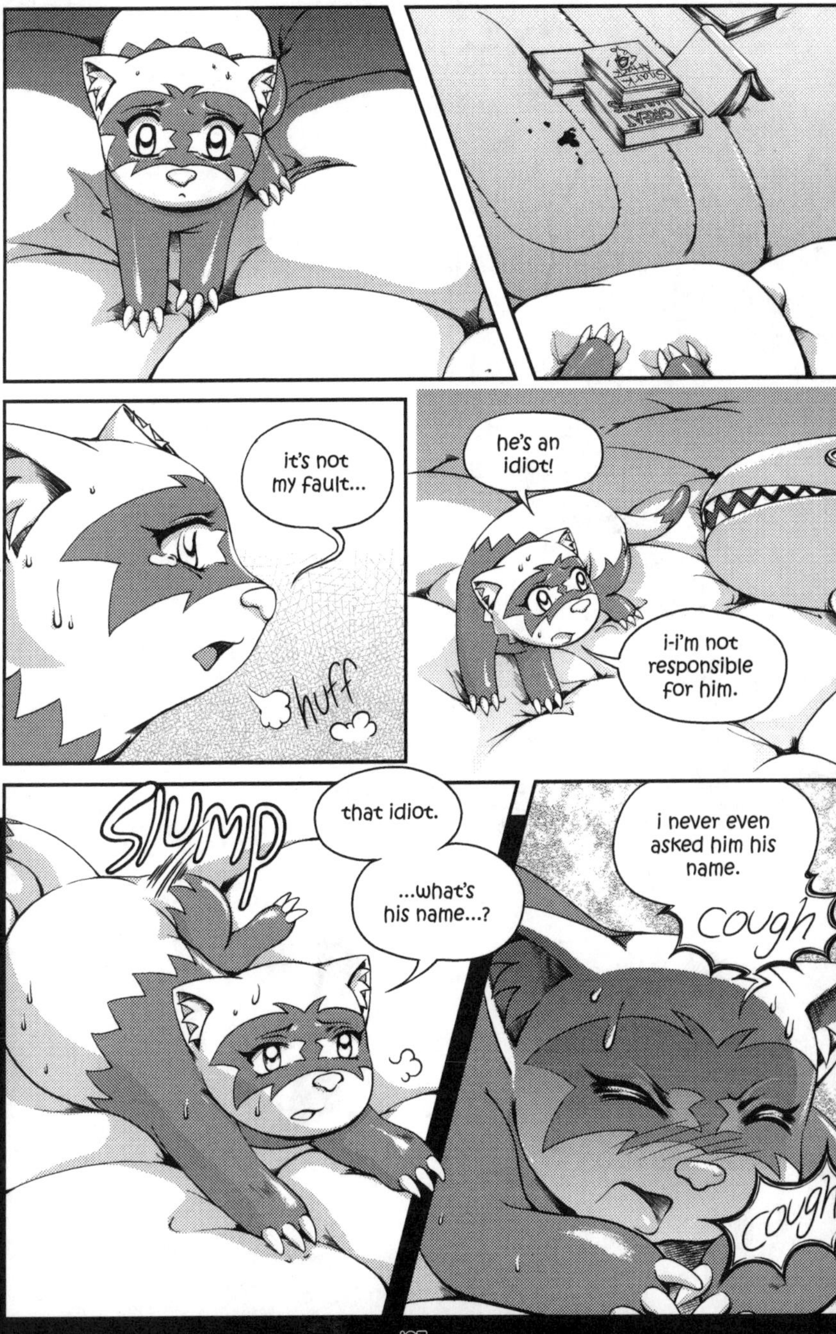
it's not my fault...
huff
he's an idiot!
i-i'm not responsible for him.
SLUMP
that idiot.
...what's his name...?
i never even asked him his name.
cough
cough

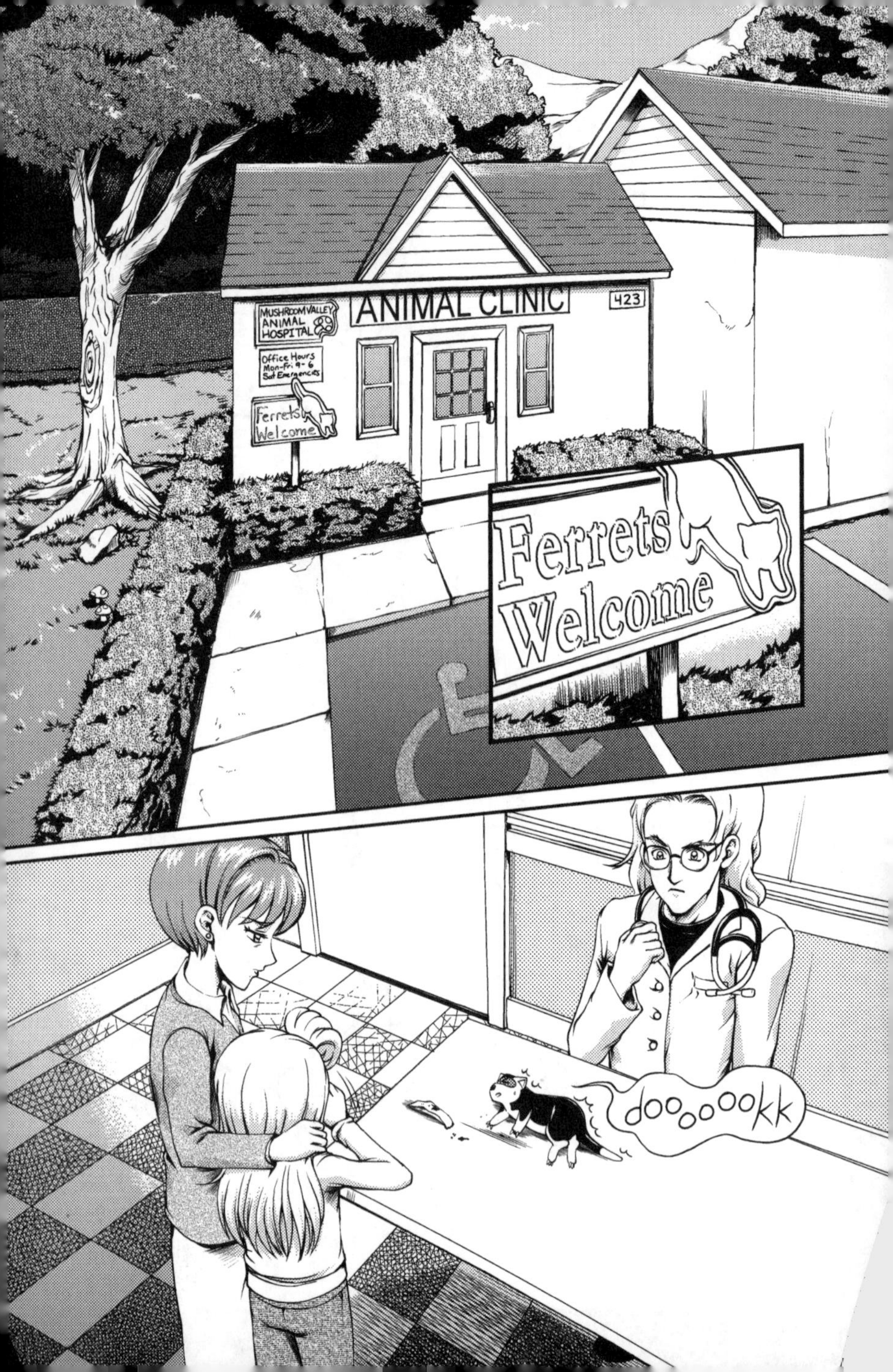
ANIMAL CLINIC
423
MUSHROOM VALLEY
ANIMAL
HOSPITAL
Office Hours
Mon-Fri 9-6
Sat Emergencies
Ferrets
Welcome
Ferrets
Welcome
dooooookk

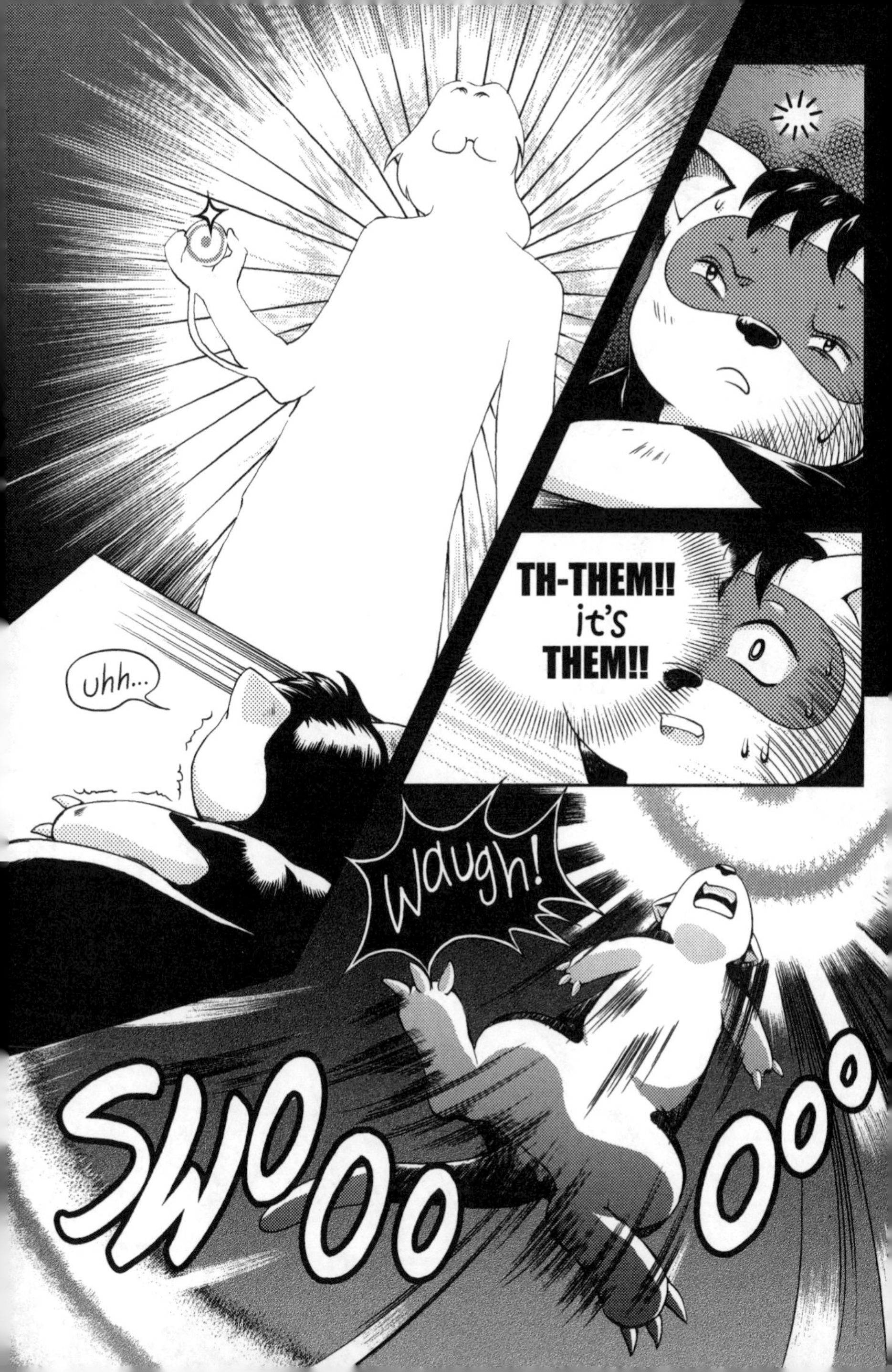
uhh...
TH-THEM!!
it's
THEM!!
waugh!
SHOOOO
OOOO

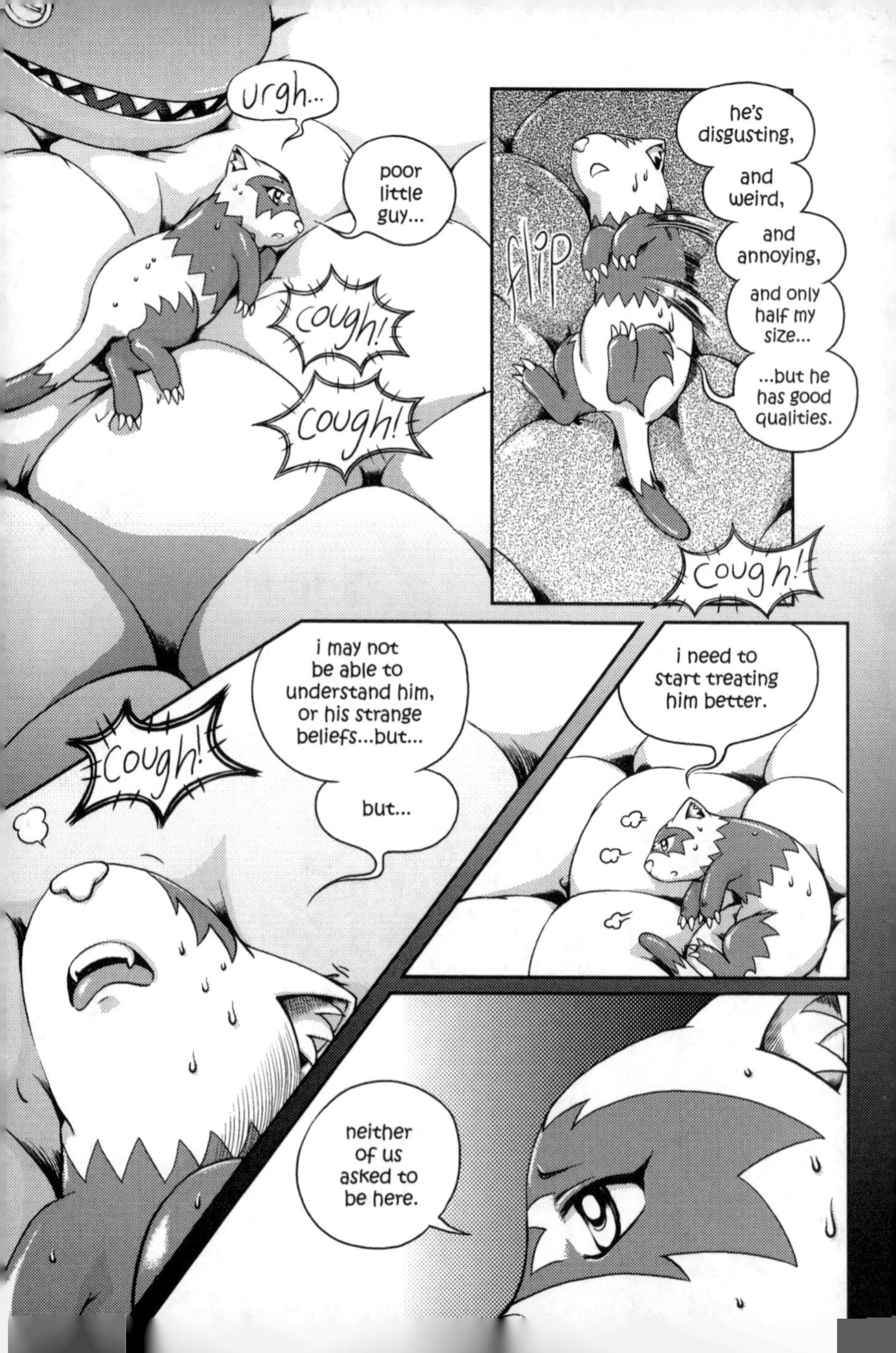
urgh...
poor little guy...
cough!
cough!
he's disgusting,
and weird,
and annoying,
and only half my size...
...but he has good qualities.
flip
cough!
i may not be able to understand him, or his strange beliefs...but...
but...
cough!
i need to start treating him better.
neither of us asked to be here.

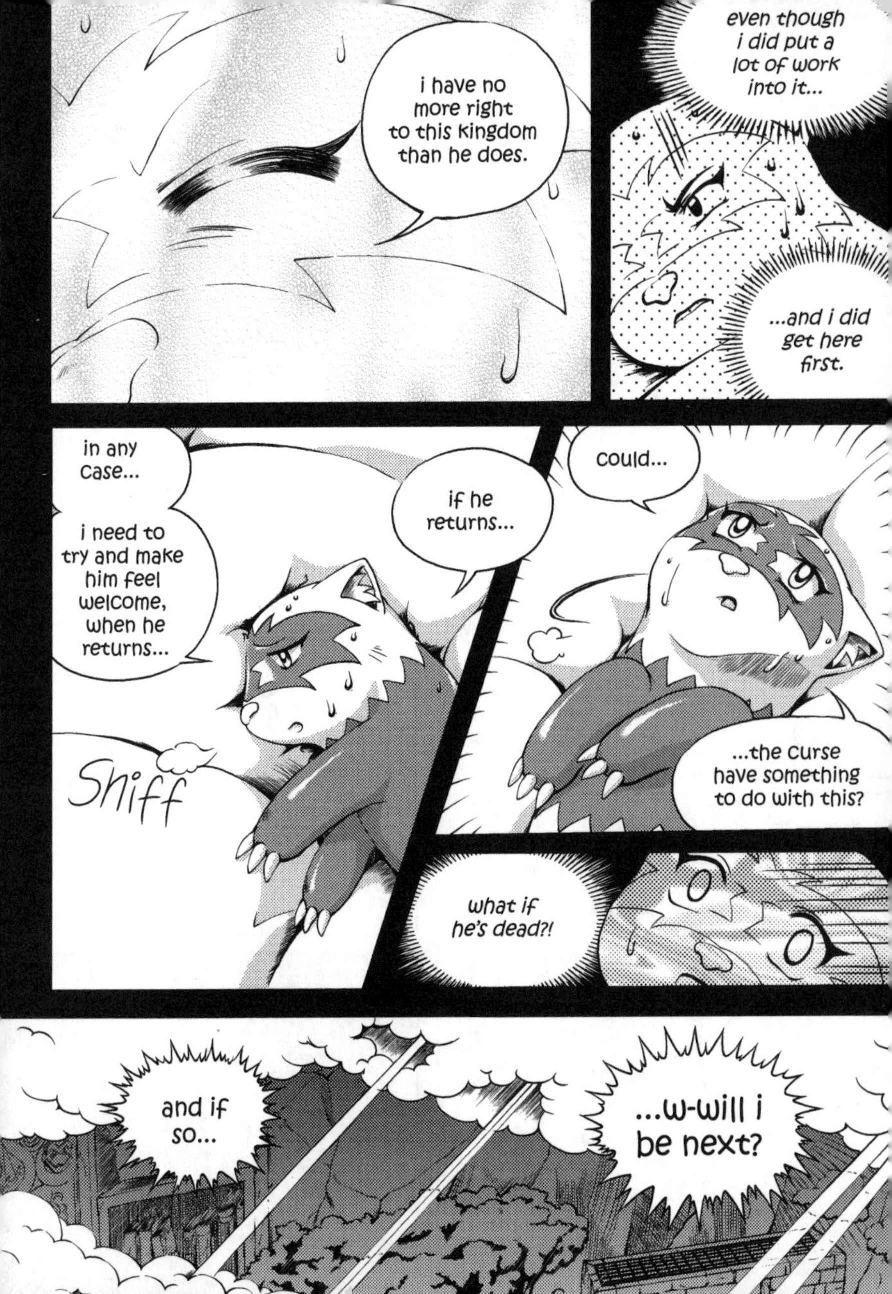
i have no more right to this kingdom than he does.
even though i did put a lot of work into it...
...and i did get here first.
in any case...
i need to try and make him feel welcome, when he returns...
Shiff
if he returns...
could...
...the curse have something to do with this?
what if he's dead?!
and if so...
...w-will i be next?

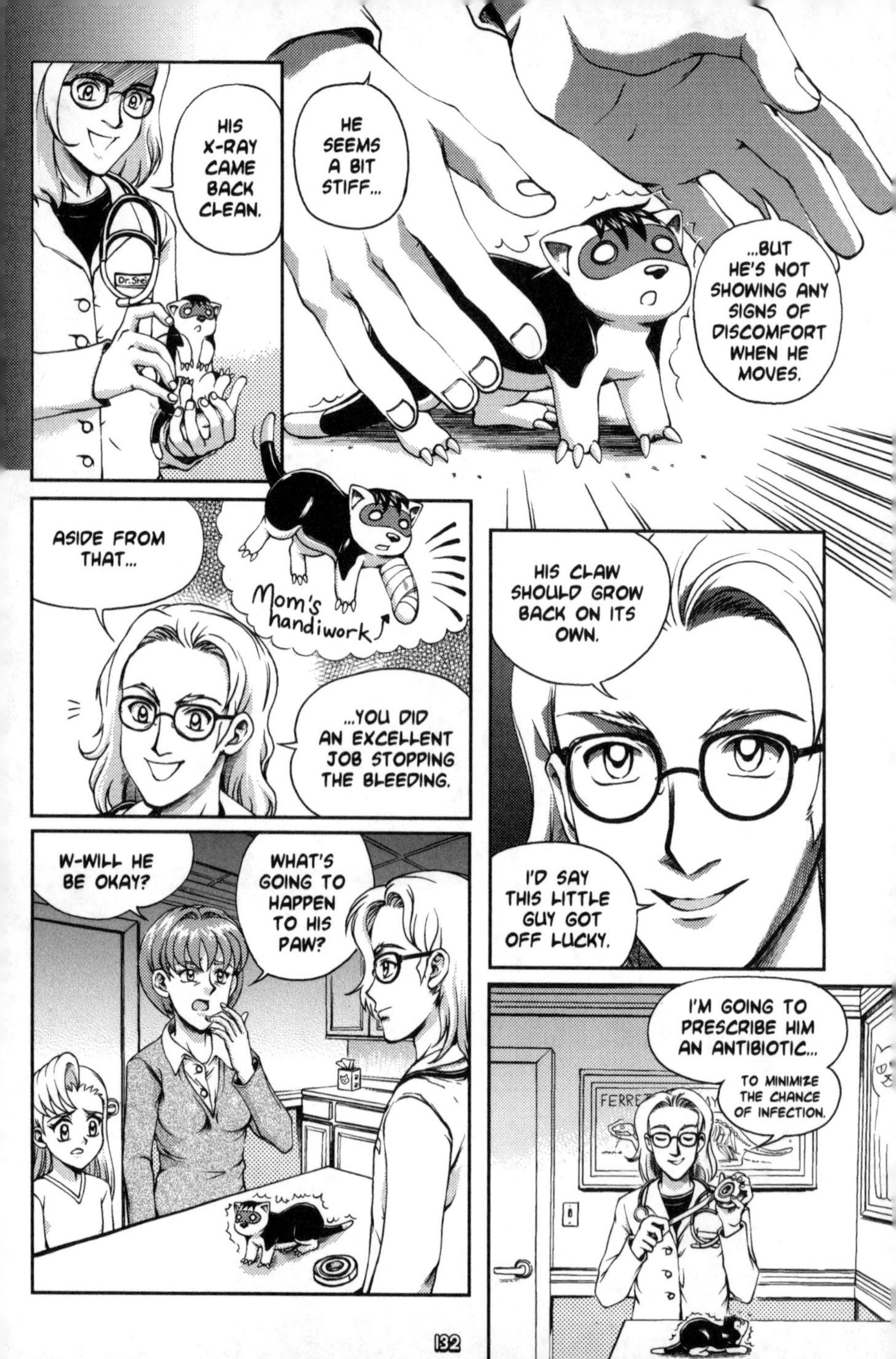

HIS X-RAY CAME BACK CLEAN.
HE SEEMS A BIT STIFF...
...BUT HE'S NOT SHOWING ANY SIGNS OF DISCOMFORT WHEN HE MOVES.
Dr. Stei
ASIDE FROM THAT...
Mom's handiwork
...YOU DID AN EXCELLENT JOB STOPPING THE BLEEDING.
HIS CLAW SHOULD GROW BACK ON ITS OWN.
I'D SAY THIS LITTLE GUY GOT OFF LUCKY.
W-WILL HE BE OKAY?
WHAT'S GOING TO HAPPEN TO HIS PAW?
I'M GOING TO PRESCRIBE HIM AN ANTIBIOTIC...
TO MINIMIZE THE CHANCE OF INFECTION.

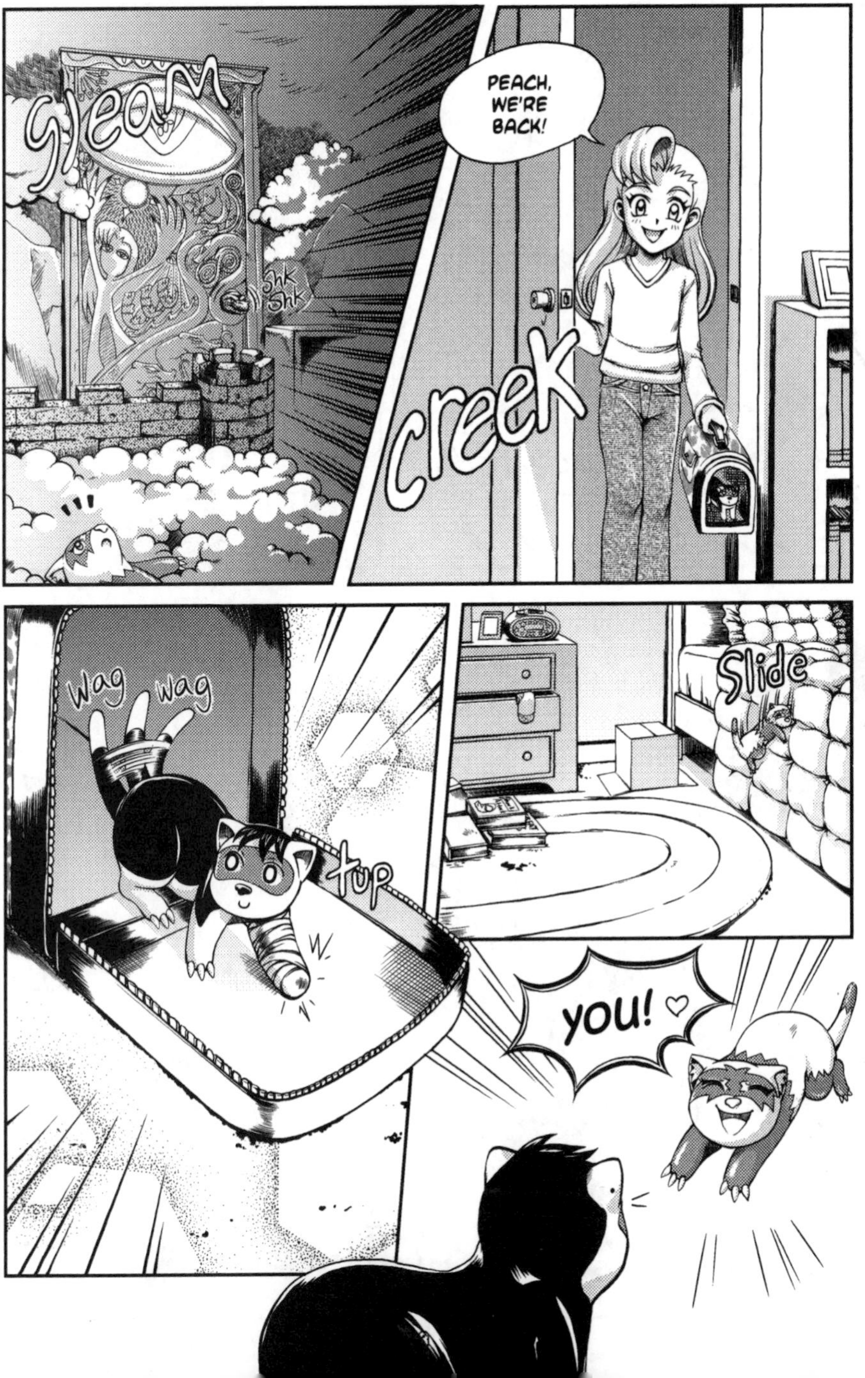
gleam
Shk
Shk
PEACH, WE'RE BACK!
creek
wag wag
tup
Slide
YOU! ♡

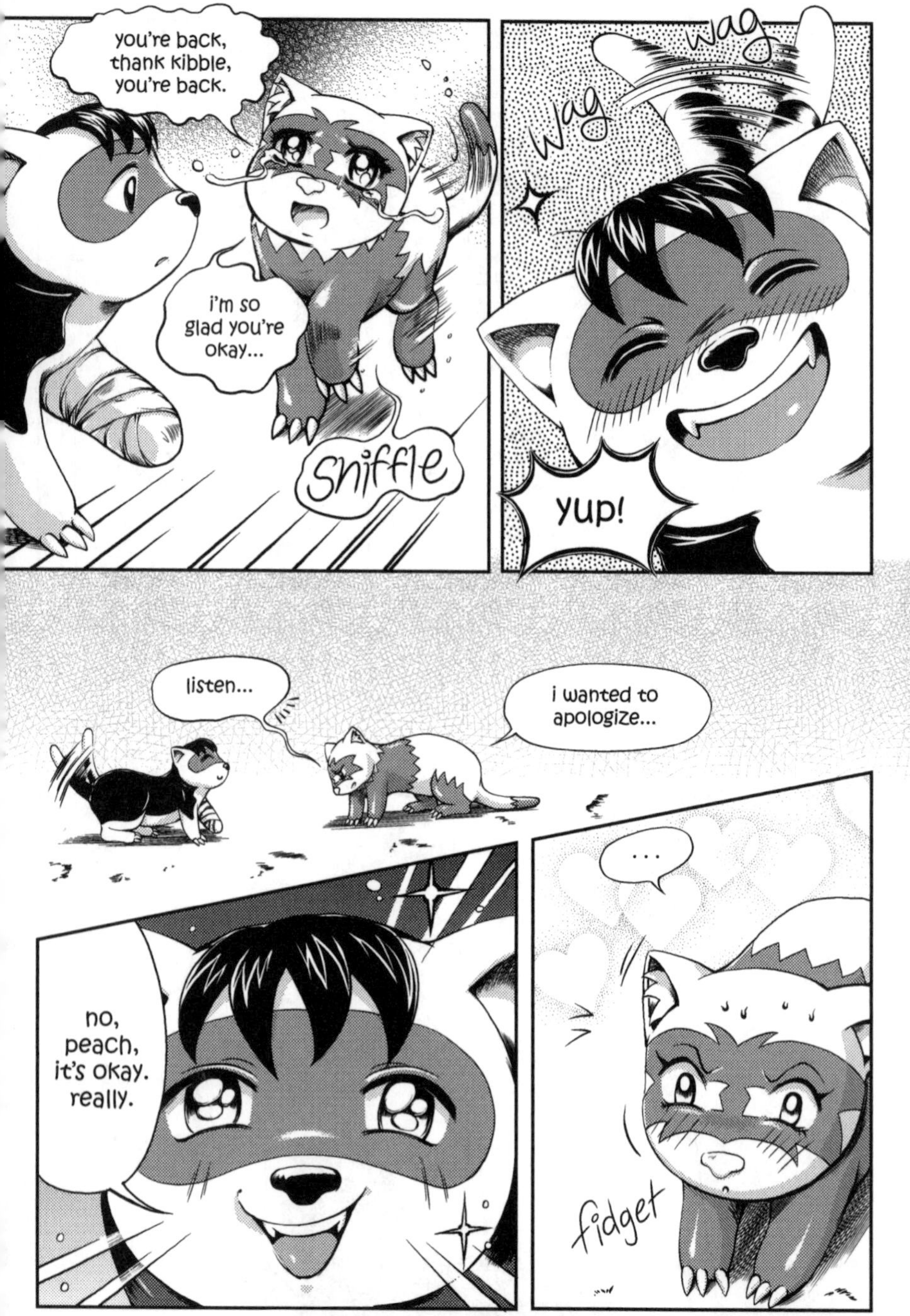
you're back, thank kibble, you're back.
i'm so glad you're okay...
sniffle
wag
wag
yup!
listen...
i wanted to apologize...
no, peach, it's okay. really.
...
fidget

SWP SWP

...

with it gone, i'm free from their control.

so, whatcha doing?

it's **THEM!**

they were using a device implanted in my claw to monitor my thoughts.

what an idiot.

i was concerned for nothing.

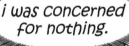

Cough

Cough

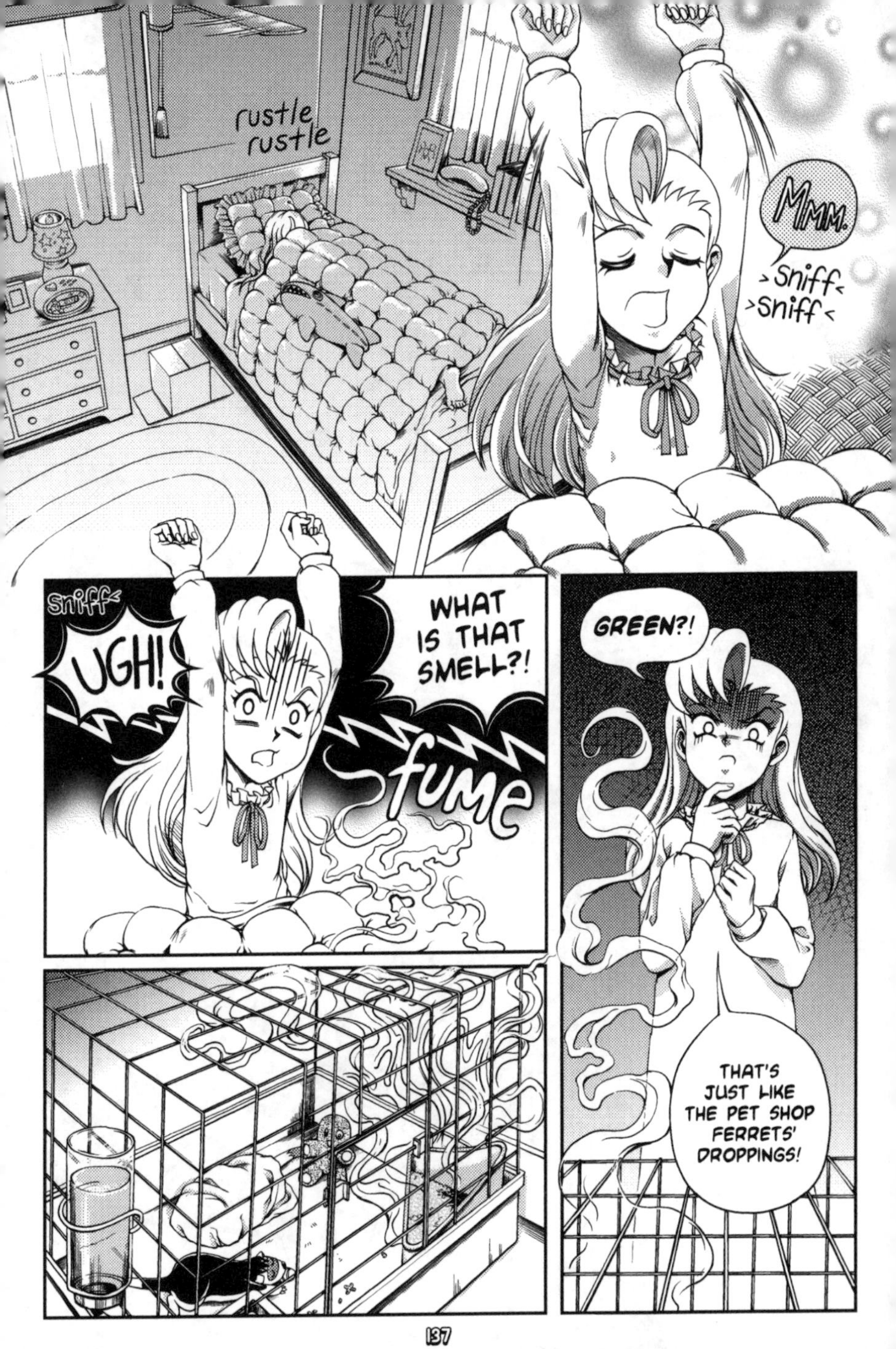
rustle rustle
MMM.
sniff sniff
sniff
UGH!
WHAT IS THAT SMELL?!
fume
GREEN?!
THAT'S JUST LIKE THE PET SHOP FERRETS' DROPPINGS!

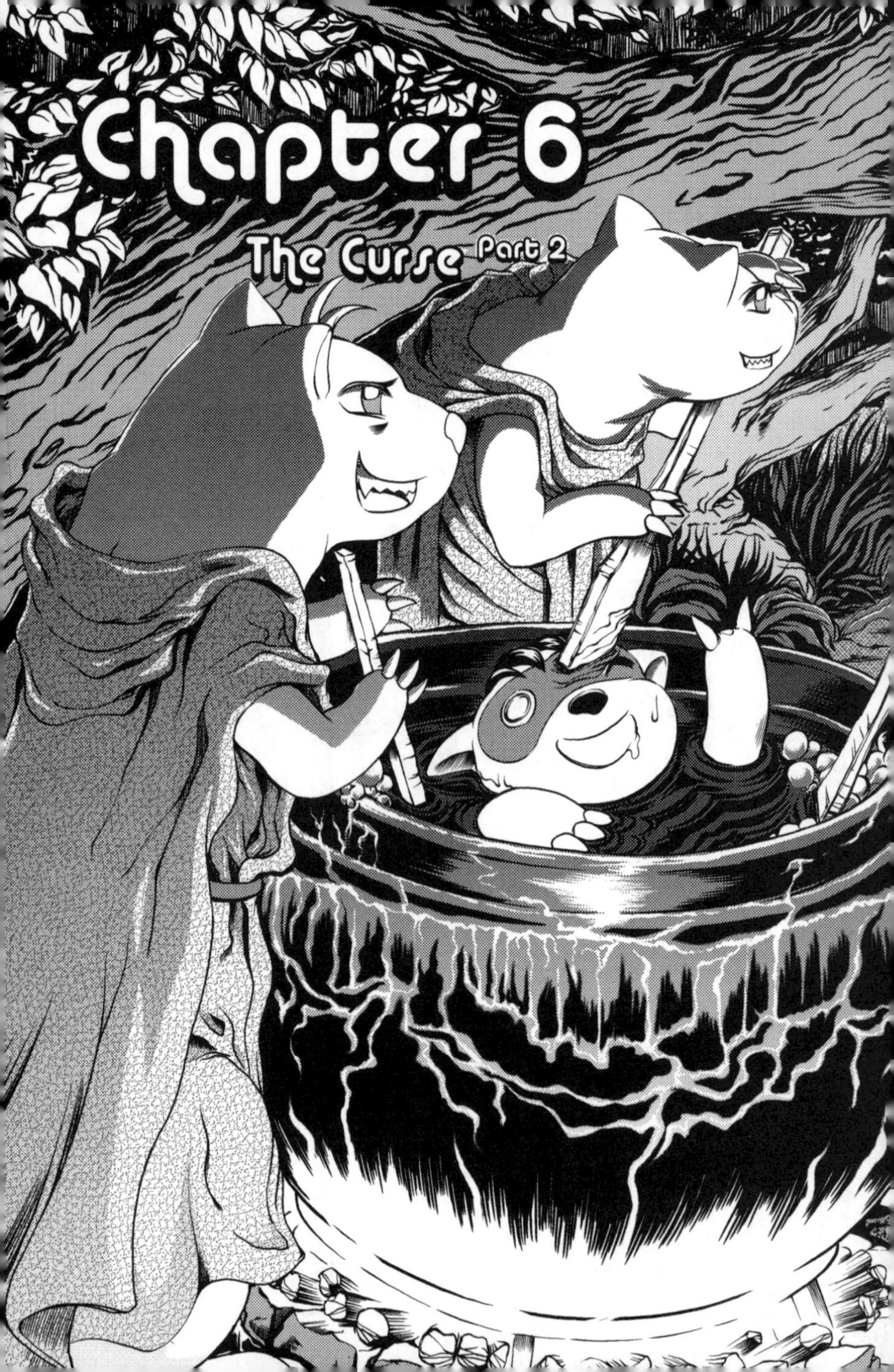
Chapter 6
The Curse Part 2

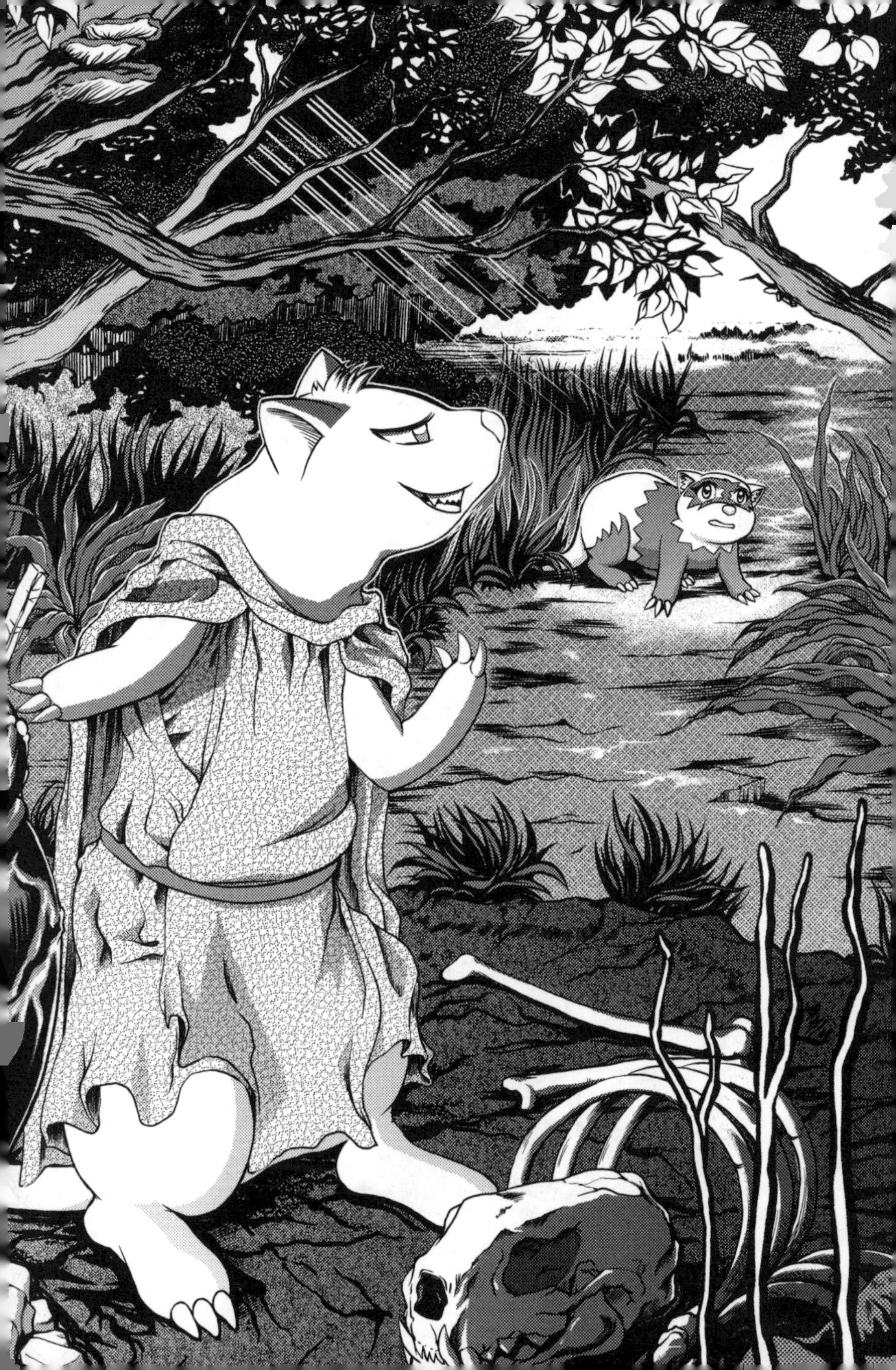

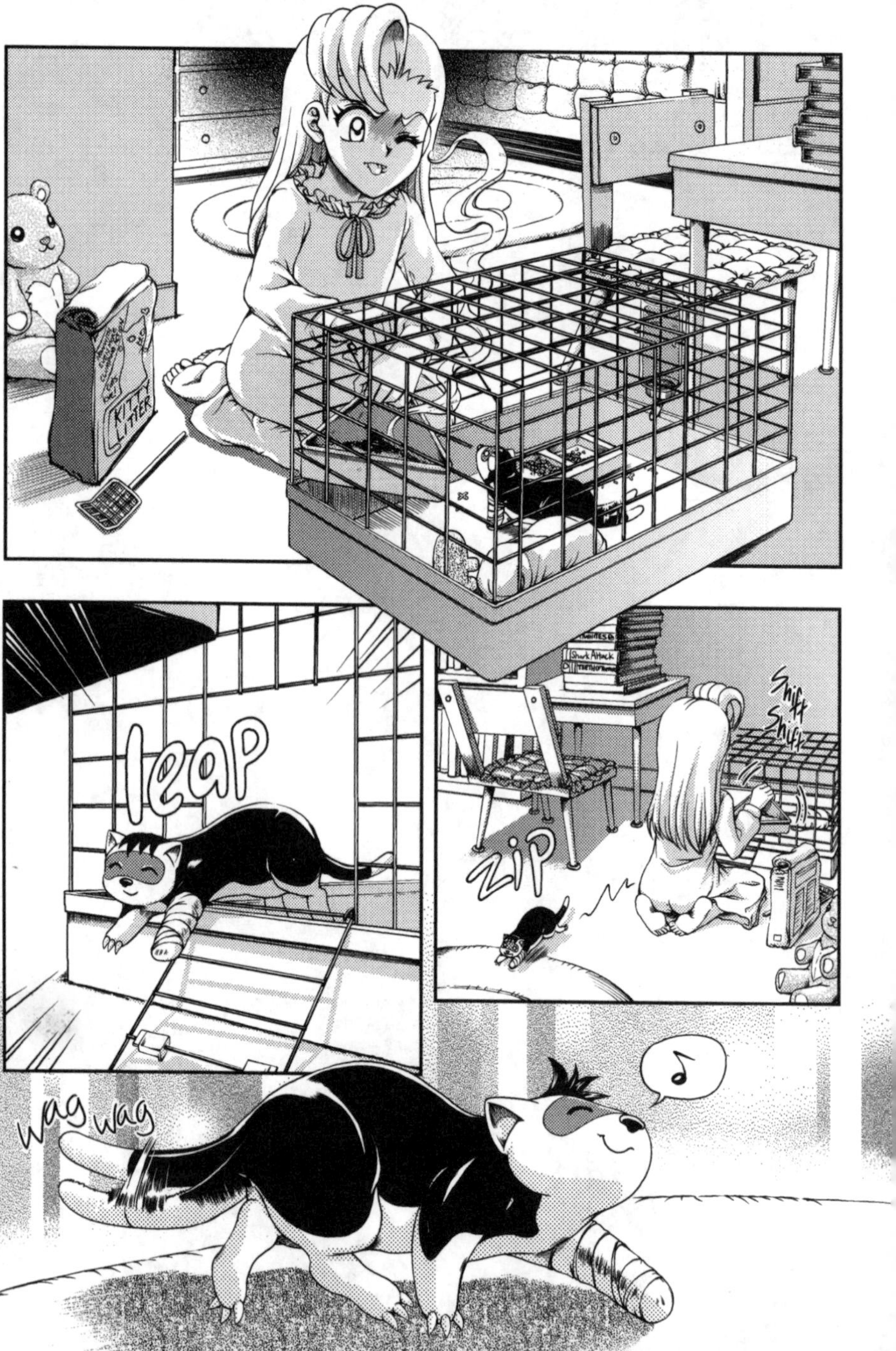
KITTY LITTER
leap
Shark Attack
Shift Shift
zip
wag wag
♪

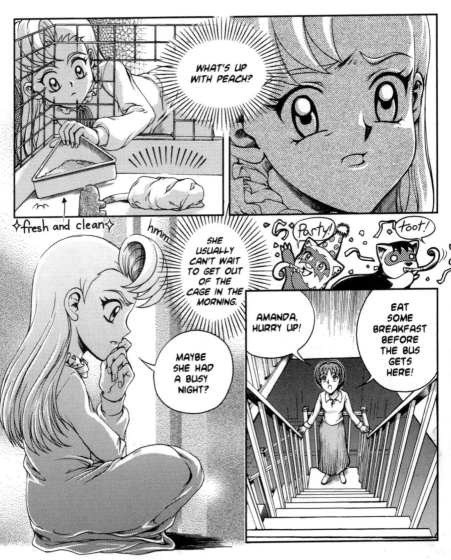

WHAT'S UP WITH PEACH?

✧fresh and clean✧

hmm...

SHE USUALLY CAN'T WAIT TO GET OUT OF THE CAGE IN THE MORNING.

MAYBE SHE HAD A BUSY NIGHT?

Party!

toot!

AMANDA, HURRY UP!

EAT SOME BREAKFAST BEFORE THE BUS GETS HERE!

...I MADE FRENCH TOAST!

COMING!

Shark Attack
TEETH of TERROR
rustle
rustle
rustle

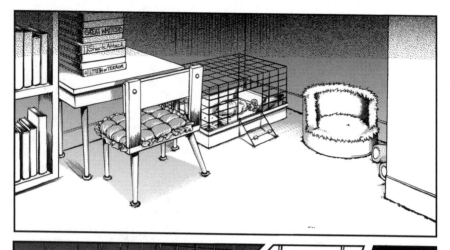

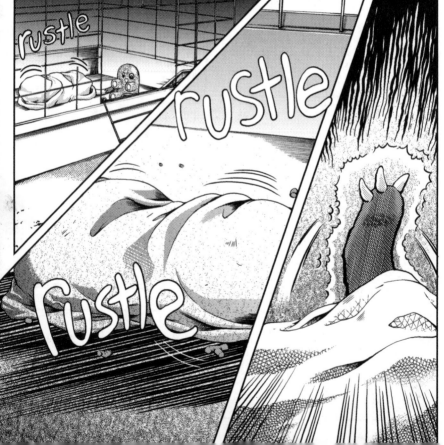

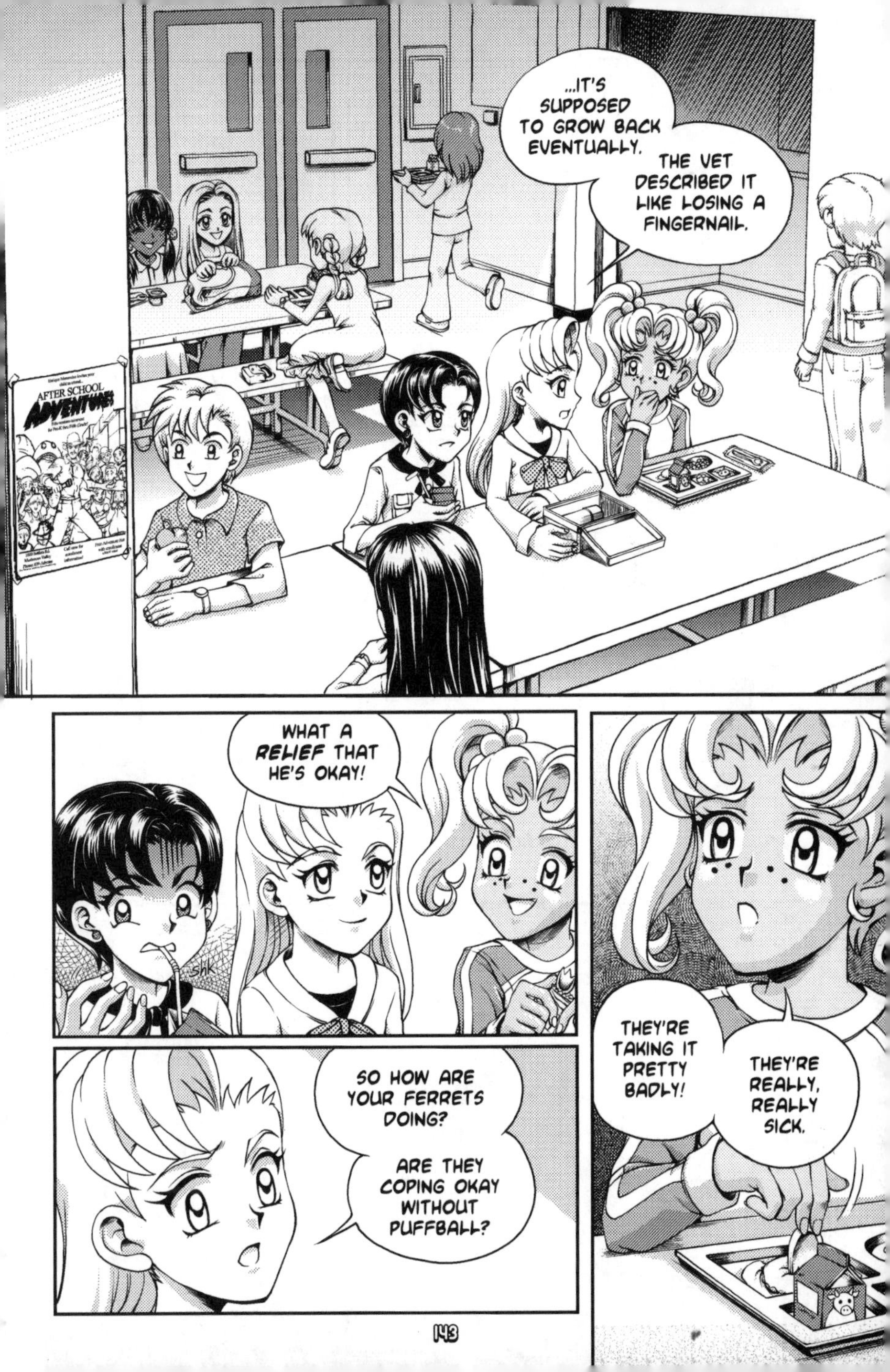
...IT'S SUPPOSED TO GROW BACK EVENTUALLY.
THE VET DESCRIBED IT LIKE LOSING A FINGERNAIL.
AFTER SCHOOL ADVENTURE!
WHAT A *RELIEF* THAT HE'S OKAY!
shk
THEY'RE TAKING IT PRETTY BADLY!
THEY'RE REALLY, REALLY SICK.
SO HOW ARE YOUR FERRETS DOING?
ARE THEY COPING OKAY WITHOUT PUFFBALL?

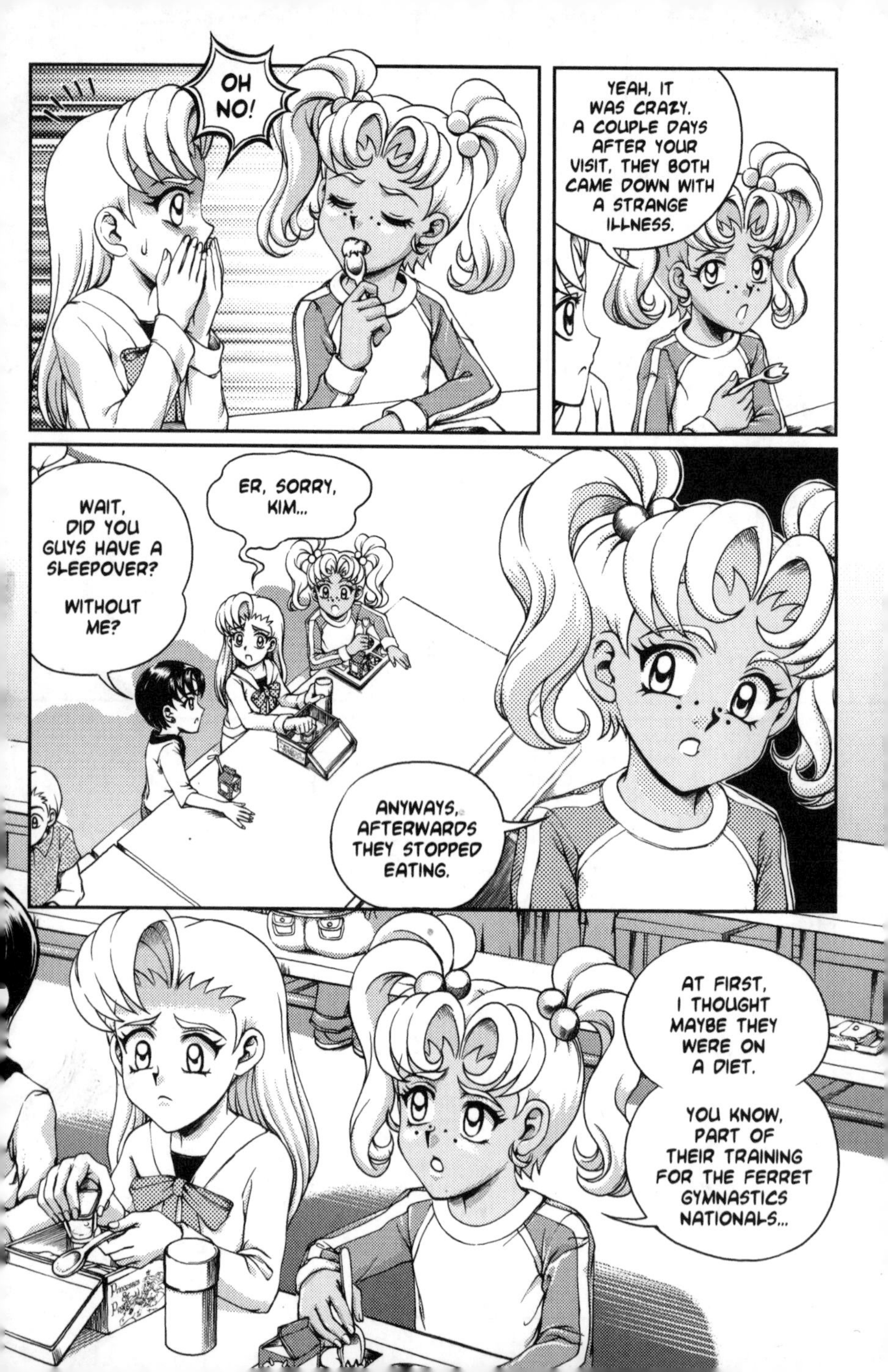
OH NO!
YEAH, IT WAS CRAZY. A COUPLE DAYS AFTER YOUR VISIT, THEY BOTH CAME DOWN WITH A STRANGE ILLNESS.
WAIT, DID YOU GUYS HAVE A SLEEPOVER?
WITHOUT ME?
ER, SORRY, KIM...
ANYWAYS, AFTERWARDS THEY STOPPED EATING.
AT FIRST, I THOUGHT MAYBE THEY WERE ON A DIET.
YOU KNOW, PART OF THEIR TRAINING FOR THE FERRET GYMNASTICS NATIONALS...

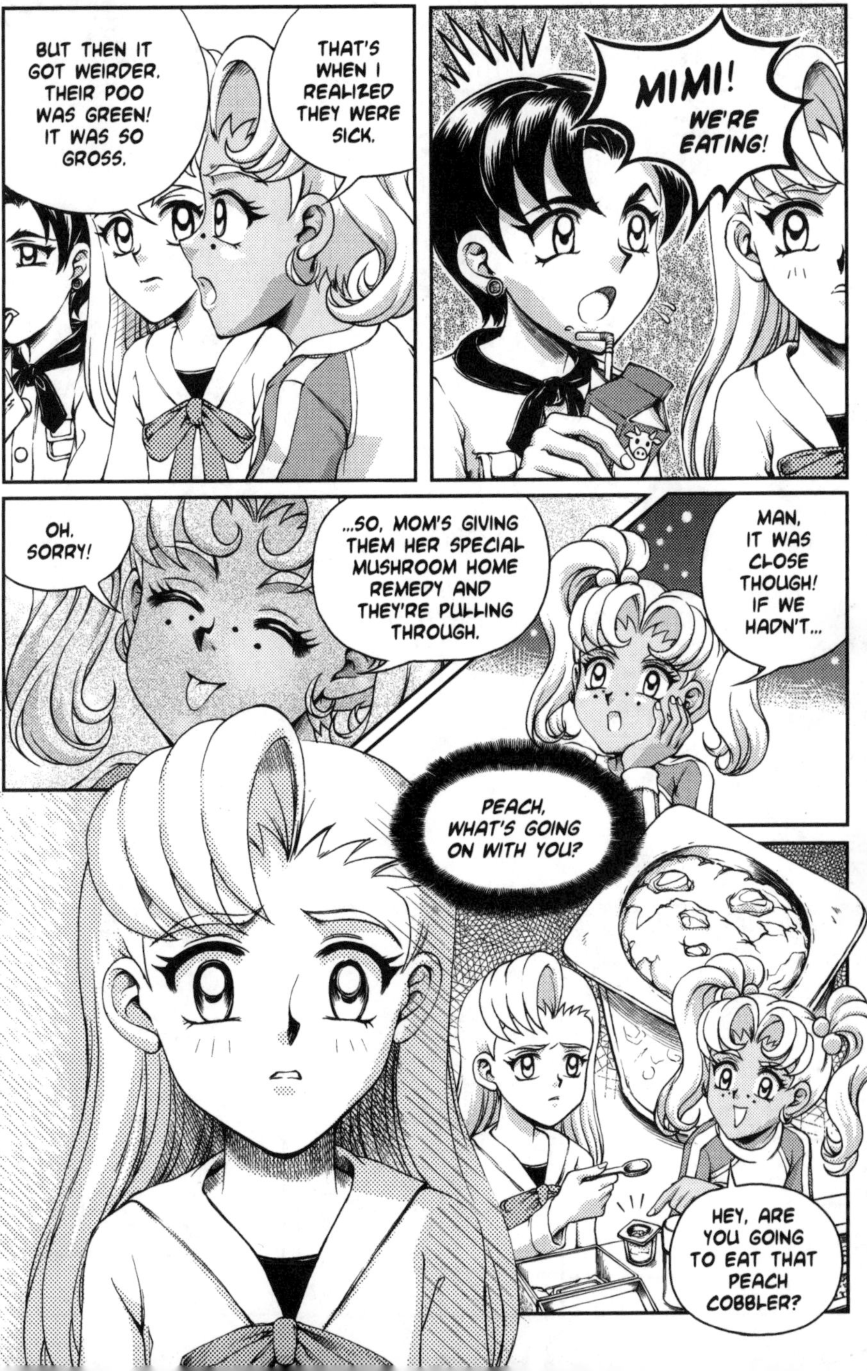
BUT THEN IT GOT WEIRDER. THEIR POO WAS GREEN! IT WAS SO GROSS.
THAT'S WHEN I REALIZED THEY WERE SICK.
MIMI!
WE'RE EATING!
OH. SORRY!
...SO, MOM'S GIVING THEM HER SPECIAL MUSHROOM HOME REMEDY AND THEY'RE PULLING THROUGH.
MAN, IT WAS CLOSE THOUGH! IF WE HADN'T...
PEACH, WHAT'S GOING ON WITH YOU?
HEY, ARE YOU GOING TO EAT THAT PEACH COBBLER?

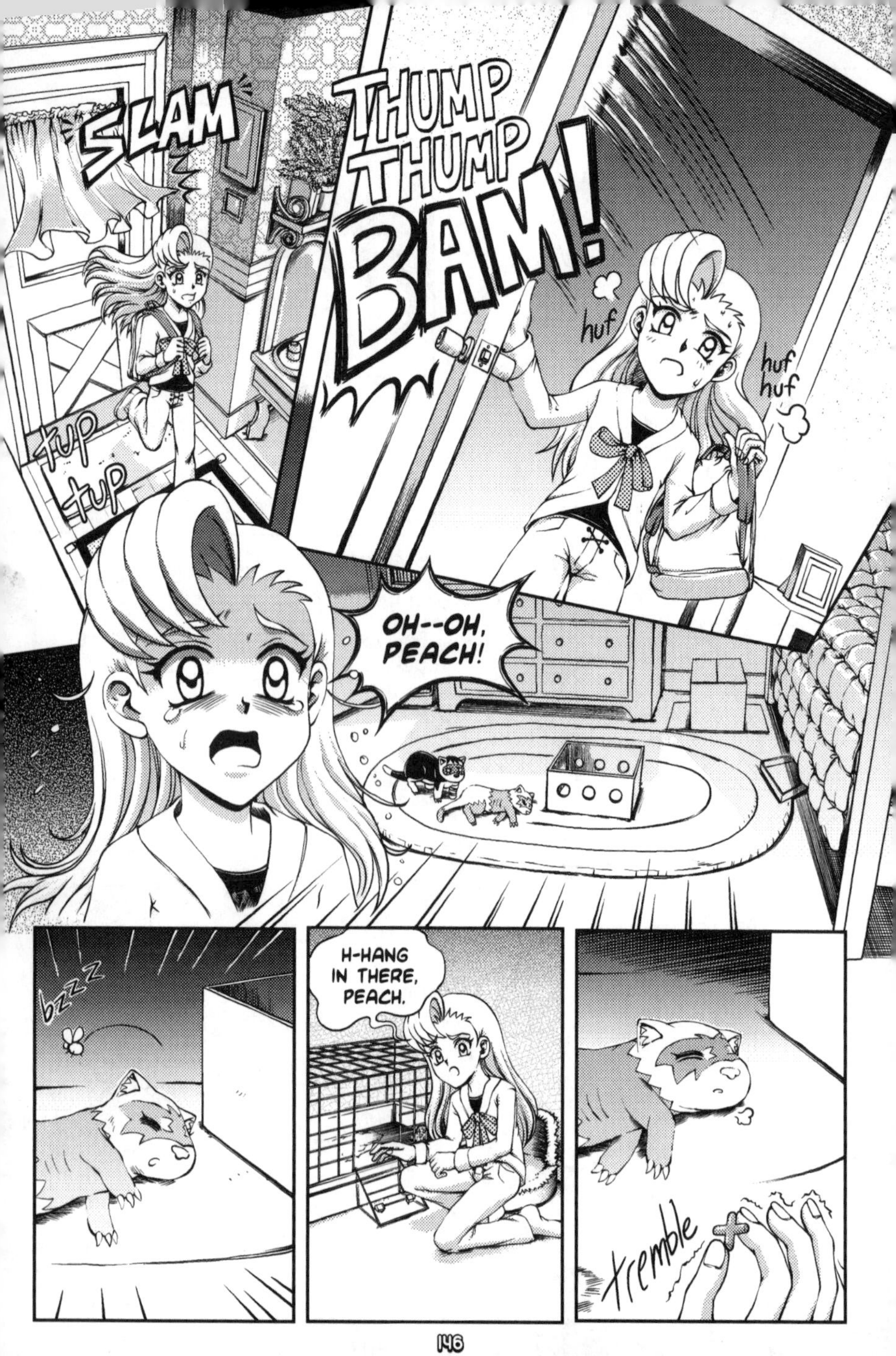

SLAM
tup tup
THUMP THUMP
BAM!
huf
huf huf
OH--OH, PEACH!
bzzz
H-HANG IN THERE, PEACH.
tremble

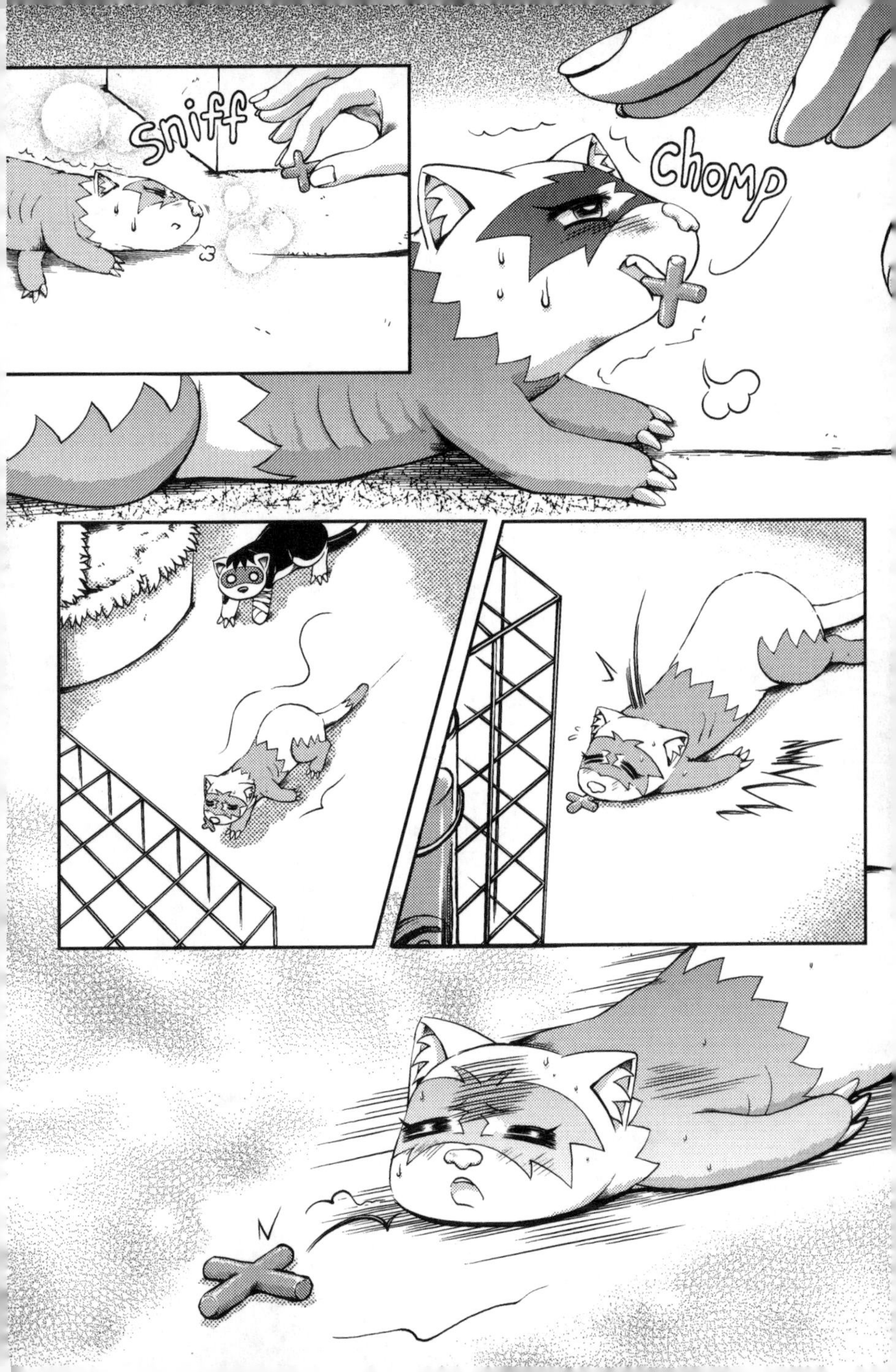
Sniff
Chomp

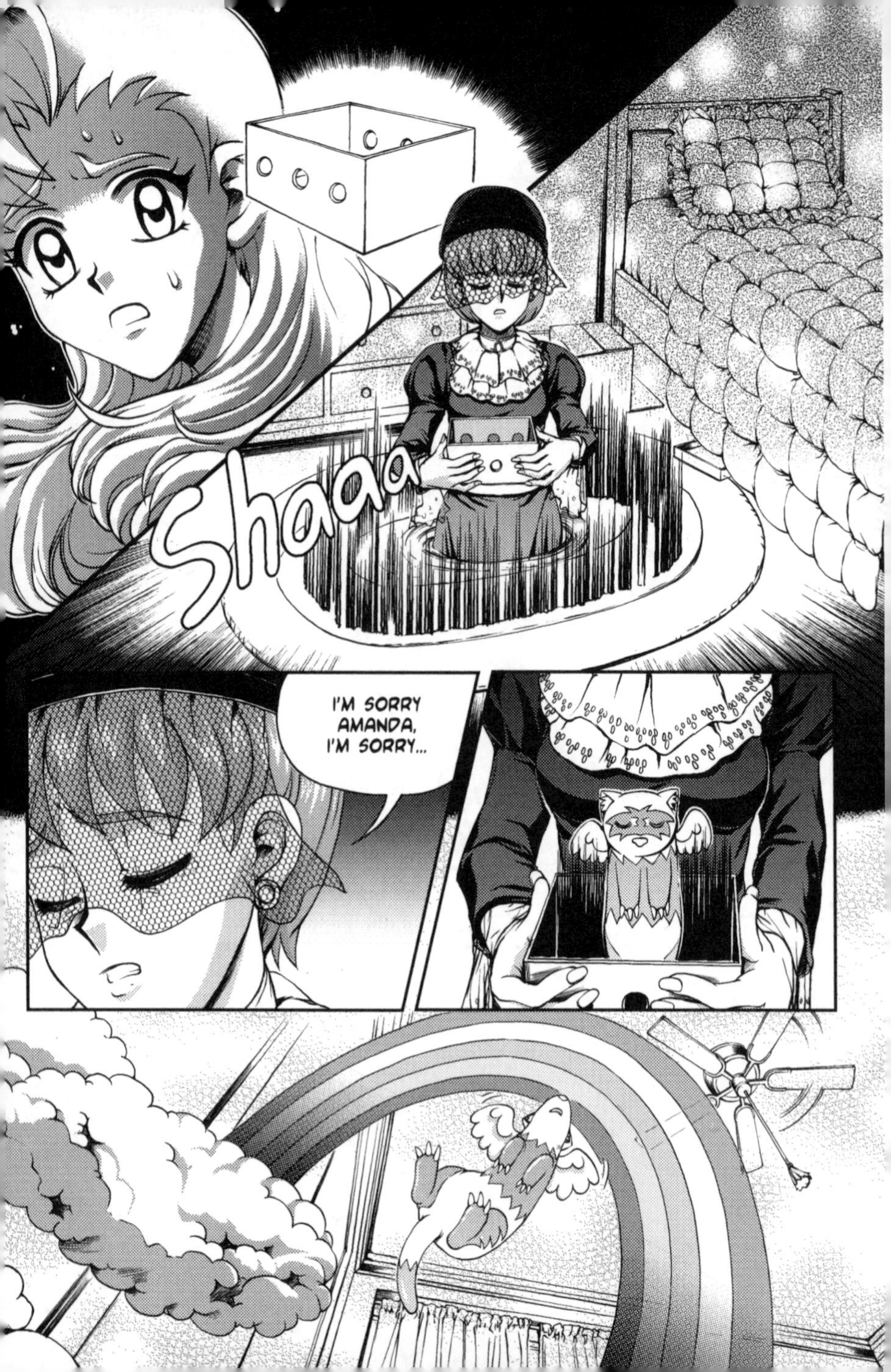
Shaaa
I'M SORRY AMANDA, I'M SORRY...

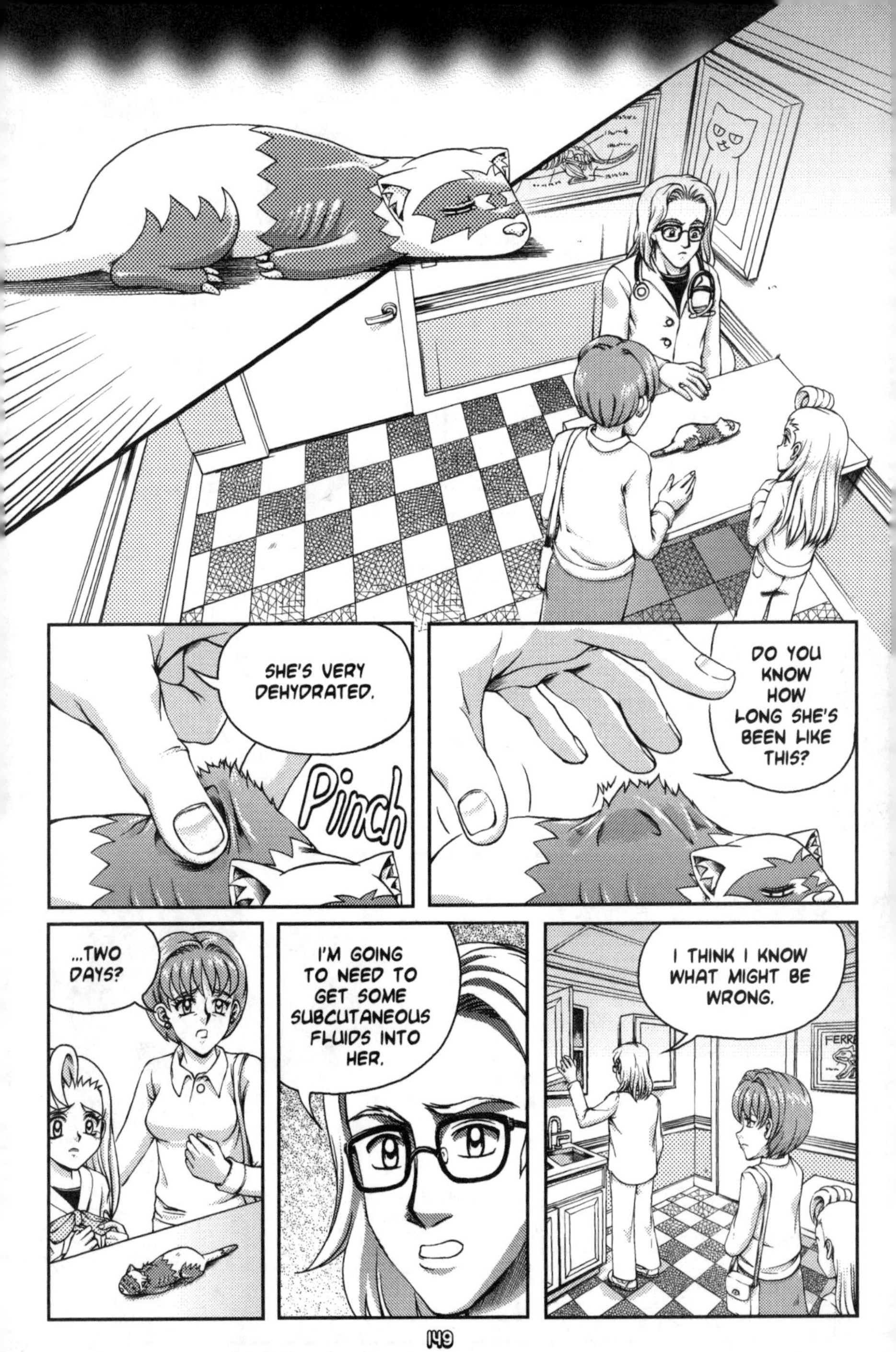
SHE'S VERY DEHYDRATED.
Pinch
DO YOU KNOW HOW LONG SHE'S BEEN LIKE THIS?
...TWO DAYS?
I'M GOING TO NEED TO GET SOME SUBCUTANEOUS FLUIDS INTO HER.
I THINK I KNOW WHAT MIGHT BE WRONG.

TAKING INTO CONSIDERATION HER SYMPTOMS...

...LETHARGY, GREEN, MUCOUSY STOOL, AND REFUSAL TO DRINK OR EAT...

...IT SEEMS LIKELY THAT YOUR FERRET HAS EPIZOOTIC CATARRHAL ENTERITIS...

...OR *E.C.E.* FOR SHORT.

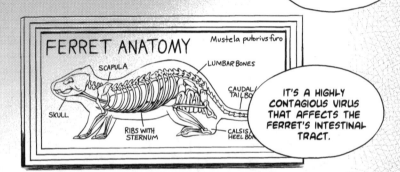

FERRET ANATOMY

Mustela putorius furo

SCAPULA

LUMBAR BONES

CAUDAL/ TAILBONE

SKULL

RIBS WITH STERNUM

CALSIS HEEL BONE

IT'S A HIGHLY CONTAGIOUS VIRUS THAT AFFECTS THE FERRET'S INTESTINAL TRACT.

IT HITS SOME FERRETS HARDER THAN OTHERS.

IT'S ONE OF THOSE DISEASES WE REALLY NEED TO KEEP A CLOSE EYE ON...

...BECAUSE IT'S A POTENTIAL KILLER.

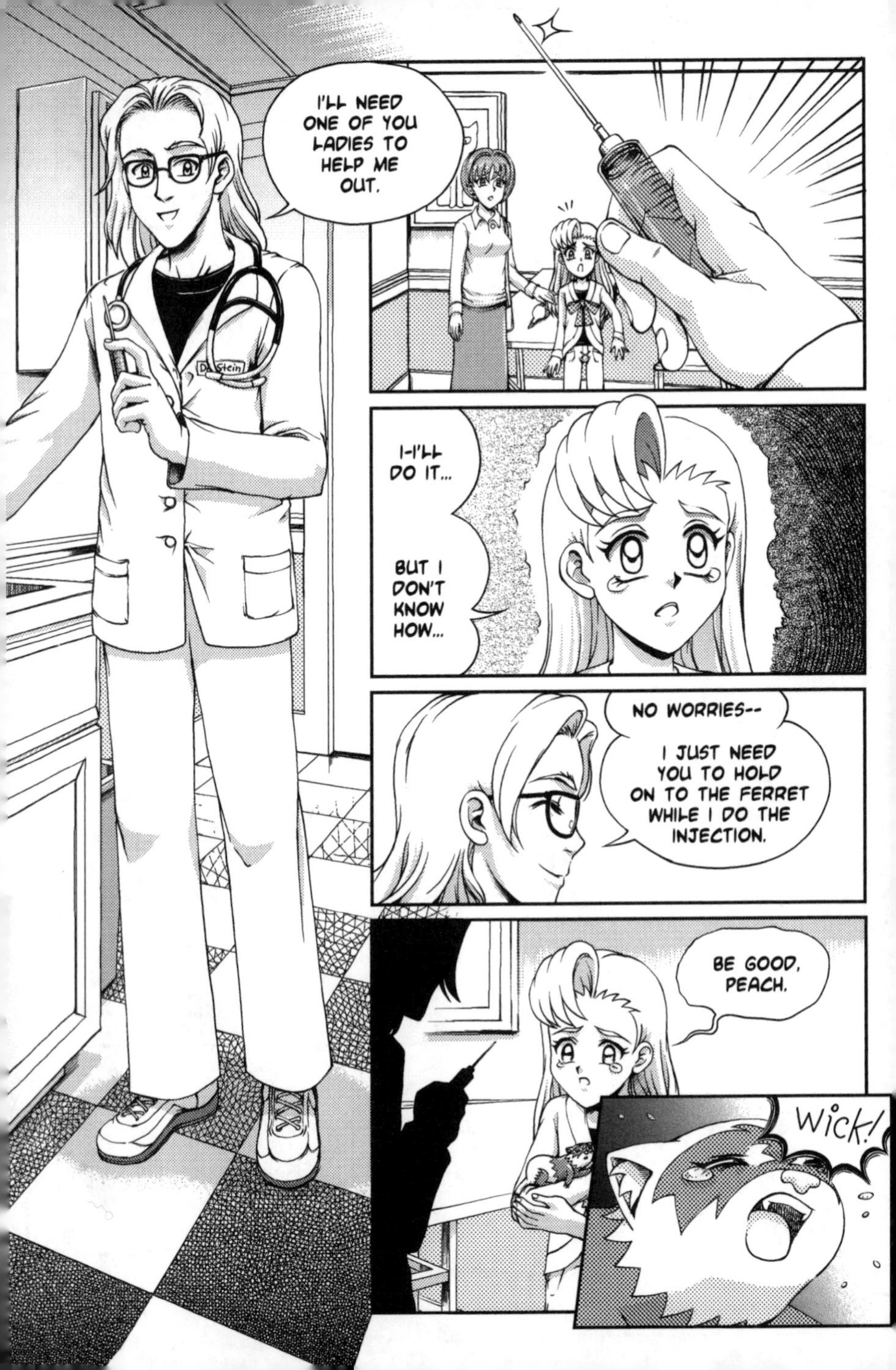
I'LL NEED ONE OF YOU LADIES TO HELP ME OUT.
I-I'LL DO IT...
BUT I DON'T KNOW HOW...
NO WORRIES--
I JUST NEED YOU TO HOLD ON TO THE FERRET WHILE I DO THE INJECTION.
BE GOOD, PEACH.
WICK!

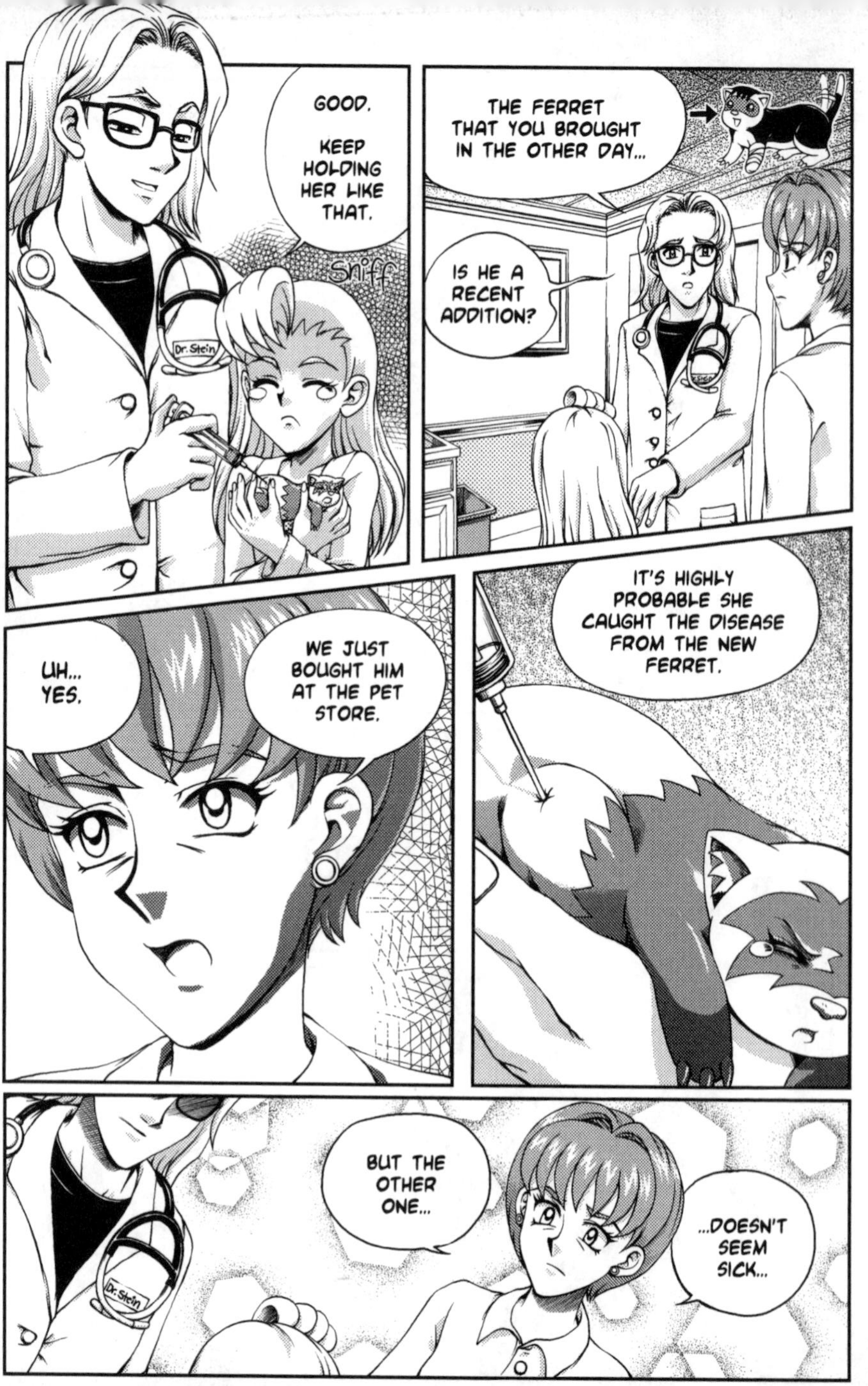
GOOD.
KEEP HOLDING HER LIKE THAT.
Sniff
Dr. Stein
THE FERRET THAT YOU BROUGHT IN THE OTHER DAY...
IS HE A RECENT ADDITION?
UH... YES.
WE JUST BOUGHT HIM AT THE PET STORE.
IT'S HIGHLY PROBABLE SHE CAUGHT THE DISEASE FROM THE NEW FERRET.
BUT THE OTHER ONE...
...DOESN'T SEEM SICK...
Dr. Stein

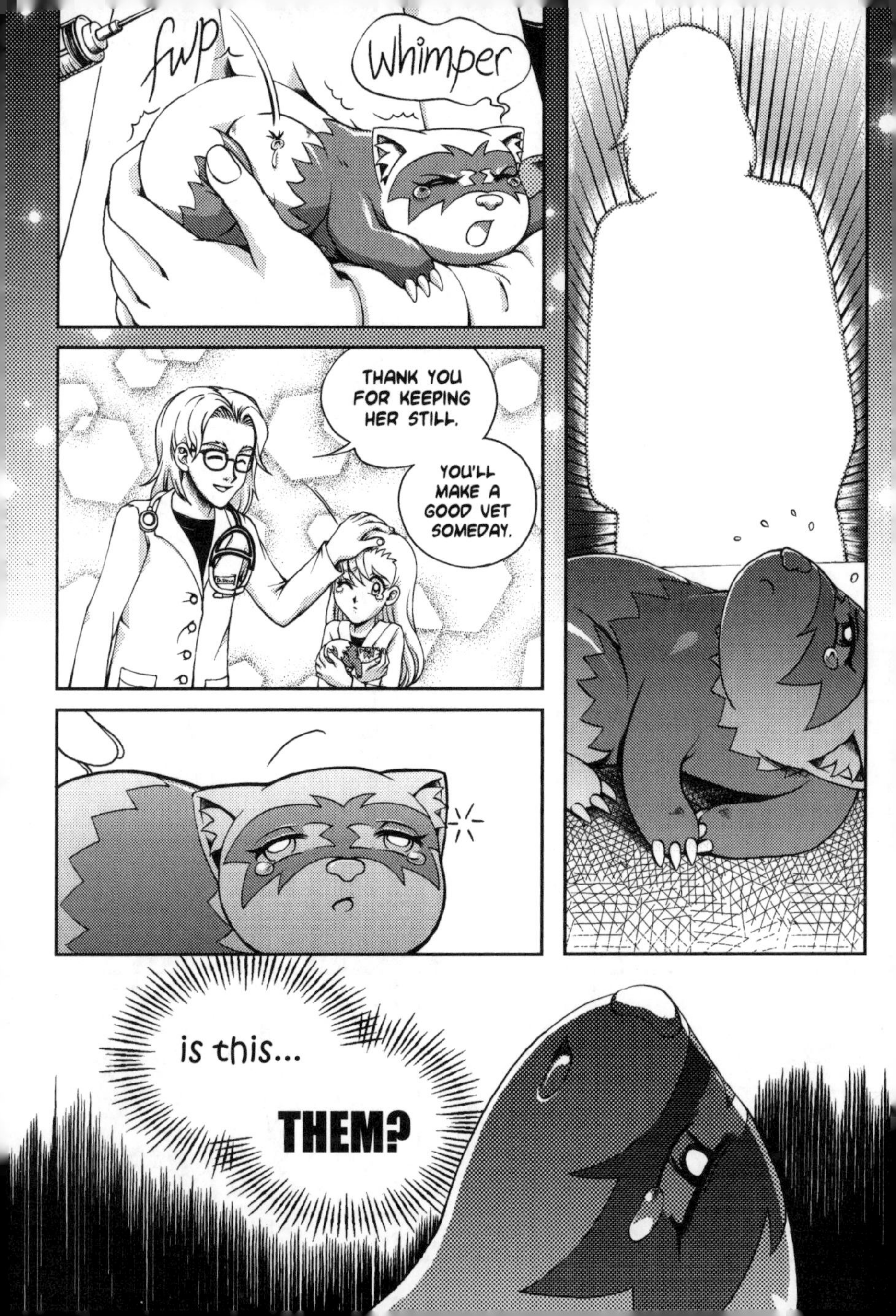
fwp
whimper
THANK YOU FOR KEEPING HER STILL.
YOU'LL MAKE A GOOD VET SOMEDAY.
is this...
THEM?

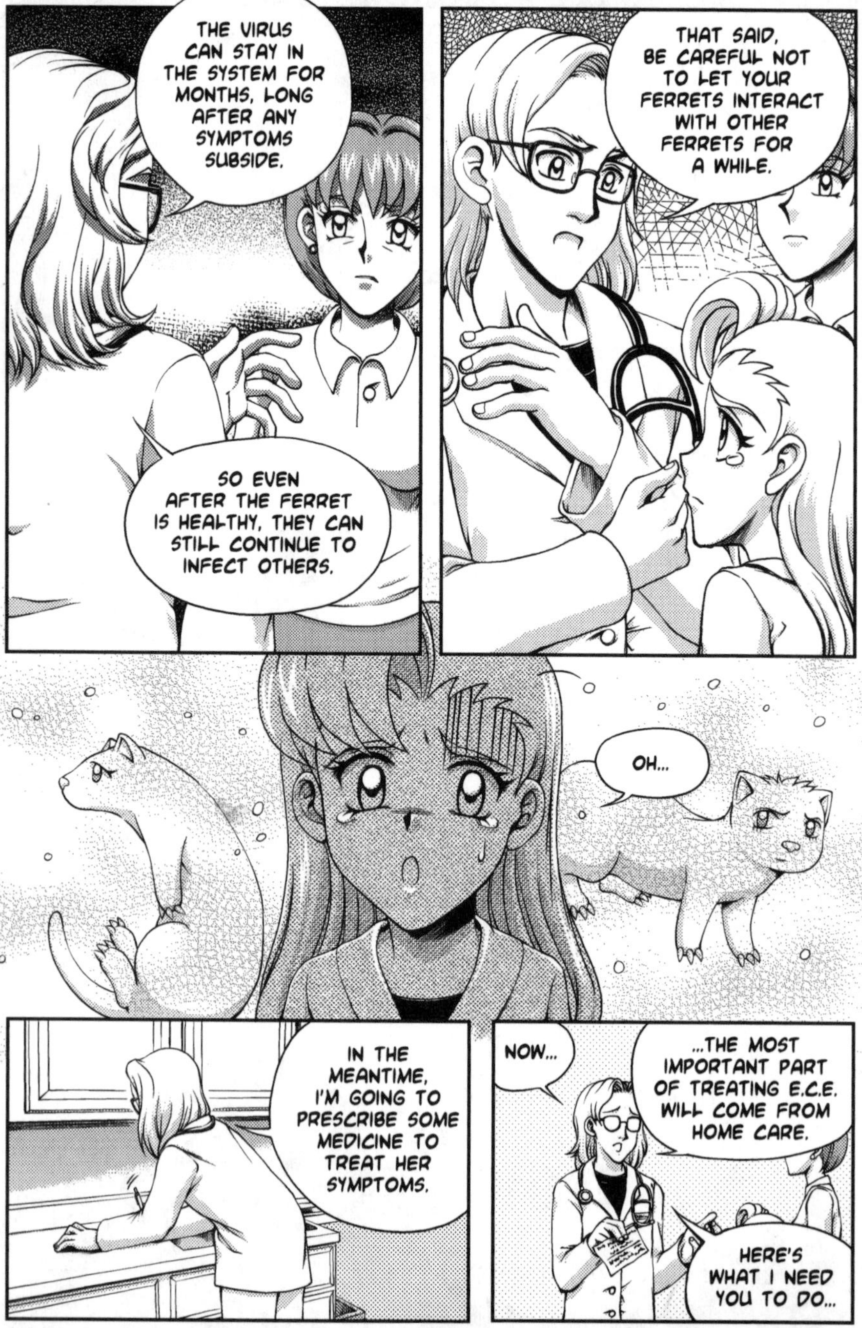
THE VIRUS CAN STAY IN THE SYSTEM FOR MONTHS, LONG AFTER ANY SYMPTOMS SUBSIDE.
SO EVEN AFTER THE FERRET IS HEALTHY, THEY CAN STILL CONTINUE TO INFECT OTHERS.
THAT SAID, BE CAREFUL NOT TO LET YOUR FERRETS INTERACT WITH OTHER FERRETS FOR A WHILE.
OH...
IN THE MEANTIME, I'M GOING TO PRESCRIBE SOME MEDICINE TO TREAT HER SYMPTOMS.
NOW...
...THE MOST IMPORTANT PART OF TREATING E.C.E. WILL COME FROM HOME CARE.
HERE'S WHAT I NEED YOU TO DO...

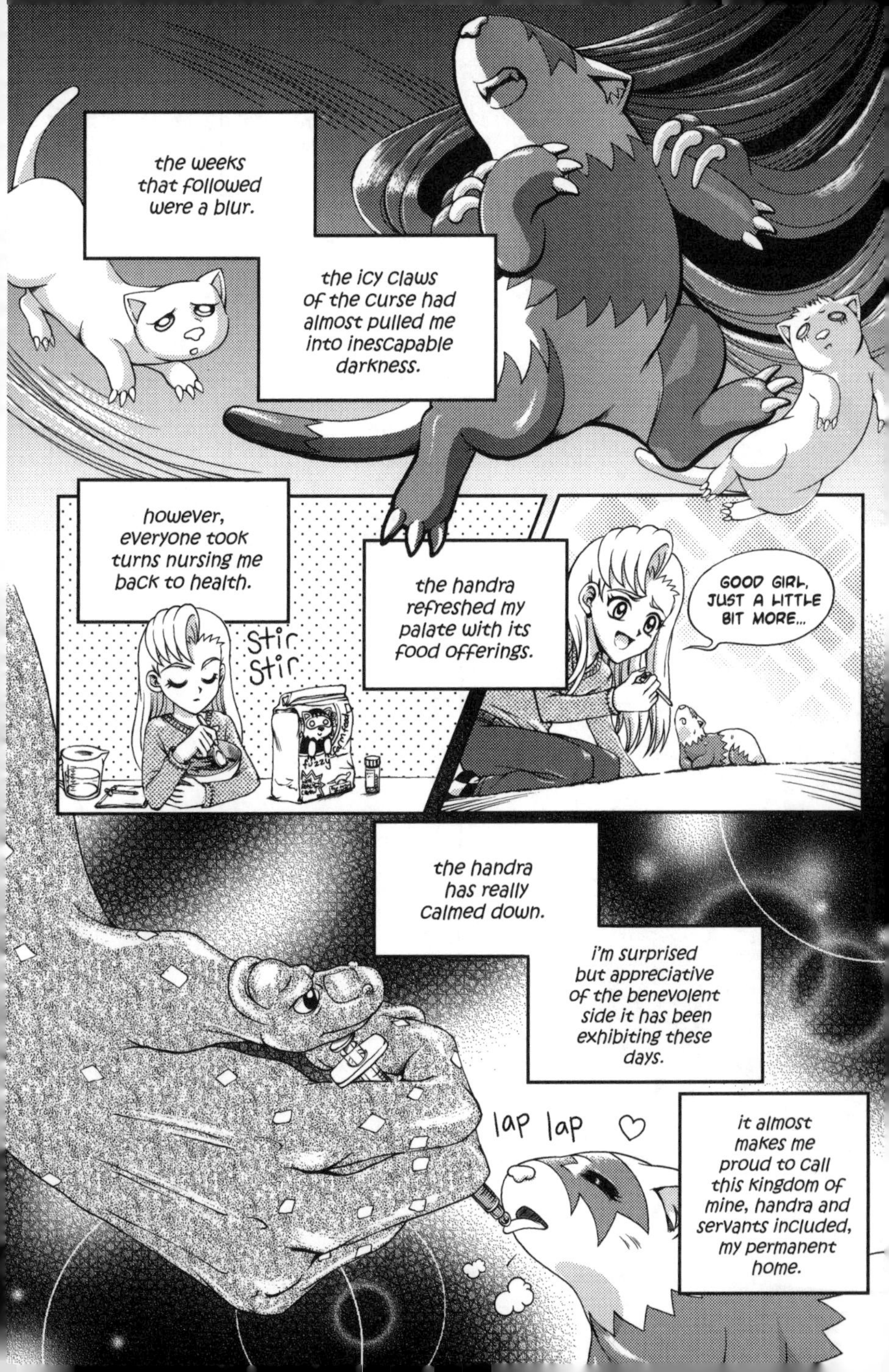

the weeks that followed were a blur.
the icy claws of the curse had almost pulled me into inescapable darkness.
however, everyone took turns nursing me back to health.
Stir Stir
fuzzy
the handra refreshed my palate with its food offerings.
GOOD GIRL, JUST A LITTLE BIT MORE...
the handra has really calmed down.
i'm surprised but appreciative of the benevolent side it has been exhibiting these days.
lap lap ♡
it almost makes me proud to call this kingdom of mine, handra and servants included, my permanent home.

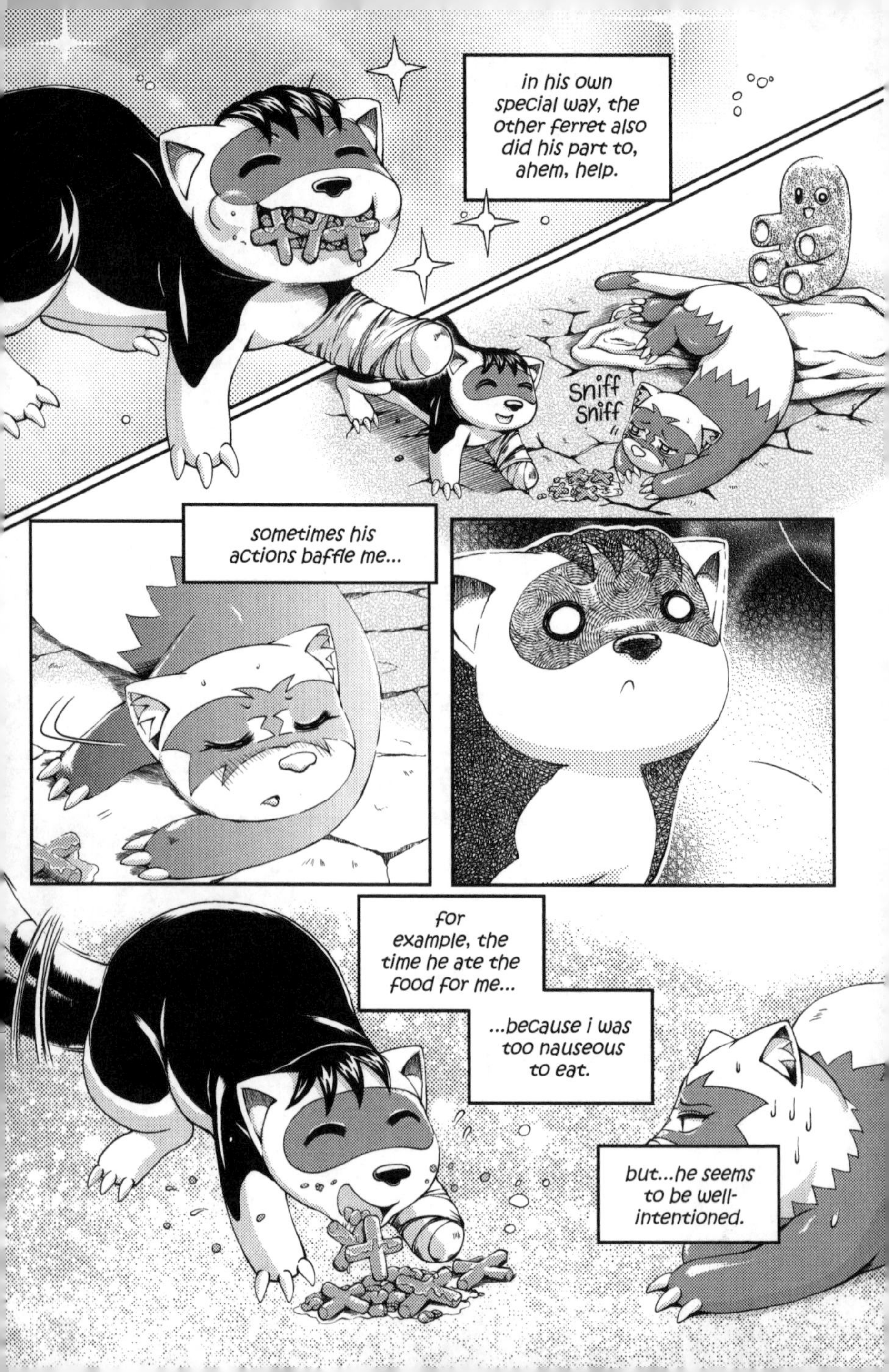
in his own special way, the other ferret also did his part to, ahem, help.
Sniff sniff
sometimes his actions baffle me...
for example, the time he ate the food for me...
...because i was too nauseous to eat.
but...he seems to be well-intentioned.

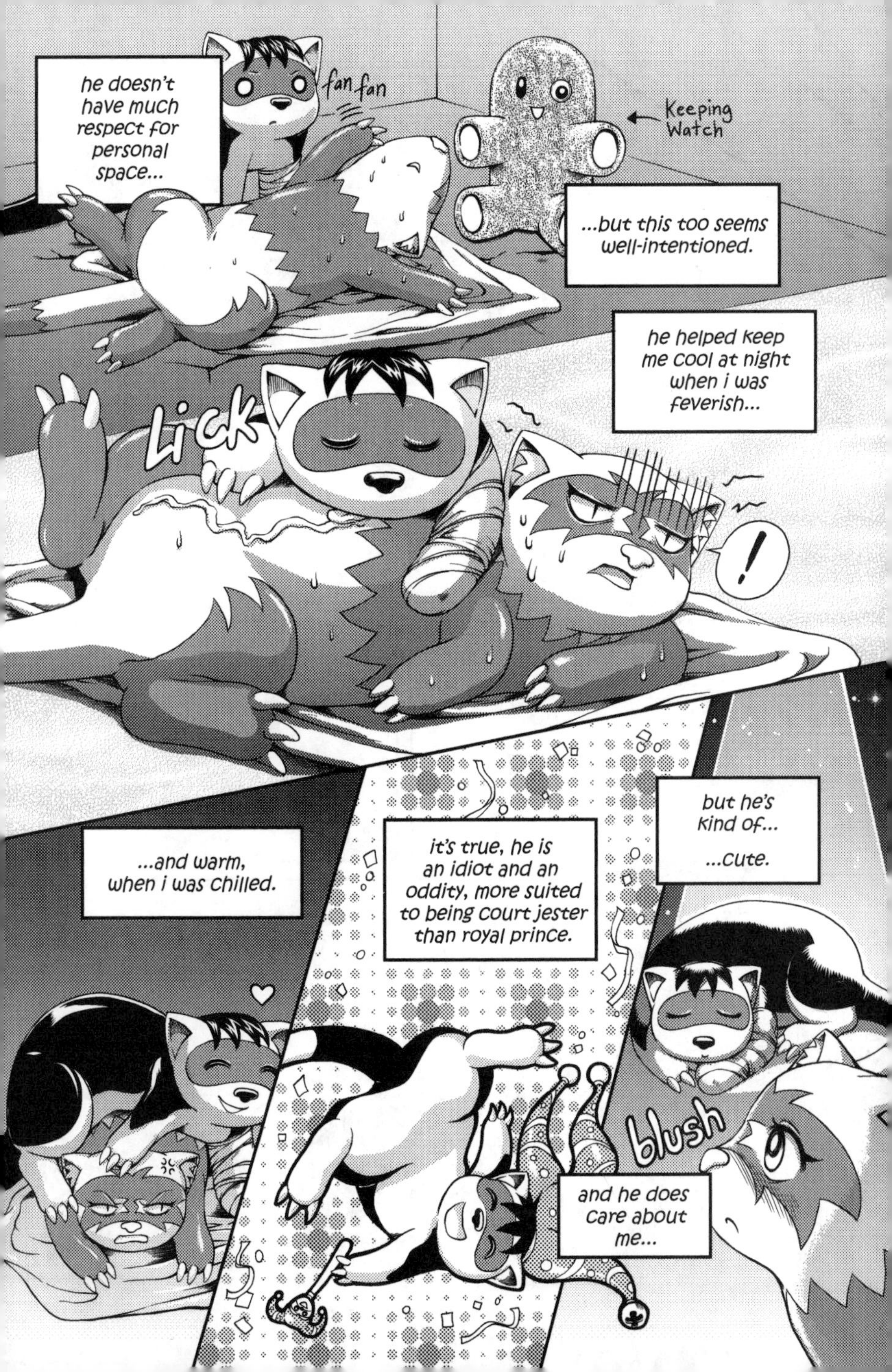

he doesn't have much respect for personal space...
fan fan
Keeping Watch
...but this too seems well-intentioned.
he helped keep me cool at night when i was feverish...
Lick
!
...and warm, when i was chilled.
it's true, he is an idiot and an oddity, more suited to being court jester than royal prince.
but he's kind of...
...cute.
blush
and he does care about me...

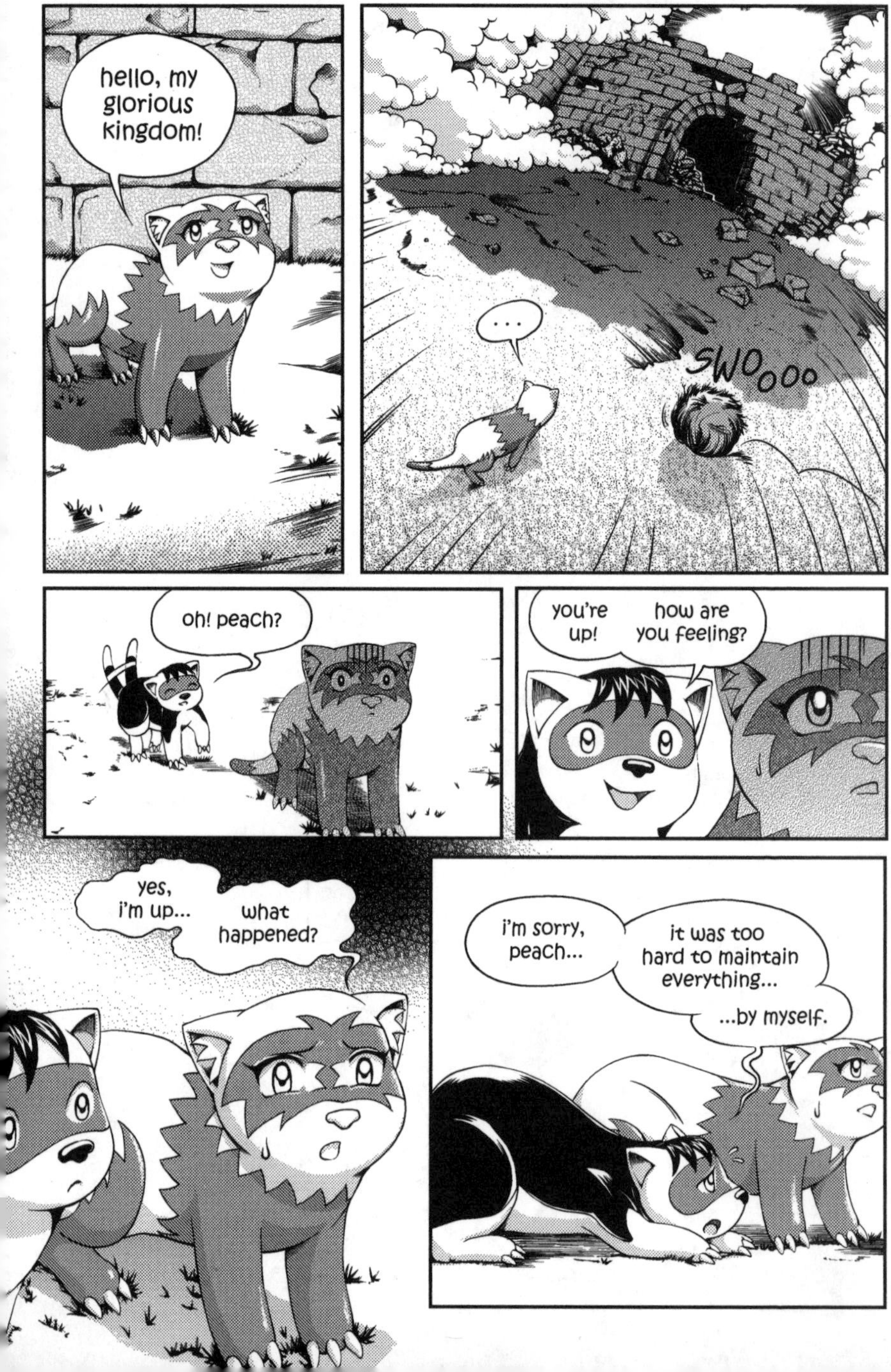
hello, my glorious kingdom!
...
SWOOOOO
oh! peach?
you're up!
how are you feeling?
yes, i'm up...
what happened?
i'm sorry, peach...
it was too hard to maintain everything...
...by myself.

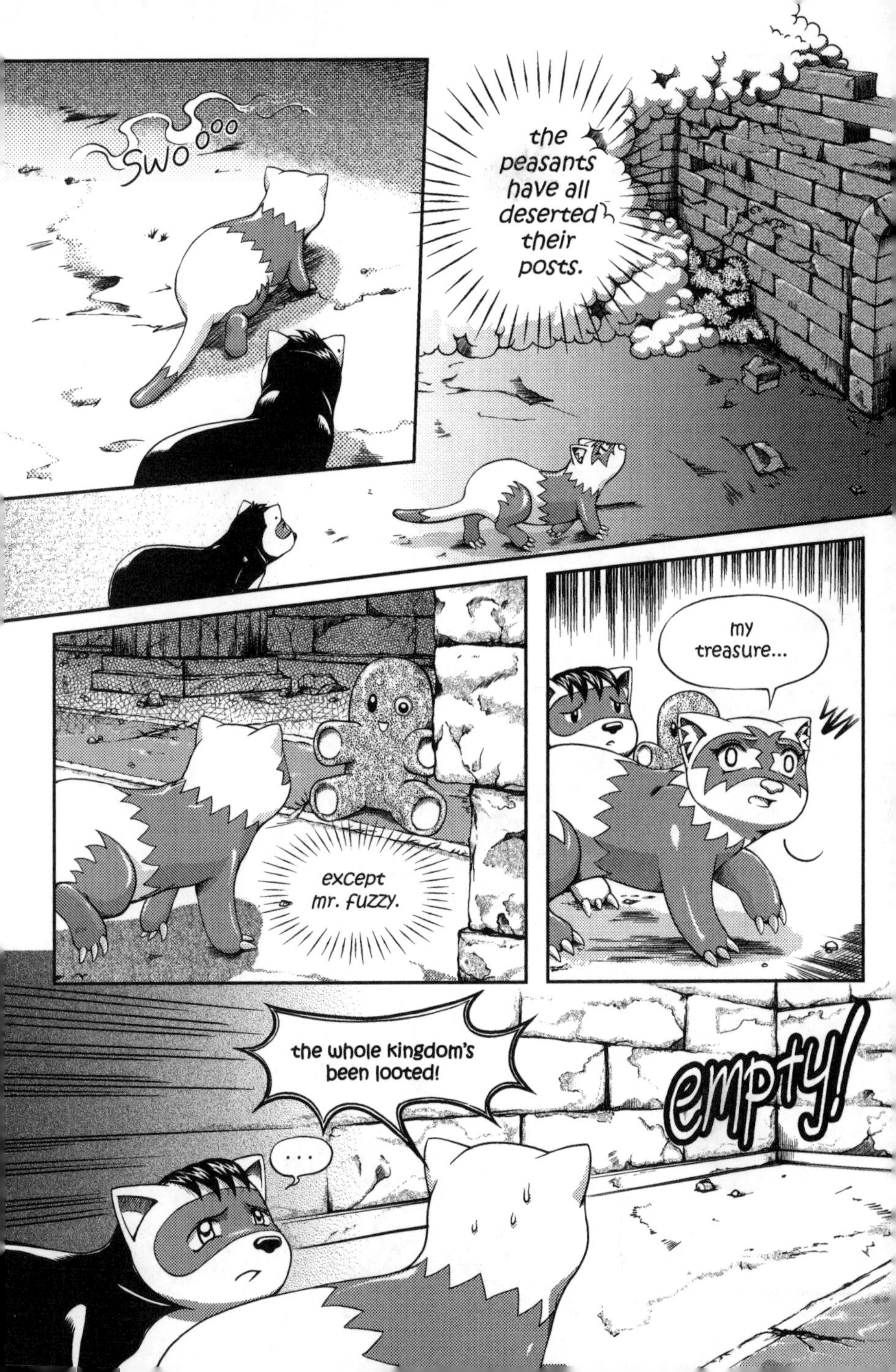
SWOOOO
the peasants have all deserted their posts.
except mr. fuzzy.
my treasure...
the whole kingdom's been looted!
...
empty!

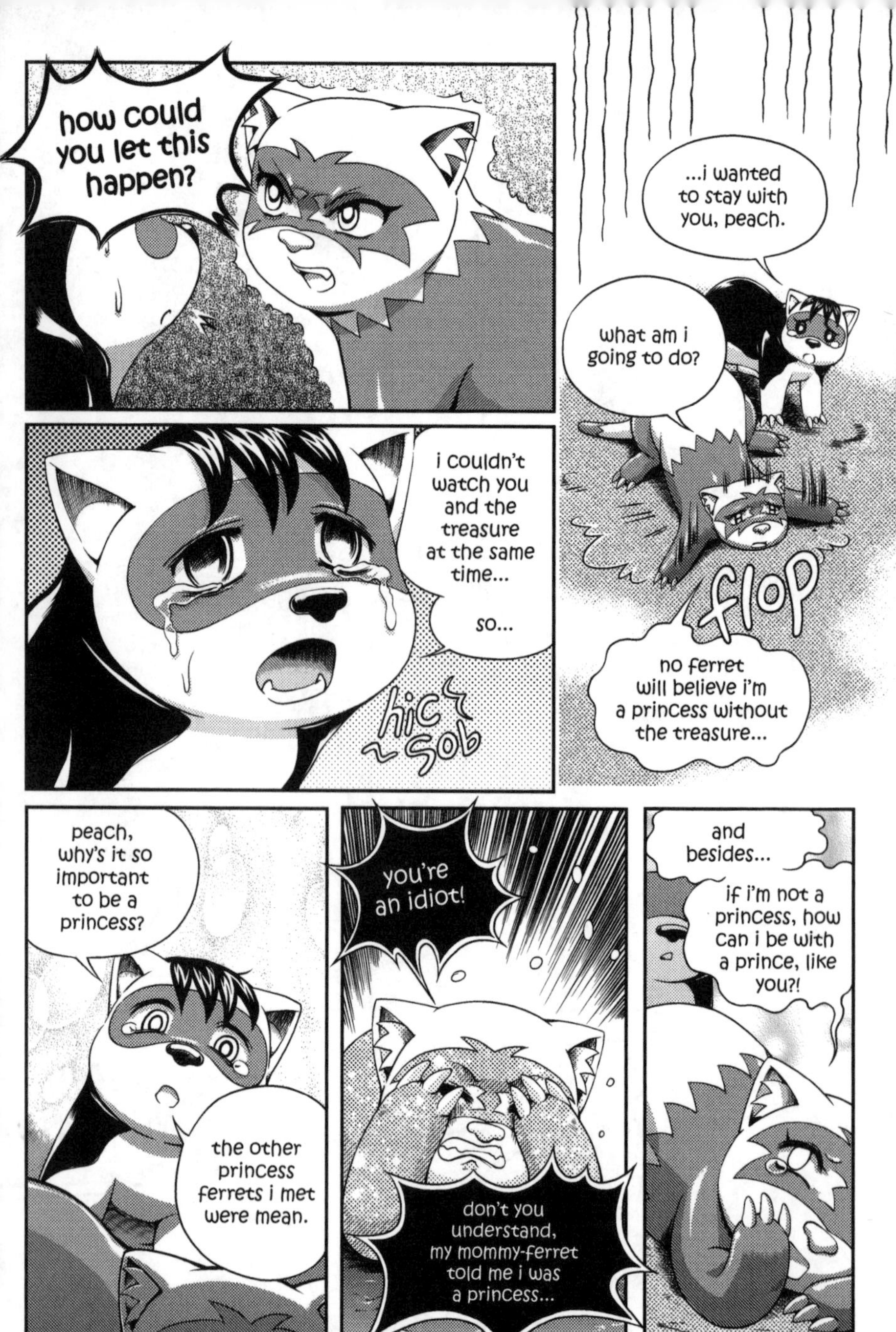
how could you let this happen?
i couldn't watch you and the treasure at the same time...
so...
hic ~sob
...i wanted to stay with you, peach.
what am i going to do?
flop
no ferret will believe i'm a princess without the treasure...
peach, why's it so important to be a princess?
the other princess ferrets i met were mean.
you're an idiot!
don't you understand, my mommy-ferret told me i was a princess...
and besides...
if i'm not a princess, how can i be with a prince, like you?!

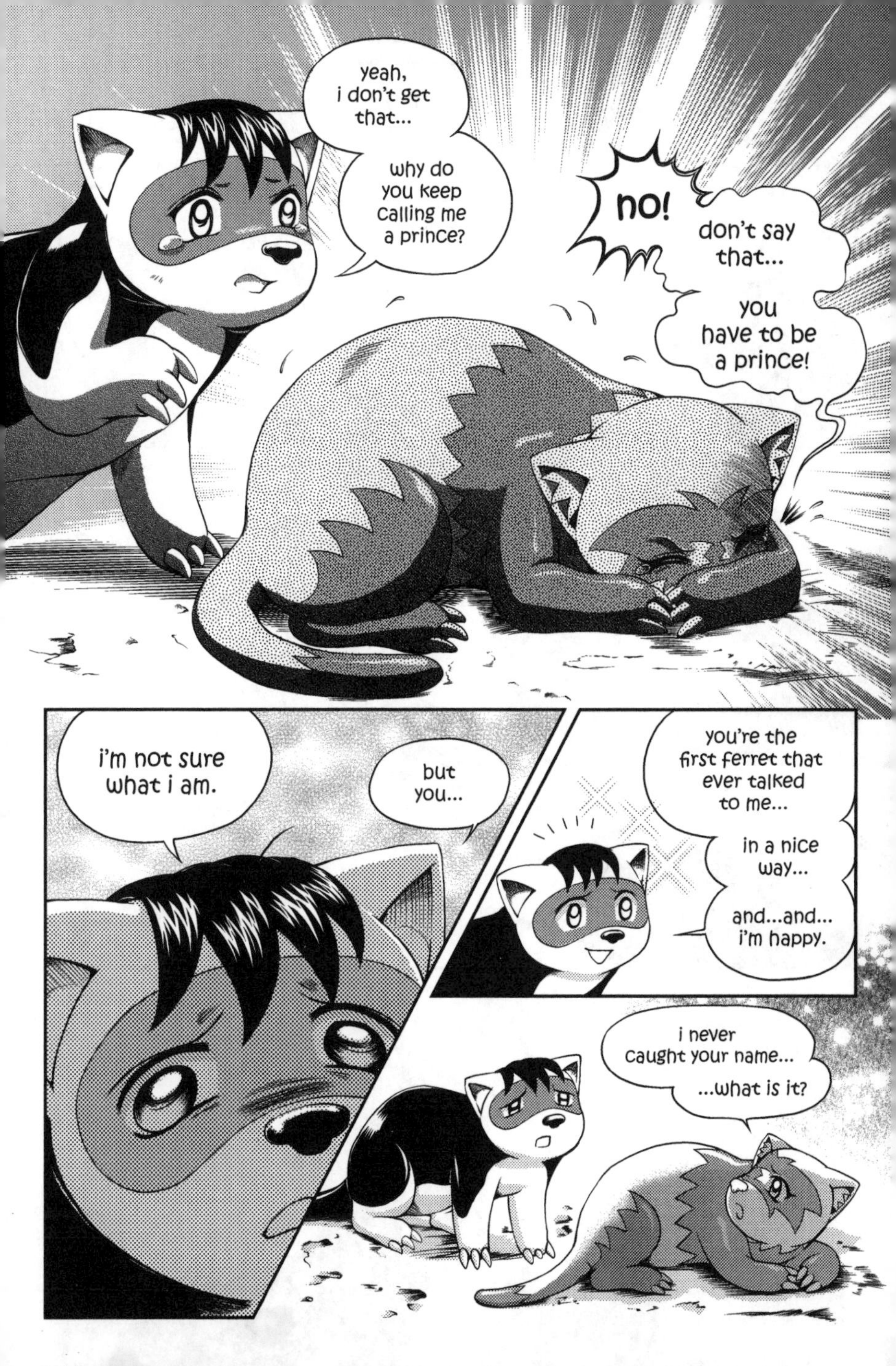
yeah, i don't get that...
why do you keep calling me a prince?
no!
don't say that...
you have to be a prince!
i'm not sure what i am.
but you...
you're the first ferret that ever talked to me...
in a nice way...
and...and... i'm happy.
i never caught your name...
...what is it?

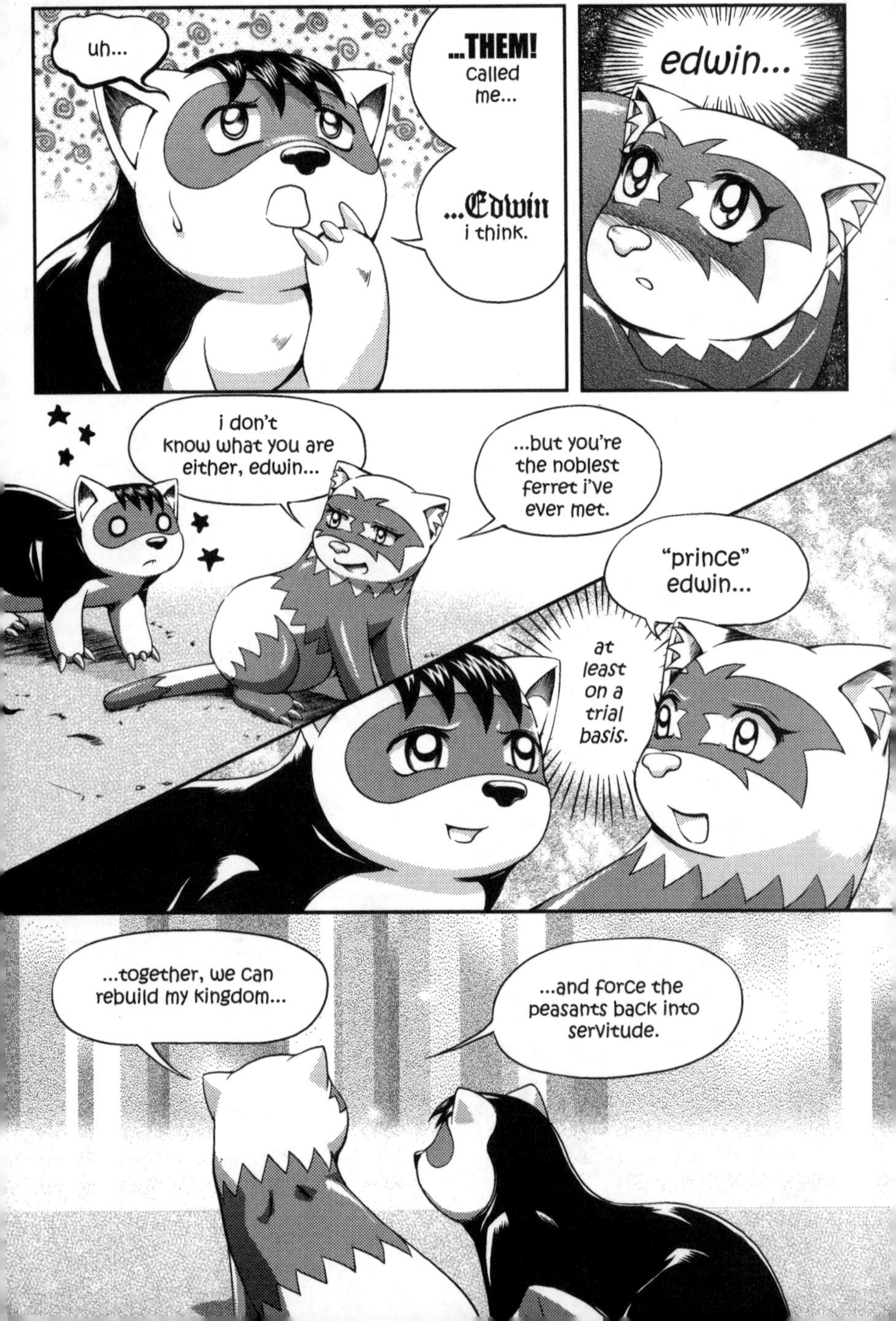
uh...
...THEM! called me...
...Edwin i think.
edwin...
i don't know what you are either, edwin...
...but you're the noblest ferret i've ever met.
"prince" edwin...
at least on a trial basis.
...together, we can rebuild my kingdom...
...and force the peasants back into servitude.

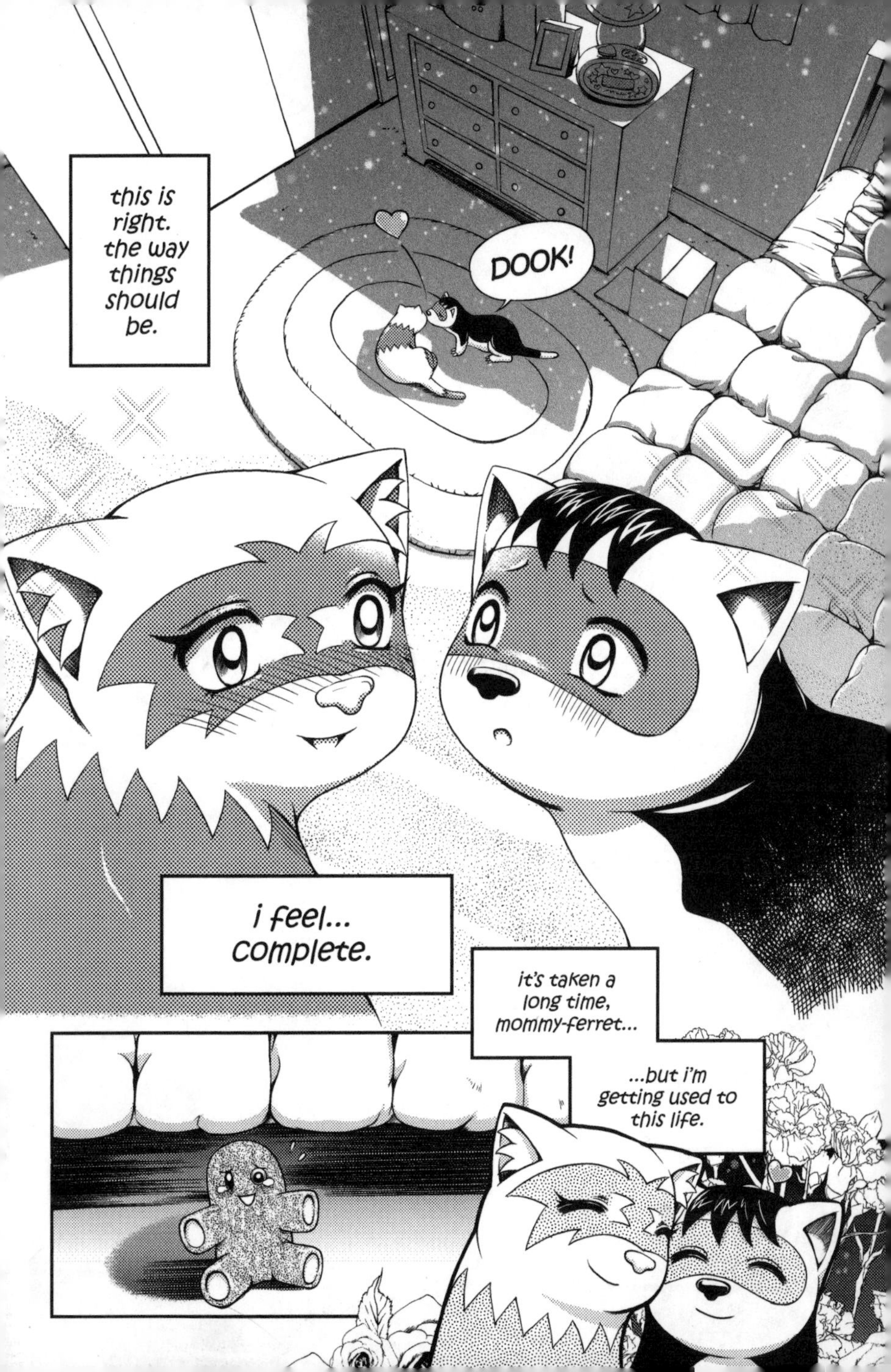
this is right. the way things should be.
DOOK!
i feel... complete.
it's taken a long time, mommy-ferret...
...but i'm getting used to this life.

The End.

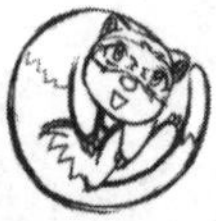

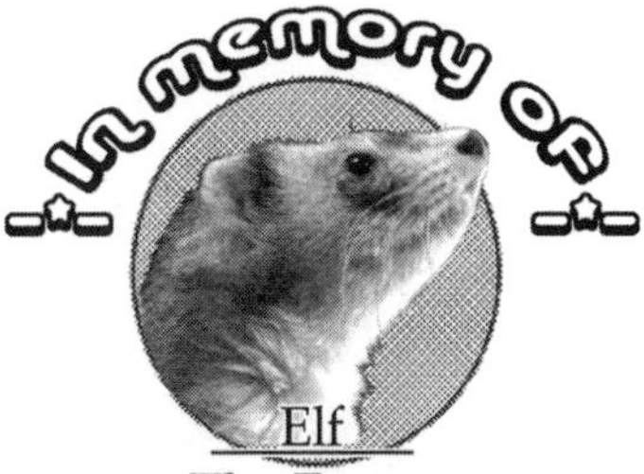
In memory of
Elf

The Ferret

AUGUST 2001-APRIL 2006

The quirky character Edwin was inspired by a real-life ferret named Elf. Born around August 9th, 2001, this little guy charmed Jared and me with his cute face and unusual mannerisms.

Elf had a funny way of drinking water. He always pawed at his water bottle to prep it for drinking, and pawed the ground before drinking from the bathtub. When eating, he would situate himself so that half of his body was still hanging out the cage. He was obsessed with a pair of headphones, and would intensely search a place from top to bottom to find them. Once retrieved, he would spend hours guarding them from would-be thieves. He never liked to be held or go on walks, but this too was a cute quirk that made Elf Elf.

In December 2005, halfway through the creation of *Peach Fuzz* Volume 2, Elf's health suddenly took a nosedive. He was diagnosed with Lymphoma (cancer of the lymph nodes). Chemotherapy and medicine helped extend his life, but eventually, after a long and difficult battle, he passed away at around 9:05 A.M. Saturday morning, April 15th, 2006.

Rest in peace, little mink, we'll miss you!

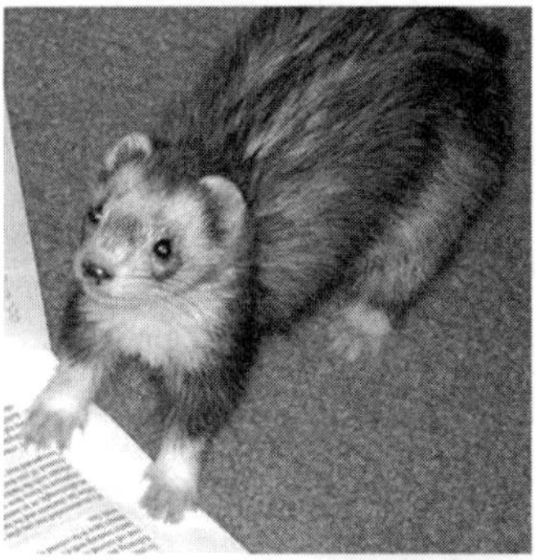

Elf, helping out with the *Peach Fuzz* volume 2 script.

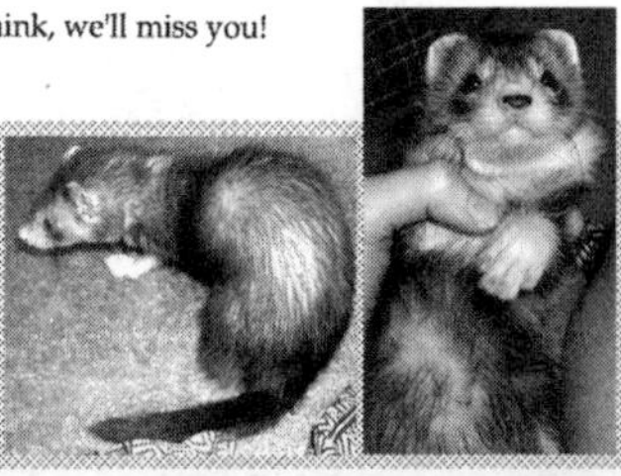

Elf as a baby ferret.

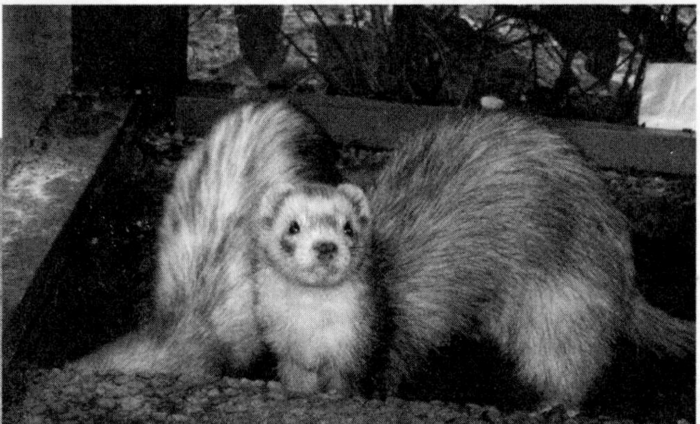

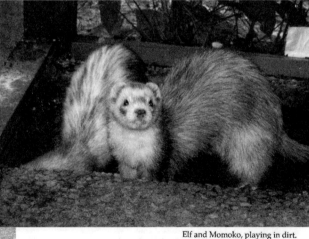

Elf and Momoko, playing in dirt.

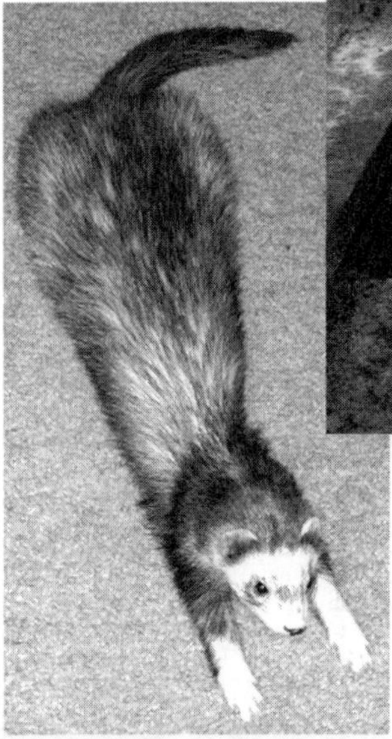

Elf in his popular sphinx pose.

Losing a loved one is difficult. If you have a special fuzzy friend in your life, give them a hug and treasure your time together.

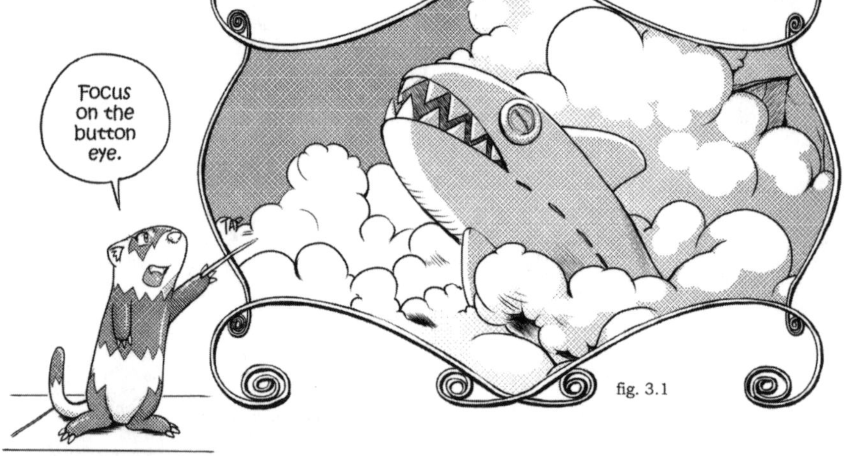
Focus on the button eye.
TAP

fig. 3.1

Mr. Shark

*A deep-sea terror...a Great White...with two rows of razor-sharp teeth, incredible agility, and a massive muscular frame...*Mr. Shark was a force to be reckoned with—even during my time as a hardened gladiator. It was only through sheer luck that I managed to escape becoming shark food in that fateful encounter. Or so I thought...

A former enemy, Mr. Shark, whose name I later learned to be Greaticus Whiticus, is a cloud shark who controls a neighboring domain, high above the boundaries of my kingdom. He looks mean and menacing, but I've come to discover that Mr. Shark is actually a big softy. His teeth, for example, are spongy and incapable of piercing, and he far prefers tea parties and cuddling to battling and bloodshed.

The Handra Connection

When I first met Mr. Shark, he was unrelenting and aggressive in his assault. Upon reflection, I've come up with two possible theories for this uncharacteristic behavior: 1) Mr. Shark felt he was threatened by my invasion of his territory, or 2) the Handra were controlling Mr. Shark at the time and forcing him to fight me, much like how the Handra forced me to battle against Mr. Fuzzy.

Mr. Shark has the quiet, patient demeanor of a great listener. His prior ties and frequent bonding with the Handra make him a somewhat untrustworthy ally, but as long as you're careful about not divulging information you don't want the Handra to know, Mr. Shark is a great go-to guy for free counseling.

Land of the Clouds

The soft clouds billowing over the walls of my castle lead up to the Domain of Greaticus Whiticus, also known as Land of the Clouds, a fluffy-white wonderland shepherded by its sole resident, Mr. Shark.

A realm of peace and tranquility, it is no wonder the Handra prefers to spend its nights sleeping there. It is my belief that the Handra and Mr. Shark have worked out some sort of time-sharing arrangement for use of the cloudland, as evidenced by Mr. Shark's patrol during the day and the Handra's presence during the night.

The domain is difficult (but not impossible) for ferrets to reach, but most of the time I prefer to keep my feet planted firmly in the safety of my kingdom.

Peach Fuzz

Concept Art Collection

Peach Fuzz began life as a short webcomic inspired by the authors' two real-life ferrets, Momoko and Elf. In 2003, a short story based on the series placed grand prize in TOKYOPOP's second *Rising Stars of Manga* contest. From there, it grew into the series you are now holding in your hands. Since then, it has been translated into other languages and even syndicated in newspapers nationwide.

The following pages showcase some of the preproduction work that went into creating *Peach Fuzz* vol. 3, including character designs, costume designs, rough sketches, scenery, and story details.

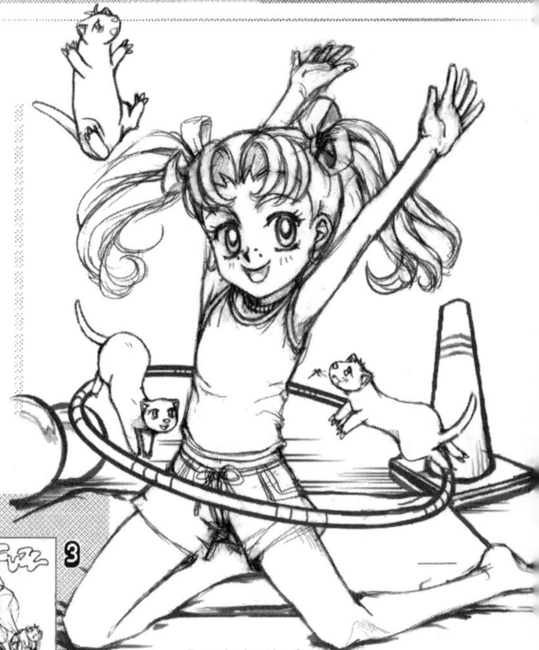

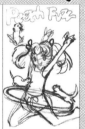

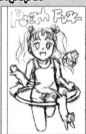

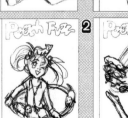

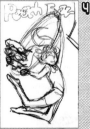

Rough sketch of Volume 3 cover.

Cover Art Concepts

Peach Fuzz
1
Peach Fuzz
3
Peach Fuzz
2
Peach Fuzz
4

Peach Fuzz volume 3's cover features Amanda's cheerful best friend Mimi and her fuzzy albino ferrets Spore, Puffball, and Truffle engaged in one of their favorite activities, gymnastics!

With the basic idea in mind, Jared and I brainstormed potential layouts and came up with four rough concepts. In each one, our goal was to create a cover design as energetic and fun as Mimi, with lots of movement and excitement. It was a difficult choice, but we eventually settled on number 1.
--Lindsay

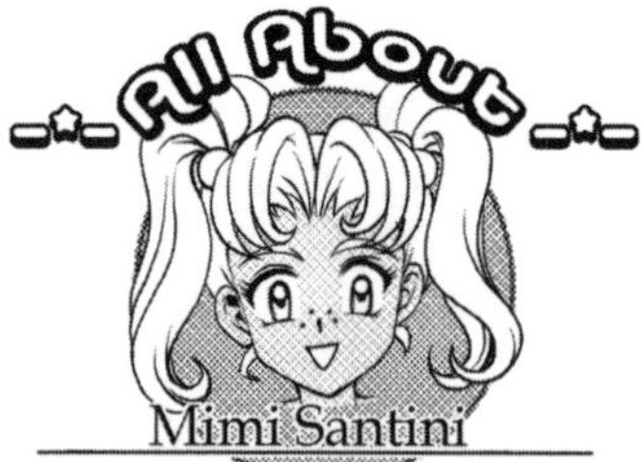
All About
Mimi Santini

Birthdate: December 21
Age: 9
Sign: Sagittarius
Birthplace: Mushroom Valley, USA
Height: 4 ft. 8 in. Weight: 72 lbs.
Religion: Devout Mushinite
Favorite Color: Pink

Hobbies: Gymnastics, biking, swimming, running, sports, and singing. Also enjoys playing board games, primarily those that are physically challenging and Mushinite approved, like "Hypae Tangle."

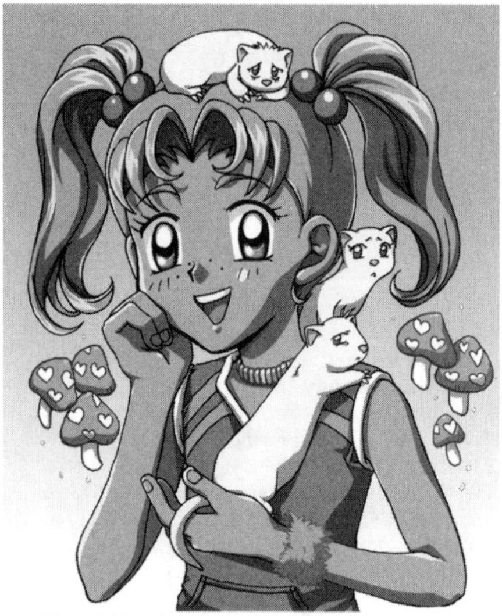

Mimi and her three albino ferrets (that's Spore on top, Truffle on her shoulder, and Puffball in her hand).

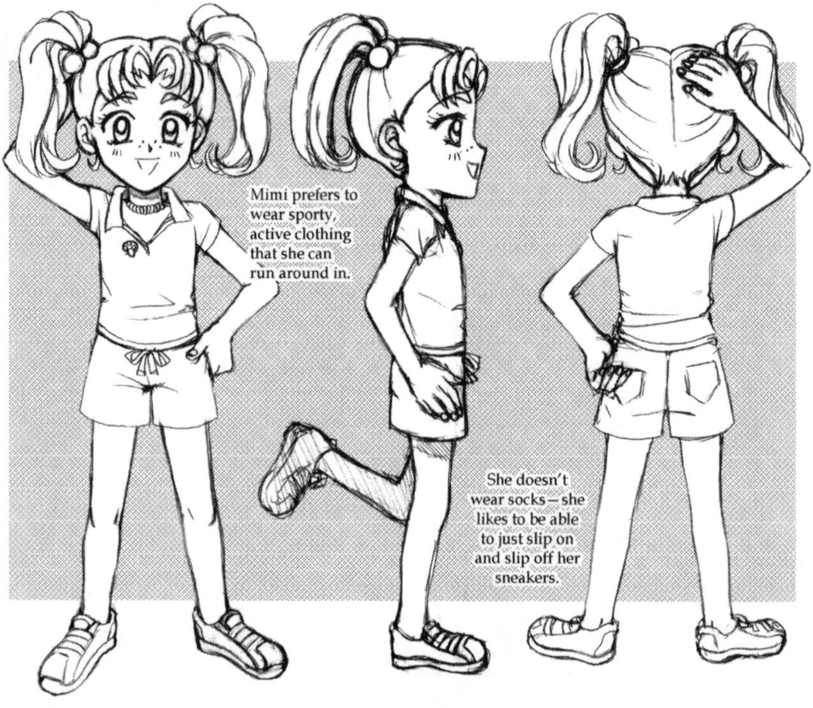
Mimi prefers to wear sporty, active clothing that she can run around in.
She doesn't wear socks—she likes to be able to just slip on and slip off her sneakers.

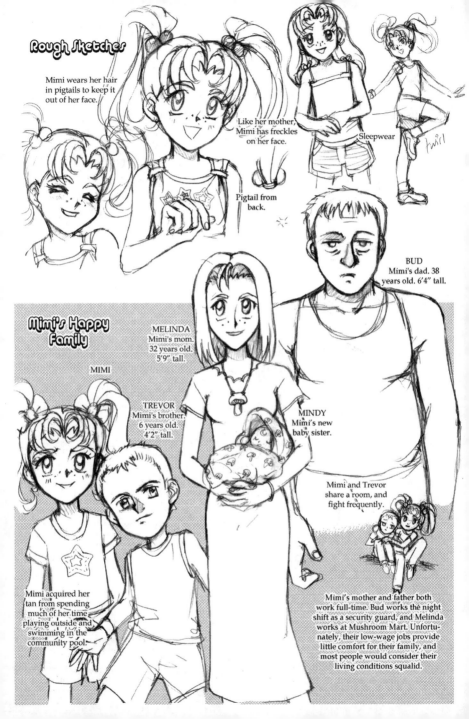

Rough Sketches

Mimi wears her hair in pigtails to keep it out of her face.

Like her mother, Mimi has freckles on her face.

Sleepwear

Pigtail from back.

BUD
Mimi's dad. 38 years old. 6'4" tall.

Mimi's Happy Family

MELINDA
Mimi's mom. 32 years old. 5'9" tall.

MIMI

TREVOR
Mimi's brother. 6 years old. 4'2" tall.

MINDY
Mimi's new baby sister.

Mimi and Trevor share a room, and fight frequently.

Mimi acquired her tan from spending much of her time playing outside and swimming in the community pool.

Mimi's mother and father both work full-time. Bud works the night shift as a security guard, and Melinda works at Mushroom Mart. Unfortunately, their low-wage jobs provide little comfort for their family, and most people would consider their living conditions squalid.

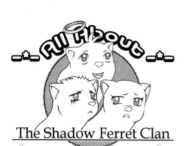

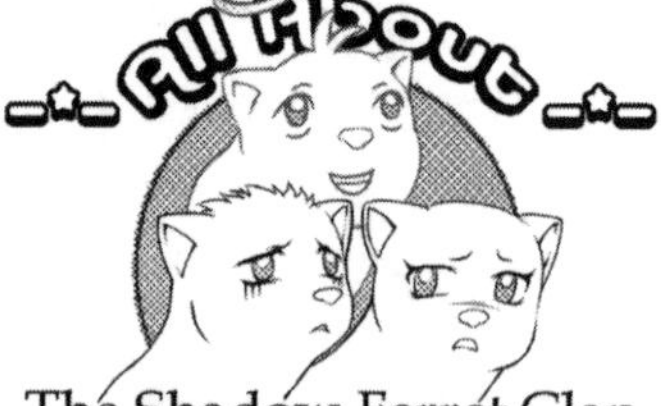
All About

The Shadow Ferret Clan

Title: Mimi's Ferret Gymnastic Troupe
Birthdate: January 26th (all three come from the same litter)
Age: Nine months old
Sign: Aquarius
Birthplace: Private breeder in MushroomValley
Length: Of the three, Truffle is the longest, Puffball the shortest.
Color: Albino

Special Skills: Trained gymnasts. Can jump farther and climb better than other ferrets.

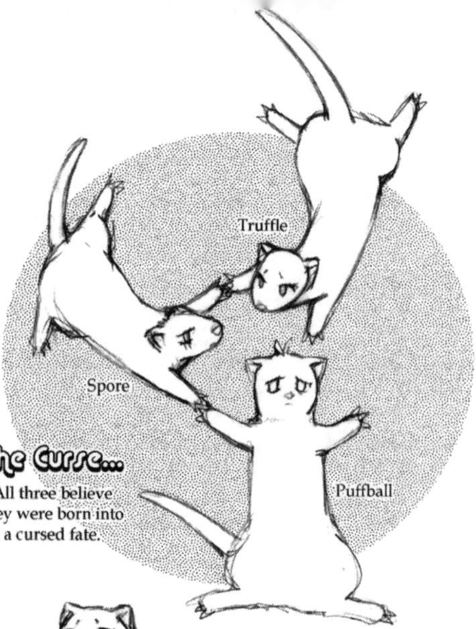
Truffle
Spore
Puffball

The Curse...

All three believe they were born into a cursed fate.

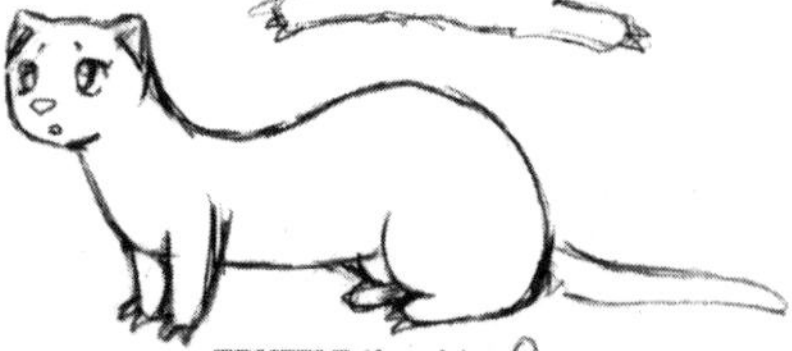

TRUFFLE (female) ♀

She's the motherly figure of the Clan. She often rubs her paws together to comfort herself, or takes part in compulsive grooming.

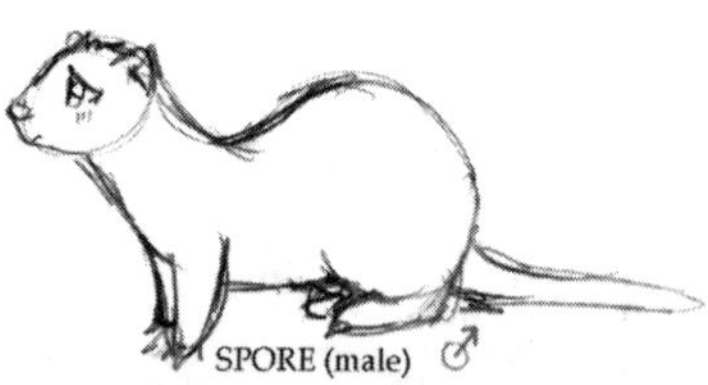

SPORE (male) ♂

He's the most athletic but also the most sleepy of the three. His manic-depressive personality swings like an unbalanced pendulum.

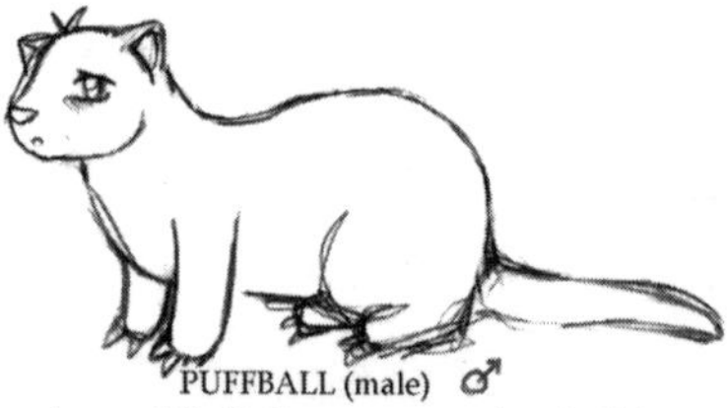

PUFFBALL (male) ♂

Now deceased, Puffball was most convinced of his impending doom and was often depressed. He indulged in food and was heavier than the others.

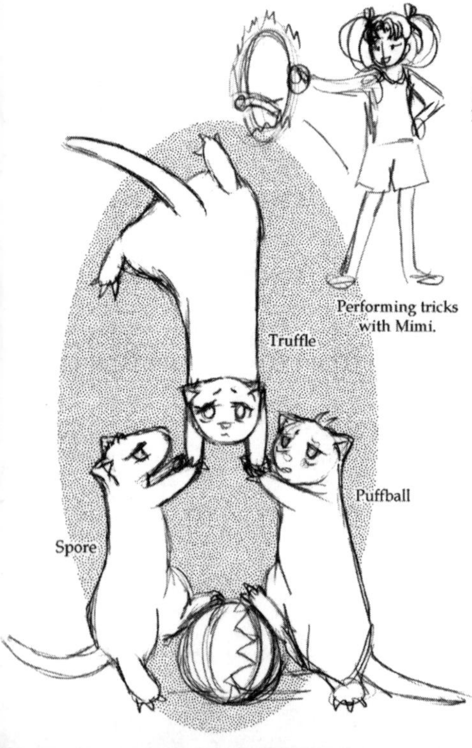
Truffle
Puffball
Spore

Performing tricks with Mimi.

Design Notes

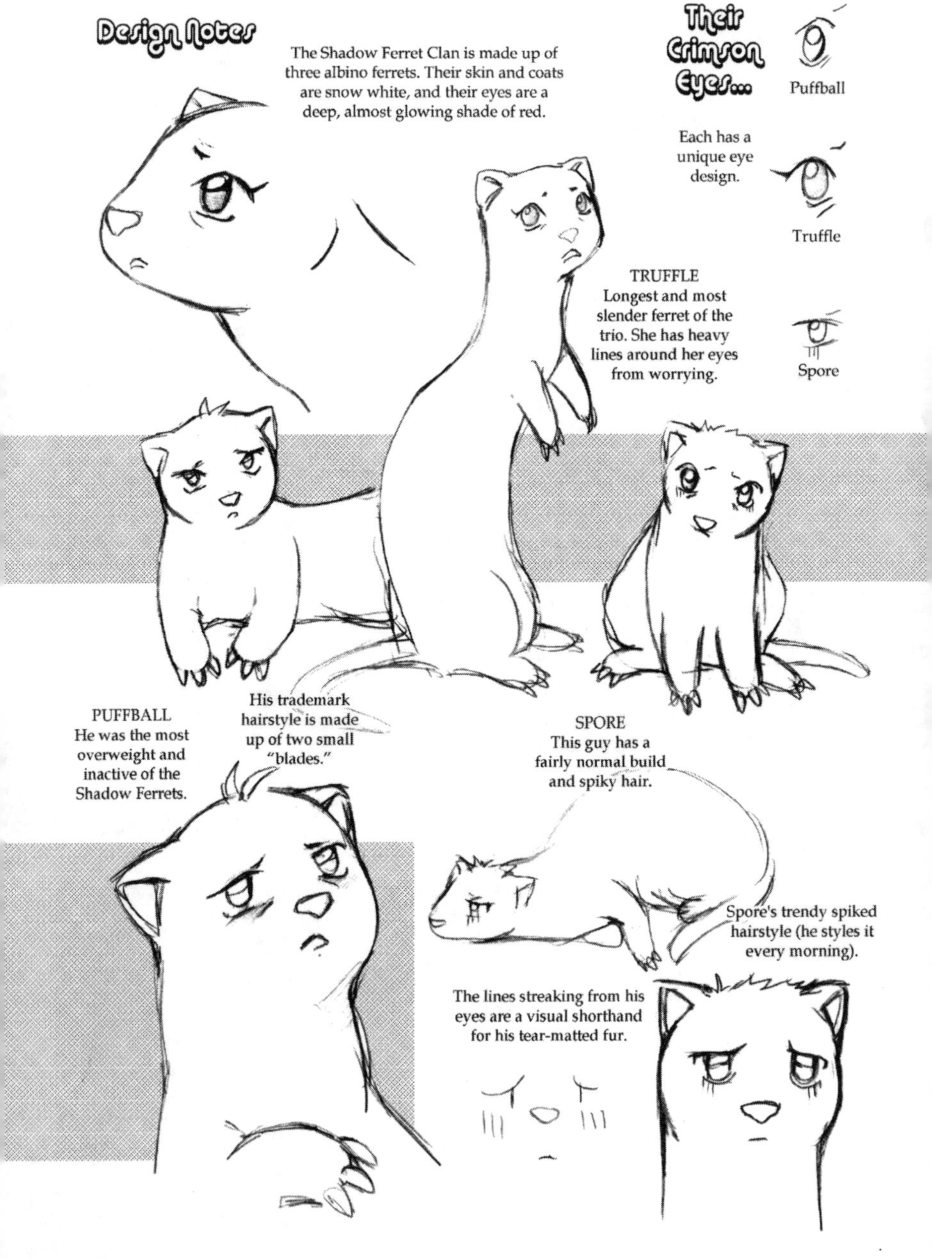

The Shadow Ferret Clan is made up of three albino ferrets. Their skin and coats are snow white, and their eyes are a deep, almost glowing shade of red.
Their Crimson Eyes...
Puffball
Each has a unique eye design.
Truffle
Spore
TRUFFLE
Longest and most slender ferret of the trio. She has heavy lines around her eyes from worrying.
PUFFBALL
He was the most overweight and inactive of the Shadow Ferrets.
His trademark hairstyle is made up of two small "blades."
SPORE
This guy has a fairly normal build and spiky hair.
Spore's trendy spiked hairstyle (he styles it every morning).
The lines streaking from his eyes are a visual shorthand for his tear-matted fur.

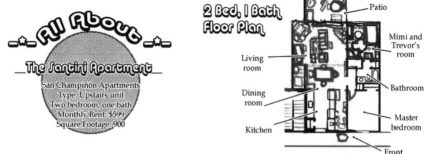

All About

The Santini Apartment

San Champiñón Apartments
Type: Upstairs unit
Two bedroom, one bath
Monthly Rent: $599
Square Footage: 900

2 Bed, 1 Bath Floor Plan

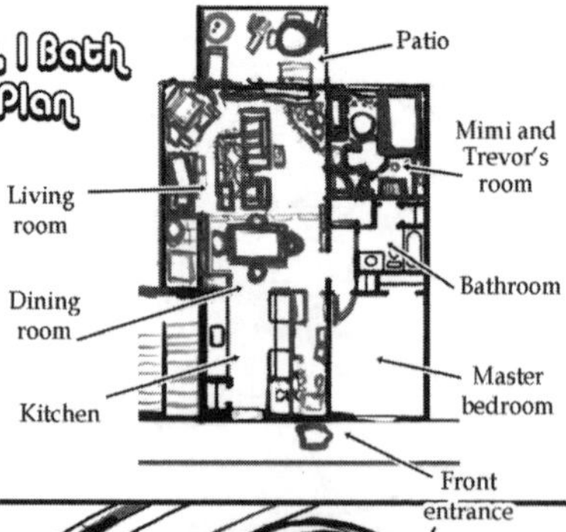

Patio
Mimi and Trevor's room
Living room
Bathroom
Dining room
Master bedroom
Kitchen
Front entrance

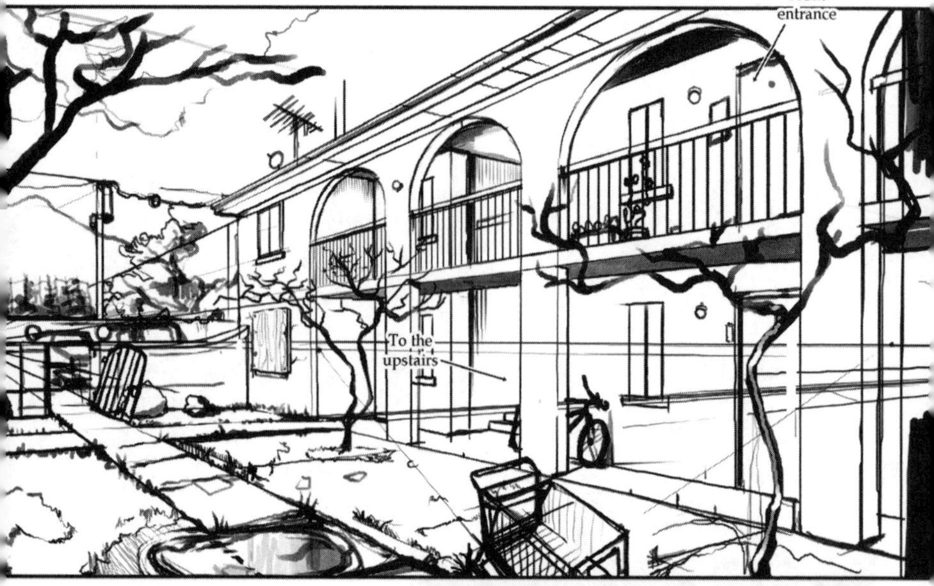

To the upstairs

Exterior

San Champiñón Apartments is a low-rent community. Management's upkeep of the grounds is poor, so it's not uncommon to see broken gates, trash, pools of still water, dead trees, or even abandoned shopping carts.

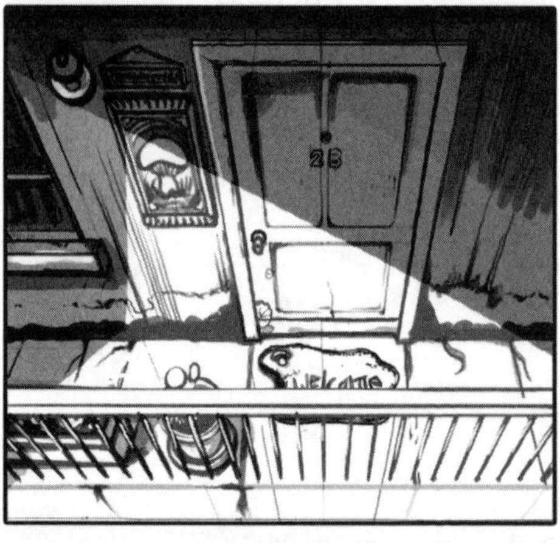

Front Porch

Melinda Santini (Mimi's mom) does what she can to keep her front porch looking nice and clean. A garden of pretty mushroom planters and a bristly mushroom-embroidered welcome mat greet would-be guests.

All About

The Santini Apartment

The Santini Family

Despite living in a rundown apartment complex, there's very little unhappiness in the home. Part of the Mushinite doctrine stresses "living close to the soil," which some Mushinites interpret to mean as living a luxury-free life.

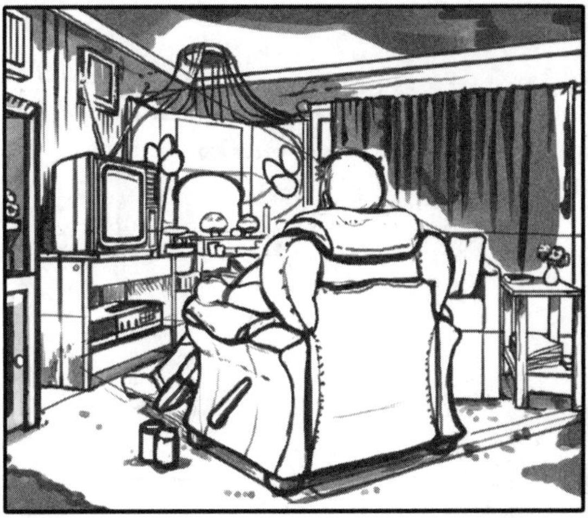

Living Room

During the day, Bud Santini (Mimi's dad) can usually be found snoozing away in his favorite easy chair, passed out after a hard night working the graveyard shift at his security guard job.

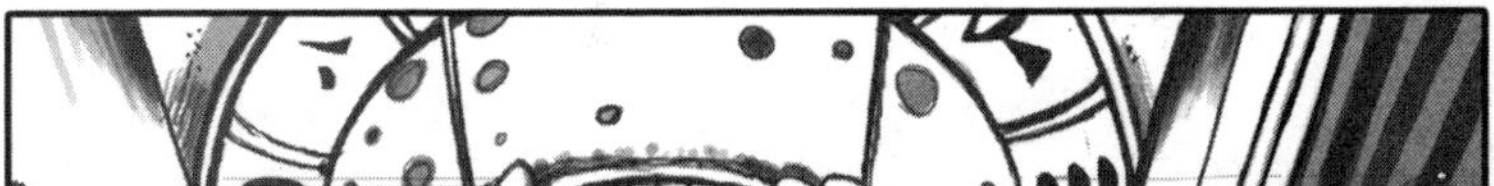
JOY

Mushinite Shrine

As devout Mushinites, Mimi's family keeps colorful and exotic mushrooms on display throughout the house.

School Lunch

Mimi is enrolled in the free lunch program at Portobello Elementary. The food is actually quite good, well-balanced, and Mushinite-approved.

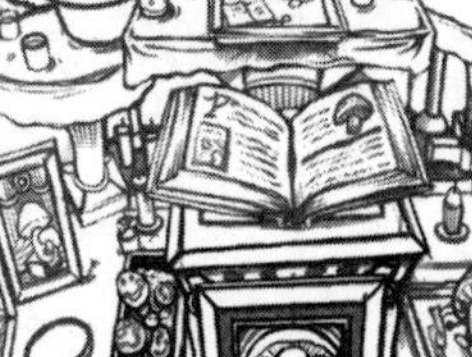

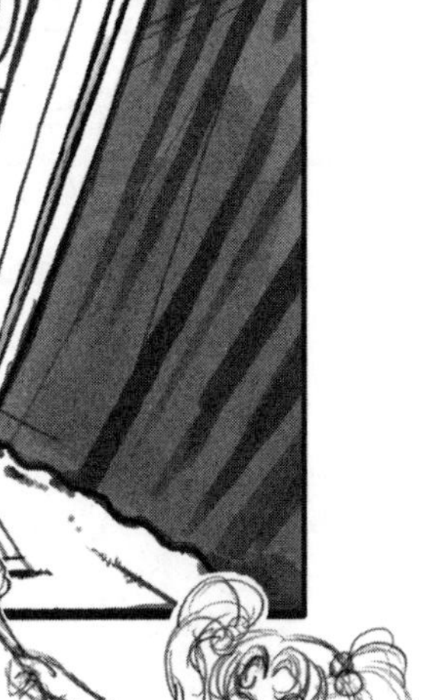

All About

Mimi's Room

Current Theme: Shroomy
Sister/Brother Room Split: 50/50
Number of Mushroom-Themed Items: 37

Ferret Cage Designs

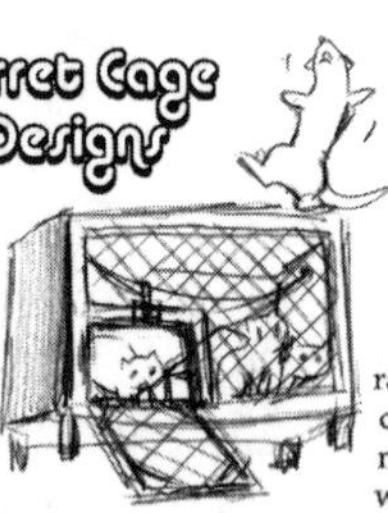

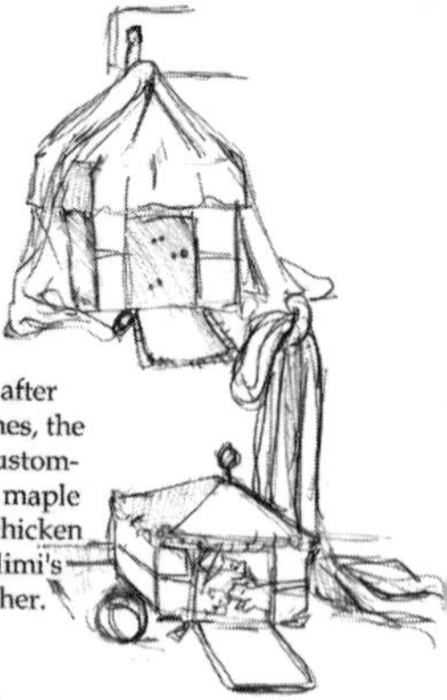

Modeled after rabbit hutches, the cage was custom-made from maple wood and chicken wire by Mimi's grandfather.

Mimi keeps a sheet partially draped over the cage to block out light.

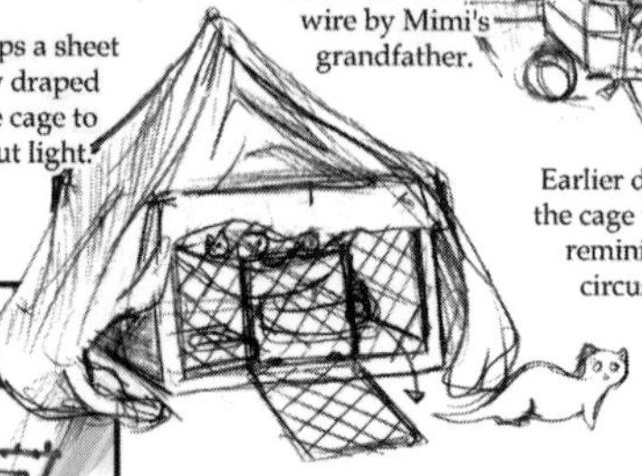

Earlier designs for the cage were more reminiscent of circus tents.

Overview

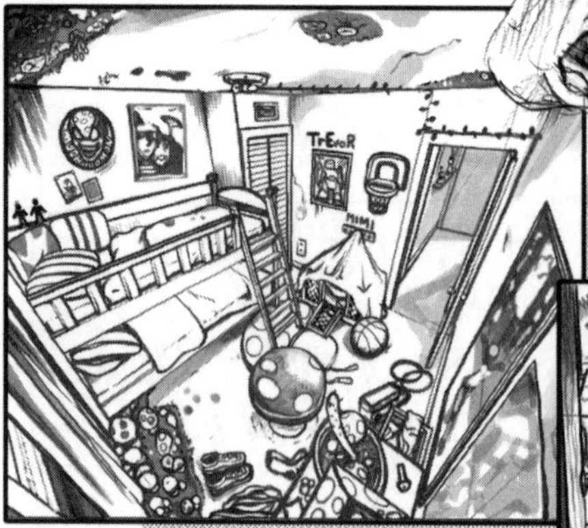

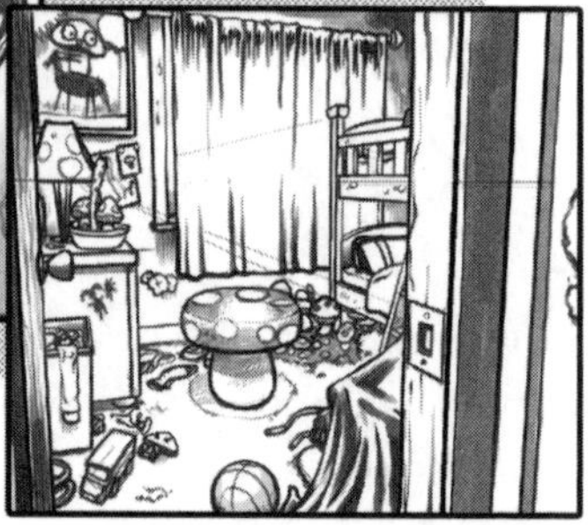

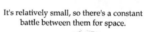

Prototype Sketches

Mimi shares the room with her little brother, Trevor.

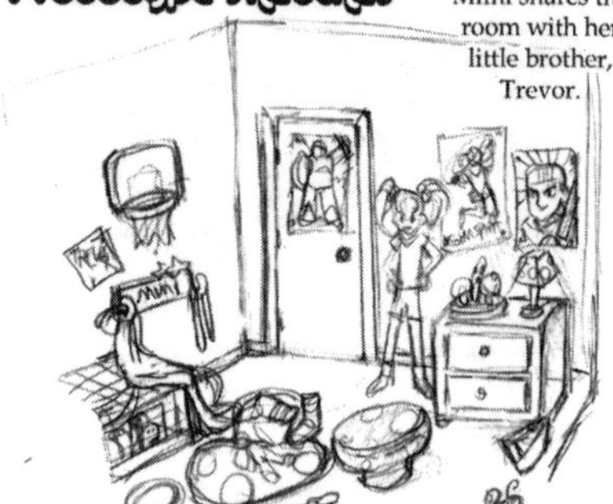

It's relatively small, so there's a constant battle between them for space.

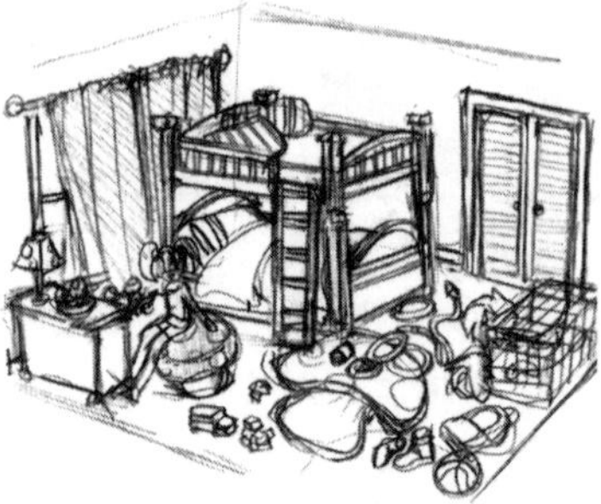

A small planter of mushrooms is kept on the desk.

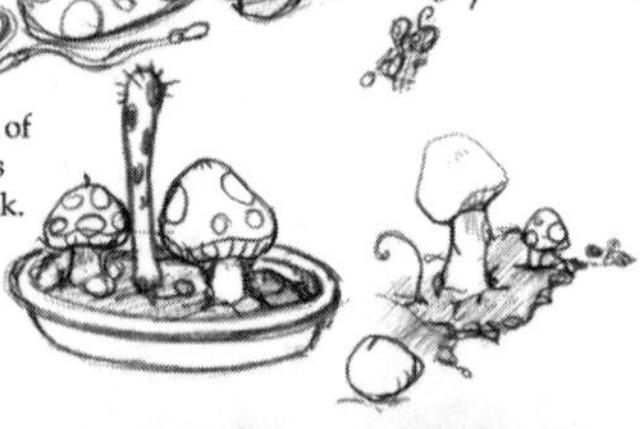

A twin bunk bed helps free floor space. Mimi sleeps in the bottom bunk.

All About Pavaratty

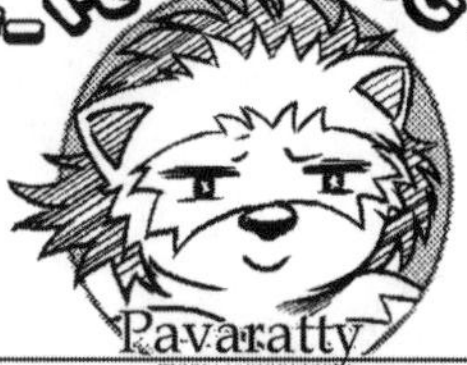

Title: Self-proclaimed "World Famous Ferret Extraordinaire"
Birthdate: April 1st
Sign: Aries
Age: One year and six months old
Birthplace: Unknown
Length: 20 inches from head to tail.
Weight: 5 ½ lbs.

Hobbies: Building his extensive wardrobe made up of all sorts of household junk. Spreading gossip about other ferrets.

Special Skills: Singing, dancing, and performing.

Expressions

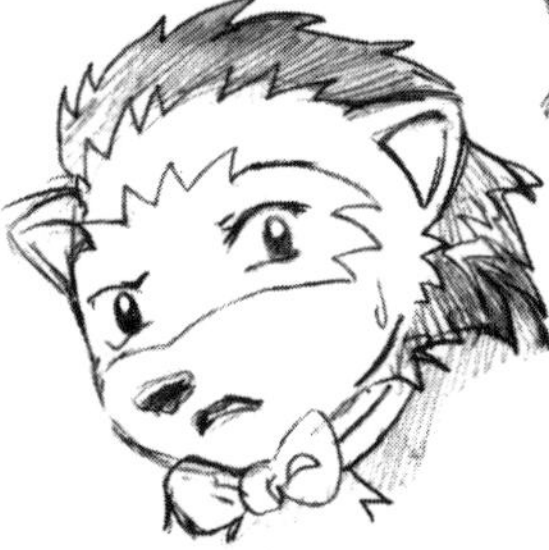

Surprised

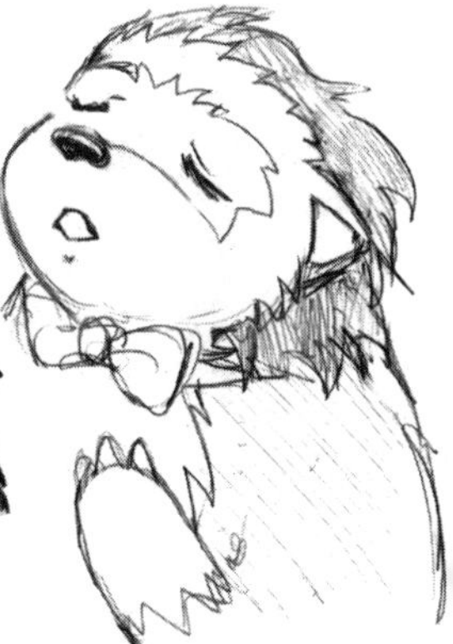

Singing

"The world is my stage."

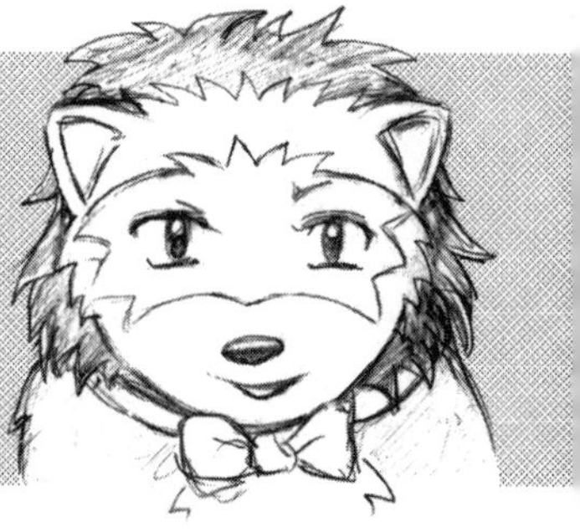

Confident

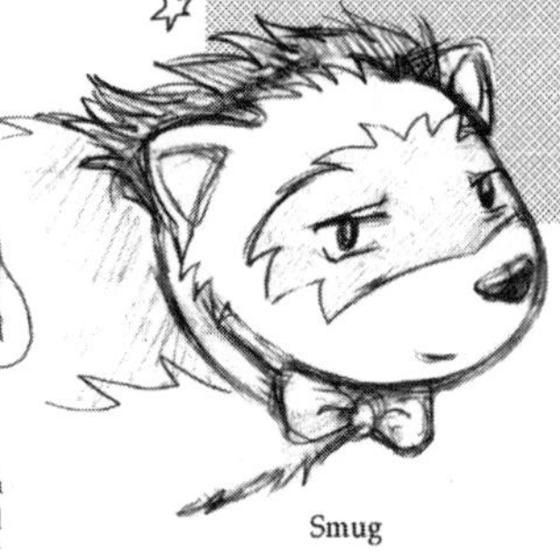

Smug

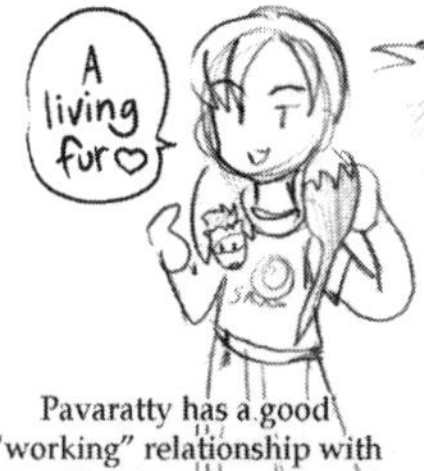
A living fur♡

Pavaratty has a good "working" relationship with Kim. They're so coordinated that watching them play together is like a ballet.

Fun Fact

Pavaratty sees human hands as white-gloved assistants, which he calls Handlers.

Size Comparison

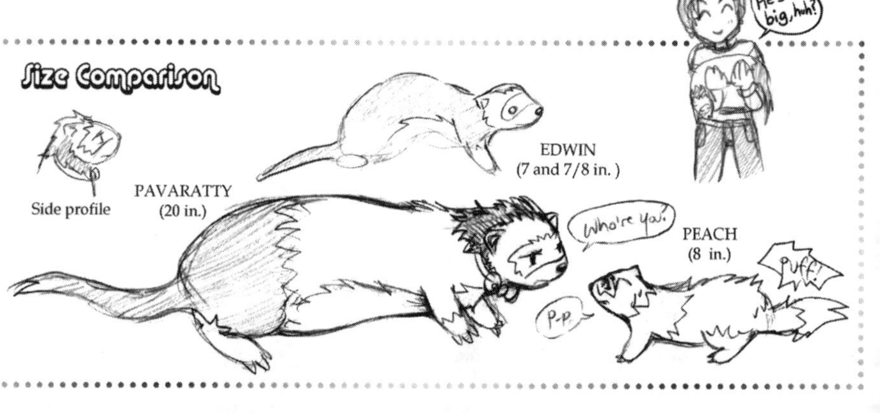
He's big, huh?
Who're you?
P-P..
Puff!

Side profile

PAVARATTY (20 in.)

EDWIN (7 and 7/8 in.)

PEACH (8 in.)

All About

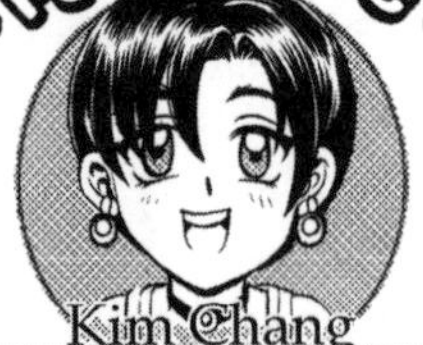

Kim Chang

Birthdate: February 5
Age: 10
Sign: Aquarius
Birthplace: West Coast, USA
Height: 4 ft. 1 in. Weight: 52 lbs.
Ethnicity: Chinese American
Favorite Color: Purple

Interests: Loves makeup, clothing, fashion, anything hip or new. Enjoys coming up with new catch phrases. Takes a passing interest in her father's musical career and enjoys listening to his classical CDs.

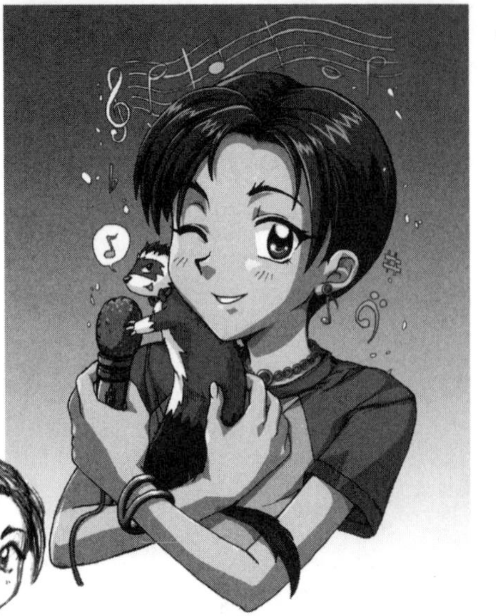

Kim and her ferret Pavaratty doing their favorite thing: being in the spotlight.

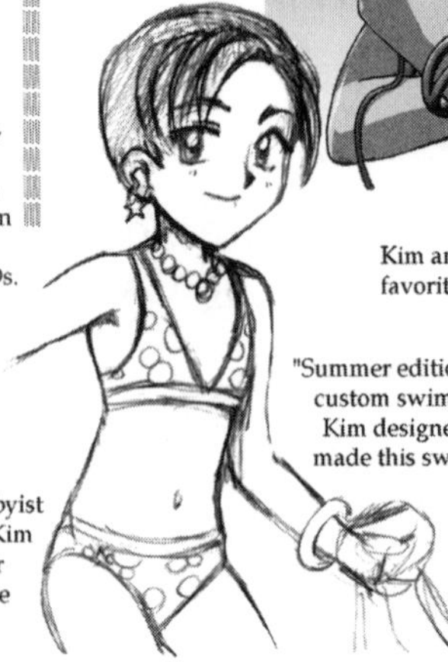

"Summer edition. Kim's custom swimwear!" Kim designed and made this swimsuit.

Fun Fact

One of Kim's hobbies is sewing and making clothing. Her mother, a hobbyist seamstress, taught her how to sew. Kim finds it difficult to get along with her mother, but sewing is one area where they really connect.

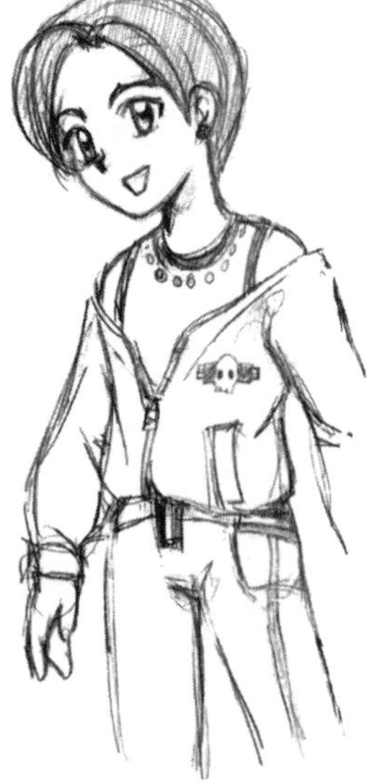

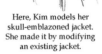

Here, Kim models her skull-emblazoned jacket. She made it by modifying an existing jacket.

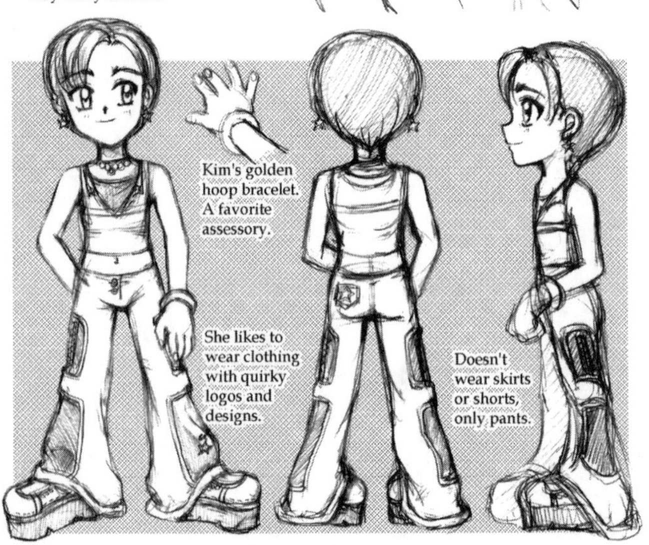
Kim's golden hoop bracelet. A favorite assessory.
She likes to wear clothing with quirky logos and designs.
Doesn't wear skirts or shorts, only pants.